Dear Reader,

Thank you so much fo̶̶̶̶̶ ̶̶̶̶̶̶̶̶̶̶̶̶̶̶̶̶̶̶̶̶̶
Black Silk. I hope you ̶̶̶̶̶ ̶̶̶̶̶̶̶̶̶̶ ̶̶̶̶̶̶̶̶̶ real page-turner
and it keeps you entertained.

If this is the first time you've read any of my books,
I do hope you enjoy it. For those of you who are
familiar with my work, you won't be surprised to
find *Black Silk* is set in New Orleans, my birthplace
and the city that continues to inspire me.

As always, one of the greatest joys for me as a writer
is hearing from readers. Your comments, opinions
and feedback on my books mean a great deal to
me. So please keep those letters, cards and e-mails
coming.

In fact, as a special way to express my appreciation,
this year I'm offering a *Black Silk* commemorative
refrigerator magnet that has been created to celebrate
the release of *Black Silk*. While supplies last, I'll be
happy to send one to each reader who writes and
requests one. To request your *Black Silk* magnet, my
address is Metsy Hingle, P.O. Box 3224, Covington,
LA 70434, or you can contact me on the Web at
metsyhingle.com.

Until next time, best wishes and happy reading!

Metsy Hingle

METSY HINGLE

BLACK SILK

MIRA®

ISBN 0-7783-2281-5

BLACK SILK

Copyright © 2006 by Metsy Hingle.

MIRA and the Star Colophon are trademarks used under license and registered
in Australia, New Zealand, Philippines, United States Patent and Trademark
Office and in other countries.

www.MIRABooks.com

Printed in U.S.A.

In Loving Memory of Missy
1991–2004
The four-legged ball of fur
who owned my heart.

ACKNOWLEDGMENTS

During the course of writing this book, I lost dear family members, a lifelong friend and my beloved Missy, the puppy who sat on my lap for every book I've written until now. It was a difficult and sad period for me that made writing all the more difficult. Were it not for the grace of our Lord and the Blessed Mother, along with the support of some very special people, this book would never have been written. My heartfelt thanks go to the following people for their help in bringing life to *Black Silk:*

Valerie Gray, my editor and friend at MIRA Books, whose continued guidance has been a blessing.

Dianne Moggy, editorial director of MIRA Books, for her friendship and support.

The amazing MIRA staff, who continue to astound me with their support.

Sandra Brown, my dear friend, for her friendship, love and for the shoulder to cry on whenever I needed it.

Erica Spindler and Nathan Hoffman, dearest of friends, for their friendship, advice and love.

Hailey North, my dear friend and fellow writer, for her friendship, love and support.

Carly Phillips, my friend and fellow writer, for her support.

Bill Capo, TV investigative reporter for Channel 4 News in New Orleans, for his friendship, support and for answering my questions about the inner workings of the newsroom.

Marilyn Shoemaker, my friend, fan and researcher.

A special thank-you goes to my children and my family, whose love and support enable me to spin my tales of love, hope and happily-ever-after.

And as always, to my husband, Jim, who is my lover, my best friend, my rock and the person who has taught me everything that I know about love.

One

She should have found him by now. Ignoring the chill of the February wind, Detective Charlotte "Charlie" Le Blanc stared down at her sister's grave. Six years had passed since an unspeakable monster had murdered her sister Emily. And still he remained free. Free to walk the streets. Free to breathe. Free to kill again.

Thunder rumbled overhead and the angry sound seemed to echo Charlie's mood. She was no closer to finding her sister's killer now than she'd been when she'd quit law school and joined the New Orleans police force almost six years ago.

"It sounds like we're in for some bad weather," her mother remarked, drawing Charlie's attention from her dark thoughts. "I wish you had worn your heavy coat like I asked you to, Gordon."

"My jacket is fine," her father replied. "Honey, this is New Orleans, not New York."

Charlie looked over at the two of them. Grief had taken its toll on both of them, she thought. Despite the grief counseling that had helped them get through the loss of their middle daughter, the twinkle in her mother's hazel eyes was never quite as bright again, her smiles never quite as wide. And although he'd never fallen apart, Emily's murder had left its mark on her father as well. The lines around his eyes had grown deeper, his hair grayer, his laughter less frequent.

When another growl of thunder was followed by a crack of lightning, her father placed an arm around her mother's shoulder. "Looks like that rain is moving in this direction. We'd better go if we want to beat the downpour."

"All right," her mother responded and walked over to the headstone. Stooping down, she placed a bouquet of yellow roses in front of it. After pressing her fingers to the marble stone where Emily's name had been engraved, she straightened and returned to her husband's side. "Charlotte, are you coming?"

"Not just yet. You and Dad go on ahead. I won't be long."

"I don't like the idea of leaving you here alone," her mother said. "It's not safe."

"Mom, I'm a cop," Charlie protested.

"You're still our little girl," her mother informed her.

"Your mother's right, Charlie," her father told her. "We'll wait and walk you to your car."

Charlie fingered the package of yellow M&M candies in her jacket pocket. It was a silly gift—her sister's favorite snack in her favorite color. It had become both a joke and a tradition since she'd fished out six of the yellow candies from a bag of the treats, bundled them up in tissue, tied it with a yellow ribbon and presented it to Emily for her sixth birthday. Emily had adored it. So every birthday that had followed, Charlie had added another candy to mark her sister's age and presented her with the gift—right up to the year that her sister was killed. And for the past six years, she had continued the tradition. Only now she placed the gift on Emily's grave. She knew it was foolish. After all, her sister was dead and as far as she knew, ghosts, if there was such a thing, didn't eat candy. But continuing the practice somehow kept the memory of her sister close. It also renewed her determination to keep the promise she'd made to both of them at Emily's funeral—to find her sister's killer and bring him to justice. "I'll be fine, Dad," she told him.

"Charlotte," her mother began.

"I'll only stay a few minutes." She kissed her mother on the cheek and then her father. "Now you two go on before the rain hits. I won't be long. I promise."

"Are you still coming over for dinner?" her mother asked.

"Yes. But I've got some paperwork to do at the station first so I may be a little late."

"That's all right. Anne got sent out on some kind of assignment at the TV station this afternoon and she'll probably be late, too," her mother explained. "We'll just plan on eating a little later than usual."

"Sounds good. I'll see you tonight," she said.

"Make sure you don't stay long," her father instructed.

"I won't," she promised again. Once her parents had departed, Charlie walked over to the marble stone that marked her sister's grave. She retrieved the package of twenty-five yellow M&Ms from her pocket and placed it beside the roses her mother had brought. "Happy birthday, Em," she whispered just before the skies opened up.

Charlie made a run for it. By the time she reached her car, the black boots she'd splurged on the week before were a mess and she was soaked to the skin. A gust of wind sent a surge of rain into the vehicle as she hurried inside. After starting the car, she pushed wet clumps of hair away from her face. She was debating whether to go home and get a dry jacket before heading to the station when her cell phone rang. "Le Blanc," she answered as she hit the defrost button on the dashboard.

"It's Kossak,"

"What's up?" she asked Vince Kossak, her partner for the past two years.

"We've got a possible 187," Vince informed her, giving her the code for a homicide.

"What's the location?" she asked.

"The Mill House Apartments in the Warehouse District," Vince replied. "I'm headed there now."

"I'm on my way." Maybe she had yet to find justice for her sister Emily, but at least she could try to find justice for someone else.

He stood across the street shadowed by both his umbrella and the trees in the small park. Smiling, he watched the activity unfold at the apartment building. It had been risky for him to hang around, but the camouflage of the rain made it too tempting to resist seeing the reaction to his handiwork.

Everything had gone according to plan. The discovery of Francesca's body by the maid couldn't have gone better if he'd scripted the scene himself. Which, come to think of it, he had—at least indirectly, he thought proudly. Maybe when he finally collected the money due him, he would invest some of it in the movie business. Making movies in Louisiana had become big business and it made sense for him to get in on some of the action. Better yet, instead of simply being the moneyman, he would act as the movie's director. After all, he had directed the players in the drama going on across the street for months now, hadn't he? And look at what a masterful job he'd done. Yes, he thought with a chuckle, the idea of directing appealed to him—almost as much as killing Francesca had appealed to him.

The M.E.'s van pulled up and he shoved his plans for the future aside. Another group of the city's gofers exited the van followed by a tall woman wearing an ugly beige raincoat. Mid-forties, moderately attractive, he thought, studying her. After speaking to the doorman for a moment, she turned and began giving instructions to the men accompanying her. The medical examiner herself, he realized, his gloved fist tightening on the handle of his umbrella. Another woman in a position of power—power that she wielded over the men beneath her. Adrenaline surged through him as he considered the prospect of showing her what real power was. He couldn't risk it, he told himself as he watched her and her minions enter the building. Besides, she really wasn't worthy of his attention.

Now the pretty, blond detective who had arrived flashing her badge was another matter altogether. He smiled. He hadn't anticipated that the police department would assign a woman to Francesca's case and certainly not one so young and attractive. Even all wet and in the bland clothes, she was a looker. And hadn't he always been partial to blondes? She was a bonus, one he hadn't expected. He was going to enjoy sparring with this one. And maybe he would do more than just sparring, he amended with a smile as he touched the black silk stocking in his coat pocket.

But the lady cop would have to wait, he decided. First…first, he had to put the next part of his plan into play. Whistling, he strode down the street toward his car.

By the time Charlie turned onto the street where the Mill House Apartments were located, the rain had slowed to a drizzle. But the wet streets had caused a slew of fender benders that had turned what should have been a ten-minute drive into twenty. With a touch of impatience, Charlie pulled her unmarked car to a stop behind a silver Rolls-Royce.

"Ma'am, this is a no-parking zone," a uniformed doorman

holding a black umbrella told her as she exited her car. "I'm afraid I have to ask you to move your vehicle."

She didn't bother pointing out that the Rolls was in the same no-parking zone as her car. Instead she flashed him her badge. "I'm here on official business. The car stays here," she informed him and strode toward the apartment building.

Nervously tailing her, he called out, "But, ma'am—"

"Detective," she corrected without breaking her stride, making her way to the building's entrance. Once a working cotton mill, the Mill House was one of several vacant buildings that had been converted into luxury apartments following the success of the city's 1984 World's Fair. The place bore little resemblance to the old mill now, she thought as she reached the porte cochere that had been part of the building's original architecture. She climbed the dozen steps and was about to open the door when the doorman practically jumped in front of her.

"It's my job," he explained when she leveled him with a look.

"Thanks," Charlie murmured as he pulled the door wide. This had to be a first, she thought. She couldn't recall ever being greeted at a crime scene in such a manner before. Then again, this wasn't the typical place for a homicide. Although New Orleans held the unwanted distinction of ranking number one in the nation for murders per capita, most of the crimes were committed in the poorer sections of the city. Nine times out of ten, where the poverty was most prevalent so were the drugs, gangs and turf wars that so often resulted in murder. It was a sad fact of life and a black eye on the city of New Orleans, despite the current efforts being made by the police chief to rectify the problem. But barely into the second month of the calendar, the murder rate had already exceeded one a day.

In her five years on the police force Charlie couldn't ever

recall a murder occurring in one of the city's upscale apartment buildings. And there was no question this one was upscale, she conceded as she marched across shining marble floors, past urns filled with fresh flowers and over to the front desk.

A nervous-looking clerk in a gray-and-red uniform that matched the doorman's looked up and asked, "May I help you?"

"I'm Detective Le Blanc," she said, flashing him her badge.

The man paled. "You must be here about poor Ms. Hill."

"That's right," she said, assuming poor Ms. Hill was the victim. "What's the apartment number?"

"Let me call Mr. Blackwell for you. He's the building manager," he explained. "He'll take you up to Miss Hill's apartment."

"That's all right. I can manage on my own. Just give me the apartment number," she told him.

"It's 513. But—"

"Thanks," she said and started toward the elevator.

"Wait! Ma'am. Officer—"

"It's Detective," she corrected, pausing at the panic in the young man's voice.

"Yes, ma'am. I mean, Detective," he said. "If you'll just wait a minute. I'm supposed to notify Mr. Blackwell—"

"It's all right, Dennis," a portly man with a horrible combover said as he materialized from a door behind the desk to stand beside the nervous clerk. "I'm Mr. Blackwell, the manager of Mill House Apartments," he advised her with a pomposity that annoyed her.

"Detective Charlotte Le Blanc," she told him with a flash of her badge. "New Orleans Homicide."

"So I see," he all but sniffed. "Several of your associates have already arrived, Detective. Perhaps you would like to remove your coat before you join them."

The disdain in his voice was clear as he surveyed the wet tracks she'd left in her wake, and Charlie suspected he would have preferred showing her the exit instead of allowing her further access. And because she'd never understood why some people thought a fancy title or money entitled them to act pompously, she said, "It's a bit chilly in here. I think I'll just keep it on." And without waiting for his response, she walked past him, down the corridor to the elevator, where she found a uniformed police officer waiting. "Detective Le Blanc," she said, showing him her ID.

"Yes, ma'am." The officer stepped inside the elevator with her and hit the button for the fifth floor.

"Why don't you fill me in, Officer," Charlie said and noted the surveillance camera inside the elevator. She made a mental note to have the tapes confiscated if Kossak hadn't already done so.

"I wasn't first on the scene, Detective. All I know is that we have a robbery/homicide in apartment 513. Any details on what went down and who was involved are being kept in there."

Moments later when the elevator doors slid open, the police officer remained where he was and she stepped out into a carpeted hallway adorned with artwork and more urns of fresh flowers. As she walked down the hall, her damp boots were silent on the thick carpet. More surveillance cameras were in evidence and Charlie was impressed by the security measures. The tapes should prove useful, she thought. As she approached apartment 513, she noted the crime-scene tape that had been stretched across the doorway and another uniformed police officer, whom she pegged as a rookie, standing at the door's entrance like a sentinel. Charlie held up her badge. "Detective Le Blanc."

"Detective," he said, all but snapping his heels together.

"Who was the first on scene?" she asked.

"I was, ma'am. My partner and I were on patrol when we

got the call. After we arrived, we confirmed the victim was dead and phoned it into the station. We secured the scene and took a statement from the woman who found the body."

Charlie quickly scanned the room, taking in the crime scene, which she guessed had been the site of a party, judging by the empty glasses and half-eaten food. The various police units were at work, sorting through it all. The forensic photographer snapped shots of empty glasses and champagne bottles on the table, then bagged the items. She spied her partner, Vince Kossak, in a far corner of the room, questioning a woman in a maid's uniform. From the look of things, the fresh-faced officer had followed procedure. His securing the scene properly would certainly make her and Vince's job easier. "Good work, Officer…"

"Mackenzie, ma'am. Andrew Mackenzie."

"You did a good job, Officer Mackenzie."

"Thank you, ma'am."

Charlie nodded, then made her way across the room toward her partner. At thirty-two, Vince was three years her senior. An average-looking man of average height with brown hair and eyes, Vince was anything but average when it came to being a cop. He had a string of commendations for his bravery in the field. Though he downplayed the awards, she knew firsthand that he deserved every one of them. Just last year he'd faced down a drugged-up junkie wielding a knife who was holding his own wife hostage. Vince got the woman away unharmed, but it had taken a dozen stitches to close the gash in his shoulder. No, Vince Kossak wasn't even remotely average, she mused. He was everything she believed a cop should be—honest, trustworthy, a man you could stake your life on.

They didn't come any more solid than Vince Kossak. And she'd been lucky to be assigned to work with him. The two of them made a good team. In the two years that they had been partners, she had learned a great deal from him. More than that, they had become friends. She trusted Vince with her life and vice versa. He was among the few people that she'd confided in about her sister's murder and her determination to track down the killer.

Looking up, she caught Vince's eye and he motioned for her to join him. "Thank you, Mrs. Ramirez. You've been a big help," Vince told the woman and waved the uniformed officer over to join them. "Now if you'll just go with the police officer, he'll get your contact information and we'll be in touch with you."

"You will find this person who hurt Miss Francesca, yes?" the woman asked, her accented voice thick with tears.

"We're certainly going to try." Once the police officer led the woman away, Vince turned to Charlie. "Jeez, Le Blanc," he said as he took in her wet hair and jacket. "Haven't you ever heard of an umbrella?"

She shrugged. "The weatherman said no rain today."

"And you believed him?"

"I was hoping he'd get it right for once." Of course, he hadn't gotten it right. Nine times out of ten, the weather forecasts were off the mark, as was typical for New Orleans. The weather was as wide-ranging as the people who lived there. You could find yourself in shirtsleeves and suffering from a drought one day only to be hit with freezing temperatures and floods the next day.

"You're lucky they even let you in the front door of this place."

"Trust me, that prissy manager wouldn't have if he could have helped it," she replied. "So what have we got?"

"The vic's wallet is empty and according to the maid there's jewelry missing."

"A robbery gone bad?" Charlie asked.

"Maybe." He gave her a quick rundown of the situation, explaining the maid had arrived that morning to help the victim get ready for her wedding, only to find the bride-to-be dead.

"Today was her wedding day?" While each case she investigated left a mark on her, Charlie couldn't help feeling sad for the woman whose dreams had ended before they'd even begun.

"It was supposed to be." He paused. "This one is going to be touchy, Le Blanc. Word from the top is that we're to handle this with kid gloves."

She wasn't surprised given the real estate. "Who's the victim?"

"Her name's Francesca Hill. Age twenty-six, a former casino hostess."

The name didn't ring any bells. Charlie glanced around the apartment. Lots of white and black, bold splashes of red, modern artwork that looked like a kid had been let loose with finger paints. It all added up to one thing—money. "Casino hostessing must pay really well."

"It does if you're marrying the boss."

Charlie arched her brow.

"The fiancé is J. P. Stratton."

"Stratton," she repeated. "As in Stratton Real Estate?"

Vince nodded. "And Stratton Hotels. The man also has an interest in two casinos and a professional football team. Our vic was supposed to become wife number five this evening."

Charlie conjured up a vague image of a gray-haired man with a George Hamilton tan. The guy was sixty if he was a day. "Apparently Stratton likes his brides young."

"Apparently," Vince replied.

"Where's the body?"

"In the bedroom."

"How'd she buy it?" Charlie asked.

"We're waiting for the M.E. to give the official cause of death," he said, a troubled look coming into his eyes. "But it looks like she was strangled."

For a moment, everything inside Charlie froze. Murder investigations were never easy. But the ones where strangulation was the cause of death were the hardest for her because it always brought back thoughts of her sister's death.

"Listen, why don't you stay out here and make sure the techies don't screw up and I'll handle things in there," he offered and urged her away from the bedroom.

Charlie narrowed her eyes. "All right, Kossak. What's in that bedroom that you don't want me to see?"

Vince eyed his partner carefully, noting the shadows beneath her dark brown eyes. In the years they'd worked together he'd watched Charlie push herself, driven by demons to find justice for the victims. He knew from the countless hours she spent poring over case files that the demon that drove her hardest was finding her sister's killer. It was the reason he was worried now about how she would respond to what was in the next room.

It had nothing to do with her toughness. He'd seen Charlie hold it together at more than one bloody homicide scene when even a seasoned vet would have lost his lunch. As far as he was concerned, there wasn't a better, smarter or more dedicated cop on the force than Charlie Le Blanc.

But for all her smarts and toughness, Charlie Le Blanc had a heart, a heart that sometimes felt way too much. And her sister's murder was like a wound with a bandage on it that had been pulled off too soon. It was painful. And it wouldn't take much to reopen that wound again.

"You going to answer me, Kossak?"

"Come on, Le Blanc. We've got a female strangling victim. Give yourself a break. Let me handle this one."

"I can carry my end of the job, Kossak," she informed him, her already husky voice dropping even lower.

"Nobody said you couldn't," he said sharply and when he noted heads turn in their direction, Vince hustled her over near a window and out of earshot of the fingerprint team. Lowering his voice, he repeated, "I never said you couldn't carry your end of the job. Hell, half the time you'd carry mine if I'd let you. But you are not personally responsible for solving every homicide in this city."

"I know that."

"Then act like it. Cut yourself some slack for once."

"I can't," she told him and looked away.

"Why not?"

"Because I can't," she insisted.

"Why can't you?" he pressed.

She whipped her gaze back to him and spat out, "Because if I don't stop him, he might kill another—" She paused, took a steadying breath. "He might kill someone else."

Vince said nothing. But he had no doubt that what she had been about to say was that he might kill another innocent girl like her sister.

"I thought you said this one was high priority," she said more calmly. "So are we going to process the scene or not?"

Vince knew any further attempt on his part to dissuade her would be pointless. So he said, "Let's do it." He headed to the bedroom, knowing she was behind him. He paused at the door and donned gloves so as not to mar any evidence. "Ready?"

"Ready," she replied as she finished putting on her own gloves.

They stepped into the room. It was huge, almost the size of his apartment, he noted as he surveyed the scene a second time. Only this room smelled of booze, perfume and sex. The virginal-white color scheme was only broken by the clothing that lay strewn on the carpet and the golden-blond hair of the woman who lay on the bed.

"She's beautiful."

"Yeah," Vince replied. From a distance she did look beautiful, like something out of a painting, a siren draped in satin sheets. Her heart-shaped face looked as if it had been carved from ivory. It was smooth and perfect. The green eyes stared glassily up at the ceiling. The long, yellow-gold hair was spread out against the pillow and fell across pale shoulders. One hand rested near her face, the diamond ring on her finger catching the light. Only the marks across her throat marred the picture of beauty. He eyed Charlie, worried about the impact of the scene on her. But other than a momentary stiffening, she gave nothing away.

"Judging by that rock on her finger, we either have ourselves a very dumb thief or robbery wasn't the motive. The way she's positioned on the sheets with her hair spread on the pillow and her hand near her face looks staged," Charlie remarked. "Our killer is evidently into showmanship—which tells me this was no robbery turned homicide. And it was no act of passion either. It was planned."

He had reached the same conclusion himself. "Given the security in this place, I'd say our vic must have known her killer."

She glanced down at the discarded underwear. "I'd say she knew him well enough to go to bed with him," Charlie added.

"I figure they started off with drinks in the living room," he began, mentally re-creating how the murder had gone down.

"Then they decided to take the action into the bedroom," she continued. She walked past the high heels that had been discarded a few feet from the door, then stopped in front of the black sequined dress that lay in a heap. "Pretty," she said and stooped down to examine the dress. She checked the label and read, "Ricardo's. I know this shop. It's very expensive."

"Why, Le Blanc, I never would have guessed that you'd go in for this kind of number," he said in an effort to distract her from what awaited.

"Oh, I'd go for it all right. The problem is I'd never be able to conceal my gun in it or be able to afford it, which is exactly what I told my sister Anne when she dragged me into the place to see a skirt she'd been drooling over."

"Did she buy it?" The question was out before he'd been able to stop it and he could have kicked himself for the slip. Anne Le Blanc was little more than a kid, but for some reason she got under his skin.

"No. I managed to talk her out of it," she said and went back to examining the dress. "We should get the techs to dust the zipper for prints. There's always the chance we'll get lucky."

But it wasn't likely, Vince thought. A killer who would take the time to pose the victim wouldn't make the mistake of leaving his prints on the dress's zipper or anyplace else.

Charlie moved farther into the room and stopped again, this time to check out a spot on the carpet. She poked at the matted section of carpet with her gloved fingertip, then sniffed it.

"My guess is it's champagne," he told her. "There was an empty bottle in the living room and a couple more bottles in the bar."

She nodded, rose and continued toward the bed. "So they get a little more frisky here. She loses the bra," Charlie said, playing out the scene just as he had. She looked at the overturned glasses that rested on the night table, eyed the panties beside the bed. Then she spied the black silk stocking draped on the bed next to the victim. Suddenly her body stiffened.

Vince was sure Charlie noted, as he had, that the stocking looked smooth, no visible snags, not even a crease, as though it had never been worn. Instead, it appeared to have been placed beside the victim for effect.

Finally she looked up at him. "The other stocking isn't here, is it?"

"No," he told her, knowing the conclusion she would draw. Her sister had been strangled, her body posed in the bed in a similar manner and a single black silk stocking found at the scene.

"He took the other one as a trophy. Just like the last time," she said and stared once more at the bed. "Just like when he killed Emily."

Two

Cole Stratton studied the floor plans of the newest Logan Hotel for which he and his firm, CS Securities, had been contracted to provide a security system. Spreading out the blueprints on his desk, he made notations to those areas where additional cameras would be needed. Logan Hotels, which had begun with a few small, luxury hotels a decade ago had blossomed into an international chain whose "L" logo guaranteed excellence in accommodations and in service. Cole had set his sights on this account nearly a year ago. Getting the call from Josh Logan telling him the job was his had been the culmination of months and months of hard work. It had been a major coup for him. He should be thrilled. He should be out celebrating.

Instead, he was sitting in his office on a Saturday afternoon trying to assuage his concern for his sister by concentrating on business. But it wasn't working. Frustrated, Cole threw down his pen and rammed his fingers through his hair. If only he had been able to convince Francesca not to file charges against his sister, Holly. But despite his efforts, the woman had been determined to follow through on her threat and have

Holly arrested for violating the restraining order. Even though
he'd sent Holly out of town for the time being, it would only
be a temporary fix. If Francesca had contacted the police this
morning, as she'd sworn she was going to do, they would already be looking for Holly. For his sister's sake, he hoped
Margee Jardine's skill as a lawyer would be able to override
J.P.'s political influence. The last thing his sister needed was
the trauma of being dragged into the police station by her father's newest wife.

"Damn," he muttered. Thinking about what Francesca was
putting his sister through infuriated him. But he couldn't lay
all the blame at Francesca's feet. No, J.P. was the one responsible for this mess. If the man hadn't fallen into lust with his
own daughter's friend, Holly wouldn't be in trouble now.

Damn you, J.P.

The selfish S.O.B. didn't care whose life he ruined as long
as he got what he wanted. If he weren't so angry at Francesca,
he might even feel sorry for the woman, because it wouldn't
be long before she discovered that being Mrs. J. P. Stratton
came at a very high price. His mother had paid it. First with
her fortune, then with her dignity and finally with her life. The
women who had followed had paid a price as well. So had
each of J.P.'s children—including himself.

Unfortunately, by the time his father's new bride discovered the cold, ruthless man behind the charming facade she'd
married, it would be too late. She would have become another
casualty of J. P. Stratton's ego and greed. But, maybe not.
After all, Francesca Hill struck him as the type of woman who
always landed on her feet. Of course, her share of J.P.'s fortune would certainly help cushion her fall.

But Francesca wasn't his concern. Holly was. And for the
time being, there was nothing more he could do but wait and
hope Francesca was too busy preparing for her wedding to fol-

low through with the charges. Reminding himself that his sister was safely tucked away for now, he picked up his pen and went back to work. Lost in the challenge of the hotel project, he didn't register the pounding on the door out front until he heard the shouting.

"Cole!"

Recognizing his brother Aaron's voice, Cole pushed away from his desk and headed down the hall to the reception area. His first thought was that there had been a warrant issued for Holly. Just as quickly he dismissed that notion. Margee Jardine's contact in the police department had promised to notify her if a warrant was issued.

"Cole, open the door!"

He frowned as he approached the door, suspecting that his brother was there to try one last time to convince him to attend J.P.'s wedding. Younger than him by four years, Aaron had been blessed with his mother's blond hair and green eyes while he had inherited his father's dark hair and blue eyes. Even though he more closely resembled his father than his four half siblings, it was Aaron who shared the closest bond with J.P. And it was Aaron who constantly tried to bridge the rift between them. Cole unlocked the door.

"It's about damn time," Aaron snapped. "I've been trying to reach you for over an hour. Why in the hell aren't you answering your cell phone?"

"Because I didn't want to be disturbed," Cole told him. "So if you're here to try and change my mind about going to J.P.'s wedding, you're wasting your time."

"There isn't going to be any wedding," Aaron told him, his voice flat. "Francesca's dead."

For a moment, Cole thought that his brother had made some sort of tasteless joke. After all, Aaron had made no secret of the fact that he thought J.P. marrying his own daughter's friend was disgusting. But one look at Aaron's face and he knew his brother wasn't joking. "What happened?"

"It looks like she was murdered."

Cole's brain tried to process the news. The determined young woman he'd tried to reason with the previous night was dead? "When? Where?"

"Sometime last night at her apartment," Aaron informed him. "The maid found her a few hours ago. Blackwell, the manager at the Mill House, called me and I had him phone the police. Then I went over to the apartment building to wait for them. Seeing that dead body shook me up. You'd think my years in the military and in the SEALs would have prepared me for something like this."

"Sit down," Cole told his brother, motioning to the sitting area where sofas and chairs had been grouped around a square marble table. Aaron sank down into one of the upholstered chairs. Cole did the same and waited for his brother to continue.

"Anyway, once the police arrived, I left and came looking for you since I couldn't reach you on the phone."

"I'm sorry about that," Cole said and meant it. "Do the police have any idea who did it?"

"Not that I know of. They think robbery might have been the motive. Francesca's wallet was empty and the maid said some of her jewelry is missing."

"A robbery at the Mill House?" Cole remarked skeptically. He knew the building and the security system. Both were excellent.

"I know. I find it hard to believe, too. But it's the only thing that makes sense. You know how the old man drapes all his women in jewelry and shows them off. He spent another chunk of change on a bracelet for her just last week. And Francesca wasn't at all shy about flashing her *little gifts* under everyone's noses. The woman might as well have pasted a sign on her back. Every thief in a five-state radius could spot her as an easy mark."

Somehow he doubted the street-smart woman would allow herself to be anyone's mark, Cole thought. But then he also couldn't see her going down without a fight. "How did she die?"

"The police say it looks like she was strangled."

Like a lightning bolt, a dark memory from his childhood flashed through Cole's mind—a furious J.P. arguing with his mother, grabbing her and choking her. He'd been no more than five at the time, too small to take on a man J.P.'s size. But he'd grabbed his baseball bat and struck J.P. across the back as hard as he could. It had earned him a backhand and a bloody mouth, but it had given his mother time to get away. "How did J.P. react when you told him?"

"He doesn't know yet," Aaron said. "That's why I was trying to reach you. I was hoping you'd come with me to break the news to him."

"We both know the news will go down better without me there," Cole told him. And it was true. He and his father were civil to one another, but just barely. Besides, they had nearly come to blows last night when he had ripped into J.P. for encouraging Francesca's actions against Holly.

"You're probably right," Aaron replied and stood. "I'm just not sure how he's going to take this. You know how he is when he thinks he's in love with a woman."

He did know, Cole admitted silently as he stood. He'd seen J.P. fall into lust more times than he could count when he'd been growing up. And each time, J.P.'s new fling had taken precedence over everything in his life—including each of his wives and his children. "I don't think you have to worry about J.P. He'll bounce back fast enough," Cole said.

"You're probably right about that, too."

I am right, Cole thought. His own mother's grave wasn't

cold before J.P. had married Aaron's mother. He walked his brother to the door and placed a hand on his back for a moment. "Don't worry about telling Holly. I'll let her know what's happened. Are you going to tell the twins or do you want me to do it?" he asked, referring to his two youngest half siblings.

"Christ! I forgot all about them. They're probably getting ready for the wedding right now," Aaron said. "You'd better tell them. I don't know how long I'll be at the old man's place and I don't want them to hear about it on the news."

"I'll tell them," Cole promised. He walked his brother out into the hall, down to the elevator bank, and pushed the button. After the elevator arrived, he rode with Aaron to the parking level.

When they exited the elevator into the garage, Aaron said, "Boy, talk about a mess. The press is going to have a field day with this and the timing couldn't be worse. We're waiting for approval on J.P.'s application for a new gaming license."

"I'd be more concerned with finding Francesca's killer than with any bad publicity her murder might generate for J.P.," Cole told him, irritated that his brother's thoughts were on business and not the tragedy of a young woman's death.

Aaron's eyes darkened and he shot him a look of annoyance. "You don't have the market on empathy, Cole. I'm just as concerned as you are. I even liked Francesca. But someone has to look out for the business."

And because Cole had walked away from his father and the career path that had been planned for him, that duty had fallen to Aaron. Unfortunately, since Aaron had earned his law degree, J.P. had taken full advantage of his son's legal skills. As a result, Aaron had never pursued the brilliant career or personal life he could have had outside of J.P.'s shadow. "I hope J.P. realizes how lucky he is to have you," Cole told him honestly.

"He's my father," Aaron said as though it was the only explanation needed for giving up his own career to work as his father's attorney and right-hand man. "He's your father, too. It wouldn't hurt for you to remember that."

"Trust me. It's something I never forget." And Cole had certainly tried. In fact, he'd spent most of his life trying to distance himself from the man. Being J. P. Stratton's son was something about which he had never taken pride. As far as he was concerned, the only good thing that J. P. Stratton had ever given him was his half siblings. It was because of them, and only them, that he maintained any relationship with the man at all. His brothers and sister were also the reason he had not destroyed J.P. as he had vowed to do following his mother's death.

The *zap-zap* of Aaron activating the door locks of his car with the remote broke into his thoughts. When they reached the vehicle, Aaron turned to him. "We're going to need all the help we can get with damage control. It would help if you'd make a call to that friend of yours at the TV station to counteract any bad press."

"J.P.'s no stranger to publicity. I'm sure he can handle it."

"It's not him I'm worried about. It's Holly. What do you think they're going to do when the story gets out about her crashing the rehearsal dinner last night and throwing wine in Francesca's face?"

Cole had heard all the ugly details from his sister last night. It had been a stupid and immature thing for Holly to do. Of course, she'd regretted her actions later. But by then the damage had been done.

"How do you think Holly's going to handle having the press in *her* face?"

Aaron was right. Holly was as beautiful as a hothouse flower and just as fragile. And ever since that mess J.P. put her through eight years ago, she had never been the same. Having the press all over her would only unnerve her. "I'll see what I can do."

Charlie stood, waiting impatiently for the M.E. to complete her preliminary examination of the body. As she did, she kept seeing that silk stocking lying next to the victim. But instead of seeing Francesca Hill's face, she saw Emily's. The memories came tumbling back like slides from a home-movie reel…back six years ago…back to another dreary and cold afternoon….

Charlie adjusted the rearview mirror of her car in an attempt to diffuse the blinding headlights from the car that was practically on her bumper. When the other driver pulled out into the oncoming lane to pass her, horns blasted as the car nearly collided with the SUV coming from the other direction. Gasping at the near miss, Charlie hit the brakes of her car when the driver pulled back into the lane in front of her.

"Idiot," she muttered when her heart began to beat almost normally again. The jerk could have gotten himself killed, not to mention the people in the SUV and her. Of course, she wouldn't even be on this road if it weren't for Emily.

Emily. Just thinking of her younger sister annoyed her.

This was payback. She knew it was. Her sister was punishing her by not answering her apartment phone or cell phone because Charlie had refused to drop everything and race over when she'd called yesterday. Emily's claim that it was urgent usually meant one thing—guy trouble. Younger than her by four years, she and Emily couldn't have been more different in appearance or personality. Emily was petite, feminine and blessed with the sexy curves that teenage boys dream about. Whereas she was tall, on the skinny side and more comfortable in jeans and T-shirts than a dress. Guys had been tripping over their tongues to go out with her younger sister from the time she'd gotten her first bra at the tender age of twelve. When it came to Charlie, the boys were more apt to ask her to play a game of catch than to go to the movies.

She didn't mind that Emily was always considered the pretty, ladylike one while she…she was the smart, athletic one. She never had minded. She was even glad to see that their baby sister, Anne, was turning out to be a good mixture of the two of them—pretty and feminine, athletic and smart. She loved both of her sisters, would do anything for them. But she resented the heck out of Emily screwing up her plans by playing stupid games.

Because that's just what she was doing by not answering her phone, Charlie reasoned. Emily knew that their mother would worry and insist that Charlie drive right over and check on her younger sister. And, of course, she would never refuse her parents—especially when her mother offered to make the drive from New Orleans to Baton Rouge if Charlie couldn't.

As a result, here she was driving clear across town and dodging idiotic drivers just to make sure that Emily was okay, when what she should be doing was studying for her criminal-law class. And she really, really needed the extra study time if she wanted to finish at the top of her class. You'd think by now their folks would be used to the fact that Emily was a drama queen, she reasoned, growing more resentful with each mile she drove. She didn't know why her sister had bothered to take premed courses when she clearly belonged on the stage. Everything in Emily's world was of major importance. Even a blemish popping up on her face the day before the senior prom in high school had been a life-or-death matter to her younger sister.

Charlie smacked the steering wheel, irritated all over again that she had to put her own life on hold to come check on her sister. Finally she turned off onto the street where Emily lived. She pulled her car to a stop in front of the small cottage that their parents had leased for Emily at the start of the new semester. When she spied Emily's Honda in the driveway and lights on inside the house, she fumed. She turned off the engine, slamming the car door as she exited, and marched up to the porch.

She jabbed the doorbell with her thumb and held it there for an extra moment or two. Five seconds, ten seconds ticked by and she hit the doorbell again. When her sister still failed to answer, Charlie pounded on the door with her fist. "Come on, Emily. I know you're in there. Open the door!"

After several moments passed and her sister failed to answer, Charlie tried to peer through the frosted glass set in the wood panel of the door, but all she could see was the glow of lights. Since the drapes were drawn, she didn't bother trying to look in the windows. Instead, she banged on the door again.

When she still got no response, Charlie began to worry. Tilting the potted fern beside the door, she retrieved the spare key that her sister kept there. Quickly, Charlie inserted the key in the lock and opened the door. "Emily," she called out as she stepped inside and pushed the door closed behind her. She could hear music coming from somewhere in the house, a mushy love song from that CD her sister had purchased a month ago and had played incessantly when she'd been home for the weekend.

"Emily," she called out again. Still no answer. A shiver of unease skipped down Charlie's spine as she checked out the combination living room/dining room, but the room was empty. Charlie hit the off button on the CD player and suddenly there was silence. Too silent, she thought.

Moving down the hall, Charlie glanced in the kitchen. The light was on, the room neat. Two empty wineglasses sat on the counter, washed but not put away. A dish towel had been folded in half and draped across the sink. But there was no sign of Emily.

Charlie continued through the house to the next room, the spare bedroom. She flipped on the light, found it empty as well. Then she came to Emily's bedroom. The door was closed, but she could see a faint light shining from beneath the bottom of the door. She tapped on it. "Emily?"

Nothing. No response. No sound at all.

With her heart pounding, Charlie opened the door.

The heavy scent of honeysuckle hit her. Charlie noted the gutted candles, recognized the silky-sweet scent that Emily loved and that had driven her crazy when they had both still lived at home. But beneath the overpowering sweetness, she detected another scent. An unfamiliar scent. An unpleasant scent.

Adjusting her eyes to the dimmer light, she saw her sister lying atop the bed, her body and face turned slightly away. At first glance, Charlie thought she was sleeping. She looked small in the four-poster bed, surrounded by the lacy yellow pillows and with the floral duvet draped over her lower body. She was wearing one of those silky, frilly nightgowns that she'd always favored over nightshirts and pajamas. A pair of matching black satin mules was askew on the floor. Although Emily's face was turned away, her long blond hair cascaded across the pillow. One arm was lifted so that her hand rested on the pillow. Within reach of her fingertips lay a black silk stocking.

For a moment, Charlie simply stared at her sister. Then she was struck by her stillness. Emily wasn't moving, Charlie realized. Not even a slight rise and fall of her chest as she breathed. Nervous, Charlie's heart began to pound like a jackhammer. A knot formed in her stomach as she moved to-ward the bed. "Emily," she said her name again, this time un-able to keep the fear out of her voice. Reaching out, she touched her sister's shoulder and Emily's body shifted. Sud-denly Emily's arm fell limply over the side of the bed; her head tilted toward Charlie like a broken doll. As she stared at Emily's lifeless brown eyes, Charlie began to scream.

Charlie yanked herself back to the present. Shaking off the memory, she tuned into what the M.E. was saying to her and Vince and hoped that neither of them had noticed her lapse in attention.

"What about a time of death, Doc?" Vince asked.

"You know I can't tell you that until I get the body back to the lab and examine it more closely," Dr. Penelope Williamson said as she stripped off her gloves.

"Come on, Doc. Just a ballpark idea," Vince responded.

"Well, based on lividity, I'd say she died sometime between midnight and four this morning. I should be able to narrow it down once I complete the exam."

"What about the cause of death?" Charlie asked her, even though she was sure strangulation would be ruled the cause—just as it had been for her sister.

"My initial assessment is death due to strangulation. But like I said, I'll know more once I get back to the lab and do a full exam." She motioned for her team and they moved in and began to bag the victim for transport back to the coroner's of-fice. "I heard this one was a robbery turned homicide. Judg-ing by some of the artwork left behind, your perp isn't very bright. There's a small fortune just on the living-room walls."

"He may have settled for the cash and jewelry because it was easier to get it out of here without attracting attention," Vince offered.

Or maybe the robbery had nothing to do with the murder, Charlie thought, because it simply didn't feel like a robbery to her. "You'll let us know if anything interesting shows up— like someone else's DNA," Charlie stated, knowing without asking that she could count on the other woman. Not only was Penelope Williamson a good doctor, she was thorough in her exams. Nothing got rubber-stamped on her watch.

"I'll let you know, Detective," Dr. Williamson assured her in that cool, calm voice that reminded her of her high-school English teacher, her words perfectly enunciated and no hint of the South in her tone. "And I'll also let you know if anything shows up in the toxicology report. From the looks of things, your victim liked to party."

If the champagne bottles and caviar in the other room were an indication, Francesca Hill liked to party in style, Charlie thought.

"Sean, just one minute," Dr. Williamson called out to one of the men with the body bag. Frowning, she said, "Excuse me, Detectives."

She and Vince watched as the other woman went over to her crew and had them wait while she tucked the victim's hair inside the bag and away from the zipper. She stood there a moment longer, giving them instructions.

Charlie had come to admire Penelope Williamson immensely in the year since she'd joined the New Orleans Coroner's Office. To her surprise, the doctor had a sense of humor—something that helped make an often gruesome job more tolerable. Charlie had seen Dr. Williamson approach the most grisly of crime scenes without hesitation. And she'd seen her handle broken and bloody corpses with the same tenderness and care she would administer to a child. Penelope Williamson cared about the dead victims. It was something the two of them had in common, Charlie thought. She also felt in her bones that if anyone would be able to provide her with the information she needed to identity Francesca Hill's killer, it would be Dr. Penelope Williamson. And her every instinct told her that when she found Francesca Hill's killer, she would find Emily's killer, too.

"I know what you're thinking, Le Blanc. And you shouldn't start jumping to conclusions," Vince warned.

But before she could respond, Dr. Williamson returned. "Sorry about that."

"No problem," Vince said.

"How quick can you get us the autopsy results?" Charlie asked.

Vince placed a hand on her arm and gave her a look. "Doc, what my partner's trying to say is that we need the results on this one yesterday. So we really would appreciate it if you could process this one right away."

"Kossak, you and Le Blanc *always* need your cases processed right away. But you're going to have to wait like everyone else. The weekend's not over yet and I've already got five bodies lined up in the crypt waiting for me," she told him, referring to the two homicides and three accident victims from the previous night.

"But this one can't wait," Charlie began, only to grimace when Vince stepped on her foot.

"The word from the top is that this case is a priority," Vince explained. "We've been ordered to solve it quickly and quietly or heads are gonna roll."

"I don't like politics, Kossak. They have no place in police business," Dr. Williamson informed him.

"I agree with you," Vince returned. "But the victim's fiancé has friends in high places and those friends are putting pressure on the captain."

The comment irritated Charlie—especially because she

knew that despite the mayor's efforts to rid the city of corruption, there were still a great many who held on to the good-old-boy system of doing business. "It doesn't matter who her fiancé was or who the man is friends with," Charlie said as she watched the body bag being carried out. "What matters is that a woman is dead and we need to catch the animal who killed her."

"You're right, of course," Dr. Williamson told her. "You'll have the autopsy results as soon as I finish."

"Thanks. We owe you one, Doc," Vince told her.

"You owe me several, Detective." She shifted her gaze to Charlie and back to him again. "Both of you do and one of these days I intend to collect by having you treat me to a lavish dinner at Commander's Palace."

"Anytime you say, Doc. Right, Le Blanc?" Vince nudged her with his elbow. "Right?"

"Um, right," Charlie said, pulling her thoughts back to the present.

"I intend to hold you to that," Dr. Williamson told them, and after she gathered her bag, she headed for the door.

"Snap out of it, Le Blanc, and start focusing on *this* case," Vince said in a low voice near her ear before heading for the tech guys in the next room and barking orders about the surveillance tapes.

Telling herself that Vince was right, that she did need to concentrate on the case at hand, Charlie made another sweep of the crime scene. Pictures had already been taken, evidence bagged and tagged. She walked through the bedroom, attempted to re-create where each piece of clothing, each shoe had been found. She looked at the bed, noted the markings on the mattress, outlining the position of the body when it had been found. She looked over to the spot where the stocking had been draped beside the body. As she did so, she called up the images forever etched in her memory from Emily's bedroom six years ago. The similarities couldn't be dismissed.

It's the same guy.

She was sure of it—could feel it in her bones. He might have gotten away the last time, but not this time, she vowed. This time she wasn't an unprepared law student who didn't know enough to preserve the crime scene. This time she was a cop, one who knew what to look for and where to look for it. If he'd made a mistake, no matter how small, she would find it.

And then she would find him.

Three

"De Nova, as soon as you process those bedsheets, get back to me," Vince told the crime-scene tech who had bagged the bed linen to take back to the lab for trace evidence.

"You got it," the younger man said and gave him a salute that seemed strange coming from a guy with spiked orange hair.

Shaking his head, Vince turned away. A quick once-over revealed that the rest of the crew were wrapping up. Satisfied, he glanced at the young officer who was still standing guard at the door. The kid looked barely old enough to drink, Vince thought. But he was tall. He had a good four inches on his own six feet, Vince estimated. His police uniform was neatly pressed; his shoes looked as if they'd been spit-polished. And he was standing so stiff and straight, it made his own spine ache. But buff and polish and baby face aside, the kid had done a good job securing the scene. He owed him one for stopping the apartment manager and staff from traipsing through the place and making everyone's job a thousand times more difficult. The kid had a brain and had used it, which in his book was a big plus. He made his way over to him. "Officer Mackenzie, wasn't it?"

"Yes, sir. Andrew Mackenzie, sir."

"You can relax, Mackenzie."

"Yes, sir," he said and shifted his stance so that his feet were separated by a foot instead of a few inches.

Vince bit off a sigh. "Mackenzie, you did a good job here today."

"Thank you, sir."

"With the murder rate up, we're a bit shorthanded in Homicide. We could use an extra pair eyes and legs on this case. How would you feel about being assigned to us temporarily?"

"You mean work with you and Detective Le Blanc on a homicide?"

"Yes, that's what I mean," Vince said. "If I can get it cleared with your captain, would you be willing to stay on for a while until we close this case?"

"Yes, sir," he said enthusiastically. "I'd consider it a privilege, sir. It's my goal to work in Homicide one day."

"Then now's your chance. Who's your captain?"

"Roussell, sir. Tom Roussell."

"I know Captain Roussell. He's a good man." He had worked under Tom Roussell himself when he'd been a rookie. "I'll run this by Captain Warren in Homicide and ask him to call and square things with Captain Roussell. In the meantime, I want you to stay posted here and make sure no one enters this place without first talking to me or Detective Le Blanc. Got it?"

"Yes, sir. Got it, sir."

Vince placed a call to his own captain first. He gave him a quick rundown of the situation, then made the request for Mackenzie's reassignment. The captain didn't hesitate and said he'd handle the duty change himself. After listening to the captain reiterate the need for them to close this case quickly and quietly, Vince ended the call. He turned back to Mackenzie. "It's all set, Mackenzie. For now, you belong to Homicide and report to me and Detective Le Blanc."

"Thank you, sir. I promise I won't let you down, sir."

Vince nodded and turned away. God, but the kid made him feel like an old man. Hell, maybe in today's youth-driven culture, thirty-two *was* considered old. Or maybe all the years of dealing with the ugly side of humanity had aged him prematurely. Then again, maybe his mother was right and he needed a woman in his life—someone to remind him of the good in the world after dealing with so much of the darkness. Fat chance, he thought. Since his divorce five years ago, his longest relationship had lasted all of three months. And the truth was, that relationship would have hit the skids sooner if he hadn't been so wrapped up in the case he'd been working on at the time.

That was his problem, Vince decided. Work always came first. It had been one of his ex-wife's major complaints—he was gone all the time. Of course, she hadn't liked the size of his paychecks either. She'd given him an ultimatum—find another job or the marriage was over. He'd opted to keep the job. Luckily for both of them, they'd had the sense to call it quits before kids came into the picture. Last he'd heard, his ex had found herself a new husband with a nine-to-five job and a fat paycheck. But he was still a cop, he reminded himself. He was also still alone.

Shoving aside his grim thoughts, Vince went to look for his partner. He found her in the bedroom, staring at the bed where the body had been. Vince frowned. There was an edginess in her stance that worried him. Charlie kept a lot bottled up inside and although she was better than most at hiding her feelings, he knew that every case claimed a piece of her. Some more than others. He knew that scene in the bedroom had hit her hard. He also knew that it had hit much too close to home.

It was what he had been afraid of from the moment he'd arrived on the scene and discovered that single stocking on the bed. He'd worked enough crime scenes to recognize a perp's signature. Every criminal, whether they were a torcher,

a safecracker or a killer, had his or her own signature. The
stocking was this guy's signature. And from the report he'd
been able to obtain on Emily Le Blanc's case, he knew the
similarities—death by strangulation and a single black stocking beside the victim—were identical to this one. Though he
had attempted to downplay the situation, he knew she hadn't
bought it. The odds that the same man was responsible for
both murders was more than good. Which meant Charlie had
no business on this case.

But getting her to see that was another story. He knew for
a fact that she'd spent countless hours during her off time
scrolling through Codis, hoping to find a match in the DNA
index system to the DNA recovered from her sister's crime
scene. And each time she'd come up empty. Until now. Con-
vincing her to back away would be next to impossible. But
he had to at least try. Walking into the room, he came to a stop
beside her. "The techs are finishing up out there. We probably ought to head over to Stratton's place and give him the
news before someone else does."

She turned to face him. "My car's out front. You want to
take it or follow me in yours?"

"What do you say I work this one solo?"

"Like hell you will," she snapped.

"Come on, Le Blanc. You've got a personal stake in this
one. You don't belong on this case."

"I've been looking for this guy for years. I know more
about him than you or anyone else."

"That might be true. But you also have a major conflict of
interest. If the captain knew there was even a possibility that
this case is connected to your sister's murder, he'd pull you
off of it in a New York minute."

"But he doesn't know. And neither does anyone else."

"You sure about that?" Vince asked.

"Very few people know I had another sister besides Anne. And the ones who do only know that my sister was murdered while she was attending college in Baton Rouge. It happened years ago, before I even joined the force."

"And once you tell the captain that the two cases could be related, do you honestly think he'll let you stay on this one?"

"I don't intend to tell him," she informed him.

"And what about me, Charlie? Am I supposed to lie, too?"

"No," she said more softly. "I'd never ask you to do that. All I'm asking is that you not say anything about my suspicions."

"You mean you want me to lie by omission," he said, pointing out the truth of what she was asking of him. Keeping silent would be the same thing in his opinion.

"Only for a few days—just until I have a chance to confirm whether I'm right, whether the guy who murdered the Hill woman is the same one who murdered Emily." When Vince didn't respond, she said, "Please, Vince. Just a few days."

Vince rubbed the back of his neck. "Suppose someone who worked your sister's case remembers it and sees the similarities? Then what?"

"One of the detectives on Emily's case retired and the other one took a position out in Texas," she countered. "Besides, Emily was killed a hundred miles from here, and she and the Hill woman were from two different worlds, *and* the case has been cold for six years. The police up there have their hands full just like we do. They won't have time to start looking for a connection between one of their old murder cases and this one. Please, Vince," she repeated.

Vince sighed. "All right. You just better hope that this doesn't come back and bite us both in the ass."

"It won't. And if it does, I'll take full responsibility," she promised. "I'll tell the captain it was all my doing, that I kept you in the dark."

"Why don't we try to keep the lies to a minimum," he suggested, because there was no way on earth he'd let her take that fall alone. "Now, what do you say we head over to Stratton's and let the man know that he isn't going to need his tux after all?"

"What do you think a place like this goes for?" Vince asked sotto voce as the two of them stood in the parlor of J. P. Stratton's palatial home waiting for the butler to announce them.

"Just the real estate this place is sitting on costs more than you and I will make in a lifetime," Charlie responded. Half the homes on this stretch of Saint Charles Avenue were more than a century old and had been carved from one-time plantations. A great many of them had been refurbished, the original architecture preserved and they were now designated as historic landmarks. The polished marble floors, sky-high ceilings and the magnificent chandelier were right out of a picture book. They screamed "money." "You can add another million or two for the house—and that's without the furnishings."

Before Vince could respond, the butler reappeared. A dour-looking man in a classic black butler's suit, the guy could have been anywhere between forty and seventy years old, Charlie thought.

"If you will follow me, Detectives," he said in a voice that sounded more British than the combination of Brooklyn and the South that typified the speech of most New Orleanians. "Mr. Stratton will see you now."

Vince exchanged a look with her and she knew he found the exchange as pompous as she had. Silently, they followed the stiff-backed butler down a long hallway with walls that were covered in peach silk fabric and adorned with oil portraits. He stopped near the end of the hall and opened a door for them to enter. Once they were inside, he pulled the door closed in the same quiet manner in which he had walked.

After identifying themselves to Aaron Stratton, they waited while J. P. Stratton barked out instructions to some poor assistant over the phone. "Aaron," the older man called out.

"Excuse me, Detectives," he said and went to his father's side.

While they waited, Charlie used the time to size up J. P. Stratton. Her initial impression was that he was a big man with an even bigger ego. He was also arrogant, chauvinistic and a self-centered ass. She pegged him at about five foot eleven inches, two hundred and ten pounds. He sported a George Hamilton tan that was set off by black hair that a man well past sixty could only have achieved with the help of a hairdresser. His eyes were a deep shade of blue, his nose sharp, his mouth thin. Due to the miracle of Botox or a face-lift or both, his face was completely void of lines. In fact, the bronze skin was so taut, she'd wager a tennis ball could have bounced off it. The suit he wore looked expensive, probably from one of those Italian designers, Charlie thought. He wore a diamond Rolex on his left wrist, cuff links with diamonds set in gold and an onyx-and-diamond ring on his pinkie finger that was so large it could have been used as a weapon. There was a coldness about him that made it easy for her to understand how he had gone through a string of wives. She couldn't imagine any woman tying herself to such a man.

When he finally ended the call, Charlie introduced herself and Vince. "Mr. Stratton, I'm afraid we have tragic news, sir."

"If you're here to tell me that Francesca's dead, you're a little late, Detectives," he said in a deep, blustery voice that he directed at Vince. "When I called to speak with my fiancée, the fool police officer who answered the phone told me she was dead."

"I'm sorry about that, sir," Charlie told him.

"You're going to be even sorrier, Detectives," he fired back. "I've just gotten off the phone with your chief of police and

I've let him know how incompetent his staff is," he added, directing his remarks to Vince again and barely glancing at Charlie.

Charlie stepped in front of the man's line of vision, forcing him to look at her. "The first officer on the scene is a new man, sir," she explained. "He'll be apprised of his error in judgment and disciplined, accordingly."

"He'll be fired, if I have anything to say about it."

"Since you're neither the chief of police nor the officer's captain, you don't have anything to say about it," she said firmly.

Stratton shot to his feet. He moved quickly for a man his age, Charlie thought. She couldn't help being grateful that she'd been the sister blessed with long legs. With the two inches her boots added to her own five foot seven inches, it made it difficult for Stratton to look down at her.

"Young woman, I—"

"It's Detective, Mr. Stratton. Detective Le Blanc."

"Dad," Aaron said, and stepping forward, he placed a hand on his father's shoulder. "As you can imagine, Detectives, the news about Francesca's death has devastated my father."

The son was definitely *not* a chip off the old block. To begin with he had a good two inches in height on his father, but he weighed at least twenty pounds less. While he had his father's mouth, his eyes were green, his hair dark blond. His slacks and shirt were well made and tasteful and, from the way they fit him, it was obvious he kept himself in shape. His hands were strong and his grip had been firm when he'd shaken her hand. Charlie guessed him to be in his late twenties. The younger Stratton had a warmth his father lacked. Yet there was also a coolness. An odd combination, she thought.

J. P. Stratton shrugged off his son's hand. "I don't need you to make excuses for me, boy. I'm not devastated. I'm furious," he informed them. "Three hours from now, five hundred people from all across the state will be arriving at the New Orleans Museum of Art to celebrate my wedding," he told her, with a sweep of his arm. "Do you have any idea the amount of time and money that went into planning that wedding? Or the headaches canceling it is causing me?"

So much for the brokenhearted groom. "I'm sure I can't imagine, sir," Charlie told him, not even attempting to keep the sarcasm out of her voice.

Vince shot her a reproving look. "We realize this is a difficult time for you, Mr. Stratton, and we're sorry for your loss," Vince said. "But I'm afraid we do need to ask you a few questions."

"Instead of wasting time questioning me, why aren't out looking for the person who killed Francesca? You probably don't even have a suspect yet, do you?"

"Not yet, sir. But we're working on it," Vince told him. "We're interviewing Ms. Hill's neighbors and checking the security tapes from her building. It would help us if you could tell us when you last saw Ms. Hill."

When Stratton started to object, Aaron said, "They're just trying to get a time line on when Francesca was killed."

"Your son's right, Mr. Stratton," Vince informed him. "If we can narrow down the last time anyone saw or spoke to her, it would help."

Stratton sat down and retrieved a cigar from a humidor on the desk, but he didn't light it. "I saw her at her apartment around nine o'clock last night. We had a rehearsal dinner earlier that evening and Francesca had a bit too much to drink. I wanted to make sure she was okay."

From the looks of the apartment, Francesca had continued to party after she'd returned home, Charlie thought as she took out her notebook and pen. "Was she okay?" she asked.

"She was fine, just tired from all the excitement."

"How long did you stay?" Charlie asked him.

"Until around nine-thirty. Francesca wanted to make it an early night so that she would be rested and beautiful for today."

"Can you think of anyone who might have wanted to harm Ms. Hill?" Vince asked.

"There was an ex-boyfriend, some lowlife she was seeing before we met. He wasn't happy about being dumped and accosted Francesca outside her apartment building a couple of weeks ago. I had Francesca take out a restraining order against him."

"Does this guy have a name?" Charlie asked.

"Schwitzer. Marcus Schwitzer," Aaron told her. "I assisted Francesca with the restraining order," he explained.

Charlie wrote down the information. "Do you know where we can find him?"

"He was working as a bouncer at the Red Slipper Club," the older man advised her. "But when the club's owner was made aware that there was a restraining order out on him, his employment was terminated. I suggested he leave town and I believe he took my advice."

In other words, he'd had the guy canned and railroaded out of town, Charlie surmised. "I don't imagine he was too happy about that."

J. P. Stratton gave her a smug look. "Would *you* be, Detective?"

She didn't bother to answer. Instead, she asked, "Did this Schwitzer make any threats against Ms. Hill before he left?"

"None that I know of."

"Can you think of anyone else who might have had a grudge against your fiancée or you?" Vince asked.

"Detective, a man doesn't get to be in my position without making some enemies along the way," Stratton told him.

"Any of those enemies hate you enough to kill your fiancée?" Charlie asked.

"You'd have to ask them," he replied.

"We'll need a list of their names," Charlie informed him.

"Aaron can provide you with them. He's my attorney. He'll know of any business deals that didn't sit well with other parties."

"I'll get a list to you as soon as possible, Detective," Aaron replied.

"Thank you," Charlie told him and directed her attention once more to the father. "What about on a personal level? Was there anyone besides this Schwitzer fellow who was unhappy about the upcoming wedding?"

"Other than my last ex-wife who's deluded herself for years that I'm going to remarry her, everyone was very happy about the wedding."

He was lying through his capped teeth, Charlie decided. She hadn't missed the look exchanged between father and son.

"Is there anything else?" J. P. Stratton asked, clearly annoyed.

"Just one more thing," Charlie said, following a hunch. "I'd like a list of the guests who attended last night's dinner party."

The older man narrowed his eyes, causing his heavy brows to form a dark angry line. "Why would you need to know who my dinner guests were?"

"Because it's possible one of them saw or heard something that might help us find the killer."

"I've tried to be cooperative, Detectives, but my patience is wearing thin. Instead of wasting time questioning me and my friends, you should be out looking for Schwitzer."

"I assure you, we'll find Schwitzer and bring him in for questioning. But I still need that list." She offered him her card and when he failed to take it, she placed it on the desk.

"I'll see that you get the list," Aaron Stratton said. "Let me show you the way out."

She directed her attention back to the older man. "Once again, we're sorry for your loss, Mr. Stratton."

Aaron Stratton hustled them out of the room. "Please excuse my father," he began, his voice sincere as they stepped into the corridor. "Francesca's death has hit him harder than he lets on. He truly did love her."

Right, Charlie thought. And she had a bridge she'd like to sell him, too. "Here's my card," Charlie told him. "Just call me when you have that list and I'll have it picked up."

"I'll do that," he replied, brushing his fingers against hers as he took the card.

"Thank you for your time, Mr. Stratton."

"Aaron," he corrected, giving her a smile that she suspected was meant to charm before he turned and extended his hand to Vince. "Detective."

Vince nodded.

"Henry will show you out," he told them and, like magic, the butler appeared almost instantly.

"This way, please," he said.

Once they exited the mansion, they remained silent while they negotiated the elaborate walkway. Starting toward the iron-lace gate that led to the street, Vince asked, "What do you think of our grief-stricken groom?"

"I think he's a pompous ass," Charlie informed him.

"You buy his story?"

"No. He's hiding something," Charlie told him. "And I intend to find out what it is."

As they neared the gate, Charlie spotted the *Channel 4 News* truck and one of the station's reporters with a microphone in hand. "Aw hell," she muttered, because it wasn't just any reporter—it was her sister Anne.

* * *

The moment Anne Le Blanc recognized the pair exiting the home of millionaire J. P. Stratton, adrenaline skyrocketed through her system. Her piece for the TV station's evening broadcast had just gone from lifestyles of the local rich and famous to something a whole lot more serious. "Kevin, set up the camera," she instructed the cameraman who had accompanied her.

The hastily planned nuptials of one of the city's wealthiest and most flamboyant businessmen to a much younger former casino hostess had set tongues wagging three weeks ago. The citizens of New Orleans liked nothing better than a juicy scandal, and despite his protests to the contrary, J. P. Stratton seemed to like providing the members of his adopted city with something to talk about. And the former Texan had given them plenty over the years with his business triumphs, lavish lifestyle and string of trophy wives. The man's exploits read like a soap opera script—lots of money, lots of sex and lots of scandal. So it came as no surprise that the wedding scheduled that evening at the New Orleans Museum of Art with a guest list that read like a who's who for the state of Louisiana had guaranteed J. P. Stratton another fifteen minutes of fame.

Personally, she didn't give a fig who the old goat married. But apparently the TV station's viewers did. And she had been assigned to satisfy the public's fascination and curiosity by providing them with a peek inside the fairy-tale affair. But when she'd gotten a tip that the wedding was off, she'd high-tailed it over to the Stratton mansion, hoping to get the scoop.

According to the rumor mill, the bride-to-be had balked at signing a prenuptial agreement that had been presented to her at the eleventh hour. She didn't blame the woman. What woman wanted to start off her marriage by planning what her take would be in a divorce? On the other hand, she supposed she could see Stratton's point. After four ex-wives and several palimony suits, the man had probably forked over a chunk of his fortune. Evidently, he did not intend to do so again. And with no prenuptial, there would be no wedding. Of course, that wouldn't be the reason given for the cancellation. No, they'd probably spin some tale about a sudden illness or business emergency being the cause for delaying the happy couple's wedding. At least that's what she had thought initially, Anne admitted. But the presence of two homicide detectives at the Stratton home told her there was a great deal more than an unsigned prenup behind the canceled wedding.

"Say, isn't that your sister?" Kevin asked as he aimed the camera on the two people leaving the Stratton house and approaching the gate.

"It sure is," Anne told him. And the hunk with the sexy swagger at her sister's side was Detective Vincent Kossak. Her heart beat a little faster as she watched him. Not for the first time, Anne wondered how an innocent kiss under the mistletoe on New Year's Eve with her sister's partner had turned into a steamy, curl-your-toes kiss that had sent her hormones into overdrive. Oh, there had always been a little spark there. She'd been intrigued by him. With a nine-year difference in their ages, he was older than most of the men she'd dated, more mature, more serious. There was a confidence about him that she'd found attractive. But he'd never given the slightest indication that he was even remotely interested in her.

Until New Year's Eve.

That night when she'd seen him standing under the mistletoe looking as if he'd rather be anyplace else than at that party, she had acted on impulse. She'd grabbed him by the tie, pulled his face down to hers and kissed him. And he had kissed her back. But there had been nothing sisterly or playful about that kiss. It had been a no-holds-barred, open-mouthed, hungry kiss. And ever since that night a month ago, she hadn't been able to get Vince Kossak out of her head.

The gate opened and her sister marched out to the sidewalk with a scowl on her face and a look in her eyes that said "back off." As the youngest of three girls, Anne had had her share of run-ins with her two older siblings when the three of them had been living under the same roof and sharing one bathroom. With six years between her and Charlie and two years between her and Emily, her sisters had had a treasure trove of grown-up girlie stuff that she couldn't wait to get into. And she had never allowed a little thing like Charlie threatening to toss her out the window to keep her from those treasures. Some things were simply worth the risk.

Like Detective Vincent Kossak.

Or a hot story. And her journalist's antenna sensed a hot story now. She had no intention of allowing a little thing like Charlie's angry expression to keep her from that story. "Detective, does your presence here have anything to do with J. P. Stratton's wedding being canceled this evening?" she asked and aimed the microphone at her sister.

"Unless you want to eat that thing, I'd suggest you get it out of my face," Charlie hissed.

"Was that a yes, Detective?"

Her sister practically snarled and brushed past her.

Unfazed, Anne pointed the microphone at Vince. "What about you, Detective Kossak? Can you tell us why you're here?"

He looked right at her, dropping his gaze to her mouth. For a moment, Anne felt that zap of awareness stretch between them like an electrical wire dangling in a storm. But when he lifted his gaze to meet hers, his eyes were calm, distant. "No comment."

Shaking off the impact of that initial look, Anne hurried after them. "Keep the camera running," she told Kevin and followed them down the street as quickly as she could in the three-inch heels that matched her suit. She caught up with them at the corner. "Detective Le Blanc, can you tell us why you were at the home of J. P. Stratton?"

Charlie glared at her and Anne was sure her sister would have given her an earful, were it not for her cell phone ringing. "Le Blanc." She covered one ear with her hand. "What? I can't hear you," she told the party on the other end of the line. "Hang on a second." Holding the phone to her chest a moment, she said to Vince, "I'm going to see if I can get a better connection. You can get rid of her."

When her sister walked away, Anne once again shifted the microphone in Vince's direction. She gave him a challenging look. "If you want to get rid of me, Detective Kossak, all you have to do is tell me why you were at the Stratton home."

"No comment," he repeated.

She decided to try another tack. "Are you and Detective Le Blanc working on a homicide case?"

"No comment."

"Is your case somehow connected to J. P. Stratton?"

"No comment," he told her and kept his eyes focused in the direction her sister had gone.

Disappointed, Anne knew she wouldn't get anything more. The man was every bit as stubborn as her sister. Turning to Kevin, she made a slicing motion across her throat, indicating he should shut down the camera. "I'll meet you back at the truck," she told him.

He nodded and walked back down the street to where the TV van was parked. Once he was gone, she turned back to

Vince. At six feet, he had nearly eight inches on her own five-foot-four-and-a-half-inch frame. So she was glad she had the extra three inches her heels provided. His dark brown hair was thick, his eyes the color of coffee. The sharp cheekbones and square jaw spoke of his Russian ancestry. He wasn't movie-star handsome, but he was a man that a woman would notice.

She'd noticed. And judging by the way he'd kissed her back, he had noticed her, too. So why hadn't he done what most red-blooded males did after a kiss that registered on the Richter scale? Why hadn't he followed through? For a second, she considered the possibility that she had been wrong, that maybe she had only imagined that Vince had felt something, too. No, she hadn't been wrong. She'd been on the other end of that kiss. And Vincent Kossak had wanted her.

"You're wasting your time, Anne. Your sister isn't going to comment on an investigation and neither am I."

"So there *is* an investigation," she said, her journalistic instincts kicking in again.

"No comment."

A canceled wedding and homicide detectives at the home of the prospective groom. A coincidence? She didn't think so. In fact, she'd stake her new Louis Vuitton purse on it. "What about off the record? If I promise not to report anything, will you tell me what's going on?"

He chuckled. "Not a chance."

"Fine. Since you refuse to discuss police business with me, what about personal business?"

He eyed her warily. "What personal business?"

"Oh, we could start with you explaining why you've been avoiding me since New Year's? Is it because we kissed?"

"No. And I haven't been avoiding you."

"Then how come every time I've set foot inside the police station during the past two months, you disappear?"

"I've been busy."

"Careful, Vince, you keep telling fibs and your nose is going to grow." She edged a little closer, just enough to get into his personal space. He moved back a step and Anne thought she detected a tinge of red in his cheeks.

"Listen, about that night. I was out of line kissing you and I should have called to apol—"

"Don't," she all but growled. "So help me, Vincent Kossak, if you apologize for kissing me, I swear I'll…I'll punch you in the nose."

"All right. I won't apologize," he said. "But that kiss should never have happened."

"Why not?"

"Because I'm your sister's partner."

"So?"

"So you and me, us…it's not a good idea," he said firmly.

"Says who?"

"Says me." He sighed. "Come on, Anne. I'm almost ten years older than you. I've been married and divorced while you're just getting started with your life. You're just a kid and I'm practically an old man."

"I assure you, Detective Kossak, I am not a kid. I am a grown woman and—"

"Kossak, we've got to roll," Charlie called out as she ran back to the car.

"No time to talk," he told her. And with a swiftness that made her blink, Anne stared dumbfounded as Vince shifted gears, seeming to forget that they were in the midst of a serious discussion, seeming to forget her. Suddenly he was all business. His body tensed, poised for action. And without another word to her, he yanked open the car door and focused all of his attention on his job. "What have we got?" he asked Charlie.

"Not what, who," Charlie told him as she pulled open the driver's door and slid behind the wheel. "We hit pay dirt with the security discs from the apartment building and—"

Vince pulled his door shut.

But she'd heard enough, Anne thought as she watched the car with Vince and her sister speed off. She raced back to the TV truck. "Let's go," she told Kevin.

"We following them?" he asked as he started the engine and pulled away from the curb.

"No. We're going to the Mill House Apartments," she told him. And with a little luck she was going to be breaking a big story on the evening news.

Four

While she and Vince waited for the electronics tech to key up the security tapes from the Mill House Apartments, Charlie scanned the visitors' log. Noting the number of people who had visited Francesca Hill on the day she was killed, she nearly groaned. It would take days to interview them all. "I'm surprised she didn't install a revolving door."

"According to the kid at the front desk, our vic was very popular," Vince said.

"I'll say. Wait until you see the tape," the whiz-kid tech named Rich replied.

"We are waiting," Charlie pointed out. They had been racing from Stratton's home to the station when the call came saying someone of interest had popped up on the security tapes. She had spent years searching for a lead on Emily's killer and at last she had one—even if it had come through another tragedy. And she wanted to move on that lead now.

"Here we go," Rich said as a view of the elevator door and hallway to Francesca Hill's apartment came onto the screen. A tall blonde in a black leather skirt, sweater and thigh-high boots exited the elevator carrying a gift bag with a frilly ribbon.

"That must be the hot chick the kid at the desk told me about before the manager showed up and put a muzzle on him," Vince remarked as the woman strutted toward the apartment. "The kid said her name's Danielle. She's a dealer at the casino where our vic worked before she hit the engagement lottery."

Danielle Marceau, Charlie noted, locating the name in the guest log.

On screen Francesca peeked inside the gift bag, then ushered the woman inside her apartment. After several moments spent staring at the closed door, Charlie asked, "Can you speed it up?"

"Your wish is my command, Detective."

She rolled her eyes. The boy wonder with peach fuzz on his chin had joined the department six months ago. Despite his weird sense of humor and even weirder fashion style, he was a walking, talking, electronics genius. He could make anything electronic sing. A few taps of his fingers and Danielle zipped down the hall in fast-forward motion. The time lapsed on the tape was thirty minutes.

"And here's our next guest," Rich said as he slowed the tape again.

"The intended bridegroom," Charlie remarked when J. P. Stratton stepped out of the elevator. He was greeted at the door with a kiss, before disappearing into the apartment. Fast-forwarding had him leaving again less than twenty minutes later.

"I guess he's not big on foreplay," Rich joked.

"Skip the commentary and just run the film," Charlie said dryly.

Aaron Stratton arrived next, carrying a briefcase, and stayed for fifteen minutes. "You remember sonny boy mentioning a visit to his stepmother-to-be?" Vince asked.

"No," Charlie replied and made a note to question Aaron Stratton about his visit. The film was fast-forwarded and when it was slowed again, an older gentleman wearing a gray overcoat, hat and carrying a bible went to the apartment. "Reverend Homer Lawrence," she read the name in the visitors' log. "I wonder what the minister wanted at that time of night?"

"I'll get Mackenzie to find out what church he's affiliated with and we'll ask him," Vince said as he scribbled in his notepad.

"Wait! Slow it down," Charlie instructed. She sat forward, studying the newest arrival. The man was tall, probably six foot three or better, two hundred pounds, early to mid-thirties, she guessed. He had an arresting face with a strong jawline, a sensual mouth and cheekbones sharp enough to cut ice. His hair was thick, straight and looked in need of a trim. Dark brows rested above knowing eyes that stared directly into the camera. Despite the grainy film, the man made an impact. "He looks familiar."

"He should. He's Cole Stratton, the owner of CS Securities, one of the fastest-growing companies in the South. The *Times-Picayune* ran a profile on him in the paper's business section a few months ago."

"What's his relationship to J. P. Stratton?" she asked.

"His firstborn, courtesy of the first Mrs. Stratton. The story is that she was some kind of heiress and it was her money and connections that J.P. used to get started."

"Divorced?" she asked.

"Dead. Cancer," Vince explained. "Apparently J.P. did a real number on her before she died. Cole Stratton was just a kid at the time, but word is he never forgave the old man and as soon as he was old enough, he walked out. Turned his back on a virtual fortune and struck out on his own. According to the grapevine, lots of bad blood there."

"With all that bad blood, one has to wonder why he was visiting his father's fiancée," Charlie pointed out and decided to find out what she could about Cole Stratton.

They sped through more surveillance tape and watched as a young woman approached the apartment. Judging by her clothes and the long, straight hair, Charlie pegged her to be in her early to mid-twenties. She didn't stay long and when she left, she was swiping at her eyes as though crying. Charlie checked the visitors' book, but there were no further guest entries to the Hill apartment. "Whoever she is, she didn't sign in."

"I'll take another shot at the desk clerk to see if he recognizes her and find out why she didn't sign in," Vince offered.

Rich fast-forwarded through more film and when the light glowed on the elevator, he slowed to real time again. A man wearing sunglasses and a hat with a brim exited. The collar of his jacket was turned up, shielding the lower half of his face, which he kept angled away from the camera. "Hold it there," Charlie instructed and glanced at Vince. "Do you think wearing sunglasses indoors at night is some kind of new fashion trend? Or do you get the feeling our visitor knew about the security camera and didn't want to be identified?"

"My guess is number two," he said. "Can you get a close-up of our shy guy?"

"Give me a sec." Rich tapped at the keys, formed a frame around the face, then magnified it. "That's about the best I can do," he said after several attempts at enlarging the image failed to yield a clearer view. "I'll see if I can get a better angle of him leaving."

But that view proved no better. Disappointed and frustrated, Charlie clenched the pen in her hand. "What about the cameras in the lobby? Maybe there's a better shot of him on those tapes? And check the camera at the delivery entrance, too, just in case he didn't come through the front door."

"I'll check them," Rich said.

"Call us if something pops," Charlie said and started to push away from the table. They had a lot of territory to cover and with each hour that passed the trail grew colder.

"Hang on a second. Don't you want to see what else I found?" Rich asked.

Charlie eased back down and waited while the whiz kid tapped the computer keys. He fast-forwarded, then slowed it to real time. One second, two seconds, three seconds ticked by showing only the same scene of the elevator door and the empty hall leading to the Hill apartment. Then she saw it—a blip in the film. The blip was so quick, it was almost indiscernible. The empty hall scene remained the same, but the time on the film had jumped forward by nearly two hours. "Wait. Back it up a few seconds, then run it."

Rich did as he was told. And there it was again—a break in the surveillance tape. It lasted no longer than the blink of an eye, but according to tape, nearly two hours had passed. "Somebody monkeyed with the surveillance camera," she said aloud.

"Someone who obviously knew his or her way around the security system," Vince pointed out.

"Good job, kid," she told the tech as she stood and grabbed her jacket from the back of the chair. "Let us know if you come up with anything else on our mystery guy."

Vince followed her to the door. "Who do you want to start with?"

They'd already interviewed J. P. Stratton and his son Aaron once. "Why don't we start with the other son, Cole Stratton. Since he owns a security company, chances are he knows how to get around one."

* * *

Sitting alone in the dark, he turned on the television and tuned in to Channel 4, knowing they would be the first to break the news story. He sipped his scotch and waited patiently for the beer commercial to finish.

"Good evening. This is Bill Capo filling in for Eric Paulsen," the veteran investigative reporter began in that deep, sincere voice that made him a favorite among the locals. "Today in Washington..."

He listened to the reporter give a rundown on the national news front, the budget deficit, the rising cost of health care and the use of steroids in professional sports before he shifted to news on the local front. After a station break, Capo's face returned to the screen.

"In other local news, the much-talked-about wedding of businessman J. P. Stratton to Francesca Hill that was scheduled to take place this evening has been canceled," Bill announced. "Live on the scene with more on that story is Anne Le Blanc."

The TV screen switched to the perky blond reporter standing at the entrance to the museum with the wind whipping her hair around her face. "Bill, I'm here at the New Orleans Museum of Art, where less than an hour from now J. P. Stratton, the founder of Stratton Hotels, was scheduled to take Francesca Hill as his bride. Inside," she continued, extending her arm toward the structure, "thousands of red roses were flown in for the event and food was prepared by some of the top chefs in the city for the guest list of five hundred. But I'm told, a short time ago the guests began receiving calls from Mr. Stratton's staff, advising them that the wedding had been canceled."

"Anne, has any reason been given for the cancellation?" Bill asked.

"Not yet, Bill. And so far, our calls to both Mr. Stratton and Ms. Hill have not been returned. But as you can see from the

cars arriving, not all of the guests received the news in time."
She walked down to the street and knocked on the window of
a sleek black limo. When the window slid down, she asked,
"Sir, you're live on Channel 4 News. *Are you here for the*
Stratton/Hill wedding?"

She pointed the microphone at him. "Yes, I am."

"No one contacted you to tell you the wedding had been
canceled?" she asked, and angled the microphone at him.

"My secretary reached me on my cell phone just as I ar-
rived and gave me the news."

"Were you told the reason for the cancellation?" Anne asked.

"No. Just that it was canceled and that Mr. Stratton ex-
tended his apologies."

"Any guess as to why it was canceled?" she asked.

He paused. "Maybe J.P. got cold feet."

"Thank you," she said and walked away from the car. "It
appears that for now the reason for cancellation of the fairy-
tale event remains a mystery. However, a source, who has
asked not to be identified, told this reporter that the police
were seen at Mr. Stratton's home this afternoon."

"Anne, do we know why the police were at the Stratton
home?" Bill asked.

"No, Bill, we don't. But I'm sure many of the guests who
were invited are wondering just as we are if the reason for the
cancellation of the wedding is something much more serious
than cold feet."

"Thank you, Anne."

"Thank you, Bill. This is Anne Le Blanc reporting live for
Channel 4 Eyewitness News."

"I'm sure we'll be hearing a lot more on this story as the
details become available," Capo said.

They would be hearing so much more, he thought, disap-
pointed that they hadn't released the real story. He'd hoped

to see the photos, hear some of the grim details and relive his triumph. He'd also wanted to get another look at the pretty detective.

Using the remote, he turned off the television. No matter, he decided. It would happen soon enough. After setting down his glass, he picked up the black silk stocking that he had taken from his treasure chest. His heart beat a little faster as he looked at it, sliding it along his fingers. There was nothing like the feel of silk. Sensuous. Seductive. Secretive. Just like the woman he'd killed. Lifting the stocking to his face, he breathed in her scent. He could feel his blood beginning to heat. A throbbing ache started in his loins and spread through his body like fire. It clawed at him, a ravenous beast demanding to be fed.

He freed himself from his pants. Closing his eyes, he pressed the stocking to his mouth so he could taste her while he closed his fist around his hard flesh and began the up-and-down motion. Up and down. Up and down. Fast. Faster. Faster still. He held the stocking in his fist, used the scent of her to bring back the memory.

And then she was there.

So beautiful. So wanton. So wicked.

Increasing the tempo, he could feel his breathing grow labored. Sweat began to trickle down his brow. Suddenly he was back in the bedroom with her. Once again, he could see the lust in her eyes turn to alarm. See the fear begin to take root as she struggled to free her bound wrists. Watch that fear turn to panic when she realized they were no longer playing a game. Best of all, he could see the terror come into her green eyes when she realized he was going to kill her. And as he recalled the feel of her body bucking beneath him and her life slipping away, he shouted as his own release came.

Later, when his breathing had returned to normal and he'd

*righted himself, he retrieved the black silk stocking and re-
turned it to the envelope marked Francesca. Opening the black
box, he placed it inside behind the envelope marked Emily.*

"Kossak! Le Blanc!"

Charlie's head came up, as did those of half of the squad
room. All eyes went to Captain Edward Warren who stood at
his office door with a scowl on his face. "Get your carcasses
in here! Now!"

Quickly Charlie hung up the telephone, not bothering to
finish dialing the number. She darted a glance over at her partner and mouthed the words *What's up?* Vince shrugged in response while he attempted to finish his phone call. Pushing
away from her desk, Charlie grabbed her black jacket from
the back of the chair and slipped it on.

"I'll get back to you," Vince told the person on the other end
of the phone line and ended the call. "What gives?" he asked
her as the two of them started toward the captain's office.

"Beats me," she said. Together they entered the office. Big,
black and bald, Captain Warren was a cop's cop who had worked
his way up the ranks. He was a tough taskmaster but a fair man
who didn't let politics get in the way of the job. And in a sue-
the-police-force mentality that had begun to permeate society,
the captain always went to bat for his officers. She respected him
for that. She also was grateful to him for believing in her and
giving her a chance to be a real homicide detective and not a
token female with the title who was stuck behind a desk shuf-
fling papers in order to meet some minority quota. She and
Vince waited in front of his desk. "You wanted to see us, sir."

"Shut the door," he ordered, then pulled open the bottom
drawer of his desk. He retrieved a bottle of antacid tablets. He
dumped out a handful of the chalky-looking tablets and
shoved them all into his mouth.

Whatever it was, it was bad, Charlie realized. Everyone in the department knew that the way to gauge the captain's mood was by the number of antacids he took. Three tablets meant he wasn't happy. Four meant he was angry and five meant you were in real trouble. But never, ever, in the three years since she was assigned to Homicide had she seen the man take an entire fistful of the things all at once. Whatever had riled the captain was major. She glanced over at Vince and saw from his expression that he knew it, too.

When the captain finished the tablets and returned his attention to them, he looked mad enough to chew nails. "Did I or did I not instruct you to use discretion in the Hill murder investigation?"

"You did, sir," Vince informed him.

When he looked at Charlie, she said, "Yes, sir, you did."

"And weren't you told that there were no statements to be given to the press until I authorized it personally?"

"Yes, sir," they said in unison.

Charlie got a sinking feeling in the pit of her stomach and she hoped that she was wrong, that her sister Anne hadn't done something stupid and landed both Vince and her in hot water. But when the captain shifted his gaze from Vince and trained it on her, Charlie knew she didn't have a prayer.

"Then how do you explain the five o'clock newscast?" he demanded.

"Sir, I'm afraid we haven't seen it," she told him. "We've been working the case."

"Then allow me to show you what you missed," he said dryly and hit the remote button for the portable TV set in the corner of the room. The set was tuned to the channel where the WWL-TV station reran the news broadcasts throughout the day. And there in living color was Anne in front of the New Orleans Museum of Art with a microphone in her hand.

"It appears that for now the reason for cancellation of the fairy-tale event remains a mystery," Anne announced. "However, a source, who has asked not to be identified, told this reporter that the police were seen at Mr. Stratton's home this afternoon."

"Anne, do we know why the police were at the Stratton home?" Bill Capo asked.

"No, Bill, we don't. But I'm sure many of the guests who were invited are wondering just as we are if the reason for the cancellation of the wedding is something much more serious than cold feet."

"Thank you, Anne."

"Thank you, Bill. This is Anne Le Blanc reporting live for *Channel 4 Eyewitness News*."

The captain turned off the TV set. When he turned his attention back to the two of them, Charlie feared the veins in his neck would burst. "Sir, I don't know who my sister's source was," she told him. "But it wasn't me or Detective Kossak."

He leaned forward, dropped his voice to a deep growl and asked, "Then who in the hell was it, Detective? Because let me tell you, I'd like to know who *is* responsible for me spending the last twenty minutes on the phone with the superintendent of police ripping me a new one because my detectives ignored a direct order from the chief himself that there was to be no information on the Hill homicide given to the press."

Charlie checked the urge to flinch. She met the captain's angry gaze. "Sir, you have my word, I did not tell my sister anything about the case."

"Then how do you explain your sister breaking the story, Le Blanc?"

"I can't, sir. But I can tell you that my sister arrived at the Stratton home as we were leaving. I refused to comment on our reason for being there."

"She's telling the truth, sir. I can attest to that," Vince said. "Detective Le Blanc made it…um…clear to her sister that she had nothing to say."

"Evidently she didn't make it clear enough," the captain remarked.

"If I might point out, sir, my sister Anne isn't stupid. She knows I'm a homicide cop and she saw me leaving the Stratton residence. My guess is she put two and two together when the wedding was canceled."

He seemed to consider that. "Then how do you explain your sister showing up there in the first place?"

"I can't, sir," Charlie told him.

"If I might speculate, Captain?" Vince asked.

"I'm listening."

"Anne…Detective Le Blanc's sister is a good reporter and like any good reporter, she has a nose for news," he began.

Charlie looked up at her partner. She knew her sister was a good reporter and she knew Anne had the instincts of a bloodhound when it came to sniffing out a story. But she hadn't realized that Vince knew it or that he had paid enough attention to Anne to discover that fact. Charlie frowned, recalling now that during the last month Vince had been commenting on her sister's reports, asking about her family. Damn, she thought. Did her partner have a thing for her kid sister?

"…and she mentioned to me last week that she would be covering the wedding for the TV station. It's possible she was there to interview Stratton before the ceremony as part of her story. That would explain her being at the house."

"And I'm supposed to believe that it was just a coincidence, her being there at the same time you were?" the captain asked skeptically.

"I'm not a big believer in coincidences either, sir. But every now and then, they happen. And I think that's what happened."

"What about you, Le Blanc?" the captain asked. "What's your theory?"

"I don't have one, sir. But what Detective Kossak said makes sense, with respect to my sister's reason for being at the Stratton house. If you want me to, sir, I could ask her."

He waited a long moment and then said, "Don't bother. I'll see what I can do to smooth things over with the chief. But I'm warning both of you, any more leaks to the press and all the slick talking in the world isn't going to save any of our asses. Understood?"

"Understood, sir," Vince told him.

"Understood, Captain," she replied.

He nodded. "Now tell me what you've got so far."

They brought him up to speed on the investigation, starting with the fact that the theory of robbery as the motive seemed unlikely. "No thief with half a brain would have left that rock behind," Vince told the captain, referring to Francesca's engagement ring.

"He's right, Captain," Charlie added. "I'm not sure what to make of the cash, credit cards and other jewelry that's missing. But robbery is not what's behind the Hill woman's murder."

"Damn! This is not going to play well with the press or with Stratton," the captain informed them. "Any leads?"

Charlie told him about the people on the surveillance video at the apartment, as well as about the gap on the tape. "We've spoken to the staff at the apartment building, to some of the neighbors, to Mr. Stratton and one of his sons. We've got someone running down addresses on the minister and girlfriend who visited her that night, as well as Cole Stratton. And we're trying to locate the ex-boyfriend, Schwitzer, and bring him in for questioning. We're also still trying to identify the other woman on the tape and the mystery guy with the shades."

"What about the victim's family?" the captain asked. "Any help there?"

"Not so far. There's a mother in Arkansas. We're still trying to locate her," Charlie responded.

"Forensics is going over the sheets, clothing and glasses from the crime scene to see if we can get a hit on any of the prints. I'm going to have the new kid Mackenzie try to run down the manufacturer on the stocking we found at the scene. It's a long shot, but there's a chance we'll get lucky and be able to trace it back to the buyer."

"Anything from the M.E. yet?" the captain asked.

"No, but we've asked for a rush and we're on the hook to her for a dinner at Commander's Palace," Vince told him.

"What about cause of death?" he asked.

"The preliminary exam indicates death was due to strangulation," Vince told him.

Charlie released a breath she hadn't realized she'd been holding when Vince made no mention of the stocking's possible connection to her sister's murder. She'd hated taking advantage of their friendship. And she felt guilty asking him to remain silent or to do anything that might jeopardize his career. But the need to find Emily's killer had outweighed her guilt. If it fell apart, she would make sure that Vince didn't take the fall with her. It was she who had made the decision to withhold the information about her sister's murder. She'd swear on a stack of bibles if need be that Vince knew nothing and that she'd done it on her own. But she prayed it wouldn't come to that. Lying wasn't something she did often and she didn't do it well. But if it was the only way she could stay on the case and try to find Emily's killer, then she would do it.

"Any suspects?" the captain asked.

"The ex-boyfriend is at the top of the list. And word is the victim didn't get along with Stratton's daughter. There was some kind of incident at the restaurant where they had the rehearsal dinner last night. Mackenzie is checking into it and getting statements about what went down," Vince said. "And depending on how J. P. Stratton's will is structured, I say we look at each of his kids since a new stepmother could impact their inheritance. My guess is that Stratton isn't going to like us questioning them."

"Anything else?" the captain asked.

"It'd help if we weren't being asked to walk on eggshells while we do our job."

"Point taken, Detective." He steepled his fingers, saying nothing for a moment. "I'll handle the chief and Stratton. You do your jobs and find me the killer."

After exiting the captain's office, Charlie said, "Thanks for backing me up in there and for not saying anything about the stocking and my sister's case."

"I told the truth—just not all of it."

"You did more than that, Kossak. And I won't forget it," she promised as they approached their desks.

For the next hour, they worked the phones and attempted to track down Francesca Hill's neighbor who had reportedly been out of town on vacation for the past week. They also tried to located Cole Stratton, the minister and the ex-boyfriend, Marcus Schwitzer. Charlie placed a call to Aaron Stratton and pressed him for the names of the dinner guests. She came away with several names to check out. In addition to Aaron Stratton, Jason and Phillip Stratton, J.P.'s twin sons from his fourth marriage, had attended the dinner party. Also present was Reverend Lawrence, Danielle Marceau and Judge William Findlay who was to serve as best man.

Vince stood and stretched. "I'm going to head over to Forensics and see if I can sweet-talk Pam into pushing our stuff up the line."

"Who's Pam?" Charlie asked, looking up from her notes.

"I swear, Le Blanc, sometimes I think you live in a cave. Pam is the brunette that came on board almost a year ago."

"The one with the tattoo?"

"That's the one," Vince responded. "She works the late shift."

Mention of the late shift made her glance at her watch. It was almost seven—which meant she was going to be even later getting to her parents' house than she'd originally thought. She also had hoped to grab Anne before she headed to their folks' and demand an explanation from her. Realizing that she'd have to wait only served to annoy her more. "I gotta go," she said and began shoving papers and files into her bag to review at home.

"Got a hot date?" he teased.

"Hardly." The truth was it had been more than two months since she'd been on a date. And that one had been a fiasco. Not that it was the guy's fault. It wasn't. She doubted if many guys would like being left in a five-star restaurant with two pricey entrées on the table because his blind date had been called to a murder scene.

"So what's the big hurry?"

"I'm having dinner with my folks. And then I'm going to toss my sister Anne off a bridge."

Five

Anne looked up from the sink in her parents' kitchen as Charlie came through the door, carrying the plates following dinner. She plopped them on the counter next to the sink. "You rinse and I'll load the dishwasher," she said in that same brusque tone she'd used with her all evening.

Anne started to argue, but decided against it. "Fine. But I set the table and did the salad because you were late, so you rinse and load the dessert dishes by yourself."

"Girls, quit fussing and finish the dishes. Your father's already setting up for the bananas Foster," her mother called from the next room.

But not even the prospect of bananas Foster—one of her favorites—did anything to lighten her mood. And it was all Charlie's fault. Fuming silently, Anne scraped the remains from the plates into the disposal. She'd known Charlie was angry with her the minute she'd come through the front door. Her sister had trained those blue eyes on her and looked as though she'd wanted to strangle her. Then she had barely said ten words to her all evening. And when she'd mentioned her coup—being the first reporter to break the news about the cancellation of the Stratton/Hill wedding—Charlie had ruined the moment by cutting her off. Since Charlie was working a case that involved Stratton, she couldn't discuss or listen to any of the society drivel that she reported if it involved J. P. Stratton.

Society drivel, my fanny, Anne thought, her irritation growing. Just because Charlie was a police detective and she was a TV reporter didn't mean her job was a piece of cake. Maybe she didn't put the bad guys in jail, but she worked her rear end off just the same. Besides not all of her stories were fluff. More than a few of them had resulted in improved conditions for people caught up in the red tape of bureaucracy or forgotten by the system. Why, she even had a file folder thick with thank-you letters from people whose lives had been changed for the better as a result of her investigative reports.

Continuing to stew over her sister's unfair attitude toward her, she attacked the next plate with a sponge and dishwashing liquid. When Charlie returned with the serving dishes, Anne practically growled as she said, "I don't know why we bother with the dishwasher at all if we have to wash everything first."

"Because that's the way Mom wants it done."

Anne shoved the washed plate at her sister for loading in the dishwasher. "Well if you ask me, it's dumb."

"Nobody asked you."

Anne threw the sponge in the sink, sending suds flying. "What is your problem?" she demanded.

"As if you don't know."

"I don't," Anne insisted.

"Fine. Play innocent. We'll discuss it later. Dad's waiting to do the flaming dessert thing."

"I want to discuss it now."

"Will you keep your voice down?" Charlie chided with a

glance toward the door. "You know how upset Mom gets when we argue. And it's been a tough enough day for them as it is."

Charlie was right. Today had been tough for their parents. Although they had moved past the grief that had paralyzed them following Emily's death, some days—like Emily's birthday—were more difficult for them than others. It wasn't all that easy for her either, Anne admitted. Even though it had been six years since Emily's murder, sometimes she still walked into the kitchen and expected to see her there. Maybe because there had been many a spat waged among the three of them over kitchen cleanups. She'd lost count of the times Emily had weaseled out of her turn to do the dishes by giving her a lipstick that she'd wanted or offering to lend her a blouse she'd admired. It had infuriated Charlie and she'd taken Emily to task for it more than once.

Anne shifted her gaze over to the breakfast nook where the same yellow and white curtains were draped across the bay window, where the garden was once again abloom with pansies in bright yellows, purples and white and camellia bushes and early blooming azaleas were bursting with red and pink flowers. The same porcelain vase was filled with fresh-cut roses and sat in the center of the table that smelled of the lemon oil her mother had used to polish it. For a moment, Anne could almost see the three of them seated at that table again as they had done so often while growing up. She could almost see them that last year before Charlie went off to college with Emily eating her egg-white omelet and lecturing Charlie on her diet. With Charlie ignoring Emily while she scraped the burnt parts off of her toast and washed it down with coffee. With her loading sugar on her cereal and following Charlie's lead by tuning Emily out.

God, but she missed Emily. And she missed being one of three.

"You going to wash that plate or just stare at it?"

At Charlie's sharp comment, Anne shut off the memories. Picking up the sponge, she began washing the plate. And as she washed, she wondered what she could have possibly done to make her sister so angry with her. Before running into her and Vince at the Stratton house, she hadn't even seen Charlie for days. And hadn't she backed off when Charlie had refused to comment? Anyone else would have dogged her heels for answers. Why, she had even undercut her own news scoop by not revealing that it had been homicide detectives seen leaving the Stratton home. So where did Charlie get off being angry with her? She was the one who should be angry with Charlie for the way she had spoken to her. Right? Right! Feeling indignant, Anne slapped the sponge against the next plate, then shoved it at Charlie.

"There's still gravy on the corner. Wash it again," Charlie said and shoved the plate back at her.

That tore it. Turning to face her sister, she snapped, "You want it washed again? You wash it." And without stopping to reconsider, she threw the sponge at Charlie. The soapy square of foam caught her right between the boobs before falling to the floor with a plop. Anne felt a moment of immense satisfaction at her sister's stunned expression—until Charlie scooped up the sponge with astonishing speed.

"Why, you little witch," Charlie began, brandishing the sponge like a weapon in her fist. "I should make you eat this."

"You can try."

"Don't tempt me, Annie. That stunt you pulled on the news this evening was bad enough—"

"What stunt?"

"—And now you've ruined my blouse."

"Your blouse isn't ruined and you know it. And what are you talking about? What stunt?"

"Don't play the innocent," Charlie told her. "You announced to a half-million people on live TV that the Stratton wedding was called off and intimated that your unnamed source told you it was because of Francesca Hill's murder."

Francesca Hill was dead?

Shocked, Anne held on to the sink. She couldn't believe it. Oh, she'd known something was wrong, even suspected that someone close to the Strattons had gotten tangled up in something bad and had died. But she'd never dreamed it was Francesca Hill or that the woman had been murdered.

"I guess it doesn't matter to you whether or not you compromise an investigation—just as long as you get your story."

Both stunned and hurt, she said, "My God, Charlie. Do you honestly believe I'd do that?"

Charlie hesitated, eyed her closely. "You saw me and Vince leaving the Stratton house. Then you go and do that report. What was I supposed to think?"

"That I would never do that to you. Or anyone."

Charlie looked away for a moment, then tossed the sponge in the sink. "Maybe I should have," she said. Grabbing a dishtowel from the counter, she dried her hands, then dabbed at the wet spot on her blouse. "But you made that crack about an unnamed source. The captain and everyone else thought you were referring to me."

"Well I wasn't. For your information, my unnamed source was a doormen at the Mill House Apartments. He said that when he came on duty, he'd heard that the police had been all over the place and in Mr. Stratton's lady friend's apartment and that they carried someone out in a body bag. I thought it was Holly Stratton."

"J. P. Stratton's daughter?"

Anne nodded. "Everyone knows that she and Francesca didn't get along. She moved out of the Mill House when her father moved Francesca in and she wasn't at all happy about the wedding. Besides I'd heard Holly has emotional problems and even attempted suicide. When I heard someone had died, I thought she tried again and succeeded this time. I also thought she'd done it where she knew her father would find her."

Charlie sighed. "I'm sorry, Annie. I shouldn't have jumped to conclusions."

"No, you shouldn't have," she said firmly. But she had never been one to stay mad for long. She couldn't do so now. More softly, she asked, "Did you really get in trouble?"

She nodded. "So did Vince. Apparently, the chief came down on the captain and he came down on us. Everyone assumed I was your source."

"Well first thing tomorrow morning, I'm marching down to the police station and telling your Captain he was wrong, that you didn't tell me a thing."

"Thanks, but you don't need to do that. I told the captain it wasn't me and Vince backed me up."

"I should hope so," she said.

"The truth is, I think Vince is the one who convinced him. He told the captain that you were smart and a good reporter, and that after you'd seen us at Stratton's house and found out the wedding had been cancelled, you put two and two together."

"He was right," she told her as a trill of pleasure went through her. "Did Vince really say that I was smart and a good reporter?"

"Yes, he did," Charlie said dryly. She eyed her closely. "You want to tell me what's going on between you two?"

Anne blinked, felt color rush to her cheeks. "Nothing. Why?"

"Because you both get this sea-sick look when I mention one of you to the other."

"Girls," their mother said as she came through the kitchen doors. "What on earth is taking you so long? And why is there water on the floor?"

"I dropped the sponge," Anne fibbed. "Don't worry, we're almost done." But as she tackled the remaining dishes, Anne's thoughts were on Detective Vincent Kossak.

"I still can't believe Francesca's dead."

"It's true," Cole told his sister Holly as he set her bag down inside of her apartment. After learning from Aaron about Francesca's murder, he'd driven to the casino resort on the Gulf Coast where he'd sent Holly the previous night. He had thought that getting Holly out of New Orleans would be the best way to ensure his sister didn't do something foolish—like crashing J.P.'s wedding—and making matters worse for herself. But once he'd learned of Francesca's death, he'd known he had to act quickly. Holly had always been fragile emotionally and he hadn't wanted her to hear the news over the phone. Nor did he want her to learn about it from the media. He'd wanted to break the news to her in person.

After the initial shock, she'd grown quiet. She'd remained quiet while she packed her bags and checked out of the resort hotel. And she had barely said ten words during the ninety-minute drive back to New Orleans. He eyed her carefully as she stood staring out of the picture window that offered a view of the Mississippi River and the night sky.

Unsure whether to be relieved or concerned by his sister's silence, Cole took off his leather jacket and laid it on the chair beside Holly's. He wasn't blind to his sister's faults, he admitted. Holly was spoiled, often unpredictable and gullible. Her emotions ran high—be they happy or sad. She also had the most tender, generous heart of anyone he knew. And despite the angry scene with Francesca the previous night, he didn't doubt for a moment that she was already regretting the ugly words that had passed between them. She was probably also feeling a loss. After all, she and Francesca had been good friends at one time.

Until J.P. had come along.

The selfish bastard. He had ruined the friendship between his own daughter and her friend simply to satisfy his own twisted ego. He hadn't been concerned about how his actions would affect Holly or anyone else. But then, J. P. Stratton had never cared about anyone other than himself. He'd learned that lesson firsthand a long time ago. What he didn't understand and never would was why Holly continued to love J.P. after everything he had put her through. But then, he'd never understood why his mother had continued to love the man who'd used and abandoned her, either. Maybe he hadn't been able to help his mother all those years ago, but he could help his sister now.

Walking over to the window, he stood beside Holly and stared out into the night. The rain that had come through earlier in the day had washed away the clouds. Stars glistened against a black velvet sky with a crescent-shaped moon that looked as though it was suspended above the river. It was a quiet, peaceful scene, but he knew the woman beside him was not at peace. "You want to talk about it?"

"No." Turning around she said, "What I want is a drink."

When she started toward the bar, Cole blocked her path. "I don't think that's a good idea right now," he told her firmly, knowing his sister had used alcohol as a crutch in the past and worried at her dependence on the stuff.

"Well, I think it's a great idea," she argued. "My nerves are shot. I need it to calm me down."

"No, you don't," he insisted and caught her hands in his. "The booze is a crutch and you don't need a crutch. You're stronger than that."

"No, I'm not," she countered and tried to pull her hands

free. "Ask anyone. They'll tell you I'm just a spoiled little rich girl who gets herself into one mess after another and has to have her daddy or big brother bail her out," she said, her self-loathing evident.

"You are so much more than that, Holly. Why can't you see that?" he asked, pained to see his sister in such distress.

"Because I can't see what isn't there. I'm not like you, Cole. I'm weak. I always have been. You're the one who can't see it."

He tipped up her chin with his fingers. "What I see is a brave, beautiful and compassionate woman who is a lot stronger than she thinks."

"I certainly don't feel brave or strong."

"That's because you've been dealt some hard blows in the past few days. Why don't you come sit down and try to relax. I'll get us both some tea."

"I don't have any tea," she said as she took a seat on the couch.

"What about coffee?"

"I have some instant."

He hated instant coffee, had never understood how people could drink the stuff. But if it would help Holly, he'd drink dishwater. "Instant's fine. You relax and I'll go fix us each a cup."

"It's in the kitchen cabinet beside the stove."

"I'll find it," he assured her.

He found it. Fifteen minutes later, neither one of them had taken more than a few sips of the horrible-tasting brew. But his sister had been able to listen without falling apart as he tried to prepare her for what would be coming. He'd had several messages already from a Detective Le Blanc, wanting to question him. It wouldn't be long before they made their way to Holly. "The news about the wedding being cancelled has already made it on the local TV stations. By morning the news of Francesca's murder will probably be out, too. I'm guessing word about your run-in with Francesca at the rehearsal dinner last night has already reached the police." And he didn't doubt that his sister violating the restraining order by showing up at the dinner and throwing a glass of wine in Francesca's face would make her a prime suspect. Needing to prepare her, he said, "They're probably going to want to question you."

"What am I going to tell them?"

"The truth. That you were unhappy about the wedding and the two of you had an argument, but that you didn't kill her."

"It's true, Cole. I didn't," she said.

"I know, kiddo. And you have nothing to worry about. You were nearly a hundred miles from here when she was killed and can prove it." At least that was in her favor, he reasoned. Also in her favor was the fact that he had waited until Holly had called to say she was at the resort before going to see Francesca and the woman had still been alive when he'd gone to see her. "Once the police check with the resort and confirm you were there, you'll be in the clear."

"What if they don't remember me or know exactly when I arrived?"

He smiled. "Trust me. They'll remember a beautiful redhead and the time you checked in will be on your receipt and in the reservation system."

"But I didn't check in right away," she told him. "I mean, there was a line at the desk, so I played the slot machines for a while."

"That's okay. They'll just check the surveillance tapes. CS Securities installed the system there. There are cameras capturing every angle of the casino and recording the dates and times. The tapes will put you in the clear," he explained.

"No they won't," she said and her eyes filled with tears.

"Why not?" he asked, a sinking feeling in his gut.

"Because I wasn't at the casino when I called you last night. I called and said I was because I didn't want you to worry. But I didn't get there until later that night."

"Then where were you?"

"In New Orleans. I was more than half-way to Biloxi when I turned around and came back. I went to see Francesca, to apologize and try to convince her not to file the charges."

"What time did you go see her?" he demanded.

"I don't know. Late. She told me that you'd already been there, pleading my case and that she'd turned you down. Then she said she wasn't going to wait until morning, that she was calling the police now and telling them I'd violated the restraining order twice that night. When she picked up the phone, I rushed out, got in my car and went to the resort. I'm so sorry, Cole. I've made a mess of everything, haven't I?"

"We'll work it out," he said, but he was worried. He didn't believe for a second that Holly had killed Francesca. But she had motive and no alibi—something that the police would latch on to quickly.

"How? What are we going to do?"

"The first thing I'm going to do is call Margee Jardine and let her know what's happened. Then I'm going to find out who else visited Francesca last night." He'd seen the bottle of champagne chilling and two glasses when he'd gone to see her. So he knew she'd been expecting someone.

"What can I do?"

"You can stay calm and trust me to take care of this."

"I do trust you, Cole," she said, her expression somber. "Whenever I've needed someone, you've always been there for me. You're the one person who's never let me down."

Only Holly was wrong. He hadn't always been there when she'd needed him, Cole thought as he hugged her close. Eight years ago when she'd been a pregnant sixteen-year-old and J.P. had forced her to have an abortion, he had been thousands of miles away. She'd gone through that nightmare all alone because he'd been on a Special Ops assignment, because he had chosen to re-up for another tour of duty instead of coming home where he was needed. While he hated J.P. for putting Holly through that, he hated himself more for not being there to protect her. He intended to protect her now.

He looked up at the television as the crime show in progress was interrupted by the sound of a breaking news report. At last, he thought and set aside the papers he had stopped by his office to pick up. He'd been disappointed when the media had failed to report Francesca's murder on the six o'clock evening news. Although phone calls had been made and favors called in by the Stratton family to handle the situation with discretion, he'd hated that no one was acknowledging his work. Instead, everyone seemed to have focused on the cancelled wedding—which didn't deserve even the fifteen minutes of attention it had already garnered. No, the real story was him and what he had done.

"Ladies and gentlemen, we interrupt this program to bring you this breaking news story," Bill Capo, the WWL-TV Channel 4 News anchor and reporter began. "Francesca Hill, the fiancée of real estate mogul J. P. Stratton, is dead, the victim of a robbery turned homicide. As reported early today, guests who were invited to the wedding of the former casino hostess and the multimillionaire began receiving phone calls shortly before the scheduled ceremony, notifying them that the wedding had been cancelled. At the home of J. P. Stratton, here is Anne Le Blanc with more on the story."

The television screen switched to a view in front of the Stratton home where a flock of reporters and news trucks

*were gathered outside the wrought iron gates. Although it was
nearly nine o'clock at night, the area was lit up like a Christ-
mas tree thanks to the news crews. And standing there bundled in a fitted red leather coat that tied at the waist and fell
just above the knee was the perky blond reporter who had
been the first to report the cancellation of the wedding.*

*He'd recognized the name, of course, and had found it
amusing to have Emily Le Blanc's baby sister reporting on
his latest accomplishment. But the one who had truly intrigued him was the older sister—Charlotte Le Blanc. In the
few weeks he'd known Emily, he'd heard all about her two sisters—especially about Charlotte, the smart and serious one
who was studying to be a lawyer. He hadn't realized that
she'd abandoned her plans to become a lawyer and become
a cop instead. Smiling, he couldn't help wondering if he had
been the one to influence her change of career. He also wondered if she would put up more of a fight than Emily had. She
would, he decided and found himself growing excited by the
idea.*

"Anne, what can you tell us?" Bill asked.

*Holding the microphone in front of her, she touched her ear-
piece and stared directly into the camera. "Bill, I'm standing
outside the palatial home of J. P. Stratton, who as you know,
was scheduled to be married this afternoon and whose wedding was abruptly cancelled without explanation. Although we
have not been able to speak with Mr. Stratton, his publicist and
a member of the immediate family has confirmed that Ms. Hill
is dead. Her body was found early today by the maid who had
come to help her prepare for her wedding."*

*"Anne, do we know how she was killed?" Bill asked as the
screen split in two, giving views of the TV studio and of the
reporter outside the mansion.*

"Bill, the police have not released any details about how

Ms. Hill died. But what we have been told is that cash and jewelry were missing from Ms. Hill's apartment. And the case is being treated as a robbery turned homicide."

Robbery turned homicide his ass, he thought, irritated. He didn't know who the prick was that had stolen Francesca's wallet and jewelry, but he had been the one who'd killed her. And the damn police better not screw up his plans. They should be looking for a murderer—not some petty thief.

Charlotte Le Blanc would be looking for a murderer, he told himself, growing calmer.

"Anne, do the police have any suspects?" Capo asked.

"None that they've reported."

But they soon would, he thought and Detective Charlotte Le Blanc would uncover them all. He was sure of it. Smiling again, he turned off the set and gathered up the file he needed. Karma had brought her to him for a reason, he decided. And once she had served her purpose, he would kill her.

Six

"This is Stratton. Leave a message and I'll get back—"

"I've already left three messages," Charlie said and slammed down the telephone without waiting for the rest of the recording. Dinner with her parents had been lovely but after Anne had gotten the call from the TV station ordering her to report on location for a story, she'd had to forgo dessert. So Charlie had skipped the bananas Foster as well and left their parents' home. Too wired to relax, she'd known going home was pointless. So she did what she often did when a case was nagging at her, she headed back to the station.

It was after eight o'clock when she'd arrived. And as was usually the case for a Saturday night during carnival season, business at the station was brisk. Most uniformed officers were pulling double shifts to handle the crowds and the problems generated by the party fever that engulfed the city for two weeks each year. When she made her way back to the Homicide Department, she hadn't expected to find Vince there working. But then she hadn't been surprised to find him, either. With the murder rate quickly approaching triple digits, there was always work that needed to be done, leads that needed to be followed up on, paperwork to be processed. They had other open cases that required attention. But the word had come down from the top that the Hill case was priority. That was fine with her, Charlie admitted, because from the moment she had seen that black silk stocking, the case hadn't been out of her thoughts.

She went back to the list of people who had visited Francesca Hill the previous night. The odds were one of them was the killer or had seen the killer. She ran her finger down the list. J. P. Stratton. Aaron Stratton. Danielle Marceau. The Reverend Homer Lawrence. Cole Stratton. Plus the two mystery guests—the crying female and the camera-shy guy with the shades. She made a question mark, knowing it was possible that whoever had monkeyed with the surveillance tape was none of the above. But for now, she had to work with what she had and what she had were a lot of people visiting Francesca Hill on the eve of her wedding. She needed to find out why.

Going back to the top of the list, she skipped past J. P. Stratton and Aaron Stratton. She had spoken to them once already and doubted she would learn much more from them tonight. Danielle Marceau hadn't been at home or at work, so she tried again and once again left a message. Next on the list was the reverend. Given the lateness of the hour, she decided to wait until tomorrow to pay him a call. Since they had yet to identify the mystery lady and the guy with the shades, that left Cole Stratton—who obviously wasn't returning her calls. Deciding to try his home number again, she had just punched in the first three digits when she heard a whoop of excitement from Vince's desk across the aisle from her. She put down the phone.

"Got it! Thanks, pal. I owe you one." He hung up the phone and swung around in his chair to face her. Holding up a slip of paper, he said, "Guess what I've got here?"

"A hot stock tip?"

"Funny," he said dryly. "It's the name of our mystery girl on the surveillance tape. I'll give you three guesses."

"Kossak." She growled out the word.

"Holly Stratton. I had the new kid, Mackenzie, take a copy of the photo we had printed from the tape over to the Mill House Apartments and show it around. The desk clerk identified her."

"Another ex-wife?" Charlie asked.

"Daughter. According to the clerk, she and the vic used to be friends. But they had a falling-out when Hill took up with the father."

"I can't say that I blame her," Charlie responded, empathizing with Holly Stratton. Having your father marry a woman who couldn't have been more than a year or two older than you would have been tough for anyone to swallow. But having him marry one of your friends had to be ten times worse.

"It gets better," Vince continued. "Hill took out a restraining order against Holly Stratton a couple of weeks ago. She showed up at last night's rehearsal dinner and she and the vic had words. Ms. Stratton ended up throwing a glass of wine in her soon-to-be stepmother's face. Apparently all hell broke loose and Hill threatened to have her arrested for violating the restraining order."

"I bet that went over real big with daddy."

"Sensitive guy that he is, daddy had hotel security escort his daughter off the premises."

Charlie flinched inwardly for Holly Stratton. She could only imagine the other woman's humiliation. "If you ask me, she should have thrown the wine in *his* face."

"She might have if the security guards hadn't hauled her out when they did. According to the waiter, Ms. Stratton didn't go quietly. She told the Hill woman she was going to regret what she'd done."

Charlie sobered at once. "Then what was she doing at the victim's apartment last night?"

"I was wondering the same thing," Vince said. "Why don't we go ask her?"

When they pulled up in front of Holly Stratton's apartment building, Vince let out a whistle. Charlie understood her partner's reaction. The address itself was a calling card that read, For Rich People Only. She'd seen advertisements for the luxury apartments located on Saint Charles Avenue when they'd first come on the market. They had started at a half-million dollars. And that had been several years ago before property values had skyrocketed.

"Exactly what did that report on her say this girl does for a living?"

"She doesn't. She lives off of an allowance paid from a trust fund."

"That must be some allowance," Vince commented. "I bet a closet in this place goes for a grand a month."

"Somehow I doubt that Ms. Stratton lives in a closet."

Holly Stratton didn't live in a closet. She lived in a two-bedroom dream apartment with vaulted ceilings, a fireplace and a terrace. The place was beautiful. So was Holly Stratton. Long red hair framed an oval face with big blue eyes and skin like alabaster. She reminded her of a young Julianne Moore, Charlie decided. She was small, no more than five foot two or three. Standing barefoot and wearing pink Juicy Couture sweats and no makeup, she looked like a teenager instead of a twenty-four-year-old woman. She also looked scared—which was why Charlie suspected she had allowed them inside and agreed to speak with them without demanding an attorney.

"We understand that you and Ms. Hill had an argument at

the hotel restaurant last night," Vince continued with the questions. "Would you mind telling us what that argument was about?"

Holly plucked at the sleeve of her sweats and sat down on the couch. "It was just a dumb argument," she insisted. "It wasn't any big deal."

When Vince signaled her, Charlie took a seat in the chair across from Holly and took over the questioning. "It was apparently a big enough deal for you to throw wine in her face and tell her she was going to regret what she'd done."

"I was angry and upset. I didn't mean it."

"Why were you angry and upset?" When she didn't answer, Charlie pressed, "Was it because Francesca was about to marry your father?"

"Yes! All right? I hated the idea of him marrying her," she said, her voice thick with tears. "Can you blame me? How would you feel if your father was going to marry someone your age, someone who had been your friend first, before she started sleeping with your father?"

"I would hate it and the two of them. And I would do everything I could to stop the wedding from happening," Charlie answered honestly. "Is that what you did? Did you try to stop the wedding? Is that why you went to her apartment last night?"

"Despite what most people think, I'm not stupid, Detective. You think I killed Francesca. Well, you're wrong. I didn't kill her and I resent you implying that I did."

"No one's implying anything, Ms. Stratton. The questions are just routine," Charlie said, attempting to calm the other woman. Holly Stratton wasn't stupid. And while she had agreed to speak with them, it didn't mean she couldn't change her mind and tell them to leave. Having her talk to them now was their best shot at obtaining information because, given her family's connections, getting Holly down to headquarters for questioning wouldn't be an easy task.

"Detective Le Blanc is right," Vince said. "These questions are routine in a murder investigation. It's by talking to people who knew or saw the victim last that usually leads us to the murderer."

Holly's face paled and she tucked her feet beneath her. "I don't see how I can help you. I can't imagine anyone I know being capable of murder."

"Everyone is capable of murder," Charlie told her. "It's simply a matter of finding what it is that would make someone feel justified in taking another life."

"And what would it take for you to justify taking a life, Detective?"

Charlie hadn't heard him enter. That bothered her. Standing, she turned and looked over at the man who stood in the entryway with a bag bearing the name of a nearby Chinese restaurant. She recognized him from the surveillance video— Cole Stratton. He'd looked good in black and white. In living color, he was gorgeous with hair the color of midnight and piercing blue eyes. He placed the bag on the table.

"Detectives, this is my brother, Cole Stratton," Holly said as she stood. "Cole, these are Detectives… I'm sorry." She looked at Vince.

Vince stepped forward. "Detective Vince Kossak, Mr. Stratton," he said and showed him his ID. "This is my partner—"

"Detective Le Blanc," Cole said, shifting his attention back to her.

"Obviously you got my messages," Charlie said.

"I did."

No apologies. No excuses. "Most people return their calls when they know the police are trying to locate them," she pointed out.

"I'm not most people, Detective."

"Maybe not, Mr. Stratton. But like it or not, you are subject to the same laws as the rest of us lesser mortals," she fired back.

A ghost of a smile played across his lips. "Somehow, Detective, I doubt that anyone would mistake you for a lesser mortal."

Charlie narrowed her eyes, unsure if he had just paid her a compliment or insulted her. But she had little time to dwell on it as he moved to his sister's side and placed a protective arm around her shoulder.

"You didn't answer my question, Detective. What would it take for you to justify taking another person's life?"

She met his gaze evenly and said, "As a police officer, I use my weapon when I have no other choice in order to save myself or an innocent."

"I'm not talking about as a police officer. I meant you, personally. You said everyone is capable of murder. I assume that includes you. So what's the trigger that would make you take another's life?"

"When that person is a threat to someone I love," she said without hesitation.

"Then you and I have something in common."

Charlie knew she had just been issued a warning. He would do whatever he had to in order to protect his sister. She understood it, even admired it. But she wouldn't let it get in the way of her doing her job.

"The detectives were asking me about my argument with Francesca last night," Holly explained.

"My sister should have been advised that she could have her attorney present," he said sharply.

"They did," Holly told him and placed a hand on his arm. "I chose not to call one. I don't need an attorney to deny killing Francesca. Because I didn't kill her."

"I know you didn't. And if the detectives have any further questions for you, they can contact your attorney, Margaret Jardine."

"What about you, Mr. Stratton? Should I contact your attorney or are you willing to answer some questions for us?" Charlie asked.

"I'll be happy to answer your questions, Detective Le Blanc. Just not tonight. It's been a long and emotional day for my sister and our dinner is waiting," he told her, indicating the bag from the Chinese restaurant. He walked to the door, opened it.

While she would have liked to argue and insist he speak with them now, she followed Vince's lead and exited the apartment. Outside the door, she turned and said, "I'd like to remind you that this is a murder investigation, Mr. Stratton. So we'll need to set up that interview as soon as possible. I'll contact you in the morning."

"I'll look forward to it, Detective," he said and then shut the door in their faces.

For a moment, Charlie simply stood there, saying nothing before turning and marching down the hallway toward the elevator. Irritated, she jabbed at the elevator down button and when it arrived, she selected the first floor.

After they exited the elevator, they headed out of the building. The night air was brisk and Charlie was glad she'd worn her leather jacket as they started down the block to the car. She could hear the sound of drums from the marching bands in a parade several blocks away and hoped they wouldn't get stuck in traffic.

"What do you make of Holly Stratton?" Vince asked her as they walked.

"I think she's a mixed-up kid and I feel sorry for her. But I don't think she's a murderer." Aside from the fact that she didn't think Holly was guilty, she also didn't think the killer was a woman. Semen had been found at her sister's crime scene and she'd stake her badge that the same man's DNA would be found on Francesca Hill.

"You have to admit the Stratton girl had motive. Her one-time friend was not only marrying her old man, but the woman was threatening to have her arrested."

"Which only proves that she has a screwed-up family," Charlie countered.

"What do you think about the brother?"

"I think arrogance runs in the family," Charlie told him, still irritated by Cole Stratton's attitude. Most people would have been intimidated or at least tried to be cooperative. But not him.

"I meant, do you think he's our guy? Do you think he killed Francesca Hill?"

"No," Charlie said without hesitation. Cole Stratton might be too sure of himself for her tastes and she didn't doubt he was capable of murder given the right circumstances, but he wasn't the killer. No. Her sister's killer and Francesca Hill's killer were one and the same. And whoever had killed her sister had been involved with Emily romantically. While she may not have kept as close an eye on Emily as she should have, she knew her sister's type. Emily had preferred men who were in awe of her beauty, who lavished her with attention— men she could wrap around her finger. Five minutes in Cole Stratton's company and she knew he was not that man.

"You sound sure," Vince countered.

"I am."

Cole hit the last leg of his morning jog as Jackson Square came into view. With his tennis shoes pounding the pavement, he started toward the historic landmark located in the heart of the French Quarter. Even at a distance, the sculpture of General Andrew Jackson on his steed, erected to honor the hero of the Battle of New Orleans, made an impressive sight. As he continued his run, he made his way down Decatur Street where the residents were beginning to stir. After yesterday's wintry weather, dawn had arrived with clear skies and spring-like temperatures. If he were superstitious, he would take the change in the weather as an omen. All he knew was that he hoped the fortune in his cookie from Saturday night's Chinese dinner had been right—that he would soon have his heart's desire. Right now his heart's desire was for Holly's happiness.

Thanks to J.P. and the cold, self-centered woman who gave birth to Holly, his sister had known little happiness in her twenty-four years. The mess during the past two months with J.P. and Francesca planning to marry had dealt her a blow. Francesca's murder had been another blow because now she had lost her friend twice—once to J.P. and again to a killer.

What worried him most though was that the police were looking at Holly as a murder suspect. Keeping a steady pace, he recalled his encounter two nights ago with the two detectives. Kossak he'd pegged as a straight shooter, probably a by-the-book cop. He'd be a man people would underestimate and that would be a mistake. Kossak was no one's fool. Detective Charlotte Le Blanc was harder to read. Lots of layers to that one. She intrigued him, Cole admitted. Perhaps because he recognized a kindred spirit. Fearless and determined was how he'd describe her. And beneath that cool control there was fire. He didn't doubt for a second that the lady would face down Attila the Hun himself to protect one of her own. So would he.

As he neared the Café du Monde, Cole caught a whiff of coffee coming from the round-the-clock café. Jogging past the sidewalk eatery moments later, he noted a number of early risers sitting at tables, sipping their first morning cups of coffee and eating beignets. He also spied a foursome who looked as though they'd done some nonstop partying and were in need of a jolt of caffeine.

Continuing his route, he ran up one side of the square and waved greetings to the horse-and-carriage drivers who were lining up, getting ready for the day. No doubt they were taking their posts early in hopes that the forecast of sunshine and warmer temperatures would spell tourist dollars for them. He turned the corner at the end of the block, started down the other side of the square where he watched the faithful ascending the steps of Saint Louis Cathedral for morning mass.

After he completed the circuit around the square, Cole decided to make another lap around. Once again, he ran along the black iron fence that encased the gardens and monument. As he did so, memories came flooding back of other days when he'd been just a boy and had started his mornings there. Like it was yesterday, he recalled ascending the steps to the cathedral with his mother where she would pray for the Lord to heal her marriage. By the time he was five years old, he'd known his mother's prayers were wasted. But he'd cherished those mornings with her and their walks through the square together. He'd relished the stories she'd told him, the history lessons really, of how the onetime drill field had been renamed to honor Andrew Jackson and how the Baroness Pontabla had been responsible for the iron fence and gardens.

He looked over at the Pontabla Apartments across from Jackson Square and remembered his mother's admiration of the baroness. Like the baroness, she had hoped to leave a legacy to the city she had loved so much. Only, Margaret Cole Stratton had never had the chance—not once she had become ill and J.P. had gained control of her fortune. The only thing J.P. hadn't gotten his greedy hands on had been the house in the French Quarter. Following his mother's death J.P. had been unable to break his grandparents' trust. The home had remained his and out of J.P.'s grasp. It had been the first time he had succeeded in beating J. P. Stratton.

Pushing the dark memories aside, Cole continued his run. When he turned the corner of the street to his home, he saw a familiar figure standing in front of his house. Detective Charlotte Le Blanc. Had he not known better, he never would have pegged her for a cop. Tall and slim with hair that was somewhere between blond and brown, she had brown eyes the color of fine brandy and a mouth that begged to be kissed. She was smart, stubborn and sexy—all attractive traits to him. There was also an intensity about her that he found appealing on that most basic level. "Good morning, Detective," he said as he reached the front of his house.

"Good morning."

He reached for the towel around his neck and used it to wipe the sweat from his face. "You'll have to forgive me, but I don't seem to recall us having an appointment this morning."

"We don't," she admitted. "But you did agree to speak with me about Francesca Hill. And since your assistant says you've been out of the office and you've obviously been too busy to return my calls, I thought it might be more convenient for you to answer those questions for me before you start your busy workday."

His lips twitched at her audacity and her cleverness. "That's very considerate of you, Detective," he replied, even though he knew it wasn't out of consideration for him that she had shown up on his doorstep before 7:00 a.m. on a Tuesday morning. No, it had been her determination to get answers to her questions. He understood her tenacity, admired it. It was another trait they both shared—a single-mindedness to go after what they wanted. In his own case, it had been to divest any hold that J. P. Stratton had over his life. In Detective Le

Blanc's case it was to find Francesca's killer. And he didn't doubt for a second that the lady had him on her list of suspects. "Since you're being so considerate, Detective, I'm sure you won't mind if I answer your questions inside," he said and unlocked the door. "I haven't had my coffee yet this morning."

She said nothing, but merely glanced down the block.

Cole stepped inside and went to the panel on his right, where he punched in the security code to deactivate the alarm system. When he looked back and saw that she remained on the sidewalk in the same place, he asked, "Coming, Detective?"

"I'm waiting for my partner. He's supposed to meet me here."

"Then you have time to join me for a cup of coffee in the courtyard before you and Detective Kossak start grilling me." He held the door open for her to enter.

"We don't plan to grill you, Mr. Stratton," she advised him as she stepped indoors. "We just want to ask you a few questions concerning your relationship with Francesca Hill."

"By relationship, I assume you're referring to something beyond her becoming my stepmother," he said and closed the door behind her. "This way."

"Was your relationship more than that?"

"I knew her slightly. My sister had introduced us shortly before she became engaged to J.P.," he explained and led her through the house, out back to the courtyard.

"How *slightly* did you know her?"

He paused with his fingers on the handle of the French door. For a long moment they stood close, close enough for him to see the gold flecks in her brown eyes and smell the hint of soap and roses on her skin. He heard her slight intake of breath as the awareness between them sharpened. He didn't step away. Neither did she. "Are you asking me if I slept with Francesca, Detective?"

"Did you?"

He liked her directness. "No, I didn't." Opening the door, he motioned for her to precede him.

When she stepped out into the courtyard onto the slate-covered ground, the mantle of cop that she wore like armor fell away. She looked around her, then began walking toward the fountain at the center of the courtyard. "This is lovely."

Pleased, Cole watched her face as her eyes flitted from the old-fashioned lampposts with gas-burning lights, to the brick archway, to the lush gardens of roses and azaleas, to the towering oaks that provided shade from the summer heat and had been ideal for climbing when he'd been a boy.

"I would never have guessed this was even here."

"Most people don't," he said, pleased by her response to his home. "It's one of the charms of this part of the city. Many of the older homes in the French Quarter have courtyards like this one tucked away at the rear of the houses."

"I suppose this was the original owner's answer to a backyard."

"Actually this was an open area at the rear of the main house, and over here," he said, pointing to a brick wall. "There used to be a stable where the horses and carriages were kept."

"Have you owned it for very long?" she asked.

"Since I was six."

She turned, looked up at him, her expression curious.

"The house was built in 1825 by my great-great-grandfather William Cole as a gift for his bride," he explained. "The property has remained in the family and has been passed down to his direct descendants. When my mother died, it passed on to me."

"And someday you'll pass it down to your own children."

"If I have any children, yes. It will go to them." Children had not been something he'd given much thought to, Cole realized. Maybe because he'd given little thought to marriage.

"Make yourself comfortable, Detective. I'll get that coffee I promised you."

"Coffee isn't necessary, Mr. Stratton. This isn't a social call," she reminded him.

Cole smiled. The cop was back. "Perhaps not for you, Detective, but it is for me." Without waiting for her reply, he turned and headed inside the house.

When he exited the house a short time later, he found her sitting at the patio table with the silver-and-white tomcat on her lap, scratching it behind the ears. "I see you've met Goliath," he said and placed the tray with a carafe of coffee and cups on the table.

"He just showed up and jumped on my lap."

Lucky cat, he mused. "So you decided to come back, did you, pal? What happened? Did Miss Morgan give you the boot?"

"He isn't yours?"

"I guess it depends on who you ask." He poured her a cup of coffee and then one for himself. "He showed up on my doorstep about a year ago and decided to stay. I've been paying his vet bills and keeping him in catnip ever since. But I suspect that Goliath believes he owns me."

She gave him a curious look. "Then who is Miss Morgan?"

"A sweet little Persian cat down the street. He's been spending a lot of time over there lately. Haven't you, Romeo?"

As if in answer, Goliath opened one eye. Just as quickly he closed it and went back to his mouse-chasing dream.

"Cream and sugar?" he asked.

"Just cream."

"Ah, a woman after my own heart," he said as he topped her coffee with cream and then did the same to his own. He lifted his gaze to hers. "It makes me wonder what other things we have in common, Detective."

"Very little is my guess."

"I wouldn't be so sure of that." Removing the saucer from underneath his cup, Cole poured some of the cream from the pitcher into it and set it down on the ground. Goliath abandoned her lap for the saucer of cream and began to lap it up greedily. "For instance, you're not afraid of going after what you want and you don't quit until you get it."

She eyed him warily over the brim of her cup. "What makes you say that?"

"You're here, aren't you? And that's despite the fact that you were probably told by your captain to tread lightly around us mighty Strattons."

"I have a job to do," she countered.

"Yes, you do." But Cole noted she didn't deny that she'd been pressured to watch her step with his family, no doubt courtesy of J.P. "And that's why you showed up here even after I threw you out of my sister's apartment the other night."

"You didn't throw me out. I left under my own power," she pointed out.

"So you did." But before he could press her further, the doorbell rang.

"That must be Detective Kossak."

Charlie was grateful that Vince had arrived when he had. She hadn't been comfortable alone with Cole Stratton. The man disturbed her and not just on a professional level. True, he was a gorgeous male specimen. In running shorts and a sweatshirt with his dark hair mussed from his run, he was a great advertisement for the benefits of staying physically fit. But she'd known other good-looking men and had not been unsettled by them. Cole Stratton was different. He was interesting, amusing and he had a soft spot for animals, which was a big plus in her books. He was also fiercely protective of his sister—something she understood. It was little wonder she felt an attraction to the man. Unfortunately, he was on her short-list of murder suspects.

"We appreciate your agreeing to speak with us at such an early hour, Mr. Stratton," Vince said and slanted her another reproachful glance. Her partner hadn't been at all in favor of her plan to show up at Cole Stratton's home when most people were just crawling out of their beds.

"Detective Le Blanc's argument was quite…persuasive," he replied as though searching for the proper word. "Please sit down, Detective. Can I offer you a cup of coffee?"

Vince hesitated a moment, then apparently the need for caffeine kicked in. "Sure. Black is fine," he said and took a seat at the table in the courtyard.

After filling Vince's cup and topping off his own, Cole sat back in the cushioned chair and turned his attention back to her. "Now, where were we?" he asked.

"You were clarifying the nature of your relationship with Francesca Hill," she reminded him.

Amusement danced in his blue eyes. "Ah, that's right. As I told you, Detective, Francesca and I were never lovers. Our relationship, if you can call it that, consisted of a total of three meetings."

"Could you tell us when and where those meetings took place as well as their purpose?" she asked as she opened her notepad.

"The first one was about four months ago, shortly after Francesca struck up a friendship with my sister. Apparently Holly mentioned me a few times to her new friend and Francesca expressed a desire to meet me. So I arranged to meet my sister at Commander's Palace where she introduced me to Francesca. The three of us had lunch."

"You said that Ms. Hill 'struck up a friendship' with your sister," Vince said. "Do you have reason to believe her befriending your sister was planned on her part?"

"I suspected that might have been the case," he answered. "Considering how quickly she became involved with J.P., I think there's a strong possibility that I was right."

"She was a young, beautiful woman. If she was looking to hook up with a rich man, I would have thought you or one of your brothers would have been a more likely target," Charlie said, wondering if Francesca had hit on Cole first.

He smiled over the rim of his cup before setting it down. "I think Francesca was smart enough to realize she'd have been wasting her time on me. I wasn't interested. As for my brothers, Aaron already has more women chasing after him than he can handle and the twins weren't in her league. J.P. was by far more suitable for her needs."

"And what would those needs be?" she asked him.

"To have someone support her in style."

"In other words, you thought she was a gold digger who latched on to your father."

"I thought she was a smart woman who had done her homework. J.P. has a reputation for falling into lust with young, beautiful women and allowing it to impair his judgment. His ex-wives and affairs have cost him a considerable amount of money over the years. I suspect Francesca knew that and hoped to cash in on it."

"As I said, you thought she was a gold digger," Charlie told him.

"I believe *opportunist* would be a better word."

"How did you feel about this opportunist marrying your father and taking another bite out of your inheritance?" she asked.

A thin smile curved Cole's lips. "It didn't bother me at all since I don't stand to inherit anything from J.P. But then I'm sure you already know that."

She did know it. She had run background checks on all of the Strattons. J. P. Stratton was an extremely wealthy man.

Even after paying a small fortune to three ex-wives in nasty divorce settlements, he still had enough money to last several lifetimes. His hotel and real estate holdings alone were worth more than two hundred million dollars. And Cole Stratton's four half siblings all stood to inherit upon their father's death. But not Cole. Deciding to move on, she asked, "When was your second meeting with Ms. Hill?"

"About six weeks ago. I was attending a fund-raiser and J.P. arrived with Francesca. While he was getting drinks, she came over to tell me that they had gotten engaged and showed me her ring. I gave her my condolences."

She chose not to comment. "And the third meeting?"

"Last Friday night at her apartment, which is also something else you already know since you would have viewed the security tapes and seen me on them."

"You're right, of course," Charlie conceded. "Can you explain then why, considering your claim to have only met Ms. Hill briefly, you visited her at her apartment so late at night on the eve of her wedding?"

"Because I thought going to see her at her apartment was preferable to trying to catch her on the morning of her wedding."

"Why the need to see her at all?" Vince asked.

"Because I had hoped to convince her not to press charges against my sister for violating the restraining order," he replied.

"Were you successful?" Vince asked.

"No. She said she intended to file a police report in the morning."

"How did you feel about that?" Charlie asked.

"I wasn't happy," he told her.

"Were you angry?" Charlie asked him.

"Not so much angry as frustrated. My sister was having a difficult time with the prospect of her father marrying one of her friends. For her to be arrested because her argument with

Francesca got out of hand would have made it more difficult for Holly."

"You're very protective of your sister, aren't you?" she commented.

"I suppose I am. It comes with being the oldest, I guess—that need to look out for your siblings. But I'm sure you understand, Detective."

Surprised and annoyed to realize he had checked up on her, she said, "Why would I understand?"

"The Anne Le Blanc who reports for *Channel 4 Eyewitness News* is your sister, isn't she? The color of the eyes is different, but the two of you share the same bone structure and similar features. Or am I mistaken?"

"No, you're not mistaken," she admitted and felt foolish for jumping to conclusions. "But we weren't discussing me. We were discussing your visit to Ms. Hill on the night she was murdered to plead your sister's case. Somehow you don't strike me as someone who accepts no easily."

"And you think that I killed Francesca to stop her from filing charges against my sister?" he asked, obviously amused.

"Did you?" she countered.

"I'm sorry to disappoint you, Detective, but I decided to try something less dramatic first. I hired an attorney to represent my sister in the event Francesca did file charges as she threatened. You're welcome to call Margaret Jardine and verify that I retained her services if you'd like."

"I will," Charlie assured him and wrote down the name he'd given her.

"Anything else?" he asked.

"Just one more thing. Where were you Friday evening between midnight and two in the morning?" she asked.

"I was at home, working on a proposal for a client until about 1:30 a.m. and then I went to bed."

"Can anyone corroborate that?" she asked him.

"Unfortunately, no, since I was alone. But if I had killed Francesca it would have been very foolish of me not to provide myself with an alibi. Don't you think?"

"Or very clever, because you would assume that we'd think just that," she said.

"Perhaps," he said, that amused glint back in his eyes.

"Your company provides security systems for businesses. Does that include apartment buildings?" she asked.

"Yes."

"Did you provide the one for the Mill House Apartments?"

"No. But I'm familiar with the system and I'm sure I'd have no trouble accessing it if I chose to," he answered.

"Did you access it?" Charlie asked.

"No, I didn't." He tipped his head, eyed her curiously. "Does the fact that you're asking me these questions mean that someone did tamper with the security system?"

"We'll ask the questions, Mr. Stratton," she told him.

He glanced at his watch and stood. "Actually any more questions will have to wait. I'm supposed to be meeting my sister in an hour and I still have to shower."

She put away her notepad and she and Vince stood. "Thank you for speaking with us," she said. "Here's my card. If you should think of anything else, please call me or Detective Kossak."

He looked at the card she'd handed him. "I'll do that."

"Thank you for your time," Vince told him.

He nodded and escorted them to the front door with Goliath, the cat, trailing them. When the cat started to follow them outside, he scooped the animal up into his arms. "Detectives," he said as they descended the steps.

Charlie turned to look up at him. So did Vince.

"I hope you find your killer."

"We'll find him," she assured him. "You can count on it." And so could Emily.

Seven

"You want to tell me what I walked in on back there?" Vince asked Charlie as they headed down the street toward her car. Parking was always a problem in the French Quarter. But with Mardi Gras two weeks away and the city filled with tourists, it proved to be even more of a hassle than usual.

She glanced up at him. "What do you mean?"

"I mean I arrived at Stratton's place, expecting to find you grilling the man about Francesca Hill's murder. Instead, you're sipping coffee and discussing the history of his home."

"For your information, I did grill him. Or at least I tried to. But when I told him you were meeting me there, he clammed up, said he didn't want to go through his story twice. What was I supposed to do—beat the answers out of him?"

The Charlie Le Blanc he knew would not have given up so easily, he thought, but he kept that to himself. Still, he had picked up a strange vibe in that courtyard and that worried him. "So what do you make of his story?"

"I say we check it out. But I think he was telling the truth."

They stopped at the corner, waiting for traffic to pass before crossing the street. "I did some more checking up on him," Vince advised her. "The man not only has a genius IQ and a knack for making money, he was also a Navy SEAL for four years before he came back to New Orleans and started his business."

"So he's smart, rich and was in the navy. What's your point?"

"My point is that he wasn't just in the navy. He was a SEAL. I've heard stories about those guys. The training is brutal and very few make it through. The ones who do are almost superhuman. They're trained in survival tactics and counterespionage and they're superintelligent. They can get in and out of a hostile country without anyone ever knowing they've been there."

"Again, what's your point?" Charlie asked him.

"The point is we're dealing with a shrewd individual who's been trained in the art of how not to get caught. The man is no pussycat."

"Neither am I."

"Trust me, no one would ever mistake you for a pussycat, Le Blanc." It was true. Charlie could handle herself as well as any man he knew. What she lacked in size and muscle, she more than made up for with smarts. "All I'm saying is I don't think you should be so quick to write off Cole Stratton as a suspect."

"My instincts tell me he's not our killer."

"Maybe he isn't. But that doesn't mean he's innocent either," Vince argued.

"Come on, Kossak. You said yourself the man is intelligent. If he was the killer, wouldn't he have made sure he had an alibi for the time of the murder instead of telling us he was home alone?"

"As you pointed out, he would also be clever enough to realize that we would think just that and purposely not bother establishing an alibi for himself."

Charlie said nothing as a group of college-age guys wearing strands of the shiny green, gold and purple Mardi Gras beads around their necks squeezed by them on the sidewalk. "In other words you think I'm off base."

"Don't put words in my mouth, Le Blanc. I'm just pointing out that there's a lot more to Cole Stratton than meets the eye," he explained. "His old man may be the one making noise and tossing his weight around, but if you ask me, the son is the one I'd worry about."

"He's not our killer," she repeated.

"That your opinion as a cop or as a woman?"

"I resent that," she fired back.

"I'm calling them as I see them. And right now you're sounding more like a female than a cop to me."

Charlie stopped in the middle of the block. "In case you haven't noticed, Kossak, I *am* a female. But I'm also a cop and a damn good one," she all but hissed.

He shrugged. "You'll get no argument from me on the cop part. And Cole Stratton certainly seemed to notice the female part," he shot back, earning himself an icy glare. When a fellow walking his German shepherd approached them from the other direction, Charlie clamped her lips closed and marched on at a quickened pace. Vince followed. He couldn't exactly blame Stratton for noticing her, Vince admitted. He had been taken aback at first when she'd been assigned as his partner. Homicide was an ugly business, one that never led to a happy ending because the victims were already dead. It wasn't the type of job most female officers wanted, and being a southern male he had been sexist enough to think Charlie wouldn't be able to cut it. He'd been wrong. He'd never known anyone more driven, more capable, or more committed to finding justice for the victims than Charlie Le Blanc. She'd proven herself time and again in the years that they'd been a team, and he considered himself lucky to have her covering his back. It was the reason he was concerned about her now.

Once the dog and his master were out of earshot, she asked, "You think I've lost my edge, Kossak? That I can't do my job?"

"What I think is that you're too close to this case. It's personal and when something is personal, emotions rule instead of logic. That leads to mistakes," he told her. "And neither one of us can afford to make a mistake. Not on this case. Not when we've got brass and politicians breathing down our necks."

"It's because it *is* personal that I won't make a mistake," she insisted.

"There's no way you can be sure something won't go wrong," he reasoned.

"And there's no way you can be sure that it will."

They reached her car and he waited for her to unlock it. "You're right. I don't know that something will go wrong. But I do know that if something does happen, it'll be better for you if it happens on someone else's shift."

She looked up at him as though he'd lost his mind. "What are you saying?"

"I'm saying that I think you should come clean with the captain, tell him you suspect the killing is linked to your sister's murder and let him assign someone else to the case."

"No!"

"Le Blanc—"

"No," she said again, this time lowering her voice. "You promised you'd give me time, Kossak. It's only been four days. You can't go and renege on that promise now."

"I shouldn't have made the promise in the first place." Relenting, he tried to explain, "I don't like the feel of this one. We've got a crime scene that's raised more questions than answers, a string of suspects who have been conveniently unavailable, and we've got our hands tied while we investigate because of political pressure."

"This isn't the first case where we've had to walk on eggshells," she reminded him. "And we still managed to do our job."

"But this one is different." He couldn't explain why. He only knew that his gut kept telling him they weren't dealing with some low-life robber or junkie, or even some hotshot kid from a rich family who had wigged out on too much meth. This time they were dealing with a cunning psychopath who, if Charlie was right and he believed she was, had gotten away with murder at least once before.

"You're right. It is different because the guy we're looking for is the same one who killed my sister. And I'm going to find him with or without your help."

"What's that supposed to mean?" he demanded.

"It means if you go to the captain and he pulls me off the case, I'll work it on my own without a badge and without you to back me up."

And she would, Vince told himself. Charlie was stubborn enough to go it alone and her working alone would be a hell of a lot worse. "All right. I'll keep quiet—for the time being. But from now on, we work this as a team. No going off on your own to investigate, no more calls at the crack of dawn telling me you're on your way to interview a suspect and that I should meet you there. Agreed?"

"Agreed," she said. "So do we try the reverend again or Danielle Marceau?"

"Why don't we see if the good reverend is in," Vince suggested.

"The reverend it is."

When they arrived at the church this time, it was to find the Reverend Homer Lawrence conducting a morning service. Quietly she and Vince eased into a pew at the back of the church. Since it wasn't Sunday, Charlie had been surprised to find the church filled with people. But apparently it was some type of feast day and the faithful had turned out to pray.

While they waited for the service to conclude, she used the opportunity to study the minister. He was somewhere in his mid-fifties, she guessed. On the short side, probably no more than five foot eight inches tall. She wondered if the slight paunch was a new acquisition, courtesy of New Orleans's fine dining. She imagined that his hair had been brown at one time, but it was giving way to gray and thinning on the top. He reminded her of a more portly version of Mr. Rogers, the one-time kids' television host. Not a bad image for a minister, she supposed. According to the data she had obtained on him, the reverend had been at his current post in New Orleans for just shy of a year. Prior to that he'd tended flocks in Mississippi, Arkansas and Alabama. He had been described by the doorman as a soft-spoken and devout man.

So what was a soft-spoken, devout man of the cloth doing in the apartment of a former casino hostess late at night?

"…And may the blessings of the Lord be with you all," the reverend said.

"And also with you," the congregation responded.

"Go forth in peace to love and serve the Lord."

The organ struck up the introductory notes of the recessional, marking the end of the service. Charlie recognized the song, it was an old standard that she used to sing in church herself during her youth. As the choir belted out praises to the Lord, she found herself remembering her last year in the church choir. She had been seventeen and a member of the teen choir at the church where she and her sisters attended services each week with their parents.

She'd enjoyed singing. Although she been no Whitney Houston or Celine Dion, she did have a good voice and, according to the choir director, perfect pitch. It was the reason she had been given a solo during one of the holiday services. Anne had only been eleven at the time and a member of the children's choir. But Emily…Emily had just turned thirteen and after chomping at the bit for months, she'd finally been able to join the teen choir. While Emily's voice was pretty, it hadn't been as good as hers, Charlie admitted honestly. But that hadn't stopped Emily from campaigning for her solo. Saying no to Emily had never been easy—especially for her. So in the end, she'd given in and convinced the choir director to allow them to sing the song together.

She couldn't help wondering if Emily might still be alive if she and her family had learned to say no to her more often instead of caving in to her wants. Because she was sure it was someone or something that Emily had wanted six years ago that had gotten her killed. And that same person had crossed paths with Francesca Hill. But who? J. P. Stratton or one of his sons? The minister? The old boyfriend that J.P. had run out of town? The mystery guy on the surveillance tape? Or someone else—someone who had been clever enough to tamper with the security tape.

Vince nudged her. "You okay?"

"Sure." Shaking off her musings, she realized that the reverend was marching past their pew and heading outdoors. The congregation began to file into the aisle and follow him outside. Impatient, she started to step out into the aisle.

Vince caught her arm. "It's better if we wait our turn."

He was right. She knew it. Still, it didn't make it any easier to wait for the slow-moving procession to reach their area at the back of the church. Finally the people in the pews in front of them stepped into the aisle. She and Vince followed. At last they exited the church and stepped outdoors into bright sunshine.

The Reverend Lawrence stood just beyond the bottom of

the church steps. He was all smiles as he exchanged greetings and pleasantries, shook hands and patted toddlers on their heads. Eager to speak with him, Charlie started forward.

"Hang on a second, Le Blanc. He isn't going anywhere," Vince said softly and once again placed a restraining hand on her shoulder. "Give the man a few minutes to chat with his congregation. After all, we don't want the minister complaining that we accosted him in front of his parishioners, do we?"

That made twice in the space of a few minutes that Vince had had to remind her to take a step back. Was he right? Was she too close to the case? Had she lost perspective because of the connection to Emily's murder?

No, she decided. The connection to Emily's murder might have made her more aggressive and given her a greater sense of urgency. But she hadn't lost focus and her goal remained the same—to find the black-stocking killer. She owed it to Francesca Hill. And she owed it to her sister Emily.

When only two women remained speaking with him, Vince asked, "Ready?"

She nodded.

"Just remember the man's a minister," he cautioned her. "Try not to bust his balls in front of everyone."

"I wouldn't dream of it," she told him and started toward the reverend.

"Reverend Lawrence?" Vince queried, taking the lead when they reached him.

"Yes," he said with a hesitant smile.

"Could we speak with you a moment?" he asked.

"If you'll excuse me, ladies. Martha, tell Rodney I hope he feels better and that I'll stop by this afternoon to see him."

"Thank you, Reverend Lawrence," the woman said, and after both said goodbye, they began to walk away.

When the reverend turned his attention back to them, Vince

said, "I'm Detective Vincent Kossak with the New Orleans Police Department and this is my partner, Detective Charlotte Le Blanc." Vince held up his badge.

He looked from one to the other. His smile disappeared. "Yes, my housekeeper said you tried to reach me yesterday while I was out visiting a sick member of our congregation. How can I help you, Detectives?"

"We'd like to speak with you about Francesca Hill."

"Ah, yes. I heard the tragic news. What a terrible thing to have happened to poor Mary Frances," he murmured.

"Mary Frances?" Charlie repeated.

"I know she preferred the name Francesca. But I still think…thought of her as Mary Frances. Forgive me," he said, a distraught expression crossing his face. "I've known…knew her since she was a young girl," he amended. "It's hard to believe she's dead."

"I hadn't realized that you and Ms. Hill were old acquaintances," Charlie said, but she had wondered if there had been a connection since the address they had obtained for Francesca Hill's mother had been in Arkansas.

"Actually, I hadn't seen her in years, then one day about six months ago, she turned up at one of my services. I can't tell you what a surprise it was to see her again after all this time," he explained, then shook his head. "I'm sorry. I didn't mean to ramble. Tell me now, how can I be of service to you?"

"Reverend, would it be possible for us to speak with you somewhere more private?" Vince asked, obviously noticing, as she had, that the two women who had been speaking with the reverend were eyeing them.

"Yes, of course. I should have suggested it. My residence is at the back of the church. We can speak there. Please follow me," he said.

They followed him to a small blue cottage that sat behind the church. It looked like something out of a storybook was Charlie's first thought. A single-story raised Acadian, the house had a porch across the front with two rockers and a window box brimming with white impatiens. A white picket fence and a flower garden bright with yellow and blue pansies and azaleas completed the picture. Following the reverend, they ascended the stairs and wiped their feet on a mat outside the door.

After fishing a key from his pocket, the reverend unlocked the door and held it open for them to enter. "Please, come in."

The inside was every bit as quaint as the exterior. Small, the place had a homey feel to it with lots of lace and ruffles. A crocheted afghan lay draped over the back of a floral couch. A country landscape and framed scripture verses filled one wall. A crucifix was mounted above one door. Green plants were scattered about the room. Many of the items looked homemade and Charlie imagined most had been gifts from members of his church. Not surprisingly, a bible sat on the wooden coffee table.

"Could I offer you something to drink, Detectives? Tea, soda, coffee?"

"Nothing for me, Reverend," Vince said. "But thank you."

"Detective…Le Blanc, wasn't it?"

"That's right, but no thank you, Reverend. I'm fine."

"Well, I hope you don't mind if I pour myself a glass of tea. The sermon left me a bit parched, which probably means that I was long-winded," he said lightly. "Please make yourselves comfortable, I'll only be a moment."

True to his word, the reverend returned within minutes with a tray containing a pitcher of tea, glasses and lemon wedges that he placed on the table. "I brought extra glasses in case you change your minds." After he had poured himself a glass, he drank deeply, then sat back with a sigh. "All right, now tell me how I can be of assistance."

Charlie took out her notepad and began, "Reverend, when was the last time you saw Ms. Hill?"

"On Friday evening. She and her fiancé, Mr. Stratton, invited me to join them at their rehearsal dinner."

"That was the last time you saw her? At the hotel restaurant?"

He paused for a fraction of a second. "Actually, I saw her again a few hours later. She was troubled about a personal matter and felt she needed spiritual counseling. She called and asked me if I could come by her apartment."

"What time was that?" she asked and noted his answer. "What was she troubled about?"

Once again he hesitated. "I suppose if you haven't already heard, you will soon enough. There was a incident at the dinner party that night, a confrontation between Mary Frances…Francesca…and Mr. Stratton's daughter. Francesca was quite upset."

"Do you know what the argument was about?" Vince asked.

"Ms. Stratton wasn't happy about her father's plans to remarry."

"Were you aware that Ms. Hill had threatened to press charges against Ms. Stratton for violating a restraining order?" Vince asked.

"Yes. Francesca was quite distraught over the situation. That's why she called me."

"Why is that?" Charlie began. "Why call you instead of her fiancé?"

"She didn't want to put Mr. Stratton in the middle between her and his daughter. So she called me and asked for my counsel."

"And do you make a practice of counseling beautiful, young women in their apartments at night, Reverend?" Charlie asked.

"I go whenever and wherever I'm needed, Detective," he said calmly.

"Judging from the guest log, Ms. Hill required your counsel rather frequently," she remarked.

"Some of God's children require more help than others," he responded.

Ignoring Vince's warning look, she pressed, "And what type of help did you offer Ms. Hill?"

He placed his glass on the table, met her gaze. "The same type of help that I offer to all of God's children, Detective. I listened to her and prayed with her."

Charlie recalled the look of Francesca Hill's apartment. There had been a great many things going on in that place on Friday night. But she doubted that prayer was among them. "Other than her problems with Holly Stratton, did Ms. Hill discuss anything else with you?"

"What do you mean, Detective?"

"I mean, was she worried about something or maybe having second thoughts about the marriage?" Charlie prompted.

"As I'm sure you're aware, Detective, conversations between a minister and a member of his church are sacrosanct. Anything Francesca may have confided in me would be privileged."

"About that minister-to-parishioner relationship," Charlie began. "I understand that Ms. Hill wasn't actually a member of your church."

"It's true. Francesca didn't attend services on a regular basis. But I still acted as her spiritual adviser and considered her one of the Lord's flock. I've continued to pray for both her and her mother ever since they first joined the church."

"Speaking of her mother, we've been trying to reach her but have been unsuccessful. Do you know how we can get in touch with her?" Charlie asked. Although J. P. Stratton's assistant had advised them that Stratton had notified Francesca's mother of her death, they had wanted to question her. But thus far none of their calls had been returned.

"I have a phone number for her," he said. "I spoke with her yesterday about the funeral service that Mr. Stratton has arranged. I understand she's to be buried once your coroner releases the body."

"If you could give us that number, we'd appreciate it," Charlie told him.

"Certainly," he said and wrote down the number for her.

"Thank you," Charlie said as she took the slip of paper from him. When she looked up at him again, she asked, "Reverend, when you last saw Ms. Hill on Friday evening, did she mention that she was expecting anyone?"

"No," he replied.

"Well, thank you for your time," she said and stood. So did Vince. "If you remember anything else, or think of something that you think could help us, please contact me or Detective Kossak. Here's my card."

"Thank you again, Reverend," Vince echoed and gave his card as well.

The reverend walked them to the door of the cottage. When they crossed the threshold and stood on the porch, he said, "Good luck, Detectives. I'll pray for your safety."

"Thank you," she murmured.

"Mary Frances was no angel, but she was one of the Lord's children. I'll pray for her and for you, that the Lord will keep you both safe. I hope you catch the person who did this to her."

"We will, Reverend," she told him. "You can count on it."

While he listened to the telephone ring on the other end of the line, he traced the letters of the name on the business card she'd given him. Detective Charlotte Le Blanc. Smiling, he called up an image of her. Tall, dark blond hair, brown eyes. She was a bit on the thin side for his tastes. He usually preferred his women with more curves. But her legs had been ex-

ceptional. Too bad she chose to hide them so often under pants. She wasn't as striking as her sister Emily had been, but she was pretty. She would even be beautiful, he suspected, if she made the effort to play up her features. And what lovely features they were—smooth skin, high cheekbones, great-looking mouth.

"This is Detective Le Blanc," the recorded voice mail message began. "I'm unavailable—"

He hung up the phone and sat back in his chair. Fingering the edges of the plain, buff-colored business card, he thought of her again. No, Charlotte Le Blanc was not at all like her sister Emily. There was nothing sweet or flirtatious about her. There was a fire in her and an independence about her that he found intriguing.

Straightening, he opened the drawer of the desk and triggered the lever to open the secret compartment. When the panel slid open, he took out the chest. Opening it, he retrieved one of the envelopes, then picked up the pen. Across the front he wrote, "CHARLOTTE." Smiling again, he took out a pair of black silk stockings.

Eight

She hadn't expected the call, Charlie admitted. When her phone call, followed by a visit to the home where the two youngest Stratton offspring resided, proved fruitless, she knew she would have to attempt to contact them again. So the call from Jason Stratton saying he and his brother Phillip could speak with her had come as a bit of a surprise.

And so had the two youngest Strattons. She'd known that Jason and Phillip were twins and had assumed that they were identical. They weren't. Oh, the resemblance was strong, but they weren't exact replicas of each other. Their personalities were also different.

Physically, both young men resembled their father, measuring about five foot ten inches and stocky. Both had medium-brown hair, weak chins and gray eyes. Jason was the more attractive of the two with a bit of wave to his hair, a glint in his eyes and a chip the size of Texas on his shoulder. Dressed in jeans, a designer sweatshirt and sneakers, he looked younger than his twenty-three years.

Phillip Stratton looked just as young, but there was a solemnness in the eyes behind the round spectacles that made her suspect he was the more responsible of the two. The short, straight hair, khaki slacks and sweater gave him a studious appearance. He was more well mannered than his twin, softer spoken and, judging from the way he handled the interview questions, he was used to keeping his brother in check. While both were graduate students studying computer technology, she suspected Phillip was the more intelligent of the two.

Seated in the ornate living room of the home they shared with their mother, Sylvia Stratton, Charlie shifted on the seat of the antique chair. Because her own mother loved antiques, she had made many a foray into the shops on Magazine Street when she was younger. As a result, she recognized the grouping—William III, walnut and ebony from the nineteenth century. The floral petit-point needlework on the seat and back of the chairs was pretty, but the chairs themselves were uncomfortable, she decided. The Stratton twins didn't look any more comfortable than she was. But she suspected their discomfort had nothing to do with their mother's pricey furniture and more to do with Vince's questions.

"When was the last time you saw Ms. Hill?" Vince asked Jason.

"We saw her at the rehearsal dinner Friday night," Phillip answered and Charlie noted once again that Phillip spoke for his brother.

"Then you witnessed the altercation between your sister and Ms. Hill?" Vince asked.

"Yes," Phillip answered.

"How did you feel about that?" he asked.

"We were embarrassed for our sister, of course. Holly shouldn't have lost her temper that way," Phillip answered.

"And Ms. Hill? Were you embarrassed for her, too?"

"We felt bad for her. It was supposed to be a happy occasion," he replied.

"I didn't feel bad for her," Jason said. Ignoring his brother's quelling look, he continued, "The bitch deserved it."

"Shut up, Jason," Phillip said, his voice sharp.

"It's all right," Charlie told Phillip, signaling to Vince with a look to let her have a go at the questions. She shifted slightly and focused her attention on Jason. "You didn't like your father's fiancée?" she asked him.

"I hated her guts."

"Why?" Charlie asked him.

"Because she was a money-hungry bitch," Jason snapped.

"Knock it off, Jason," Phillip told his brother.

"Why should I? It's true. Everyone knew she was only marrying the old man for his money."

"My brother didn't like the idea of having a stepmother who was only three years older than us," Phillip explained.

"How did you feel about it?" she asked Phillip.

He shrugged. "Francesca was okay and my dad was crazy about her. But I think it would have been better if he'd been with someone closer to his own age."

Someone like his mother, Charlie thought, recalling J. P. Stratton's claim that his last ex-wife had been convinced they would remarry. She couldn't help wondering if Phillip had thought the same thing—until Francesca had come along.

"I'm not sure we should answer any more questions without legal representation," Phillip remarked. "My brother Aaron is an attorney and he's supposed to be on his way here. Maybe we shouldn't say anything else until he gets here."

The kid was definitely not a chip off the old block, she thought. Unlike his father and two older brothers, he was nervous. And judging from the way he kept stealing looks at his twin, she suspected his brother's answers were causing the case of nerves. "That's certainly your prerogative. As Detective Kossak told you, you're not being charged with anything and you're welcome to have an attorney present. If the three of you will meet us at the police station," she began. Closing her notepad, she stood. So did Vince. "We'll just continue our interview there."

Phillip blinked. The eyes behind his horn-rimmed glasses were so huge, he reminded her of an owl. "You mean we'd have to go to the police station?"

"Our captain likes to keep things more formal when there are lawyers involved," she hedged, earning her a "since when" look from Vince.

"And if we don't have an attorney present?" Phillip asked.

"We'll just ask you a few more questions and be on our way. As Detective Kossak told you, neither of you are being charged with anything. We're simply gathering information and establishing a time line to help in our investigation. Since you were among the last people to see Ms. Hill alive, your observations could be important."

"So you're talking to everybody who was at the rehearsal dinner?" he asked.

"Yes," Charlie told him. "We've already spoken to your father, your two brothers and your sister, as well as the minister. We also plan to speak with Ms. Marceau and Judge Findlay since they were among the dinner guests." She paused, gave him a moment to digest what she'd said and weigh the options. "Would you like to wait for your attorney?"

Phillip exchanged a look with his twin. "No. Let's just finish now. What else do you want to know?"

Charlie sat down again and flipped open her notepad. With her pen in hand, she asked, "What time did you leave the rehearsal dinner?"

"Around seven-thirty," Phillip said. "After that blowup with Holly, everyone pretty much left."

"Where did you go once you left the hotel?"

"Home," Phillip told her.

"Do you know around what time you got home?"

"Somewhere around eight o'clock, I guess. I didn't pay that much attention to the time," Phillip answered.

"Did you stay in for the rest of the evening?"

"Yes."

"What about you, Mr. Stratton?" she asked, directing the question to Jason. "What time did you leave the rehearsal dinner?"

"Jason left with me," Phillip told her. "We drove home together."

"Mr. Stratton, is that right?" she asked Jason.

"Yes. Phillip and I left together and came home."

"And you both stayed in all evening?"

"Yes," Jason told her.

"That's right," Phillip replied.

"Are you sure? Because one of your neighbors remembers seeing one of you leave around ten o'clock."

"You went out to pick up some cigarettes, Jason. Remember?" Phillip prompted.

"Yeah, that's right. I forgot about that," Jason said, obviously following his brother's lead. "Phillip's right. I ran out to pick up some smokes."

As though to prove his point, he grabbed a pack of cigarettes from the coffee table and lit one up. So much for the antismoking campaigns, Charlie thought. She also couldn't help wondering what Sylvia Stratton would say about her son contaminating her fancy drapes and antiques with tobacco smoke.

"What's the name of the place where you got the smokes?" Vince asked.

Panic came into the kid's eyes. He looked over at his brother.

"I don't remember the name of the place. It was just some convenience store."

"How about where it was located?" Vince pressed.

"Jason was upset about the argument between Holly and Francesca," Phillip explained. "When he's like that, my brother doesn't pay much attention to things."

"I know what you mean. When I get ticked off about something, I don't pay much attention to where I'm going either. I just go on automatic pilot," Vince said.

"That's what I did," Jason said, jumping on the out being offered.

"The good thing about being on automatic pilot is that the body follows our routines, it knows where to go even when the brain's not working."

"Yeah," Jason responded. "That's what happened to me."

"I figured as much. So where do you usually buy your smokes when you run out?"

Charlie almost felt sorry for the kid because he knew he'd been caught. "I…um, I buy them different places," Jason answered.

"But there must be someplace close by that you go to buy them when you're in a pinch and it's late," Vince suggested.

When Jason said nothing, Phillip offered, "There's this gas station/convenience store a few blocks from here that Jason goes to sometimes."

"Thanks," Vince told him after he gave him the address.

"So once you came back from buying the cigarettes, you stayed in the rest of the evening?" she asked Jason.

"Yes."

"He was here with me. We were working on a new computer program most of the night," Phillip explained. "Neither one of us left the house again until morning."

"Can anyone verify that you were both here all night?" she asked.

"Our mother was here," Phillip told her.

Charlie made a notation and closed her pad. "Good. We'll just need to speak with her for a moment and have her confirm you were both here. Is she at home?"

"No. She's out," Phillip told her. "And I'm not sure she'll be of any help. I mean, she took a sleeping pill that evening and was in bed when we got home. She didn't wake up until late the next day."

"But you said you both got home around eight o'clock. Does your mother usually go to bed so early?" she asked.

"She did that night. She was upset about Dad remarrying," Phillip replied.

"Then I suppose she wasn't unhappy to hear that there would be no wedding."

"She wasn't glad that Francesca was dead, if that's what you mean," Phillip said. "She was more concerned about my dad."

"I'm sure she was," Charlie said in an effort to calm him. "You said your mother was out. Do you know when she'll be back?"

"I don't know. Probably a while. She's at my dad's. When she heard about what happened to Francesca, she went over to, you know, comfort him."

And maybe to figure a way to get back into her ex's life, Charlie thought.

Phillip stood. "If that's all of your questions, Detectives, my brother and I have to get back to that computer program we've been working on."

Charlie shot a look over to Vince. They'd worked together long enough that he knew she needed him to get Phillip away so she could question Jason without his brother's interference.

"You know, I'm a bit of a computer junkie myself," Vince

told him as they stood. "I've always admired you guys who could actually write your own programs."

"It's not that hard if you know what you're doing," Phillip said modestly.

"Maybe it's not hard for you. But for us normal Joes it's not so easy. In that article I read on your brother Cole he claims one of the reasons his security company is skyrocketing is because his computer systems are cutting edge. You help him with it?"

"No. I'm nowhere near as good as Cole. He knows his way around a keyboard. He can make the thing sing," Phillip said proudly.

"You know, I sure would like to see your setup. Maybe you could give me a few pointers on mine," Vince suggested.

He hesitated, looked at his brother. "I don't know. We have a lot of work to do…"

"Come on, it'll just take a minute." He shifted his gaze to her. "You don't mind, do you, Le Blanc? Since you like these old houses, maybe Jason could give you a tour."

"I'd love that," she said. "Would you mind?"

He shrugged. "Sure, why not."

"We won't be long," Vince said, talking about hard drives, bytes and memory as he and Phillip headed toward the far end of the house.

"I really appreciate this," she told Jason.

"Like I said, it's no big deal. I guess we might as well start in the dining room."

Charlie followed along, listened to him give a dry and un-appreciative tour of the dining room, which had been beautifully outfitted with a genuine Chippendale dining table—not a reproduction—Louis XV chairs, a crystal chandelier. The china alone would have cost her a year's pay, she thought, while making the necessary oohs and aahs and trying to put him at ease. "It's lovely."

"I suppose," he remarked. "The parlor is this way."

The parlor was equally impressive, more antiques, damask drapes, silk wall coverings. A mahogany Gainsborough library armchair caught her eye. She ran a fingertip along the hand-carved arm supports, noted the cabriole legs carved at the front with a shell motif and acanthus at the knees. She couldn't help thinking that her mother would have loved it. So would Emily who had shared her mother's passion for antiques. At the thought of her sister, she returned her focus to Jason Stratton, determined to get him to open up before Vince returned with his brother. "Are these paintings of family members?" she asked about the oil portraits on the wall.

"Yeah. My great-grandfather and great-uncle on my mother's side."

"It must be nice being able to trace your ancestors, to have such strong family ties," she commented.

"If you ask me, family isn't all it's cracked up to be."

"I understand Francesca didn't have much family, only her mother, and the two of them weren't close. That must have been pretty lonely. I guess it helped that she had people like Reverend Lawrence and Danielle Marceau as friends."

"I'd hardly call those two friends," he said.

"What do you mean? The reverend said he'd known her since she was a little girl and he'd been counseling her."

"Yeah, right. Trust me, that guy didn't look at her the way a minister should."

"How did he look at her?" she asked.

"The way a man looks at a woman. And as for Danielle, some friend she was. I saw her hitting on my old man just last week," he said. "She also stole a pair of Francesca's earrings. She claimed that she'd been trying them on and they fell in her bag. But I saw her take them."

"Did you tell Francesca?"

"Sure did. And she was really ticked off about it. I heard her giving Danielle hell outside the restaurant Friday night and demanded she give them back."

Interesting, Charlie thought. She certainly intended to follow up on Danielle's relationship to the deceased.

"This is the kitchen," Jason told her as they entered the next room. He showed her the double ovens, the commercial refrigerator, the island stove complete with a grill.

"Your mother must love cooking in here."

He made a snorting sound. "My mother doesn't cook. She can't even boil water. Our housekeeper Shirley does all the cooking."

"What about Francesca? Was she a good cook?"

"She could do breakfast stuff. She made lost bread for me once. It was really good," he told her.

Man oh man, Charlie thought and bit her lip. The kid had it bad. She couldn't help wondering if Francesca Hill had known that her intended stepson thought he was in love with her. "It sounds like you were a good friend to her."

"I tried to be and for a while we were friends. Until she met my Dad. Then she didn't have time for me or Holly anymore," he said, his voice bitter.

"Maybe she fell in love with your father," Charlie suggested.

"I told you, she didn't love him," he fired back. "It was his money. Everything was about money with her."

"Be careful, Jason. Or you'll give Detective Le Blanc the wrong impression," Aaron Stratton said from the doorway of the kitchen.

Today he wore another suit, this one a deep chestnut that brought out the blond in his hair. "Hello, Mr. Stratton," she said.

"It's Aaron, Detective." He walked into the room, stopped in front of her. "As you've probably already gathered, my brother Jason wasn't exactly thrilled about Francesca marrying our father."

"So he's told me. What about you, Mr. Stratton?" she asked, making a point of addressing him formally. "How did you feel about your father remarrying?"

He crossed his arms and the corners of his mouth curved slightly. "I thought my father was making a mistake," he responded. "But then, when it came to women, my father didn't always exercise the best judgment."

"He did with my mother," Jason defended.

"Yes. Sylvia was one of his wiser choices," he said gently. "Unfortunately, most of them weren't. Whenever my father fell in lust or love, logic went out the window."

"Along with part of your inheritance?" she prompted.

He smiled, a real smile this time. "That's true. But then, I don't need my father's money, Detective. I'm a rich man in my own right—which I'm sure you already know since you would have run a background check on me, as well as the rest of my family."

It was true. She had checked on each of the Strattons. And Aaron was indeed a wealthy man—thanks in great measure to the fortune he'd inherited from his mother. The second Mrs. Stratton had been savvy enough to negotiate a sweet deal with J.P. when they married and Aaron reaped those rewards upon her death. In addition, he drew a high six-figure salary as the lead attorney for Stratton Industries and wise investing had more than doubled his net worth. No, Aaron Stratton didn't need his father's money.

"Charlie," Vince called her name. "We need to roll."

"Thank you again for your cooperation and for the tour of the house," she told Jason.

"Sure."

Turning to Aaron, she said, "Mr. Stratton, I would like to

speak to you again. I have a few questions that I'm hoping you can clear up for me."

He dipped his head. "Of course, Detective."

"I appreciate that. We'll show ourselves out," she said and started to walk away. Pausing, she looked back. "Oh, and Mr. Stratton, I really could use that list we discussed, the one with the names of people who might possibly have a grudge against your father."

"I'll see that you get it," he told her.

After she joined Vince and they exited the house, she asked, "What's up?"

"The M.E.'s report is in."

Cole sat back in the chair at his desk. Locking his fingers together, he stretched his arms out in front of him to ease the muscles in his back that had tightened from sitting so long in front of the computer. He flexed his fingers, heard the satisfying crack of knuckles, then he straightened and went back to work.

He typed in the name Charlotte Le Blanc and sent his fingers flying across the keyboard. As a security expert and with the special skills he'd acquired during his tenure with the military, he knew where to look and how to get into databases that were normally inaccessible. He tapped into those sources now.

Forty-five minutes later, he had what he wanted. He'd found a record of her birth twenty-nine years ago to Elizabeth and Gordon Le Blanc. He read through the list of milestones that included her high-school and college graduations. She'd entered law school eight years ago and her application reflected she'd been interested in a career in criminal law. A family history on file with the school listed her parents' occupations as banker and schoolteacher. She had two younger sisters, Emily and Anne.

Cole grinned as he read the names. Charlotte, Emily and

Anne. The names of the three Brontë sisters. He'd wager his sailboat that Elizabeth Le Blanc had taught English.

He continued checking the data banks and learned Charlotte had completed two years of law school. Her grades had been excellent initially, but had nosedived in the last semester in her second year. He searched but found no record of her completing law school. But he did find a record of her graduation from the police academy a year later, finishing at the top of her class. She'd been a cop for five years, he realized. There were several citations, her promotion to detective and a transfer to the Homicide Division three years ago. There were two accounts of her being wounded in the line of duty. A more recent article on a hostage/murder situation was accompanied by a photo of her exiting a house and carrying a child in her arms. The lady didn't lack courage. But then, he hadn't needed the accounts of her bravery to tell him that. He'd come to that conclusion already.

He pulled up her data from the DMV, which gave her date of birth, current address and listed her height at five feet seven inches and her weight at a hundred twenty-five pounds. Under hair color "brown" was typed. But the color was closer to caramel, he decided, that elusive shade somewhere between blond and light brown. Her eyes were brown, but the driver's-license photo didn't reflect that hint of gold in them that made them look like amber. The photo also didn't tell him what made the lady tick.

But the article on her sister's murder did. He'd been both surprised and curious by her response when he had mentioned her being an older sibling. Such a strong reaction to his innocent remark had seemed odd at the time, especially when anyone who looked closely could see that she and the TV reporter were related. The news clipping explained why. She had lost a younger sibling. He pulled up the first article onto the computer screen. Dated six years earlier, it had run in a Baton Rouge, Louisiana, newspaper:

College Student Found Dead

The body of nineteen-year-old Emily Le Blanc of New Orleans, a premed student attending Louisiana State University in Baton Rouge, was discovered yesterday morning in her off-campus apartment by her sister, Charlotte Le Blanc. Charlotte Le Blanc, a second-year law student at the university, stated that she had gone by her sister's apartment to check on her when she was unable to reach the younger woman by phone. No details about the cause of death have been released, pending an autopsy. The police said they are classifying the death as a homicide. No suspects or motive are reported at this time.

Cole studied the photo of Emily Le Blanc that accompanied the article. Long blond hair, wide brown eyes, a kittenish smile. She looked young, innocent and very pretty. A girlie girl. He could see the resemblance between the sisters as well as the differences.

His fingers flew across the computer keyboard as he continued his search. Moments later another article on the murder appeared, giving much of the same information. This one had an accompanying photo of Charlotte standing outside her sister's apartment with police officers. He tapped the keys, enlarging the photo. Six years ago, Charlotte's hair had been longer, but the delicate jawline and tempting mouth were the same. So was the serious expression and the wide eyes that looked straight at you and into your soul. He suspected it was Emily Le Blanc that people would notice first. But it would be Charlotte Le Blanc that they would remember.

He had certainly remembered her. From the second he had seen her in his sister's apartment, he'd found her difficult to ignore and even more difficult to forget. This morning's encounter had only served to reaffirm his opinion of her as well as his attraction. He recalled that moment when they had stood at the doorway. Desire had hit him like a one-two punch. Two steps and their bodies would have been touching. A dip of his head and he could have tasted her mouth. And judging from the way her eyes had darkened, she had felt it, too.

Continuing his search, he typed in the name Emily Le Blanc and requested items dating from six years ago to the present. He pulled up a string of articles about the murder, most a repeat of the earlier ones. The majority of them were dated six years ago. No details about the murder were revealed. The cause of death was listed as strangulation. Cole frowned as he thought about Francesca's murder—another strangulation victim. A coincidence? His gut told him it wasn't.

Another sweep through the system rendered only one more article about the death of Emily Le Blanc. The piece had been written three years earlier and the case was classified as open. A cold case that had been filed away, a murder that had gone unsolved, a killer for whom no one was searching.

Except for Detective Charlotte Le Blanc. She would not have given up. He'd sensed that about her. He certainly understood it. Just as he'd sensed that she would not give up until she found Francesca's murderer—a murder for which she had him marked as a suspect. Finding himself attracted to a homicide cop who was looking to pin a murder rap on him didn't exactly make for a good relationship, he mused. But then, he'd always enjoyed a challenge. And Detective Charlotte Le Blanc would certainly be that. Of course, before she would consider any personal involvement with him, he'd have to convince her he wasn't a killer. He supposed the best way to do that was to do some hunting on his own.

Cole was still mulling over how to proceed with Detective Le Blanc when his cell phone rang. "Stratton."

"Cole, it's Phillip. The police were just here, asking me and Jason all kinds of questions about Francesca and where we were the night she was murdered. They acted like they thought one of us killed her."

"I doubt that," he said, trying to ease his younger brother's concerns. "They're probably talking to everybody who knew her or saw her that last day. There's nothing to worry about. You and Jason told them where you were, didn't you?"

"Yeah. But Jason sort of messed up."

"What do you mean?" Cole asked.

For the next several minutes Cole listened while Phillip relayed the detectives' visit, the questions they'd asked, how they had known that Jason hadn't been home all night like he'd first told them and that he had gone out to buy cigarettes. "Is he going to be in trouble for saying that he was home when he actually went out?" Phillip asked.

"No. He'll be fine," Cole assured him. "They'll check out the place where Jason bought the cigarettes and, hopefully, whoever was on duty that night will remember him."

"What if they don't remember him?"

"Well, most of those convenience store/gas stations have surveillance cameras. They'll just check the footage for that night to verify he was there." When Phillip didn't respond, Cole got a bad feeling. "Phillip, was Jason lying about where he was?"

"I don't know. He might have been. He's been acting weird for the past couple of weeks. He's been skipping classes, and when I tried to tell him to get his act straight or he'd flunk out, he bit my head off, said he didn't care if he got another degree. I'm worried about him, Cole."

The last two times Cole had seen him, Jason had seemed moody, secretive. Since Jason had always been on the quiet side, he hadn't thought much about it. And when he had, he had attributed his brother's mood to Sylvia's reaction to J.P.'s upcoming marriage. After all, the woman had made no secret about her desire to remarry the man and had used her sons in her quest. It was the reason both of them still lived at home instead of going out on their own. Now he couldn't help wishing he had tried to find out what was bugging Jason. "You just concentrate on acing that midterm," he told Phillip. "And let me worry about Jason and the police."

"So what have you got for us?" Charlie asked Dr. Penelope Williamson as she and Vince stood with the medical examiner in the autopsy lab. Stretched out on the stainless-steel examining table was the body of Francesca Hill. While Charlie had seen her share of dead bodies as a homicide detective, she never got used to seeing anyone cheated out of the life that should have been theirs. But it was the young ones like Francesca Hill that were the hardest to accept.

"First off," the doctor began, "I can tell you that your victim's last meal was quite an enjoyable one. In addition to steak and grilled shrimp, she had caviar, a Caesar salad and wild rice. She also had bananas Foster and quite a bit of champagne. Her blood alcohol level was .90."

"Any drugs?" Vince asked.

"No. Not so much as an aspirin."

"She did have two tattoos—a butterfly on the left buttock and a rose on the right ankle."

"Dr. Williamson, as fascinating as all this is, do you think we could skip the show-and-tell and get to the good stuff?" Charlie asked. "Like the cause of death?"

"You really suck the fun out of this job, Detective," she said dryly.

"Next time, I promise you can dazzle us with all the little details," Charlie said.

"I intend to hold you to that—over the meal you two promised me."

"You've got it," Charlie assured her and made a mental note to plan something with Vince for the doctor.

Putting away her clipboard with the rest of the facts, figures and reports about the body fluids, stomach contents, identifying marks or scars and a multitude of other information, the doctor said, "The cause of death was strangulation."

"Any idea what was used?" Charlie asked.

The moment of levity in what was a job that provided few light moments was gone. "While there is some bruising, there are no definitive markings on the neck, which indicates your killer probably used some type of soft material or fabric to strangle her."

"Something soft like a stocking?" Charlie asked and ignored the look from Vince.

"Yes. A stocking would have worked and not left any definitive marks. Panty hose or a silk scarf could also have been used."

"What about defensive wounds, Doc?" Vince asked.

"None that I could find. There were no foreign skin cells under her fingernails that would suggest she tried to fight off her attacker. There is some bruising around the wrist areas though," she said, and with her gloved hand she lifted the victim's arms to show the discoloration at the wrists. "There are no ligature markings, but the bruising around here could mean that your victim was restrained during the attack and unable to fight back."

"Was she raped?" Charlie asked.

"It's hard to say for sure. The victim did have sexual contact with two different partners before she died," Dr. William-son reported. "But the vaginal area didn't reveal any bruising or trauma that would indicate the sex was forced. There was semen present and I did a rape kit. I've sent it on to the lab for a DNA analysis."

"Two guys the same night," Vince remarked and it was clear he didn't approve. "Makes you wonder just how serious she was about those vows she was supposed to be taking, doesn't it?"

"For all we know, the other guy could have been Stratton's idea," Charlie told him, feeling the need to defend the woman lying dead on the slab who could not defend herself.

"Come on, Le Blanc. You met the man. Did he strike you as someone who likes to share?"

Vince was right. J. P. Stratton didn't strike her as a man who shared. Rather, he struck her as selfish and demanding. He would have regarded Francesca Hill as his property and would not have tolerated anyone trespassing on what he considered his turf.

"If you two are finished speculating about the sexual pro-clivities of the victim's fiancé, there is one more thing you might be interested in," Dr. Williamson told them.

Charlie immediately shifted her attention back to the doc-tor. So did Vince.

"Your victim was seven weeks pregnant."

Charlie looked over at Vince, saw that he was as stunned by the news as she was. She also couldn't help feeling even sorrier for Francesca Hill. The woman had had even more to live for than she'd first thought. "I wonder if J. P. Stratton knew he was about to become a daddy again?"

"I think an even more important question is whether he was the baby's daddy," Vince countered.

God, he was right, Charlie realized. The child might not have been Stratton's. If it wasn't and Francesca was seeing someone else, J. P. Stratton didn't strike her as the type of man who would tolerate such a betrayal or the humiliation. "Doc, the fetus—"

"I've already ordered a DNA test."

"Thanks." She turned to Vince. "What do you say we go pay another visit to the grief-stricken fiancé and find out whether or not he was planning diaper duty?"

Nine

Once again Charlie found herself and Vince being ushered into J. P. Stratton's study by the ever-so-proper butler. "Mr. Stratton will be with you shortly, Detectives. He asked that I offer you something to drink while you wait. Wine or perhaps a brandy?"

"No, thank you," Charlie said.

"Sir?"

Charlie elbowed Vince in the ribs. "No, thanks," he responded as he looked longingly at the brandy.

"This isn't a social call, Kossak," she reminded her partner when the butler retreated from the room.

"I know that. But do you realize how much that stuff goes for?"

"No, and I don't want to know."

"Five hundred bucks a bottle. On my salary, how many chances do you think I'll get to taste the stuff?"

"My guess is never."

"That's what I figure, too," he said resignedly.

Charlie laughed.

"I'm glad one of us finds it amusing," he told her.

But in truth, she suspected that Vince was amused, too. It was one of the few light moments either of them had had since being assigned the case four days ago. Murder in itself didn't lend itself to lighthearted moments. The fact that she was sure this particular murder case was linked to her sister's murder made it even darker than normal. She knew Vince was aware of her feelings about it, just as she was aware of his. To top it off, it was a high-profile case that was generating pressure on all sides. The entire situation made for a lot of tension, she admitted. And both she and Vince were feeling that tension.

Glancing at the label on the brandy, she recognized the pricey brand name. "You know, Anne dated a guy who was a sales rep for a liquor distributor. If you want, I could ask her to call him and see if he can get you a bottle at cost or at least at a discount."

"Thanks, but I think I'll pass."

"Suit yourself," she said and wandered over to the bookcases. Stratton had quite a collection, she noted as she scanned the titles on the shelves. Classics, bestsellers, books on business and art, sports statistics, several of the hot books from a few years back on how to make millions using other people's money.

"So is Anne still seeing that guy?" Vince asked.

"The liquor-sales rep? I don't think so. I haven't heard her mention him for a while now."

"She seeing anyone special?" he asked.

Charlie looked over at her partner who was studying a painting of an English hunting scene. In the three years she'd worked with Vince, he'd never shown any interest in art that she could recall. "Not that I know of. Why?" she asked, realizing this was the second time in as many days that he'd brought up her sister.

"No reason. Just wondering," he said casually.

Too casually, Charlie thought. Was it possible Vince was interested in Anne? The notion of her partner and her baby sister hooking up came at her out of left field. But now that she thought about it, Anne had gone all weird on her the other night when she'd mentioned Vince. And now Vince was acting almost as weird. "Kossak, is something going on between you and my sister?"

"No," he said quickly. "I mean, what could be going on? She's just a kid."

"She's twenty-three," Charlie pointed out.

"And I'm thirty-two."

"Yeah, you're practically ready for the retirement home."

"Real funny, Le Blanc."

She certainly thought so. But before she could tell him as much, the door opened and in walked Aaron Stratton. She had to say one thing for J. P. Stratton—he had good-looking kids. Aaron was handsome in that all-American-guy kind of way, reminding her of a young Robert Redford. Once again, the man was impeccably dressed and looked as if he'd stepped off the pages of *GQ* magazine. Today he wore a steel-gray suit that was a perfect foil for his green eyes and dark blond hair. His smile was charming. After meeting Cole, she could see a resemblance between the brothers—the shape of the eyes and the forehead, she thought. But she couldn't help noticing the differences between them, too. Cole wasn't quite as smooth, not quite as polished. He seemed more real and yet more dangerous.

"Detectives, I see we meet again," he said and extended his hand first to her and then to Vince.

"So we do," she commented.

"You sound suspicious, Detective Le Blanc. You needn't be," he assured her with a smile as he moved behind the bar and picked up the bottle of brandy. "I had some documents for my father to sign. You're sure I can't offer you something to drink?"

"We're on duty," Charlie answered quickly.

"Ah, of course. Then I'll pass as well," he said and set the bottle down. "So tell me, how can I be of assistance?"

"Actually, we're here to see your father," Charlie told him.

"So Henry told me. But I'm afraid that's not possible, Detective. As you can imagine, Francesca's death has devastated him. He isn't accepting any visitors."

Charlie didn't buy the song and dance for a minute. She'd seen just how devastated J. P. Stratton was over the loss of his intended bride. The man had seemed more annoyed by the inconvenience the cancellation had caused him than by the death of the woman he supposedly loved. "We're not visitors, Mr. Stratton. We're homicide detectives conducting a murder investigation and we need to ask your father some questions."

Vince stepped forward. "What Detective Le Blanc means is that we don't want to intrude on your father's grief, but it is important that we speak with him."

Aaron narrowed those green eyes. "Why? Has something happened? Have you picked up Schwitzer and charged him with Francesca's murder?"

"Not yet. We're still trying to locate him," Vince informed him.

"In the meantime, we're continuing to interview anyone who had contact with Ms. Hill or who might have had a motive for killing her," Charlie added.

"Are you saying my father's a suspect?"

"At the moment everyone is a suspect," she told him. "Now, if you don't mind, we really do need to speak with your father."

"As you know, Detective, I am my father's attorney," he reminded her. "Which means I am his legal representative. Anything you have to say to him, you can say to me on his behalf."

Her patience wearing thin, Charlie said, "You're welcome to remain present while we speak to your father if he wishes.

But he is the one we need to speak with. If he's unable to speak with us now, then we can have him come down to the station and we'll speak with him there." Not bothering to look at Vince because she knew he would have used more tact, she continued, "Enjoy the remainder of your evening, Mr. Stratton."

"We'll see ourselves out," Vince said and Charlie could have kissed him.

"Detectives, wait."

Charlie paused and looked back. So did Vince. For several long seconds, Aaron Stratton simply stood there, looking at her, measuring her, Charlie was sure.

Finally, he said, "I'll see if my father is up to seeing you."

Once Aaron had left the room, she turned to Vince. "Thanks," she told him.

He shrugged. "I was getting tired of the runaround, too. Let's just hope the old man is up to seeing us," he said, using Aaron Stratton's description.

A few moments later, the door to the study opened again and Aaron entered. "My father will be down shortly." He paused. "Detectives, my father is a complex man who believes showing emotion is a sign of weakness. But he is grieving. I hope you'll take that into consideration when you speak with him."

"Of course," Vince told him.

"While we're waiting for your father, perhaps you wouldn't mind clearing something up for us," Charlie said.

"I'll certainly try. What is it you'd like to know?"

"When we were here on Saturday, why did you fail to mention that you'd been to Ms. Hill's apartment the night she was murdered?" Charlie asked.

"It didn't seem relevant at the time. I assume you saw me on the surveillance video?"

"Yes," Charlie told him. "Why were you there?"

"To get her to sign the prenuptial agreement."

Charlie arched her brow. "That's leaving it kind of late, isn't it? I would have thought the prenup would have been handled before then."

"It should have been. But the wedding was planned rather quickly and Francesca wanted some changes to the original agreement. By the time we ironed out those changes, the wedding day was almost here. So I agreed to bring the document to her apartment that night for her to sign."

"Wouldn't it have been simpler for you to have her sign the thing earlier that evening when you were at the rehearsal dinner?" Vince asked.

"Yes. It would have been—if I'd had the document. I didn't. As I said, the changes were extensive and my assistant was still working on them when I left for dinner," he explained. "I arranged to have the document delivered to me at the hotel. Unfortunately, after the incident with my sister, the party ended early and Francesca left. So I took the prenup to her apartment that evening for her signature."

"Did she sign it?" Charlie asked.

"No. She still wasn't happy with some of the terms of the agreement," Aaron explained. "She asked me to leave it with her and said she wanted to speak with my father again before signing it."

"You left the agreement with her?" Vince asked.

"Yes."

But they had found no prenuptial agreement at the murder scene. She could only wonder why. "What was it that she objected to in the agreement?"

"Several things, but mostly what her share of my father's assets would be if there was a divorce."

"What would have happened if she didn't sign the prenup?" Vince asked.

"I would have advised my father not to go through with the wedding," he told them. "My father's a very wealthy man, Detective, and Louisiana is a community-property state. Without a prenup, Francesca would have been able to claim a significantly larger share of my father's assets if they were to divorce."

And with three divorces, one widow and numerous affairs to his credit, the odds of J.P. suffering another divorce were better than good, Charlie thought silently.

A smile curved Aaron's lips. And as though he'd read her thoughts, he said, "Considering my father's track record with women, the possibility of a divorce was certainly something for which precautions had to be made."

"Would it be possible for us to get a copy of the prenup you left with Ms. Hill?" Vince asked him.

"Of course. I'll have my assistant send it over to you."

"Mr. Stratton, where were you Friday evening between midnight and two o'clock in the morning?" Charlie asked him.

He tipped his head to the side, a look of amusement crossed his handsome features. "Why, Detective, do you think I killed Francesca?"

"Did you?"

He laughed. "No. But I imagine I do have as much motive as my brothers and sister, don't I? Francesca would have taken a bite out of my inheritance, too."

"So where were you Friday night between midnight and two in the morning?" she asked again.

"I was here."

"I didn't realize you lived with your father," she said.

"I don't," he said, his lips curving as though amused. "I came here after leaving Francesca's to let my father know that she hadn't signed the prenup and to suggest that he postpone the wedding."

"What did he say?"

"Very little since he wasn't exactly in a condition to think clearly."

"How come?" she asked.

"Because he had a few friends over, gentlemen friends," he clarified. "They were giving him a bit of a send-off before he gave up his bachelorhood. By the time I arrived, my father and his friends had finished off several bottles of scotch. Things broke up sometime around one-thirty and I helped get my father to bed. I left here around two-fifteen and went to my own apartment."

"We're going to need a list of names of those present at the bachelor party."

"That shouldn't be a problem," he said. "Anything else?"

Before she could respond, the door to the study burst open and in strode J. P. Stratton, who didn't appear to be the least grief-stricken. "Detectives, I hope you're here to tell me that you've found the person who murdered my fiancée."

"Not yet. We're still working on it, sir," Charlie told him, even though he had directed his remarks to Vince. She stepped into his line of vision. "That's why we're here. Some new information has come to our attention that we wanted to ask you about."

"What information?" he asked, his voice filled with suspicion.

"Did you know that at the time of her death Ms. Hill was seven weeks pregnant?"

"What?" Aaron said, shock washing over his features.

"Francesca Hill was seven weeks pregnant at the time of her death," she repeated. She turned her focus back to the father. "Did you know about the pregnancy, Mr. Stratton?"

"Of course I knew," he spat out the words. He walked over to the bar and poured himself a scotch. He tossed it back in one swallow.

"How long have you known, sir?" she asked him.

"Long enough," he fired back and poured himself another drink, downed it.

He was lying. And Charlie knew it. "Was it yours?"

The entire room went still. The only sound she could hear was the beating of her own heart as she stared into the face of an enraged J. P. Stratton. "What are you implying, young woman?"

"It's Detective. And I'm not implying anything. I'm merely asking whether or not you were the father of the child Ms. Hill was carrying."

He slapped the glass down onto the bar so hard that Charlie was amazed it didn't shatter. "How dare you?" he demanded, his voice a snarl. "I'll have your badge. When I finish with you, you won't even be allowed to issue parking tickets."

"Detective Le Blanc meant no insult," Vince said, trying to diffuse the situation. "But we have to ask. Was the baby yours?"

"Of course it was mine!"

"Then you won't object to a DNA test so we can confirm that," Charlie said.

Aaron Stratton had grown quiet. But he was watching her closely, Charlie noted. Finally, he said, "Francesca and my father were in a committed relationship and they were about to be married. Why would you question the paternity of the baby?"

Charlie looked directly at J. P. Stratton and said, "Because the autopsy revealed that on the night she was killed, Ms. Hill had sex with two different men."

Seated in his car down the block from the Tulane University campus, Cole watched as students made their way into the building for classes. Unable to get Jason to return his calls for the past three days, he'd gotten a copy of Jason's schedule from Phillip. Hopefully he could track him down at school before classes broke for the four-day Mardi Gras holiday. According to Phillip, Sylvia had finally left J.P.'s side long enough to come home to get more clothes. And for once, the woman had actually behaved like a parent. She'd called Jason on his skipping classes. Of course, it had been in conjunction with him wasting his father's money by not attending the school for which J.P. was paying. On second thought, Sylvia had probably acted like a parent for J.P.'s benefit. Either way, she had set a fire under Jason and he'd left for class.

Cole checked his watch, noted that it was already ten past the hour. The computer lab had started ten minutes ago. If Jason was going to show, it would have to be soon.

And if he doesn't show?

Then Cole was going to park himself outside of Sylvia Stratton's home and wait until his brother surfaced. Because he fully intended to speak with Jason and find out what kind of trouble the kid had gotten himself into. He thought about his conversation with Phillip. If Detective Le Blanc and her partner hadn't already found out that Jason had lied to them about where he had been the night of the murder, they soon would.

Drumming his fingers on the steering wheel, he thought about Charlotte Le Blanc. The chemistry between them had surprised him. While he didn't consider himself as having a type, most of his relationships had been with women in his own business and social circles. Finding himself attracted to a cop who had him at the top of her list of murder suspects was a first, he thought, amused by the irony of the situation. But then, he had always liked adventure. It was why he had decided to become a Navy SEAL. Something told him that a relationship with Detective Charlotte Le Blanc would be a hell of an adventure. The lady had lots of layers to her. The smart and determined cop. Guilt-ridden sister. Vulnerable and passionate woman that she thought no one could see.

But he had seen it. And he fully intended to explore each and every one of those layers that made up Charlotte Le Blanc. But before he could do that, he had to keep her from tossing his brother in jail.

Glancing in his side-view mirror, he caught a glimpse of Jason coming down the block. Even though he was late for his class, his brother appeared to be in no hurry. In fact, the kid looked as if he had the weight of the world on his shoulders. At twenty-three, his brother should be looking forward to each new day and the future. But thanks to J.P. and Jason's mother, the kid felt like a loser. Cole could have kicked himself for not seeing what was happening sooner. Somehow, some way, he had to make things right.

When Jason was less than ten yards away, Cole exited the car. He removed his sunglasses and planted himself directly in his brother's path. He didn't miss the momentary hesitation in Jason's step, nor the flash of anger that came into his eyes.

"You're in my way," Jason told him. Cole had to give him credit. The kid didn't back down.

"I've been trying to reach you."

"I've been busy," Jason said.

"We need to talk."

"I'm late for class," Jason fired back and started to move past him.

At six foot three inches, he had five inches on his brother. He used his height to his advantage and blocked Jason again. "From what I hear, you've missed a lot of classes lately. One more won't make a difference."

He could see Jason wanted to argue, and gave him credit for knowing it was a losing battle. "All right," he finally said. "Talk."

"Get in the car," Cole told him and walked around to the driver's side and slid behind the wheel.

"Where are we going?" Jason asked as he buckled his seat belt.

"Not far."

Cole drove them to Audubon Park, located near the Tulane University campus and off of Saint Charles Avenue. He pointed his car down the winding road lined with live oak trees draped in moss. Several joggers were taking advantage of the springlike temperatures. Jason stared out the passenger window, saying nothing as they drove in silence. Finally, Cole pulled his sports car to a stop across from the path leading to the old-time train that had been a favorite of locals and tourists alike.

He shut off the engine. For several moments he said nothing. Neither did Jason. He simply stared at the big black locomotive that spoke of another time, another era that had fueled the dreams of a young Jason. "Remember when we used to come here?" he asked.

Jason shrugged.

"You had that train conductor's cap with the stripes. And you used to climb up to the top of the engine and pretend to blow the horn. You'd tell me to hop on, that we were going to hit the rails and see the country. Remember?"

"I was just a kid."

"You were five." And Cole himself had been fourteen and about to be shipped off to military school. "You wanted to be a train conductor. Whatever happened to that dream?"

"I grew up and realized there was no money in running a train."

"What about those adventures we were going to have on the trains?"

"You left," Jason said, accusation in his voice.

"Yeah, I did." Instead of trying to make peace with J.P. for his siblings' sake, he had allowed himself to be banished halfway across the country. He hadn't been there to look out for Jason and Phillip or Holly and Aaron. "I'm sorry I let you down, buddy."

"It's no big deal," Jason told him. "It was dumb anyway."

"Dreams are never dumb, Jason. You should never let anyone or anything take away your dreams."

"There's no money in dreams. All that matters in this world is how much money you're worth."

"Money isn't everything," Cole told him.

"Easy for you to say," he fired back. "You've never lost something you wanted because you weren't rich enough."

"Is that why you think Francesca turned you down?"

"I don't know what you're talking about," Jason told him and looked away.

"Come on, Jason. I was there when you told me about meeting Holly's friend Francesca. Remember? You liked her."

"Maybe I did. But that was before I found out that all she cared about was money. That's why she was marrying him, you know. She didn't love him. She was using him. Just like she used everyone else."

And like she had used Jason? Was it possible Francesca had been having an affair with his younger brother? Although Jason and Francesca had only been a few years apart in age, the woman had been years beyond Jason in life experiences. While he hadn't considered that possibility before, it would explain his brother's moodiness. "Jason, I'm going to ask you something and I want you to be straight with me. Okay?"

He shrugged.

"Were you and Francesca having an affair?"

"No," his brother practically shouted. "It wasn't like that between us. Besides, she was engaged to Dad."

"I know. But you met her first and you told me the two of you hit it off."

"We did. But then she met Dad."

And J.P. had seen something he wanted and taken it without considering the consequences or caring who he hurt, Cole surmised. "Jase, I know you told the police that you went out that night to buy cigarettes. Is that the truth? Or did you go to Francesca's apartment?" When he didn't respond, Cole pressed, "Jason, I need you to tell me, did you go to her apartment?"

"What if I did? It's not like I was the only one."

"What do you mean?" Cole asked, confused by his brother's animosity.

"Come off it, Cole. I saw you going into her apartment that night."

"You're right. I did go to Francesca's apartment to try to convince her not to file charges against Holly for violating the restraining order. But she refused and I left."

"But she said…and I thought…"

"What? That I was sleeping with her? Is that what she told you?" he asked.

"No. She blew me off at dinner when I told her I needed to talk to her later, said she already had plans."

"And you thought she meant me," Cole said. "Did you think I killed her, too?"

"I don't know what I thought. All I know is that with her everything was about money. You have plenty. So does Dad. All I have is a trust fund that I can't touch until I'm twenty-five. Maybe if I'd been rich like you, then she would have…"

"She would have what? Married you? Loved you?"

He jerked his chin up defiantly. "She might have. I know she liked me. She told me so."

"And I'm sure she meant it." But Francesca Hill would never have settled for Jason. She was out for a big fish with deep pockets and J.P. had fit the bill. Not wanting to embarrass his brother, he didn't bother asking why he had gone to see Francesca that night. Instead, he asked, "Did you see anyone else go into her apartment that night?"

"I didn't stick around."

"Where did you go?"

"Nowhere. I was angry. So I drove around for a while."

"Did anyone see you?" Cole asked.

"No."

"What about when you left the apartment building? Did the doorman or desk clerk see you?"

He shook his head. "I didn't want Dad to know I'd been there. So I used the delivery entrance at the back of the building and took the stairs to the fifth floor."

"Should I even ask how you got past the security system?"

"Some security system. They haven't changed the code in over six months and there's only one camera. A six-year-old could sneak through and not worry about anyone seeing them."

Which meant just about anyone familiar with the building could have made it through the security system. "Jason, you're going to need to tell the police you were there, that you saw me and left."

"No. I can't. That lady cop already thinks I had something to do with the murder. If she finds out I lied about being there, she'll try to pin it on me."

"Jason, listen to me. They probably already know you lied about being there. Don't wait for them to come to you. Go to them. Tell them what you know."

"I can't. If I tell the police, I'll have to explain why I went to Francesca's. I can't do that. If Dad finds out…I can't."

"Screw J.P."

"You don't get it, Cole. I'm not like you. How Dad feels about me matters. I don't want him to hate me."

"All right," Cole said. "I'll talk to the detectives, see if there's some way they can keep your visit out of things. But you need to tell them, Jason. Come on, I'll go with you."

"Not now. Later, I need to get to class now. If I miss any more, I'll get kicked out."

Cole hesitated. "All right. But after your class, we go to the police. Agreed?"

"Sure," Jason said. "But I need to get back to school."

Cole made the short drive to the university. As his brother got out of the car, he said, "Jason, is there anything that you're not telling me?"

"No. I'll meet you at the police station in an hour," Jason said and shut the door.

As Cole watched Jason walk away, he wanted to believe his brother, wanted to trust him. But his gut told him that Jason was hiding something. The problem was, he had no idea what it was.

Ten

"Look, there's a spot on the next corner," Charlie told Vince as they circled the block in search of a place to park.

"You do realize this is a no-parking zone," Vince remarked as he pulled the car to the curb and shut off the engine.

"I know, but the way the streets are filling up, we'll still be circling the block tomorrow. Just put the police sign on the dash," she suggested as they exited the vehicle. "With any luck, we'll catch Ms. Marceau at home and be back before the meter maid makes a pass."

"We'd better be because Joe Varusso over in Robbery told me that little sign on the dashboard doesn't mean squat. They towed his car just last weekend."

"You won't get towed," Charlie assured him and hoped she was right because the meter maids in the Quarter were a fierce lot known for issuing tickets and towing vehicles in record numbers. Even the installation of the controversial parking meters hadn't slowed them down. If anything, they were more diligent.

"This is the 400 block," Vince said after locking the vehicle. "Her apartment should be three blocks down."

As they started down the street Charlie's thoughts returned to Francesca Hill. In the week since the murder, an image of the slain woman had begun to emerge. And that image was filled with contradictions. One of those contradictions had come from her personal digital assistant. According to the electronic techs, the slain woman's PDA had revealed a meticulously kept calendar.

"What do you make of the info on the Hill woman's PDA?" Vince asked.

"I'd say the lady may have had questionable taste in men, but she certainly was organized." They crossed the street and started down the next block. "I mean, I get scheduling the hairdresser, the caterer and all the wedding stuff. I even get her marking her spa appointments. But scheduling her weekly trip to the bank? If you ask me, that's seriously overdoing it."

"Maybe she was anal. Or maybe the PDA was a new gizmo and she got a kick out of using it," Vince offered. "It's a great way to keep track of your schedule. I use mine all the time."

"Well, I keep track of my schedule with my Filofax. But I never, ever bother penciling in mundane things like making a bank deposit."

"You're kidding? You still use a Filofax?" Vince asked.

"What's wrong with the Filofax?"

"Nothing if you live in the Stone Age. You need to get with it, Le Blanc. The rest of the world has moved on to PDAs and iPods."

"How the rest of the world keeps track of things is their business. I'll stick to pen and paper. I find those little screens annoying."

"That's because you let anything electronic intimidate you," Vince told her.

"I'm not intimidated by the computer. I use it all the time."

"Because you know your way around computers. PDAs

and iPods aren't much different." They stopped at the next corner and Vince looked over at her. "Why don't you let me recommend a good PDA for you? I'll even show you how to use it."

"Thanks, but no thanks. My Filofax works just fine."

Kossak shook his head. "That's pitiful, Le Blanc. Just pitiful. It's a wonder you get anything done."

She gave him a cheeky smile. "Is it now? Look, there's number 723." They crossed the street and Charlie did her best to ignore the stench of urine and liquor coming from the adjoining alleyway. New Orleans was a great place to live and she had never considered living anywhere else. But both the locals and tourists alike who flocked to the French Quarter had no compunction about relieving their bladders in public alleys when they'd had too much to drink. The situation became especially bad during carnival season. Perhaps it was the spirit of revelry and anything-goes attitude that prevailed during the pre-Lenten period that accounted for the problem. All she knew was that far too much liquor was consumed during the weeks of celebration. And people who were normally pillars of the community seemed to lose all their inhibitions.

They stopped in front of the apartment building. The place was old, as were most of the buildings in the French Quarter. While many had been renovated and preserved, others had been allowed to deteriorate. What damage the termites didn't do to the old buildings, the tenants did. The two-story walk-up where Danielle Marceau lived had definitely seen its share of both. She wasn't sure if the iron gate that barred entrance to the building was there as a safety measure or to protect the place from vandals. Probably both, she decided.

"Not quite the showplace her pal Francesca lived in, is it?" Vince remarked.

"No." It wasn't. To begin with, the location was in a seedier part of the city that hadn't yet made the transition to a high-rent district. There was no doorman to open the door, no fancy lobby with a front deskman, no fresh flowers and fancy artwork. Charlie couldn't help remembering Jason Stratton's comment about Danielle being jealous of Francesca. She could see why the disparity in their living situations might be cause for envy. She pressed the doorbell marked C where the name D. Marceau had been written with a black marker on a piece of masking tape and stuck next to the buzzer. When no one answered, she tried the buzzer again. "Maybe she's not home."

"The manager at the casino said she's not due at work until eight o'clock this evening. Since she worked until four this morning, she's probably sleeping."

"She must be a sound sleeper." Either that or the woman was dodging them, which is what Charlie suspected. Charlie pressed the buzzer again, but still got no answer. She was debating trying one of the other tenants when the door to the apartment marked A opened a fraction. Charlie could just make out a pair of faded brown eyes behind old-fashioned Coke-bottle glasses peering at them. She glanced at the name R. Russell printed on the masking tape. "Miss Russell?"

"It's Mrs. Russell," the woman said, opening the door a fraction wider.

"Mrs. Russell, I'm Detective Le Blanc with the New Orleans Police Department." She held up her badge. "This is my partner, Detective Kossak. We were trying to reach Ms. Marceau. Do you know if she's home?"

Mrs. Russell stepped out into the community stairwell. The lady looked to be somewhere between seventy and eighty. Her skin had enough lines to fill a road map. Tufts of yellow-gray hair escaped a bright red kerchief on her head. Holding her flowered housecoat together with one hand, she shuffled close to the gate wearing old-fashioned white terry-cloth slippers that had seen better days. She pushed the glasses up on her nose. "Let me see those badges again."

Charlie held up her badge. So did Vince. And she had to give the old girl credit, she really did look them over closely.

"All right. It looks like you're who you say you are. A lady just can't be too careful these days."

"You're absolutely right," Vince told her. "It's too bad more citizens aren't as cautious as you, ma'am."

Preening at the compliment, she said, "Most people think I'm just being nosey. But I'm being cautious. That's all."

"Yes, ma'am," Vince said.

"Do you know if Ms. Marceau is at home?" Charlie asked.

"That one," she said. "I knew she was going to get herself in trouble. I told her she should get herself a respectable job instead of dealing cards in that casino. It's just not a proper job for a young woman."

"She's not in any trouble," Charlie said. "We just want to ask her some questions. She's not answering her buzzer. Do you know if she's home?"

"Oh, she's up there, all right. She woke me up when she came in around five o'clock this morning. She let the gate slam coming in." She frowned. "She's probably sleeping. The girl hardly ever shows her face before noon."

"We really do need to speak with her, Mrs. Russell," Vince told her. "If you could buzz us into the building, maybe we can knock on her door and wake her up."

Mrs. Russell hesitated only a moment, then buzzed them inside. She walked back to her own apartment. "Just don't tell her I'm the one who let you in. She gets a little nasty if she thinks I'm sticking my nose in her business."

"We won't say a word," Vince assured her.

They climbed the steep staircase and walked the short hall to apartment number C. Charlie knocked on the door. When several moments passed with no answer, she pressed her ear to the door. "I don't hear anything."

Vince knocked harder on the door. He waited a minute, then pounded on the door again. He was about to knock once more when he heard what sounded like a chair tumbling over and a woman letting out a string of four-letter words.

"Something tells me Sleeping Beauty is awake," Charlie remarked. "And I'd say she's not in a good mood."

She was in a foul mood, Charlie decided when the door opened and a scowling, half-dressed blonde demanded, "Who are you?"

Charlie held up her badge. "I'm Detective Charlotte Le Blanc with the New Orleans Police Department. This is my partner, Detective Vincent Kossak," she said, motioning to Vince, who held up his credentials. "I left a couple of messages for you, telling you we wanted to talk to you."

"I've been busy at work. Two of our dealers quit and because of the Mardi Gras traffic, I've been pulling double shifts for most of the week," she explained. She shoved the hair from her face.

"We understand," Vince said.

Charlie studied her. She was young, mid-twenties at best, but there was a hardness about her that said she was much older than her years. She was pretty. Not a natural blonde, but she was able to pull off the look. Her eyes were brown and almond shaped. Beneath the remnants of eyeliner and mascara that she had obviously not bothered to remove before going to bed, she had nice skin. The Angelina Jolie lips were probably courtesy of collagen and she suspected the enormous breasts that the silky black robe did a poor job of covering were the work of a plastic surgeon.

"We'd like to ask you some questions about Francesca Hill," Vince told her. "May we come in?"

"I guess so," she said and stepped back from the door to allow them entrance. "But I'm not sure how I can help you. I mean, I heard that it was that old boyfriend of hers, Marcus Schwitzer, who killed her. I thought you'd be looking for him."

"We are looking for him," Charlie assured her. "But in the meantime, we still have a murder investigation to conduct."

She shivered at the word *murder.* "It's still hard to believe Frannie's dead," she said. "I need some coffee. Have a seat."

"Not exactly the Mill House, is it?" Vince remarked after Danielle disappeared into what must have been the kitchen.

"No. But it's really not bad." And it wasn't bad, Charlie thought as she looked around her. Oh, the place was a mess all right. It smelled of cigarettes, booze and perfume and what Charlie suspected was marijuana. The coffee table was piled high with fashion magazines. An ashtray with several half-smoked cigarette butts sat next to an empty wine bottle and a pair of wine stems. Sky-high black heels with tiny straps had been dumped in the middle of the floor. A pair of black stockings were draped over the arm of another chair.

The furniture itself was nice. Not the top-of-the-line stuff at Francesca Hill's apartment, but not bargain-basement or garage-sale stuff either. A vase filled with a bouquet of spring blooms sat on an accent table in front of a silver-framed mirror. A copy of a Degas ballerina painting took up the opposite wall. Charlie walked over and stood in front of the picture.

Vince joined her. "Looks familiar."

"It's a copy of a Degas work."

"Nice. But not what I expected to find in the apartment of someone who deals cards for a living."

"No, it's not," Charlie told him. But it was what you would expect to find in the apartment of someone who'd had dreams of being a ballet dancer. And it was that realization that gave Charlie some insight into who Danielle Marceau was.

Danielle returned to the room with a cup of coffee in one hand and a lit cigarette in the other. "Oh, I'm sorry. I guess I'm still not operating on all cylinders. I should have asked if you'd like some," she said, indicating the coffee.

"That's all right, Ms. Marceau. We're fine," Charlie told her.

"I'm sorry the place is such a mess. I've been working so much, I haven't had time to clean. Listen, just dump that stuff on the floor and have a seat."

Charlie pushed aside the coat and sat on the edge of one chair while Vince took the other one. They waited for Danielle to settle.

She opted for the couch. Setting the coffee cup on the end table, she curled her feet beneath her. She sat back, took a long drag on her cigarette. "I'm not sure what it is I can tell you that will help."

Charlie pulled out her pad. "Why don't you start by telling us about your relationship with Francesca Hill."

"We were friends."

"Would you say you were good friends?"

"We were best friends. I was going to stand up for her at her wedding," Danielle told her.

"Really? From what we heard, the two of you had a big falling-out because you stole some earrings from her," Charlie countered.

Danielle stubbed out the half-smoked cigarette with such force that Charlie knew she had hit a nerve. "I suppose that little twerp Jason told you that," she accused.

Charlie neither confirmed nor denied the accusation.

"Well, it's not true. I never stole anything from Frannie. Like I told her, they must have fallen into my bag when I was at her place. I didn't find them until later and when I did, I didn't see any harm in wearing them for a few days. I mean, it's not like she needed them. She bagged a lot of really expensive stuff once she hooked up with J.P. Anyway, it was no big deal. I gave them back and Frannie and I worked things out."

"So there were no hard feelings?" Charlie commented.

"None. As a matter of fact I even went to her apartment that night after the rehearsal dinner to bring her a little gift. We had a little bachelorette party to celebrate her last night as a single woman."

"That was a pretty quick party," Vince remarked. "The surveillance video showed you were at her apartment for less than an hour."

"That's because I had to go to work. Saturdays are our busiest days and the only way I could get off the whole day for the wedding was if I worked Friday night. Besides, Frannie made some lame excuse about needing to get her beauty sleep."

"You didn't believe her?" Charlie asked.

She smiled. "A woman in full makeup wearing a sexy negligee isn't usually going to bed to sleep. I thought she was expecting someone."

"Any idea who?" Charlie asked.

"With Frannie, you never knew. She liked keeping her little secrets."

"What kind of secrets?" Vince asked.

"The kind that made it possible for her to arrive in town broke and without a job, then within a few weeks of me letting her move in with me, she's wearing expensive clothes and paying me her share of the rent a month in advance."

"I heard she was a hostess at a casino. The tips are supposed to be good," Vince remarked.

"Not *that* good," Danielle said. "I ought to know, I got her the job and if there had been any real money in it, I wouldn't still be dealing cards."

"Do you know where she got the money?" Vince asked.

"Like I said, Frannie liked her little secrets. Once when I asked her where she was getting the money, she just smiled and said people liked to give her things, that she was lucky," Danielle told him.

"Did you believe her?" Charlie asked, sensing there was something that the woman wasn't telling them.

She shrugged. "Why not? I mean, what are the chances that she'd rescue little Miss Rich Girl Stratton from a goon at a club one night and the two of them would become such big buddies. The next thing you know she's going out with the girl's father and he's moving her into her own apartment and the two of them get engaged. I should be so lucky."

"Oh, I'd say you are lucky, Ms. Marceau," Charlie told her. "After all, you're not the one who was murdered."

Cole stood on the corner in front of the police station and watched as two officers helped two men from the back of the squad car. Based on the way the guys in cuffs were weaving, Cole figured they were drunk. He'd been watching similar scenarios for the past half hour. He looked at his watch. Already past noon.

Where in the hell was Jason? He should have been here by now.

Irritated, he paced along the side of the police station, barely noticing the springlike weather or the squad cars pulling into the parking lot. His thoughts were filled with his brother. He knew Jason hadn't wanted to come, that he was holding something back from him. But he hadn't thought that Jason would lie to him. Yet he had a feeling that's exactly what his brother had done—lied. Even if the class had run long or he'd hit traffic, it shouldn't have taken this long for him to get here. Nor did it explain why his brother wasn't answering his cell phone.

Damn! Why hadn't he listened to his gut and just insisted that Jason come with him down to the station right then and there?

Three squad cars came out of the parking lot at the back of the station, sirens blaring. Cole watched them take off, no doubt called to some emergency situation. For several more minutes, he watched the comings and goings to and from the station. Then he walked back up to the corner in front of the entrance, hoping to see Jason rushing down the block to meet him.

But there was still no sign of Jason. Deciding there was no point in calling his brother again he was about to leave and go search for him when he sensed her. Cole wasn't sure if it was his military training or the simple fact that Charlotte Le Blanc had become a fixture on his radar, but he knew without turning around that she was the person approaching him from the rear. Just before she reached him, he turned around.

"Good morning, Detective."

"Actually, it's afternoon," she informed him.

Prickly, he thought, and because he liked the way her eyes went all fiery when she was annoyed, he made a point of glancing at his watch. "So it is. Looks like you're right. Good afternoon, then."

"Were you going inside or just leaving?" she asked.

"Neither."

She frowned. "So do you make a habit of hanging around outside police stations?"

"No, not usually," he said, amused. He noted that today she wore a cream and chocolate sweater and a coffee-colored skirt that did wonderful things for her legs. And he found himself wondering where she kept her gun.

"Listen, Stratton, if you're here to complain to the captain about me hounding you and your family and my insensitivity to your family's grief, you're too late. Your father's already been on the phone with the mayor, two city councilmen and the chief of police. But if you feel the need to get your shot in, go right ahead. Just make sure you tell the captain your beef is with me, that I'm the one responsible for showing up at your house the other morning, not Kossak."

Cole tightened his hand into a fist at his side and wished it were J.P.'s neck. "Let me make something clear, Detective. As far as I'm concerned, J. P. Stratton is and always has been nothing more than a sperm donor. So I suggest that you not make the mistake of assuming that I share his overinflated sense of self-importance because I assure you, I don't."

"I'll be sure to remember that," she told him. "So if you didn't come here to file a complaint, exactly why are you here?"

"Perhaps I just wanted to see you again, Detective. After all, you're a beautiful woman."

She narrowed her eyes. "I'm a homicide detective investigating a murder for which you're a potential suspect. So why don't you save the flattery and tell me the real reason you're here."

"It's hardly flattery, Detective. You are a beautiful woman and I'm sure I'm not the first man to tell you so. And while I am attracted to you and did want to see you again, that's not why I'm here."

"I didn't think it was," she told him.

"Very astute of you," he said, enjoying the sparring. "I'm supposed to meet my brother Jason here. He wants to amend his statement regarding his whereabouts on the night of Francesca's murder."

"That's good because as I'm sure you already know, his alibi didn't check out."

Just as he had suspected, Detective Le Blanc had been thorough and checked the convenience store Jason had claimed to have visited. It would be just a matter of time before she found out that Jason had gone to Francesca's apartment that night—if she hadn't done so already.

"So where is your brother?"

"I'm not sure. Something must have come up."

"And I don't suppose you're going to tell me where he really was on the night of the murder, are you?"

"You're right. I'm not."

Her cell phone began to ring. "Le Blanc," she said. "Hang on."

"Stratton, it'll be better for your brother if he comes in on his own. If he doesn't, I will have him picked up."

While he waited for the valet to retrieve his car from the garage, he thought about Detective Charlotte Le Blanc. She was a smart one, he admitted. But then her sister Emily had been smart, too. It was because Emily had been smart enough to figure out his secret and then tried to trap him that she was dead. Somehow he didn't think her big sister would be so careless.

It had been such fun watching her sift through the evidence, searching for leads. He hadn't expected her to try to track down the origin of the stockings. But then, he'd covered his tracks. He'd purposely chosen a brand available at dozens of outlets and made sure the purchase was charged to someone else. He couldn't wait to see where she went with that information.

Too bad he couldn't have sat in on the interviews with her other suspects. But then, he'd gotten the gist of those interviews secondhand. He'd have to be satisfied with that, he told himself. Besides, the real fun was his own sparring matches with her. That and watching her try to make sense of the clues, fitting the pieces to the puzzle, trying to figure out who had killed Francesca and knowing that if she found him, she would find her sister's killer.

The valet pulled his car up to the entrance. Exiting it, the young man held the door open for him.

"Here you go," he said and handed the fellow a five dollar bill.

"Thank you, sir," he said, beaming at the generous tip.

He nodded, pleased to have brightened the guy's day. As he drove away, he wondered if Charlotte Le Blanc was enjoying their game as much as he was. Because that's what it was—an exciting game they were playing—one in which the stakes didn't get any higher, one in which the loser ended up dead.

And he didn't intend to be the loser.

Eleven

Charlie reported to the squad room, along with Vince and Mackenzie, the rookie officer assigned to her team, for a briefing on the Hill case. At the front of the room was a large white board on which they had drawn a chart, outlining Francesca Hill's movements during the last twenty-four hours of her life. Also on the board was a list of possible murder suspects.

"Okay, people," Captain Edward Warren addressed them. "Where are we on the Hill case?"

"We're still looking for the ex-boyfriend, Schwitzer," Vince began. "So far he's managed to stay off our radar. We've got an APB out on him, but with Mardi Gras this weekend it wouldn't be hard for him to hide behind a mask."

"What about other suspects?" the captain asked.

"You can take your pick," Charlie began and pointed to the diagram on the board. At the center of the diagram was Francesca Hill's photo with arrows branching out to photos of the other suspects. She pointed to the box with J. P. Stratton's photo and name. "We have the fiancé, J. P. Stratton. The man is a narcissist and a control freak. If he found out she was sleeping with another man, his ego wouldn't have tolerated it. Over here we have Holly Stratton," she continued, using the pointer to indicate the photo of the young redhead. "The victim befriended the daughter and probably used her to get to the father. The two women had a fight the evening of the murder and the victim threatened legal action. We also have Sylvia Stratton, wife number four," she said, pointing to the other woman's photo. "The victim's engagement to Stratton derailed her plan for a reconciliation. With the victim out of the way, Sylvia Stratton is now free to pursue her ex-husband again."

"And apparently, it's her shoulder that J.P. has been crying on during his time of grief," Vince added.

"Over here, we have Danielle Marceau, a blackjack dealer and the deceased's former roommate. She worked at the casino with our vic before she hit the engagement lottery. There was definitely some jealousy there. And the two of them had a falling-out when a pair of the vic's diamond earrings fell into Ms. Marceau's bag," Charlie explained.

"You think the killer's a woman?" the captain asked.

"No," Charlie told him. "But we're not ruling anything out at this point, including the possibility of a woman paying someone to kill Hill."

"What's the story with the minister?" he asked, motioning toward the box with the Reverend Homer Lawrence's photo and name.

"We don't know yet," Vince told him. "According to the doorman at the Mill House the reverend made quite a few visits to the victim's apartment. And the reverend's housekeeper claims the victim was a regular visitor to the rectory. He claims to have been counseling her, but I don't buy it."

"You think they were having an affair?" the captain asked.

"I don't know. But Le Blanc and I both think something's off there," Vince told him. "We're trying to get access to the records from his previous posts, but we're hitting lots of red tape."

"Give me the names of the churches and I'll see what I can do," the captain said. "Who else have you got?"

"Jason and Phillip Stratton, J. P. Stratton's two youngest sons," Charlie told him. "In addition to the fact that a new wife would have impacted their inheritance, Jason had it bad for his intended stepmother. And Phillip was as nervous as a long-tailed cat in a roomful of rockers when we questioned him about his brother's whereabouts."

"Go on," the captain prompted.

"Aaron Stratton, the number-two son," Charlie said pointing to his photo. "He's his father's right-hand man as well as his attorney. He claims he was at Hill's apartment that night to get her to sign the prenup, but she refused. According to him, if the old man had gone through with the wedding without a prenup, it would have had a big impact on his and his siblings' inheritance. With a baby on the way, that impact would have been even more significant."

"But I thought the old man was loaded," the captain countered.

"He is. But apparently, he's not as loaded as he used to be," she said. "With the exception of wife number one, the other Mrs. Strattons were all given a chunk of stock and cash as wedding gifts. They also took a bite out of his assets when they divorced. In addition, another chunk went to trust funds set up for each of the kids. The guy has also had several liaisons that he settled hefty sums of cash and gifts on over the years."

"For a multimillionaire, he doesn't sound too bright," the captain remarked.

"Apparently it isn't his business sense that J.P. uses when it comes to dealing with women," Charlie said.

The captain nodded. "Who's this?" he asked, indicating the fuzzy still from the surveillance tape that the electronics techs had blown up for identification.

"He's our mystery man. He didn't come through the front door and avoided the camera, so I think it's safe to assume he had been there before," she said. "We think he probably came in through the delivery entrance at the back of the building. There's only one camera and from what I understand they haven't changed the access code in months. Anyone with a pair of binoculars would have no trouble getting it."

"Any idea who he is?" the captain asked.

"It could be Jason or Phillip Stratton. They're the right height. Both of them know their way around computer systems and they'd be familiar with the building."

"Cole Stratton also knows his way around security systems," Vince pointed out. "He owns his own security firm, so getting past the building's security wouldn't be a problem for him. He was also part of a rescue unit with the Navy SEALs. His specialty was electronics, so tampering with the surveillance tape would be a piece of cake for him."

"You see the inheritance as his motive, too?" the captain asked.

"No," Charlie answered. "He's estranged from his father and supposedly not a beneficiary. But he's very protective of his half siblings, in particular, his sister. He went to the victim's apartment the night she died to try to convince her not to file charges against his sister."

"Was he successful?" the captain asked.

"No," Vince responded. "And he doesn't strike me as a man who takes no for an answer."

"Killing the woman because she refused to drop the charges against his sister seems like pretty weak motivation to me," Charlie offered.

"Not if you take into account his hatred for his father," Vince countered. "You said yourself, he hates his old man. Francesca's death kills two birds with one stone. It prevents charges being filed against his sister and it also takes out his old man's intended bride, even makes the old man a suspect."

"You'd have to be pretty cold-blooded to plan something like that," she said.

"From what I've heard, a SEAL doesn't let emotion get in the way of him doing his job," Vince reasoned. "It's why they're so good at what they do."

Her every instinct told her that Vince was wrong. She thought of Cole, recalled the way he had looked at her with both hunger and challenge in those blue eyes. Her stomach tightened and she felt the stirring of desire. Realizing what she was doing, Charlie gave herself a mental shake. Was Vince right? Was this attraction or whatever this thing was she felt for Cole interfering with her judgment? God, she couldn't afford for that to happen.

"What about the theory of robbery being the motive?" the captain asked.

Vince shook his head. "No robber would have left that rock on the vic's finger. I think the killer took the money out of the wallet and some of the jewelry to throw us off."

"How about alibis? They all check out?" the captain asked.

"J.P. and Aaron Stratton alibi each other. We've confirmed with a hotel employee that Holly Stratton was at a resort on the Gulf Coast at the time of the murder and Danielle Marceau was on the casino floor dealing blackjack for a group of high rollers from L.A.," Charlie reported. "Sylvia Stratton was out of town and has an alibi. Jason and Phillip Stratton alibied each other, but there are some holes in their story. We still don't know about the ex-boyfriend, Schwitzer. The reverend claims to have been home, preparing a sermon. And Cole Stratton says he was home alone."

"Well, if you're sure the killer is one of these people," the captain said, pointing to the board of suspects, "then somebody's lying. So I suggest you find out who and that you do it soon. We're taking a lot of heat on this one."

"We're working on it, sir," Charlie told him. "Mackenzie ran down the manufacturer of the stocking and came up with some names."

"What have you got?" the captain asked him.

The rookie straightened. "Sir, that particular brand is carried by Saks, Dillard's and three local boutiques. It's the company's most popular seller. You wouldn't believe how many pairs of those stockings they sell here."

"The names, Mackenzie," Charlie prompted.

"Yes, ma'am," he said. "Three names came up. Two were former wives of J. P. Stratton—Sylvia and Laurel—the other one was the victim."

"I think it's safe to assume that J. P. Stratton has a thing for black silk stockings," Charlie remarked. "It would make sense that it would be his weapon of choice."

"If he's the killer," Vince pointed out.

"Do *you* think he's the killer?" the captain asked Charlie.

"I think it's a possibility," she responded—especially since the man obviously preferred young blondes and Emily had always preferred older men.

"Then get me some real evidence and bring him in. And do it soon. I want the chief and the mayor off my back."

"Yes, sir," Charlie said. "We're waiting for the M.E. to get the DNA test results back on the semen found in the victim and the results from the fetus to see if J. P. Stratton was the father."

"The doc knows this is priority?" he asked.

"She does, sir," Charlie replied.

He let out a sigh and ran a hand over his bald head. "Too

bad we can't use that equipment they've got on the cop shows. Damn TV has people thinking we can give them answers and solve crimes in an hour."

"I know, sir," she said, at the captain's reference to the speed with which DNA results were returned on fictional series. Even though Louisiana had gotten its own DNA-testing facilities several years ago following a long run by a serial killer and rapist who had terrorized the state, in truth, it took weeks to get back the analysis of DNA—and that was when it was done quickly.

"All right. Keep me posted," he told them and exited the squad room.

Once he was gone, Charlie turned to Mackenzie. "Mackenzie, you want to check with Dr. Williamson to see if she's gotten anything back yet? I'm afraid if she sees my or Vince's face again, she'll toss us out."

"No problem," he assured her and left.

"You really think J. P. Stratton's our killer?" Vince asked her.

"I think there's a strong possibility," she told him. "Listen, Kossak, I promise you I'm not ruling out anybody at this point—including Cole Stratton. All right?"

"All right," he said. "So you hear anything back from the forensic accountants on those bank records for Francesca Hill yet?"

"No. If you'll try to reach the mother again, I'll go upstairs and see if I can light a fire under them," she offered.

"Tell you what, why don't I go upstairs. I'd like to stretch my legs."

"Sure," she said. She was about to return to her desk and attempt to reach Francesca Hill's mother again when the phone in the squad room rang. "Le Blanc."

"Detective, there's an Aaron Stratton here to see you," Sergeant Joe Thibodeaux at the front desk informed her. "You want me to have someone bring him back?"

Charlie thought about the zoo-like atmosphere out front, a result of the increase in arrests for drunkenness and myriad minor offenses that came with the Mardi Gras revelry. "I'd appreciate it, Sarge," she said.

When Aaron Stratton was shown into the squad room a few minutes later, she was surprised to see him dressed in a tuxedo. "Something tells me you didn't dress like that because you were coming to the police station."

He smiled. "Actually, I'm on my way to a dinner party. Is it always like that out there?"

"Pretty much during this time of year," she told him. "So what brings you here?"

"I stopped by to give you this," he said and handed her a manila envelope. "It's that list I promised you, the names of people with whom my father had dealings that didn't end happily."

"I appreciate you bringing this down," she said as she opened the envelope.

"It wasn't a problem," he assured her. "I knew you were anxious to get it and with Mardi Gras almost here and things shutting down, I decided to stop by on my way and drop it off to you."

"That was very considerate of you," she told him as she withdrew the list of names. It was quite a list she thought as she scanned the two pages of names and the detailed references about the deal that had resulted in hard feelings.

"Ah, I see that I made your list of murder suspects," he said, looking at the board of suspects. "I'm not sure whether to be flattered or insulted."

"Neither," she suggested. "I'm just being thorough."

"Which I'm sure accounts for you having the fewest number of open cases in your department."

"Checking up on me, Mr. Stratton?" she asked, annoyed.

"It's Aaron," he told her. "May I?" he asked, indicating the chair.

She nodded. "Were you checking up on me?" she repeated.

"Guilty."

"Why?" she demanded.

"I see I've offended you," he said apologetically. "That wasn't my intent, Detective. I merely wanted to be sure that the best detective on the force was assigned to Francesca's case. As it turns out, my instincts about you were right. You are the best and I have every confidence you'll find Francesca's killer."

"For your information, it's a team effort, Mr. Stratton. My partner and I and the various departments work as a team."

"But something tells me you're the driving force," he told her.

She didn't bother acknowledging his remark. Instead, she studied the list of names. She recognized a number of them. "Looks like your father has made quite a great many enemies."

"My father isn't the easiest man to get along with, Detective. A man with his money and power attracts a lot of people. They think the Stratton name alone will guarantee them fame and riches. When it doesn't, they feel cheated and the person they blame is my father because it's easier than admitting they couldn't cut it."

"So anyone in particular you think I should talk to?"

"Honestly?"

"Yes."

"No one on that list has the nerve to go up against my father, let alone murder his fiancée for revenge."

Charlie noted Sylvia Stratton's name on the list, the twins' mother. "Including Sylvia Stratton?"

He chuckled. "Sylvia is an insipid woman who's never had an original thought in her entire life. She could never have planned a murder, let alone carry one out."

"So who do you think killed her?"

He looked at the board of suspects again. "I'd say one of them is your killer."

"Anyone in particular?"

His lips twitched in amusement. "You mean other than me?"

"Other than you."

"Well, you can forget about my sister or Danielle," he said. "Holly may be spoiled and immature, but she has trouble swatting flies. As for Danielle, she'd probably be capable of murder and she was jealous of Francesca. But her friendship with Francesca gave Danielle entrée to the good life. Killing her would have been like cutting off her nose to spite her face."

Curious to hear his assessment and hopefully to gain information, Charlie said, "There are still a lot of suspects up there."

"So there are. Well, there's your mystery man whom I'm assuming you think is the robber. But my guess is you've ruled out robbery as the motive."

"What makes you think that?"

"Come now, Detective. We both know any robber with a grain of salt for a brain wouldn't have left that rock on her finger. It cost my father a quarter of a million dollars."

"Point taken," she said.

"Schwitzer would be the most likely suspect, I suppose. The man was a scam artist, always looking to make a quick buck. I suspect Francesca was bait for some of those scams. Her hooking up with my father put an end to his meal ticket. I only met him once, but he was mean enough to want to get even."

"And your father?"

"He'd be a good candidate. If he found out Francesca was sleeping around, he would have killed her or made her wish she was dead," he said nonchalantly. "There's also my brother Jason who thought he was in love with her. He was really angry about the wedding. Or then again, it could be the reverend. She'd definitely cast a spell on the man," he told her and smiled.

"What do you mean?"

"Use your imagination, Detective. Francesca was a beautiful woman. He wouldn't be the first man to be tempted by a woman. Look at Adam and Eve."

"And you? Were you tempted, Mr. Stratton?"

"Aside from the fact that she was sleeping with my father, Francesca wasn't my type. I prefer a woman whose beauty is more…subtle," he told her.

"What about your brother Cole?"

"Ah, Cole…he's definitely the hard one to figure, isn't he?" He brought one fist up under his chin as though considering that possibility. "The man is brilliant and is successful at everything he tries. But beneath that soft-spoken charm, Cole's a lot like our father. He goes after what he wants and he can be ruthless when he's crossed."

"Did Francesca cross him?" she asked.

"Not Francesca, our father. Or at least that's the way Cole sees it. He hates him and it if weren't for me and my siblings, I suspect he would have acted on that hatred a long time ago."

"I heard there was some resentment after his mother died and your father married your mother," she said, hoping he would tell her more.

"It wasn't my mother or the marriage that Cole resented. It was our father. He hates him and blames him for his mother's death."

"But I understood she died from cancer."

"Margaret did have breast cancer, but they caught it in the early stages and she was in remission. But when my father told her he was divorcing her so that he could marry my mother and be with us, she committed suicide."

Talk about a bombshell. Stunned by the revelation, she said, "I didn't know."

"Few people do. Cole's the one who found her in the bathtub. She'd slit her wrists."

Charlie felt an overwhelming sadness for Cole. She couldn't even imagine how traumatic that must have been for a young boy. But would it be motive for the man to kill an innocent woman?

"Cole has hated our father ever since." He paused, watched her. "So I suppose if Cole wanted to hurt our father, destroying something or someone he wanted would be a good way to do it."

"Is that what you think happened? Do you think your brother killed her?"

He hesitated. "I think Cole is capable of murder. Whether or not he killed Francesca, well, I think that's something you'd need to ask him."

"Looks like ya'll are doing big business tonight," Anne told the sergeant stationed at the front desk of the police station as she took in the organized chaos.

"You can say that again. This time of year we've got almost as many people in here as they do out on the streets," he responded, then yelled to one of the officers to keep an eye on his charge because the man was sliding down to the floor in a drunken stupor.

It was close, Anne thought as she looked around. The place was crawling with people in various states of dress and levels of sobriety being led by tired-looking police officers. "Cheer up, Joe. It'll all be over soon," she told him, because despite all the excess partying and debauchery, on Wednesday morning the faithful would line up at the churches to get ashes on their foreheads to mark the beginning of the Lenten season.

"Can't be soon enough for me. So how are you doing? That TV station working you too hard?"

She laughed. "Let's just say you're not the only one who'll be glad to see Wednesday arrive." She liked Joe. He was a nice guy, a family man, and with his florid coloring and silver hair, he fit her image of the old-fashioned, neighborhood cop from the late fifties. In the years since her sister had transferred to the Homicide Department, he had never failed to greet her by name or with a kind word.

"So when are those suits at the TV station going to wise up and put you behind that anchor desk instead of running you all over the place doing those live reports?"

"Soon, I hope," she said, because she did hope to one day fill an anchor slot.

"Well, if you ask me, the station's ratings would go up in a heartbeat if they was to put you behind that desk." He leaned forward slightly and lowered his voice and said, "The truth is, you're a lot prettier to look at than that Eric Paulsen."

She laughed. "Thanks, but you know if I'm stuck behind an anchor desk, I won't get to come visit you. Then I'd pine away from missing you," she said, hamming it up.

He flushed. "You're a sassy one, Anne Le Blanc. How come you're still single, girl? Those young bucks must be lining up around the block to see you."

"I'm still waiting for you," she teased. While she had her fair share of dates, none of them ever led to anything serious. Probably because she found it hard to feign interest in a relationship when the man she wanted to be with was Vincent Kossak.

Joe signed some papers one of the officers handed him and once the man was gone, he told her, "Then something's wrong with the men in this town because if I was single and thirty years younger, I'd be on your doorstep."

She leaned forward and whispered, "And I'd let you inside." She winked at him, thought it was cute the way he flushed again. "Is Charlie around?"

"Yeah. Should be at her desk. Want me to call her and tell her you're here?"

"Would it be okay if I just went on back?"

"Sure. Just sign in and let me give you a visitor's pass."

"Thanks," she said as she clipped on the pass and started back to the Homicide Department. She was worried about her sister. She'd spoken to her twice during the past week and both times Charlie had seemed on edge. While she knew it wasn't uncommon for her sister to become absorbed in a case, she couldn't shake the feeling that something was wrong. She also wanted to give her a heads-up on the press conference. Drawing nearer, she noted that Charlie's desk was empty but not Vince's. He sat with his back to her and a phone to his ear.

Anne stared at him, noted the way the blue dress shirt he wore spanned his shoulders and how his dark hair curled at the ends where it brushed his collar. She remembered how his brown eyes had gone nearly black just before he'd kissed her. And the man had barely spoken to her since, she reminded herself.

Well, Anne Marie Le Blanc, what are you going to do about it? Are you going to spend another two months pining over the man and waiting for him to make a move? Or are you going to make a move yourself?

Drawing in a breath, she walked over to him as he hung up the phone. "Hi, Vince."

He went still, then slowly turned and looked up at her. "Anne, what a surprise."

"A good surprise or a bad surprise?"

Damn, she thought when he hesitated and wished that she could just squeeze her eyes shut and disappear.

"It's not good or bad," he said finally. "It's just a surprise. That's all."

Deciding there was no point in beating around the bush, she asked, "Vince, do you or don't you like me?"

"Of course I like you. Why would you even ask?"

"Oh, I don't know," she said, noting that he'd gone back to looking at the papers on his desk. "Maybe it has something to do with the way you practically bolt every time I come within fifty feet of you or it could be because of the way you're avoiding looking at me now."

Slowly, he turned his head and stared directly into her eyes. "All right, I'm looking. And I'm not bolting out the door."

Anne felt her heartbeat quicken as he held her gaze. She swallowed and hoping that her college drama class paid off, she feigned nonchalance and said, "So you are."

"If you're looking for your sister, she's in the lab."

"I can wait." Deciding to test her theory that Vince wasn't immune to her, she hopped up on the edge of his desk and crossed her legs. Anne felt her confidence kick up a notch as she watched him watch her legs.

"There's a chair over there," he told her.

"That's all right. I'm comfortable."

"Suit yourself," he told her.

"I usually do," she responded. "By the way, I never did get to thank you."

"For what?" he asked.

"For going to bat for me with your captain. Charlie said the two of you got in trouble because he thought you'd tipped me off on the Stratton-Hill story."

He shrugged. "It was no big deal. If the captain didn't chew us out about something at least once a week, we'd worry he was sick."

"Somehow, I doubt that." She paused. "But thanks for

thinking that I'm smart and a good reporter and that I can put two and two together and come up with four."

"All I did was state the obvious. You don't need me to tell you that you're smart or that you're a good reporter."

"You're right. I don't. But it's nice to know you think so anyway."

"Anytime." Pushing away from his desk, he stood and began to gather files.

It was now or never, she told herself, because Detective Vincent Kossak was about to disappear again. She took a deep breath and decided to go for broke, to ask him out. What was the worse thing that could happen? she asked herself. He could say no. He could tell her she's not his type. He could tell her he wasn't even remotely interested in her. And if he did any of those things, she would feel like an idiot. But then she already felt like an idiot for pining after him like a schoolgirl. "Vince, how would you like to go out with me?"

He dropped the files. Stooping down, he began to scoop up the papers and stuff them back in the folders. Anne slid off the desk and knelt beside him and gathered up papers and files. When she handed them to him, she saw his expression. She had shocked him. She could see it on his face, read it in his eyes. The man looked like a deer caught in the headlights. She closed her eyes a moment and for the second time since she'd arrived, she wished she could simply disappear.

"By going out, do you mean like on a date?"

Opening her eyes, she said, "Yes, I mean on a date." But the nerves hit her again and she waffled. "I have tickets for the Hornets game Wednesday night and I remembered that you liked basketball. So I thought maybe you'd like to go with me."

"Anne, I'm not sure that's a good idea."

"Why? You don't like the Hornets?" she asked as they both stood.

"No. I mean yes." He let out a breath. "I'm crazy about the Hornets. What I meant is I don't think you and me are a good idea."

Her heart sank. "I see," she said and seriously considered crawling under the desk.

He tipped up her chin. "No, I don't think you do. Anne, you're an incredibly sexy woman and I'd have to be dead to not be attracted to you."

"I hear a but coming," she said.

"But I'm almost ten years older than you and you're also my partner's kid sister. I just don't think you and I, the two of us, it's just not a good idea."

Anne stared at him, wondered if she had actually heard him right. "Let me see if I've got this straight. You're saying that if I was an old hag of say thirty instead of twenty-three and I wasn't Charlie's sister then you would be interested in a relationship with me?"

"That's right."

Because the man looked so darn serious and because her heart was soaring, she said, "Then we don't have a problem. You see, I'm thirty years old and an only child."

He laughed. "Is that supposed to make sense?"

"Sure." She beamed at him. Retrieving a business card from her jacket pocket, she snatched a pen from his desk and wrote down her home address and phone number. "You can pick me up Wednesday night at six."

He stared at the card, then looked up at her. "Anne, I don't know about this."

"What's the matter, Detective? Don't tell me a tough guy like you is afraid," she challenged. She leaned closer, just enough to invade his space, and whispered, "Don't worry, I don't expect sex on the first date."

The man actually blushed. Stepping back, he yanked at his tie.

"Relax. I was only kidding," she said with a laugh.

"I know that."

"So are we on for Wednesday or are you going to back out?"

His mouth tightened slightly. "I'll pick you up at six on Wednesday."

Twelve

Returning from the lab, Charlie rounded the corner and saw them. Anne and Vince. The two were deep in conversation and when they spied her heading their way, Vince immediately put distance between them. Darn it if they didn't look like a couple of lovesick schoolkids who'd been caught necking. Don't go there, she told herself. After all, she had been the one to point out to Vince that her sister wasn't a kid anymore. But she was still her baby sister. And she didn't want to see her get hurt.

Feeling like a mother hen, she considered talking to Vince. And if he didn't tell her to butt out, Anne would. This was Vince, she reminded herself. For years the man had been her closest friend, the brother she'd never had. He was a good guy. Sure, he carried some baggage from his divorce. But every divorced person that she knew carried baggage. It was part of who they were, a part of the life they had lived. She also knew that Vince hadn't lacked for female company since his divorce. In fact, his girlfriends changed with such frequency she no longer bothered to ask their names. As for her sister, Anne was no helpless lamb. She had seen her sister cut more than one wolf down to size. And Vince sure beat some of those clowns she'd dated over the years. Besides, the two of them might actually work, she reasoned. If there was anyone who could get Vince Kossak to risk his heart again, it was Anne. Her sister's bubbly personality and kind heart made it hard for anyone to resist her.

"What's going on?" she asked as she reached them.

"Nothing much. Anne came by to see you," Vince said.

"Vince was sweet enough to keep me company while I waited," Anne said and there was no mistaking the gleam in her eye.

Vince yanked on his tie as though he were being choked. "I'm going to see if Mackenzie's had any luck with the pawnshops on the jewelry."

"Bye, Vince. I'll see you Wednesday night," Anne said.

"Right. See you," he said and left.

"So what's going on Wednesday night?" Charlie asked her sister.

"Vince and I have a date," she said, angling her chin up defiantly. "I asked him to go to a Hornets game with me and he said yes."

From her expression, it was clear Anne was expecting a reaction. Charlie didn't give her one. She simply went over to her desk and picked up the file with the list of names that she'd received from Aaron Stratton.

"Aren't you going to say anything?"

Charlie looked over at her sister. "What would you like me to say?"

"I'd like you to tell me if you're okay about me seeing Vince."

"Would it make any difference if I wasn't?"

"Actually, it would," Anne said, some of the sass and starch going out of her. "I'm nuts about him, Charlie. But I don't want to disappoint you."

"I'm not disappointed, just a little worried." When Anne started to object, Charlie held up her hand. "You're my baby sister and I don't want to see you get hurt."

"You think that Vince is going to hurt me?"

"Not intentionally. Don't get me wrong. I think Vince Kossak is a terrific guy, they don't come any better. But his divorce did a real number on him. He's dated a lot of women, but none of them last long. He doesn't let anyone get close."

"That's because none of those women were me," Anne told her and Charlie knew her sister really believed that.

"You know, you just might be right," Charlie said.

"I am. You'll see."

And for the first time since she'd gotten the call to Francesca Hill's apartment a week ago, her spirits lifted. She had been so consumed by the case and its similarities to Emily's murder that she felt as though she'd been in a dark tunnel. Anne was a light in the darkness, a reminder of happier times, of a time when she hadn't been wishing she could go back six years and answer Emily's call. But it was because she had failed Emily then that she needed to be focused now. She needed to find Emily and Francesca Hill's killer before he stole another woman's life. "Listen, Annie, as much as I'd like to watch you get all goo-goo eyed over my partner, I've got to get back to work."

"You still working the Hill murder case?"

"Yes. And the captain's got the chief and mayor breathing down his neck and demanding an arrest be made, which means the captain's breathing down our necks."

"Actually, that's the reason I came by," Anne said. "I wanted to give you a heads-up. I heard J. P. Stratton plans to call a press conference first thing Wednesday morning if you still haven't made an arrest. The word is he's going to lambaste the police department and the detectives handling the case for not making a stronger effort to find Francesca's killer."

"Thanks for the warning. But the man has already threatened to have my badge. I doubt if he can do much worse."

"Don't be so sure of that, Charlie. The man has a lot of clout, not just in the city, but in the state and even in Washington. He may not be able to get you fired, but he could make things tough for you. I'd hate to see you or Vince get caught in the fallout."

"I appreciate the concern. But if I were to let people like Stratton dictate how I do my job, then I might as well hand in my badge. What I am going to do is my job—which at the moment is to find Francesca Hill's murderer."

"All right," Anne told her. "But you don't have a corner on the market when it comes to worrying about people. I worry about you, too, you know."

Her sister's declaration touched her. "Hey, which one of us is supposed to be the big sister here?" she teased.

"You are. But sometimes it doesn't hurt for even a big sister to take a night off and let someone else worry about the rest of the world. Okay?"

"Okay," Charlie told her.

Anne hugged her. "If there's anything I can do to help, you know all you have to do is ask. I have a lot of resources and contacts through the TV station. You'd be amazed at the amount of information that's at my little fingertips," she said and wiggled her fingers. "There's very little that goes on in New Orleans that we don't know about."

"The last thing I need is for you to start playing amateur detective."

"I know. But I've been covering some of the people you're dealing with for the past two years. I know a lot more about them than you're going to find in your computer records." She lowered her voice and said, "In other words, I know the dirt."

Charlie considered that. Her sister was right. She would be able to provide her with some insight that she couldn't find in a data bank. "What can you tell me about Aaron Stratton?"

"You mean besides the fact that he's one of the city's most eligible bachelors?"

"Yes, besides that," Charlie told her.

"Well, let's see," Anne said as she dropped into the chair next to her sister's desk. "Aaron is the golden boy. He graduated near the top of his law school class at Tulane and clerked for a federal judge. He could have gotten on with any of the major law firms here, but he opted to work as his father's counsel instead."

"Anything else?"

"He's great looking, of course, never been married, but he has been linked to several debutantes and a senator's daughter."

"Anything beyond the social-scene hype?" she asked.

"Well, I did hear that when he was younger, he got into some kind of trouble."

"What kind of trouble?" Charlie asked.

"He supposedly got a little rough with a girlfriend. But there were never any charges filed that I know of. So it may not be true."

Charlie intended to find out if there was any truth to the rumor. "Anything else?"

"Other than a few speeding tickets, which he paid, he appears to be a model citizen. He's quite the darling on the social scene and he's invited to every event in the city that matters. He's charming, wealthy and clearly his father's favorite. When J.P. retires or kicks the bucket, Aaron will most likely take over his father's hotel operations and other investments since he's been running things for the most part anyway over the past couple of years."

"What about his siblings? Won't they have some say in who runs things?"

"The only one who might would be Cole Stratton. Rumor has it that J.P. all but offered to make him the head of the company, but Cole refused. He won't have anything to do with his father."

"And the other three Stratton kids?"

"None of them are particularly interested in the business as long as it provides them with an income. So they'll probably let Aaron run things and live off their trust funds, which Aaron administers already."

"So I guess gaining control of the business really isn't an issue," she said, more to herself than to Anne. "The money keeps coming in and the rich keep getting richer."

"Maybe. Maybe not," Anne commented.

"What do you mean?"

Anne leaned closer. "I heard that J.P. has been spending money as fast as he makes it. And between what he's forked over to his exes and what he continues to shell out to them and his kids, his P & L is not as healthy as it should be."

"What do you know about Cole Stratton?" Charlie asked.

"Ah, the dark prince," her sister said with a smile.

"The dark prince?"

"That's what I heard someone call him once. It seems to fit, don't you think? I mean, he's got that dark hair, the brooding blue eyes and that air of mystery about him."

"Sounds like a character from a romance novel if you ask me."

"He'd certainly make a good one," Anne told her.

Charlie rolled her eyes. But the truth was, her sister was right. Cole Stratton did have a dangerous and mysterious quality about him.

"Your problem is you have no romance in your soul, Charlotte Le Blanc."

"You have enough for both of us. Now spill."

Anne squinched her nose. "Okay. Well, in addition to

being gorgeous, he supposedly has the Midas touch. That security firm he started has gone through the roof. The man is loaded."

Charlie remembered what Cole had told her about inheriting his home in the French Quarter when his mother had died, that it had been the one thing that J.P. hadn't been able to steal. She couldn't help feeling admiration for Cole. Instead of risking his relationship with his siblings by fighting J.P. to get back what had been taken, he'd made his own successes and fortune.

"He's a big supporter of the arts and a lot of charities, but he's very low key about it. I'm told that most of the time he asks that he not be identified."

"Unlike his father."

Anne nodded. "He's single, never been married, never lived with anyone or been engaged. Although," Anne added as an aside, "there are a number of women who would love to change that."

"He's not involved with anyone?" Charlie asked and could have bit off her tongue.

Anne didn't call her on it. She simply arched her brow. "If he is, he's managed to keep her hidden. He's no monk, but there doesn't appear to be anyone special in his life." She paused a moment, then continued, "People say he's fiercely loyal, generous, and a friend you can count on. He's also very close to his half siblings."

"Yes, I noticed." She'd also noticed that he was very protective of them.

"He also is said to hate his father with a passion because of what he did to Cole's mother."

"I know. I heard about her suicide," Charlie said.

"The suicide was what finally broke things between them, but there was a lot more leading up to it."

"You mean J.P.'s affair with Aaron's mother."

"That, too. But there were other women before Edie Stratton came along. J.P. wasn't exactly discreet. What made things worse was the fact that it was Margaret's money that he used to start his financial empire."

"That's what I heard," Charlie said. "But how is that possible? Why wasn't someone protecting her assets?"

"Because Margaret was virtually the poor little rich girl. She was an only child with elderly parents who died and left her a fortune. She was a naive, convent-educated girl and a very wealthy heiress when J.P. met her. He literally swept her off her feet. She ignored her attorney's advice and married him without a prenup. She got pregnant with Cole almost immediately. She was so caught up with being a wife and mother that she wasn't paying attention when J.P. brought home papers for her to sign, telling her he didn't want her to have to worry about business."

Charlie couldn't help feeling sorry for Margaret Stratton. She also wondered how the woman could have allowed herself to be so foolish and put not only her own future at risk but that of her child. "What about her friends? Her employees? Why didn't someone tell her what was going on?"

"Because J.P. was smart enough to keep her isolated from everyone. Her entire world consisted of him and Cole. Before she knew it, J.P. had complete access to her money, her property, all of her assets. And by the time Margaret realized what had happened and discovered J.P.'s infidelities, he had drained most of her bank accounts and cashed in her stocks. Not even the hotels were hers anymore. She'd signed them over to him as anniversary gifts."

Disgusted, Charlie said, "What a snake. Why in the devil didn't she divorce him and have the lawyers fight to get her money back?"

"Pride and the fact that she was a devout Catholic. The Catholic religion doesn't condone divorce."

"The hell with pride. And she could have gotten an annulment. People get annulments all the time," Charlie argued.

"True, but from what I was told she still loved him. And after that breast cancer diagnosis, she was afraid of being alone. So she stayed. Two days after she died, J.P. married Aaron's mother. Six months later, Cole was shipped off to a boarding school."

Poor Cole, Charlie thought.

"Except for holidays, he never really lived here again—until about eight years ago when he moved back and opened his business. And while he's got a good relationship with his brothers and sister, he's barely civil to his father. He hates him."

Was that hatred so deep that Cole would resort to murdering the woman who was a pawn in his father's game?

"You know, in a lot of ways you and Cole Stratton are alike."

"Right. He's a multimillionaire and I pull down a cop's salary."

Anne shook her head. "I'm not talking about money. I meant that you're both very focused. You're both loyal to your friends and family and you both have this annoying trait of thinking that you're the ones responsible for everything and everyone—especially your younger siblings."

"Why don't we skip the analysis?" she quipped, annoyed by her sister's remark.

"Let's not. You think I don't know you blame yourself for Emily's death, that you think you could have saved her?"

"Annie—"

"No, there's no one in here but us and you're going to listen. The guilt has been eating at you for years. That's why you quit law school and became a cop. It's the reason you push yourself the way you do on every case, the way you're pushing yourself now. You're trying to make up for not saving Emily."

"I don't have to listen to this," Charlie told her and pushed away from her desk and stood. "I've got work to do."

"All right." Anne sighed, gave her a sad look and stood. "But no matter how many bad guys you put away, you can't bring Emily back."

"Wait, there it is," Vince told the captain as the man flipped through the channels on the old TV set in his office in search of Stratton's press conference.

Charlie stood beside him, her expression somber as the three of them watched J. P. Stratton's face fill the screen. Standing in front of the Stratton Arms with four of his children flanking him, Stratton lifted his arms to quiet the flock of reporters and TV crews who had been summoned to the press conference. "Ladies and gentlemen, thank you for coming here this afternoon," Stratton began.

The sound sputtered. "Ah, hell," the captain grumbled when the audio kicked in and out, causing only every other word to be audible. "Damn piece of junk," he muttered and punched the volume on the remote.

While the captain went to work trying to fix the sound problem, Vince tuned out the static from the TV set and his thoughts once again drifted to Anne.

Anne.

Jesus, how had he allowed himself to agree to a date with her? She was a kid, Charlie's baby sister, he reminded himself just as he had done for the past month. Then he had an image of Anne, the way she had looked in that short pink skirt perched on the corner of his desk with her legs crossed and that wicked glint in her eyes.

"There, I think I've got it," the captain announced triumphantly.

Vince shut off the picture of Anne and forced himself to concentrate on the problem at hand—J. P. Stratton. He'd known it was coming. Charlie had told him that Anne had warned her about the press conference. Still, knowing you were going to get hammered didn't take the sting out of the punch. Damn, but they didn't need this, he thought as he watched the man posture for the press. This case already had proven to be a real bitch. More pressure from Stratton certainly wasn't going to make it any easier on him and Charlie or the captain.

"…And I want to thank all of you for your many phone calls and notes of condolence, for the support and friendship you have shown to me and my family during what has been such a difficult time for us," J.P. said.

"He looks real broken up," Charlie remarked.

"To lose the woman I loved and planned to spend the rest of my life with in such a horrible way, it has been—" his voice broke and he made a show of swallowing before he continued "—it has been a very dark time for me personally. It is only because of the support of my children and friends that I have been able to continue."

"Oh, give me a break," Charlie grumbled.

"Put a cork in it, Le Blanc," the captain told her.

"I know that we live in a violent world. We live in a city where violence is rife, where guns are sold on street corners, where our children are no longer safe in their schools or even in their own backyards. I also know that our brave police officers put their lives on the line every day in their effort to keep us safe," he told them. "But sometimes, despite their best efforts, even they are unable to protect us and those whom we love. While I stand here, before you today, the animal who robbed and killed my Francesca remains free. He's free to rob and kill someone else's fiancée, someone else's wife, someone else's mother or daughter. And while there is nothing I can do to bring back Francesca, with your help, I hope we can save another family from suffering the heart-wrenching loss that I and my family have suffered."

"I don't like the way this is sounding," Vince commented.

"Neither do I," the captain replied.

"That is why I have called this press conference today, to ask you to help me and to help our police officers find the person responsible for killing my Francesca before he claims another life. So I am offering a reward of one-hundred-thousand dollars to anyone who can provide reliable information that will lead to an arrest in this case."

"Shit," the captain muttered.

"Shit is right," Vince told him.

"The fool," Charlie hissed. "He's going to have every Tom, Dick and Harriet from here to Texas calling him and claiming they know who the murderer is."

"I don't think he much cares," Vince said and knew it was true. It wouldn't matter to J. P. Stratton that they would waste precious hours running down a bunch of false leads instead of searching for the killer.

"Mr. Stratton, are we to understand that you are offering the reward personally?" a reporter in the crowd asked.

"Yes, I am. I'm willing to do whatever I can to help the police apprehend this monster."

"If someone has information, who should they call?" another reporter asked.

"They should call the New Orleans Police Department and ask for Detectives Charlotte Le Blanc or Vincent Kossak in Homicide. They're the detectives assigned to the case."

The captain picked up the remote and shut off the TV with

such force, Vince suspected he wanted to throw it. Instead, he returned to the chair behind his desk and sat down. "I don't have to tell you that your job just got a lot tougher."

"Captain, isn't there anything we can do?" Charlie asked and raked her hand through her hair as though she wanted to pull it out.

"What would you suggest, Le Blanc? Families of victims offer rewards all the time. Stratton's not breaking any laws."

"All right," she said, her frustration obvious. "But since he's the one offering the reward, let him take the calls instead of having them come here."

"Even if I were able to convince the chief to do that, which I have about as much chance as I do of becoming the next Brad Pitt, do you really want to have Stratton and his staff feed you whatever leads that come in?"

"The captain's right," Vince told her. "That would be an even bigger mess."

A knock sounded at the door and the captain's assistant stuck her head inside. "Captain, the phones are ringing off the hook out here. People are calling in from all over, claiming to have information on the Hill murder."

"See if the sarge can get us a couple of rookies to help cover the phones for now," the captain instructed.

"Yes, sir." She shut the door.

"Looks like the fun's already started," Vince said.

"Unfortunately, it's only going to get worse," the captain said. "I'll see if we can get some help with the phone lines. In the meantime, bring me up to date on the case."

After bringing the captain up to speed on the investigation, he and Charlie exited the office. As they did so, they could hear the phone lines ringing off the hook. "Damn!"

"You can say that again," Charlie told him. "I swear, for two cents I'd shoot J. P. Stratton."

Vince retrieved a quarter from his pocket and held it out to her. "Here you go."

She snatched the coin from his hand. "I hope you don't expect any change."

"I never thought I'd say this," Vince told her as they headed to the church on Thursday morning for Francesca Hill's funeral service. "But I'm actually looking forward to this funeral."

Charlie glanced across the car at him. "You're starting to worry me, Kossak. Is this morbid fetish of yours something new?"

"Nope. The truth is, you could take me anyplace—just as long as I don't have to answer any more phones. Hell, right now I'd even sit through one of those fashion-show things if it would save me from another round at the phones."

"I've got news for you, pal," she told him as he turned onto the street where the church was located. "With all the society types who will be there, you'll probably see that fashion show."

But she knew how Vince felt, Charlie admitted. Thanks to J. P. Stratton's offer of a reward, they were both exhausted. After hours of fielding calls from everyone from a psychic grandmother to a guy who claimed his Pomeranian had told him who the killer was, she'd gone home and collapsed in her bed. She'd barely closed her eyes before the alarm went off. And it was only going to get worse.

Vince finally located a parking spot two blocks from the church. After exiting the car, they started down the sidewalk toward the church. It was another one of those days in New Orleans when the weather couldn't decide if it was spring or winter. Yesterday's sunshine and mild temperatures had given way to overcast skies and cool temperatures. A perfect day for a funeral, Charlie thought.

"Hey, I just realized something," Vince said as they neared the church.

"What?"

"This makes twice this month that I've gone to church. I need to tell my mother. She thinks I don't go enough and worries I'll go to hell."

Charlie almost laughed at the satisfied expression on his face. "I hate to burst your bubble, Kossak. But I don't think going to church so that you can question murder suspects actually counts as 'church.'"

"Sure it does. Church is church. It doesn't matter why you're there, just as long as you go."

Charlie shook her head at the remark. "Is that some kind of twisted male logic?"

"There's nothing twisted about it," he countered.

"I beg to differ," she said and shushed him as they climbed the steps of the church and went inside.

"…and it is with great sadness that we, the family, friends and loved ones of Francesca, are gathered here today to mourn her," Reverend Lawrence said as he addressed those present. Positioned at the lectern with an open bible before him, he looked suitably pious—just the way a man of God should look, she thought.

Standing at the rear of the church, Charlie scanned the mourners. They were a sea of people dressed in black. Black suits, black dresses, black skirts. Even the women who were wearing hats had chosen solid black with only an occasional brim trimmed in color. Sprays of flowers in every color had been placed near the altar and along the walls of the church. An enormous spray of red roses, shaped like a heart, rested atop the white marble casket that stood in the center aisle at the front of the church. Charlie rubbed the tip of her nose and felt her eyes water as the scents of flowers and perfumes and colognes made the air stifling.

"There's a seat over there," Vince whispered, motioning to an empty pew at the far side of the church. As quietly as possible, they took their seats.

"…and her death is all the more painful because she was taken from us at a time when she was about to begin a new journey in life," Reverend Lawrence continued.

While the reverend spoke of God's plan, Charlie used the opportunity to study the people who had come to mourn Francesca. She recognized a number of them—business leaders, local politicians, judges. There were even several sports figures present. At the very front of the church sat a stoic-looking J. P. Stratton. His son Aaron sat beside him and next to Aaron was a middle-aged woman who bore a faint resemblance to Francesca Hill. She leaned toward Vince. "Check out the woman in the front row with the Strattons. I think she's Mrs. Humphreys," she said softly, referring to the victim's mother whom she had spoken to only briefly. And that was after more than half a dozen phone calls.

"Doesn't exactly look overcome with grief, does she?" he responded.

Vince was right. No tears, no puffy eyes. Not at all like her own mother at Emily's funeral, Charlie thought. Seated in the pew directly behind J.P. was Holly Stratton, the twins and the twins' mother, Sylvia Stratton. Holly dabbed at her eyes with a handkerchief. Jason sat as still as stone, his eyes fixed on Reverend Lawrence while his twin kept looking over at his father. On the opposite side of the church near the middle she spied Danielle Marceau, wearing a fitted black dress that looked more appropriate for a cocktail party than for a funeral.

Charlie continued studying the people until she felt a tin-

gling at the base of her neck. She shifted her gaze to her left
and three seats back, she saw Cole. He looked directly at her.
For a long moment, their gazes locked. And just as she had
that day at his home, she felt her skin heat, her heartbeat
quicken.

Vince nudged her and whispered, "Five o'clock."

She looked to her right and standing there in the shadow
of a pillar was a man wearing a black overcoat and dark
glasses.

"Look familiar?"

"Yes, he does." She was fairly sure he was the mysterious
visitor from the surveillance tape. The organist struck up the
first notes of "Amazing Grace" and they stood with the rest
of the people present. While the congregation began to sing,
she told Vince, "I'm going to see if I can get closer and catch
him before he leaves."

"No. You stay and talk to the mother. I'm no good at that
stuff. I'll follow our mystery man."

Charlie nodded. And as Vince slipped out of the pew, the
second verse of the hymn began. J.P., Aaron, Jason and Phillip Stratton, along with two men she didn't recognize, took
the position of pallbearers. They started down the center aisle
of the church with the coffin. Following behind them was Mrs.
Humphreys, then Holly and Sylvia Stratton. Instead of waiting for her row to exit, Charlie broke into the procession and
followed them outside.

Outdoors she spied a large cluster of people around J. P.
Stratton. Then she located Mrs. Humphreys, standing with
Reverend Lawrence, who held her hand in what appeared to
be a comforting manner. As Charlie started toward them, she
sized up Gertrude Humphreys. Unlike her daughter, the
woman did nothing to enhance her appearance. Her hair was
a nondescript shade of brown peppered with gray. She'd

pulled it back into a severe bun that made Charlie's head ache just looking at it. She didn't wear a lick of makeup, but she had the same lovely green eyes that her daughter had had. Although she was somewhere in her mid-forties, she dressed like a woman twenty years her senior. The plain black dress she wore was shapeless and fell to midcalf. Her shoes sported a clunky heel that was serviceable, not fashionable. And just as she had noted in church, her eyes were dry and there was no sign of any tears. When she reached them, Charlie said, "A lovely service, Reverend."

"Thank you, Detective."

When he didn't introduce her, she asked, "Mrs. Humphreys? You are Gertrude Humphreys, Francesca's mother, aren't you?"

"Her name was Mary Frances," the woman said. "And yes, I'm her mother."

"I'm Detective Charlotte Le Blanc with the New Orleans Police Department. We spoke on the phone. Please accept my condolences on your loss."

"I lost Mary Frances a long time ago, Detective, when she chose to lead a life of sin instead of service to the Lord."

"I don't want to intrude upon your grief, Mrs. Humphreys. But I'd like to ask you a few questions about Fran—about your daughter."

"Detective, I'm not sure this is the right time," the reverend began. "We'll be leaving for the cemetery in a few minutes."

"I promise this won't take long." When the woman didn't respond, she pressed, "It is important."

"Very well," Mrs. Humphreys responded.

"If you'll excuse me then, I'll go check with Mr. Stratton and find out when he wants to leave for the cemetery," the reverend said.

"What is it you want to know, Detective?" she asked once they were alone.

"I was hoping you could tell me about your daughter, when you spoke with her last, if you know of any enemies she might have had."

"I hadn't seen my daughter for more than ten years, not since she left home and took up her life of sin."

"I see," Charlie said, realizing that Francesca couldn't have been more than sixteen when she'd run away—a young, pretty girl out on her own. With no one to protect her, she would have been an easy target for the monsters who preyed upon vulnerable and desperate girls.

"Don't judge me, Detective. Mary Frances's father abandoned us when she was five and I was left to raise her on my own. She was a rebellious girl who gave in to the sin of vanity. Instead of seeing her beauty as a gift from the Lord, she used it to tempt others to sin. No punishment I gave her, not even meetings with the Reverend Lawrence, could save her."

"So you've had no contact with your daughter at all?" Charlie asked and was disappointed because she had hoped that Gertrude Humphreys would know if there was anyone from Francesca's past who could be responsible for her murder.

"I didn't even know if she was alive until about three months ago when she called me out of the blue to tell me that she'd come into some money and was expecting a lot more. She wanted to buy me a house."

Three months ago. Before she had become involved with J. P. Stratton. And hadn't Danielle said that Francesca had suddenly been flush with cash?

"I told her I didn't want money that she'd gotten by breaking the Lord's commandments."

Once again, Charlie found herself pitying Francesca Hill. To have a stern, cold mother who believed pleasures were a sin would have been tough for any young girl. It made her realize how fortunate she had been to have parents who loved her. "Did she say where she'd gotten the money?"

"She claimed she'd earned it a long time ago and that the person who owed her was finally paying off their debt. Of course, it was a lie."

"Was that the last time you spoke with her?"

"She called me about a month ago to tell me she was getting married. She wanted me to come to the wedding."

"Were you planning to go?" Charlie asked.

"No. She wasn't marrying in the church. So as far as I was concerned it would never be a real marriage if it wasn't blessed by the Lord."

"Detective Le Blanc," Aaron Stratton said as he came to join them. "It was very kind of you to come to the service." He turned to Mrs. Humphreys. "Gertrude, the reverend has some questions about the service at the grave site."

"Thank you for your time, Mrs. Humphreys. And again, my condolences on your loss," Charlie said. "I would like to speak with you again later," she continued and shoved her business card at her. "If you could tell me where you're staying—"

"You should go see the reverend," Aaron told the other woman.

Charlie started after her when Aaron caught her arm in a firm grip. "Now is really not the time, Detective."

She looked down at the hand holding her arm and then back up at him. "Unless you want to lose your fingers, Mr. Stratton, I suggest you get them off of me."

His jaw clenched. His fingers tightened. For a long moment, he held her gaze. And then he released her. "I meant no offense, Detective Le Blanc."

But he had wanted to offend her, Charlie thought as she brushed past him. There had been a moment when she'd seen something in his eyes—a fury, a cruelty. And she'd known he'd wanted to hurt her, too. Beneath the handsome face, nice clothes and charm, there was a darkness about him, something evil. She was so wrapped up in her thoughts about Aaron Stratton, she didn't see Cole until she practically ran into him.

"Whoa," Cole said and caught her gently by the arms to stop her from plowing him down. "Where's the fire?"

Charlie blinked, looked up into those incredible blue eyes. Unlike his brother, Cole's touch was gentle. Yet she could feel the heat of his touch through her jacket like a brand. "I'm sorry. I didn't see you," she said and took a step back. To her surprise she was almost disappointed when he released her.

"Do you usually attend the funerals of people you didn't know, Detective?"

"I do when they're the victim of a crime I'm investigating." He lifted his brow. "May I ask why?"

"Because not everyone has family and friends to mourn them. No one should be buried without someone to mourn them."

"You have a kind heart," he told her.

"I'm no saint, Mr. Stratton."

"It's Cole. And I'm glad you're no saint because neither am I," he said. "Francesca obviously has people to mourn her. So why are you really here?"

"Because you can learn a lot by studying a victim's family and friends."

"And what have you learned today, Detective?"

"That while a lot of people claimed to have loved Francesca Hill, very few did."

"You're very perceptive," he told her. "I like perceptive women."

Choosing to ignore the comment, she said, "You'll need to excuse me, I need to find my partner."

"I saw Detective Kossak headed down the block after someone. I'm sure he'll be back soon. Have dinner with me tonight."

The invitation caught her off guard. "I can't," she told him and started past him, heading away from the church in the direction of the car.

He walked along beside her. "Lunch tomorrow then?"

"No."

"What about the theater next Saturday?"

"No," she said firmly.

"Charlotte, I want to see you again."

She stopped, looked up at him. "I don't date murder suspects."

"Am I still a suspect?"

"Yes," she told him because he was. "You were seen at the victim's apartment the night she died and you have an alibi that no one can verify."

"The surveillance tape shows that I left before she was murdered."

"I won't ask how you know that. But since you're an electronics expert, you could have easily rigged the camera, doctored the tape and then returned later to kill her."

"You're right. I could have. And if I had, you would never have known there was a splice in the tape," he informed her.

"Maybe." She began walking again. So did he.

"There's no maybe about it. I'm very good at what I do, Detective."

"I'm sure you are." From everything she'd learned about him the man didn't do anything in half measures.

"And what have you decided my motive was for killing Francesca?"

She glanced up at him. "It's no secret that you dislike your father."

"I despise the man," he corrected. "But you don't honestly believe that I'd kill an innocent woman to get back at him, do you?"

She didn't. "Maybe you didn't intend to kill her. Maybe things got out of hand."

"Wait a minute," he said, stopping. "What do you mean, 'got out of hand'?"

"She was a beautiful, sexy woman and from what I understand she was interested in getting to know you better."

"But I wasn't interested in her."

"I suppose you're going to tell me she wasn't your type," Charlie countered.

"I don't have a type," he informed her. "But lately I seem to be partial to pretty homicide detectives with amber eyes and long legs."

"I…" The comeback stuck in her throat.

"Le Blanc," Vince called her name.

Charlie stepped back, grateful for the interruption, then left him standing on the sidewalk as she hurried toward Vince. "Did you catch him?" she asked Vince, referring to the mystery man at the church.

"He gave me the slip. But we need to get back to the station."

"Why? What's happened?" she asked.

"We got a hit on one of Francesca's credit cards and they're holding the woman who was caught using it."

Thirteen

Cole watched Charlotte and Detective Kossak walk away. The woman fascinated him. She had from the first moment he'd met her. It was more than the packaging, he admitted as he headed back toward the church. Although he'd thoroughly enjoyed that as well. She was beautiful, but not in an obvious way. No perfect features, no picture-perfect hair, no chic clothes. No, her beauty was far more subtle. Of course, a man had to get past the prickly exterior first to see it. But once he had, there was a lot to appreciate. Peaches-and-cream skin with a faint dusting of freckles across the nose. A delicate jawline, the sexy mouth. Long legs and just enough curves in all the right places. But it was the woman herself who intrigued him. Charlotte Le Blanc was a study of contrasts. Soft and vulnerable and at the same time strong and resilient. She was tough enough to face down a murderer, yet sensitive enough to attend a funeral service for someone she'd never met so their death would be mourned. She was stubborn and determined, qualities he understood and even admired. She hadn't allowed J.P. or any pressure that he'd exerted keep her from doing her job. Beneath the cool, no-nonsense cop, Charlotte Le Blanc was a woman of deep passion.

He wanted to tap into that passion. And he fully intended to do just that. But first he had to get himself removed from her list of murder suspects. He also had to make sure his brother Jason didn't jump to the top of that list. To do that, he would have to do some investigating of his own. And he intended to start with Jason. He scanned the crowd of people flocking around J.P. to offer their condolences. While he saw Phillip and Sylvia, he didn't see Jason. Then he spied Holly standing off to the side, looking totally miserable. He walked over to her and put an arm around her shoulders. "You doing okay?" he asked.

She leaned into him, rested her head against his shoulder. "I just keep thinking if I'd never met Francesca and introduced her to Dad that she might still be alive."

Cole eased Holly away from him, tipped her chin up so that he could see her face. "It's not your fault she's dead. She became involved with J.P. all on her own and there's no reason to think her involvement with him got her killed."

"She was killed during a robbery," Holly reminded him. "They stole her money and jewelry. Before she hooked up with Dad she didn't have anything worth stealing."

"You don't know that the robbery is what got her killed," Cole pointed out.

"But that's what the police said…"

"Francesca was into a lot of things before she came here. And not all of them were good," he told her. Once he had found out about Jason's involvement with the woman, he had begun doing some checking on Francesca. Thanks to his military training, he'd been able to tap into sources that Aaron, J.P. and even the police would have difficulty accessing. As a result, he'd uncovered a charge of blackmail against her in

Texas five years ago. Using an alias, she and a boyfriend had lured businessmen to her hotel room and taped them having sex with her, then they'd claimed she was underage and demanded a payoff for return of the tape. He just wished he'd thought to look more closely at the woman before, he thought. But then he hadn't cared whether she scammed J.P. But his brother Jason was another matter.

"If you're talking about her running away from home and changing her name, Dad and I both knew about that. And I can't say that I blame her with that woman for a mother," she said with a nod in the direction of Gertrude Humphreys.

Seeing no reason at this point to divulge what he'd learned to Holly, he said, "I'm sure her life wasn't easy. But I think there's a lot no one knew about Francesca. Things she did, problems that she had. It could very well be that something or someone from her past is responsible for her murder."

"I guess you're right. Maybe I didn't really know her as well as I thought I did. She certainly didn't turn out to be the friend I thought she was."

He stroked her hair. "I know and I'm sorry."

She shrugged. "Dad wants us to go to the cemetery. Are you coming?"

"No. I only came to make sure you were okay and to speak with Jason. Have you seen him?"

"Last time I saw him, he was heading around to the back of the church."

"Thanks." He gave her a kiss on top of her head and said, "You call me if you need anything. Okay?"

She nodded and wrapped her arms around him for a second before leaving to join J.P. and he went in search of Jason. He found him standing under an oak tree behind the church smoking a cigarette. His shoulders were slumped and he looked as if he had the weight of the world on them. At the funeral service, he had noted his brother's edginess, the blood-shot eyes. The kid had looked absolutely miserable. He didn't look any better now. If anything, he looked worse. Jason looked up. And when he saw him approaching, Cole thought he saw a flicker of fear in his eyes before his brother straightened and assumed a defiant stance.

"I missed you at the police station," Cole said.

"I changed my mind about going."

"You might have returned my calls and let me know that," he pointed out.

"I've been busy. You know, with Mardi Gras and stuff."

"You know those things will kill you," Cole said, motioning to the cigarette.

Jason shrugged. "I can think of worse ways to go."

"So can I. But I don't see any point in hurrying things along. Not when you have your whole life ahead of you."

"Yeah, well, my life isn't all that great anyway."

"Maybe not, but I'd hate to see you spend any of it locked up in a jail cell for making false statements to the police," Cole told him.

Jason flung the cigarette down, crushed it with his shoe. "I'm not afraid of going to jail."

"You should be," Cole told him. "Because you wouldn't last an hour in jail. Do you want me to tell you what they do to young guys like you in prison?"

"I don't have to listen to this," Jason said and started to push past him.

Cole grabbed him by the shirtfront and shoved him back against the tree. "You do have to listen because the police know you lied about where you were the night Francesca was murdered."

"Only because you told them," he accused.

"I didn't have to tell them. They already knew. The only

reason they haven't hauled you in already is because I told them you wanted to amend your statement." He released Jason's shirtfront, stepped back. "Now, tell me the real reason you didn't show up at the station like we planned."

"I already told you. I changed my mind."

Concerned by his brother's agitated state, Cole said, "Let me help you. We'll go—"

"Don't you get it? I can't tell the police why I was at Francesca's because then Dad will find out. And if he does, it'll ruin everything."

"What are you talking about?"

"My mom and dad. For the first time in years, they're close again. They might get back together. But if he finds out that I had the hots for his girlfriend, it'll ruin everything. He'll want nothing to do with any of us because of me."

"Is that what Sylvia told you?" Cole asked, growing angry with the woman for manipulating her son in such a way. "Is she the reason you didn't come to the station?"

"I didn't come because I changed my mind," he told him. "And if you tell anyone what I told you, I'll deny it. I'll swear you're lying."

"Jason—"

"Just leave me alone," he said and, pushing past him, he hurried back toward the front of the church.

Damn you, Sylvia.

Would the woman never give up her obsession with J.P.? How could she do something like this to her own son? Because J.P. had always been more important to Sylvia than her sons or anything else in her life, he answered silently. Just as he had done to his mother and others before her, J.P. had crushed any sense of self from the woman until she believed that her life was nothing without him.

He followed the path Jason had taken and as he rounded

the church, he noted a small group still gathered around J.P. Sylvia stood by his side, her hand on his arm. Standing behind them were Jason, Phillip and Holly. Off to the side was Aaron in conversation with a judge. Aaron chose that moment to look up and when he saw him, he excused himself from the judge and began walking in his direction.

Aaron caught up with him as he neared the parking lot. "I was surprised you came to the service," he told him. "So was Dad. He was glad you came."

"I didn't come for him," Cole informed him. "I came for Holly." He saw no reason to tell Aaron that he'd also come for Jason.

"Yeah, I know what you mean. I'm not sure what hit our little sister harder—Francesca's engagement to Dad or her murder."

"What's that supposed to mean?" Cole demanded.

"Nothing. I was just pointing out what a fragile creature our Holly is."

"I'd say she's entitled," Cole defended, remembering how shattered his sister had been after J.P. forced her to have the abortion.

"Hey, I didn't say she wasn't."

"Sorry," Cole said and raked a hand through his hair. "It looks like they're getting ready to leave for the cemetery."

Aaron turned, looked over at J.P. and the others heading for the limos. When he turned back to him, he said, "I need to go. But I wanted to talk to you about Jason."

Cole tensed. "What about him?"

"I'm not sure how to say this," Aaron began.

It surprised him that Aaron appeared unsure how to proceed, Cole thought, because his brother seldom had trouble finding the right words. "Then why don't you just say what's on your mind."

"I think Jason's in trouble."

"What kind of trouble?" Cole asked.

"Serious trouble. I think he knows something about Francesca's murder."

"What makes you think that?"

"Because our little brother had a thing for the woman. And I'm not so sure she didn't string him along a bit," Aaron told him.

"What's your point?"

"The point is, Jason was in a strange mood the night of the rehearsal dinner. He was really upset about the wedding and Phillip told me he wasn't home all evening like he told the police. I think he might have gone to Francesca's apartment that night." He paused. "Ever since the murder, he's been acting weird. And I'm not the only one who's noticed. Dad's noticed, too."

That was a first, Cole thought, because J.P. seldom noticed anything except when it directly related to him. "You're off base. Jason is no more guilty of murdering Francesca than I am."

"I didn't say he was. But he did have motive," Aaron reminded him.

"Because he had a crush on her? Give me a break."

"People have killed for a lot less," Aaron advised him. "And don't forget, if he knew about her pregnancy that would have been a double blow to his ego. I can't imagine he'd be happy at the idea of having another little Stratton brother or sister running around."

"If that's the case, then you had a pretty strong motive, too, since another baby for J.P. would have meant another slice out of the inheritance pie."

Anger flashed in his brother's green eyes for a moment. Just as quickly it was gone. "There's more than enough to go around," Aaron told him. "Besides, I like being second in command."

Cole wished he believed him. But Aaron had always been competitive and placed far more importance on the money than the rest of them. "But is it really worth having to put up with J.P. and his demands? You don't need him, Aaron. You're a good attorney. There's not a firm in the city that wouldn't hire you."

"And start at the bottom? No thanks," Aaron said. "I like my big salary and the perks that come with being second in command. And sooner or later the old man will either retire or die. When he does, I'll be the one at the helm, calling all the shots."

"Is that what he promised you?" Cole asked, because just six months ago J.P. had dangled that carrot in front of him. Of course, he had turned him down.

"Yes, he did," Aaron said proudly. "I don't know why you're surprised, I've been running things for the most part for years anyway. Besides, who else would he appoint to the position? You've made it clear you want no part of the business and we both know that the twins don't have the balls for the job. And Holly certainly isn't equipped to run it. So that leaves me."

But given J.P.'s track record, he wouldn't put it past him to use Aaron, then kick him to the side. "Just watch your back," Cole told him.

"I always do. And you should watch yours, too," Aaron told him. "Because from the questions that sexy Detective Le Blanc was asking about you, I'd say she's got her sights set on pinning Francesca's murder on you."

"Based on the description of the guy she claims to have bought the credit cards from, it sounds like Schwitzer," Vince told Charlie after interrogating Kaitlyn Biblow, the woman picked up for using Francesca Hill's stolen credit card.

"And I think it's safe to assume he's our mystery guy in the surveillance video and the same guy who was at the church," Charlie said, since Schwitzer had apparently altered his appearance since his mug shot. The man had packed on twenty pounds, streaked his hair blond and gained a pair of glasses since his stint in prison. But the height, weak chin and the thin smirk were the same.

"You think she's telling the truth about not knowing where he is?" Vince asked with a nod toward the woman seated in the interrogation room.

Charlie looked through the one-way glass at the woman. Long black hair, dark eyes and fake boobs, she didn't look any older than Anne, but there was a hardness about her that said she was far wiser than her years. "She knows the score. If she knew anything that she could use to cut a deal for herself, she would have told us."

"Then I'm going to call the assistant district attorney and tell her to cut her loose if she makes bail."

"All right," Charlie told him, still disappointed that they were no closer to finding out who killed Francesca Hill than they had been nearly two weeks ago. While Vince returned to his desk and got on the phone with the D.A.'s office, Charlie sat down at her own desk. She had a mountain of so-called leads to check out thanks to J. P. Stratton's offer of a reward and more were coming in each hour. Yet, she couldn't seem to muster the energy to go through them. Instead, she picked up her pen and studied her list of suspects.

She drew lines through the women's names. A woman hadn't been responsible for Francesca's murder. That left Schwitzer, Reverend Lawrence, J.P., Aaron, Jason and Phillip Stratton. And Cole. If she was right and one of them had murdered Francesca, then one of them had also murdered Emily.

She put a question mark next to Schwitzer's name and

made a note to see if she could place him in the Baton Rouge
area six years ago. If he'd been in the vicinity, it was possible his path had crossed Emily's. And according to what the
police detective who'd arrested him in Texas remembered
about him, Schwitzer had been good at spinning lines about
his business interests. Emily was trusting enough that she
might have believed him. She tapped her pen on J. P. Stratton's name and drew another question mark. She couldn't
imagine her sister with a man who'd been old enough to be
her father. But then a lot of women found the man attractive.
And Emily had always liked older men. She made another
note to herself to check J.P.'s whereabouts six years ago.

She considered Aaron Stratton. He was certainly handsome and charming enough to have appealed to Emily. He had
been attending law school at Tulane six years ago. A drive
from New Orleans to Baton Rouge wouldn't have taken much
more than an hour. She made another question mark next to
his name.

Jason and Phillip Stratton. The twins would have only been
seventeen back then, younger than Emily by two years. It was
possible, but not likely, she thought. She couldn't ever remember her sister dating anyone her own age, let alone someone
two years younger. She didn't see either of them as a killer.
She drew a line through their names.

That left Cole Stratton. Tall, dangerous good looks and an
air of mystery about him. He definitely would have been
Emily's type. She imagined very few women had turned him
down. Emily wouldn't have. And the truth was, she had found
it hard to turn down his offer herself. She drew another question mark next to Cole's name.

Sitting back, she stared at the names that remained on her
list. One of them was a killer. She knew it, could feel it in her
bones. But which one? Which one of them had crossed paths

with her sister? And why had he killed her? She was missing something. She knew it. But what? What was it that had linked both her sister and Francesca and drawn the focus of a killer?

"Okay, I talked to the ADA," Vince said as he hung up his phone and turned around to face her desk. "She's going to make sure the woman stays in town so that when we find Schwitzer, she can ID him."

"Sounds good," she said and shoved her notes in a file.

"You okay, Le Blanc?"

"Sure," she said. "Just tired, I guess."

"I hear you. I'm going to call it quits and tackle the rest of those leads in the morning," Vince told her and began shutting down his workstation.

"You want to grab something to eat?" Charlie asked.

"I…uh…I would, but I'm supposed to go to a Hornets game with Anne tonight."

"That's right. I forgot tonight's the big date," Charlie teased.

"It's just a ball game," he told her.

"Uh-huh." Based on her conversation with Anne, she suspected it was more.

"It is," he insisted. "I mean, it's not like it's a real date."

"I've got news for you, Kossak. Anne thinks it's a real date. According to her, she made that pretty clear."

"What I mean is it's not serious," he explained and it was clear that he was rattled.

She almost felt sorry for him. The man wasn't going to know what hit him. When her baby sister went after something, she usually got it. And Anne had decided she wanted Vince. "Well, have fun on your not real, not serious date."

Vince stood. He turned off the lamp at his desk and locked his drawer. "Le Blanc, you sure you're all right about this? About me going out with your sister?"

"Anne's her own person. And as she's pointed out to me,

she's all grown up and doesn't need my permission to go out with you or anyone else."

"I know that," he told her. "But are you okay with it? We work together and I don't want it to mess things up between us."

She had already considered that and decided that whatever happened, Anne would still be her sister and Vince would still be her partner and friend. "I'm okay with it," she finally said and let him off the hook.

"Good. Then I'm out of here. I'm supposed to pick up Anne in half an hour." He grabbed his jacket from the back of his desk chair. "I thought you were leaving," he said as he slipped his jacket on.

"I'm going to stay for a bit, return a few of these calls," she said, indicating the stacks of phone slips generated by the reward. "Who knows, maybe one of them really will know something."

"Yeah, right. And the Saints are going to win the Super Bowl next year, too," he said, referring to the city's beloved but losing football team.

"We can always hope," she said. "Now, if I were you, I'd get out of here because I'd hate to see you get on Annie's bad side by showing up late for your first date."

"I'm gone."

Once Vince had left, she thought about her partner out on a date with her sister. And she couldn't help thinking about Cole. She had had relationships before, one that was even semiserious. She knew what it was to have sexual chemistry with a man, to feel that tug of attraction. But she couldn't remember feeling drawn to a man so strongly before that she was tempted to break her own rules. She'd never considered blurring those lines before, but she had been tempted today. And it would have been a huge mistake.

Shutting off thoughts of Cole Stratton, she picked up the

phone slips, then set them aside when she saw the light flashing that she had voice mail. Charlie picked up the phone, punched in the numbers and listened.

"Detective Le Blanc, this is Dwight in Forensics. I'm the accountant who's been going through bank records in the Hill murder case and I think I've found something. Give me a call back and I'll tell you what I've got."

Adrenaline pumping through her, she exited voice mail without listening to any other messages and began punching in the number left by the accountant. "Come on, come on. Pick up," she said. She glanced at her watch, saw it was forty minutes past closing time and prayed someone had decided to work late.

Finally the ringing stopped and a man said, "Richards."

"This is Detective Le Blanc in Homicide. I need to speak with Dwight."

"I'm sorry, Detective, but Dwight's already gone for the day. If fact, I was just on my way out the door myself," he told her.

"Richards, what's your first name?" she asked.

"Greg."

"Greg, I really need your help. I got a message from Dwight and he said that he'd found something for me with regards to the Hill murder case. Could you pull the file for me and tell me what it was he found?" she asked. "It really is important."

He sighed. "All right. The Hill case you said?"

"Yes, Francesca Hill. She was killed ten…eleven days ago."

"Hang on a second while I go to Dwight's desk." After what seemed an eternity but was probably no more than a couple of minutes, Greg was back on the line. "Okay, according to his notes, he found a pattern in your vic's bank deposits. They're pretty straightforward actually. It looks like every Monday for the past six months, she's been making $2,500 deposits into one of her accounts."

She considered that a moment. "Were the deposits checks from J. P. Stratton or one of his companies?"

"No, it looks like those started about six weeks ago. And those amounts varied and were all drawn on Stratton company accounts. These other deposits started before those. And like I said, they were all cash and all made on Monday like clockwork."

Six months ago, Charlie thought. Hadn't Danielle said that Francesca had arrived in town just over six months ago, broke and with no job? Then within weeks she was flush with cash, but wouldn't say where the money had come from.

"Detective Le Blanc, you still there?"

"Yes. I'm here, Greg."

"If there's nothing else, I really need to go. My girlfriend's waiting for me."

"No, that's it, Greg. You've been a big help. Thanks a lot." After she hung up the phone, Charlie grabbed the file and pulled out the calendar printout from Francesca's PDA. Every Monday at twelve-thirty, she had made the notation "bank deposit," which Charlie had thought anal at the time. Picking up a yellow marker, she went through the Monday appointments month by month, highlighting those that appeared at least three times each month prior to the bank deposit. Two came up. A ten o'clock facial each Monday morning, which was followed by an eleven-thirty meeting. And each of those Monday meetings had been with the same person—the Reverend Homer Lawrence.

Fourteen

"Detective Le Blanc. Detective Kossak," Reverend Lawrence said as they entered his office on Friday morning. "I must say, I didn't expect to see you again. Please, have a seat," he said and motioned to the two tweed-covered chairs across from his desk.

"We need to ask you some questions, Reverend," Vince told him as he and Charlie sat down. Looking across the desk at the man with his hands clasped together and a genial expression on his face, he had to admit that the reverend looked like what he was supposed to be—a man of God. He didn't look like a man who had been paying blackmail money to Francesca Hill. But based on the dead woman's bank accounts and a review of the weekly donations listed in the church's bulletins for the past year, it certainly looked like blackmail to him, Vince thought. The Sunday coffers were down ten percent. And the drop in donations coincided with Francesca's arrival in New Orleans and her reunion with her childhood pastor. It was also at that same time that Francesca's cash flow improved. Charlie was right. This was no coincidence.

"Now, tell me, Detectives, how can I help you?" he asked.

"Why don't you start by telling us the real nature of your relationship with Francesca Hill," Vince suggested.

"I thought I'd already established that. I was her spiritual adviser."

"You know, that's one of the things that confused me, Reverend," Charlie began. "You claimed that she was one of your parishioners. But no one we spoke with ever recalls her going to church."

"I'll admit she didn't attend services regularly, but then not everyone feels they need to attend church to pray to our Lord. Mary Frances…Francesca was one of those people."

"But she apparently did feel the need to visit with you every Monday. Why is that, Reverend?" Vince asked.

"I was Francesca's spiritual adviser. She wanted spiritual guidance."

Although his voice was calm, Vince noted beads of sweat beginning to form on the reverend's brow. Since the room was on the cool side and the temperature outdoors had barely tipped above sixty on the thermometer, he doubted the reverend's perspiration had anything to do with the heat. "Do you make a practice of going to the apartments of young female parishioners to offer spiritual guidance, Reverend?"

"I resent the insinuation, Detective," he said indignantly.

"Then why don't you explain it to us," Charlie suggested.

He eyed them warily, then sat back in his chair. "As I told you, I knew Francesca when she was just a girl. Her father abandoned the family when she was very young. And her mother, Gertrude…well, Gertrude found her daughter's spirited nature difficult to deal with. I did what I could by counseling and I tried to set Francesca on the right path. Then she ran away and I had to face the fact that I had failed her. When she showed up at my church six months ago, I felt the Lord had given me a second chance to save her soul," he said with conviction.

"At her apartment?" Charlie remarked. "According to the guest log at the apartment building you visited her five times in the past two months."

"Detective, I would have met her in a bar, on a street corner, wherever I needed to go if it meant helping a lost soul find their way back to the Lord."

"Tell me, Reverend," Vince said softly, "how did paying her $2,500 a week help Francesca's lost soul find its way back to the Lord?"

The man's already pasty complexion grew ashen. "I don't know what you're talking about," he said and pulled a handkerchief from his pocket and mopped his brow.

"I'm talking about the money you've been stealing from the Sunday collections for the past six months and giving to Francesca Hill," he informed him.

"That's absurd," the man said and shoved to his feet. "I am a man of God. I would never steal from the church. That would be like stealing from the Lord."

"Then how do you explain the ten percent drop in your church's Sunday collections? A drop that coincided with Francesca Hill's arrival in New Orleans and your becoming her spiritual counselor again?" Charlie asked.

"I assure you I have no idea what you're talking about."

"She's talking about this," Vince told him and slapped the file folder on his desk. He opened it and said, "Take a look, Reverend. Those are the church's weekly bulletins for the past year where you list the Sunday collections."

He sat down, stared at the damning figures. "What of them?"

"If you look closely, Reverend, you'll notice that until six months ago, those collections always tipped just over $25,000 each week. Then six months ago after you began counseling Francesca again, those collections suddenly began averaging $22,500 each week. How do you explain that?"

"Apparently collections have been down. Probably a result of the economy."

"Except that the economy has been pretty good. But you want to know what's most interesting?" he asked. "It just so happens that at the same time the church's donations decreased by $2,500 per week, Francesca's bank account increased by that exact amount each Monday—after her spiritual session with you."

The reverend looked like a drowning man, Vince thought. And just when it appeared he was going to go under for a third time, he pushed away from the desk and stood again. "All of this proves nothing," he said with a wave of his hand at the folder. "And I take offense at what you're implying. If there has been any decrease in donations to the church, I assure you I know nothing about it. And I certainly don't know anything about Francesca's finances."

"Then I don't suppose you can explain why it's the church's cash donations that have decreased and that the money Francesca Hill deposited each week into her account was always in cash," Vince said.

"No, I can't," he said. "My job is spreading our Lord's word. I leave the collection of any monies for the support of the church to others. My time is better spent ministering to those in need."

"That's funny, Reverend Lawrence," Vince told him. "Because I happened to speak to a few of the ushers who pass around the money baskets at the Sunday services. And according to them, they used to sort the checks from the cash and tally the funds for deposit for you. But about six months ago, you told them you would handle it yourself. Why is that?"

"I…" He swallowed. "They were making mistakes in addition on the deposit slips and I wouldn't find it out until I went to the bank. So to eliminate the problem, I decided to handle it myself. Now, if there's nothing else, I have another engagement."

Vince stood. So did Charlie. "Just one more thing," Vince said. "During your counseling sessions with Francesca, did she happen to mention where she was getting so much cash?"

"No, she didn't. And as I've told you repeatedly, my relationship with her was that of a spiritual adviser and nothing more."

"Thank you for your time, Reverend," Vince said. "If you happen to think of anything that might help us, please give me or Detective Le Blanc a call."

"Of course."

Once he and Charlie exited the church office and stepped outside, Vince turned to his partner. "What do you think of his story?"

"I think the man is lying through his teeth."

"So do I," Vince replied. "Let's go see if the captain has had any luck getting those church records and see if we can prove it."

She was missing something, Charlie admitted. After spending the remainder of the day trying to figure out what it was that Francesca had on the reverend, she was no closer to finding the answer than she had been when she'd started. So far, the captain had hit brick walls trying to get access to the records from the other churches where he'd served. And the closest thing to a red flag that she had turned up was that the man had been transferred frequently during his tenure as a minister. If there was a sinister reason behind the transfers, she wouldn't be able to find it because the church hierarchy of most religions closed ranks around their own.

The interview with Gertrude Humphreys had been of no use either. She'd pretty much confirmed everything the reverend had said about her daughter—that Francesca was a willful girl on the wrong path. According to Gertrude, she hadn't believed in sparing the rod and spoiling the child. Based on her two conversations with the woman, she'd concluded that Gertrude also hadn't believed in showing love or affection to her daughter, either. It was no surprise that Francesca had run away. The poor kid must have thought anything was better than the life she'd had. Unfortunately, it looked as if Francesca had traded one set of problems for another. She'd fled a stern, cold mother in search of the love and affection she'd been denied only to find herself in relationships with stern, cold men who exploited her beauty but never loved the woman herself.

So who killed Francesca Hill? And why? And how did her murder connect to Emily's?

What was she missing? Charlie asked herself for what had to be the tenth time. Opening the case file, she took out the crime-scene photos. She studied shot after shot taken at the murder scene. The bed where the victim had been found, the carpet where her clothing had been discarded. The empty champagne glasses and bottle. She continued going through the photos, noting the bookshelves, the stereo system and entertainment center, the ashtray on the table.

It has to be here. But where? What is it?

She was getting nowhere, Charlie admitted. Shoving the photos back into the file, she locked it in her drawer and turned off her desk light. After slipping on her jacket, she headed for the parking lot. But as she drove away, she couldn't get those pictures from the crime scene out of her head. Braking for a red light, she called up the images of the rooms in the apartment one by one. And she kept going back to the living room. Something about that particular room bugged her. But for the life of her, she couldn't figure out what. Whatever she was missing, it was there. She knew it. When the light turned green, Charlie flipped on her turn signal and instead of going home, she headed for the Mill House Apartments.

There was something eerie about returning to a place where someone had been murdered, Charlie thought as she took the elevator up to the fifth floor. She could almost feel a presence, a victim's spirit lingering. Sometimes Charlie wondered if these feelings were the result of the French blood that ran through her veins or if they were simply a by-product of growing up in a city entrenched in superstitions and with a healthy respect for ghosts. Whatever the reason, she hoped by returning to Francesca's apartment now she would find the answers she sought in those rooms.

Exiting the elevator, Charlie took out the key she'd gotten from the manager. As she walked down the corridor, she was keenly aware of the quiet. According to the manager, Francesca's neighbor had been too frightened to return to her apartment since the murder and was staying with friends until she could find a new place. She couldn't say she blamed the woman. Even the hallway had a spooky feel to it.

When she reached the apartment, Charlie noted the broken yellow crime-scene tape. Since the police department's personnel and finances were stretched thin, they'd removed the guard two days ago. She removed her weapon from its harness. She held it in one hand and gently turned the knob on the door. It was unlocked. Slowly, she opened the door. Giving her eyes a moment to adjust to the darkness, she was grateful for the moonlight spilling through the window.

She scanned the room and spied the master-bedroom door slightly ajar and the shifting beam from a flashlight dancing in the shadows. Holding her gun with both hands, she lifted it and moved in the direction of the bedroom. As she drew closer, Charlie could hear someone rummaging through things in the room. Pressing her back flat against the wall, she inched her way to the bedroom. When she reached the door, she kicked it open, aimed her gun and yelled, "Freeze!"

Jason Stratton dropped the CD case and flashlight he was holding and held his hands up above his head. The kid's face drained of color. "Don't shoot!"

Keeping her gun aimed at him, she hit the light switch. "You want to tell me what you're doing here?"

"I…I was looking for my CD. I lent it to Francesca and I wanted it back."

"Didn't you see the crime-scene tape? It means that no one's allowed in here. I should arrest you right now."

"I didn't mess with anything. I swear it. I just wanted to get my CD back," he insisted. "And it's not like I'm trespassing or anything. My dad owns the building."

"I don't care if the governor owns the building. This is a crime scene and no one is allowed in here." She eased her stance, lowered her weapon. "How did you get in here anyway?"

"I used the delivery entrance out back. I spent a few summers working at my brother's security firm, so the lock on the door was a piece of cake."

"So what's so special about the CD that you'd break in here to get it back?"

He shrugged. "Nothing. I just wanted it back."

"And he knows he made a mistake and it won't happen again. Right, Jason?"

Charlie spun around and aimed her weapon at the man standing a few yards behind her—Cole Stratton. "You want to tell me what you're doing here?" she demanded, both irritated and alarmed that she hadn't heard him.

"Looking for my brother to discuss his amending his statement to you and Detective Kossak about his whereabouts on the night of Francesca's murder." He paused. "Would you mind putting that away?"

Charlie reholstered her weapon. She looked at Cole. She didn't doubt he had been looking for his brother, but she couldn't help wondering if there was another reason he was there. "And you just figured you'd find him here?"

"I thought it was a possibility. Then I got a call from Maintenance telling me that his car was parked near the delivery entrance." He looked over at his brother. "Jason, since Detective Le Blanc is here now, why don't you tell her what you told me about where you were on the night Francesca was killed."

"I don't know what you're talking about. I already told her where I was," Jason tossed back.

"You might want to rethink that," Charlie advised him. "Because your alibi didn't check out. No one at that convenience store remembers seeing you that night and you weren't on the surveillance video."

"So maybe I made a mistake about which store I went to. I'd had a few drinks at dinner," he said huffily. "Listen, if you're going to arrest me, go ahead and do it."

"I'm not going to arrest you. At least not at the moment," Charlie told him.

"Then I'm out of here."

"What about your CD?" she asked when he started to bolt.

"I couldn't find it," he told her and brushed past her.

Cole blocked the doorway, halting his exit. "You're only making things worse for yourself, Jason. Let me help you."

"I don't want your help," he said. "Now get out of my way."

For a long moment, Charlie thought Cole would refuse. His face was serious, his blue eyes hard. Then he stepped aside and Jason rushed from the apartment. Once his brother was gone, he looked back at her. "He didn't kill Francesca."

"Then he has nothing to worry about." She walked over to the case of CDs that Jason had dumped on the floor and wondered what he had really been searching for, because she didn't buy his story about the CD. Removing a pair of gloves and an evidence bag from her pocket, she slipped on the gloves, then stooped down and began picking up the CDs.

Cole came over and knelt beside her. "Need some help?"

She looked up. He was so close, she could see the trace of five o'clock shadow on his jaw, smell his scent—that combination of forest and spice. It was there again. That sting of awareness that made her belly tighten, her skin heat whenever he was near. "No, and you shouldn't be here," she said, determined to ignore whatever this thing was between them. "This is still a crime scene and you're trespassing."

He held out his wrists. "Want to cuff me?"

"Somehow I doubt it would be the first time."

"You're right. It wouldn't."

She didn't ask him to explain. She sealed the bag, then stood. She looked around the room and knew any hope that the rooms would speak to her were lost for now. "I'm going to close up here," she informed him. "And you don't belong here."

"Point taken," he said and followed her out of the apartment. "I was here looking for Jason and Jason was here looking for his CD, but you never did say what you were doing here, Detective."

"You're right, I didn't," she told him as she locked the door. Satisfied the scene was secure, she headed for the elevator with Cole beside her. They stepped inside the elevator and when the door slid shut, the space seemed to have shrunk. And just as it had a moment ago in the apartment, Charlie could feel her pulse quickening.

"I haven't eaten dinner yet and I'm guessing neither have you. There's this great little pizza place a few blocks from here. What do you say we share a pizza?"

"I'd say it's not a good idea," she said and exited the elevator.

"Why not?" he asked as he walked beside her again.

"Because I'm a detective investigating the murder of a woman closely connected to your family, a murder for which, I might add, you're still a suspect."

"Do you think I killed Francesca?" he asked her directly.

"What I think doesn't matter. What matters is that I can't afford to have any association between us misconstrued as something personal."

"I hardly call sharing a pizza an association."

She paused at the desk to return the key and after giving instructions that no one was to be allowed access to the apartment without clearance, she headed for the exit. When she stepped outside, the cool night air felt good on her cheeks.

"What if I let you grill me while we eat?" he asked as he followed her to her car. "You'd be killing two birds with one stone. You get to eat *and* pump me for information."

"I also could just bring you down to the police station and question you."

"True. But you'd be surprised how much more cooperative I am on a full stomach," he said.

Charlie considered his offer. It wouldn't exactly be the wisest thing to do. Then again, he would know where all the Stratton skeletons were buried. Maybe by agreeing to pizza, she could learn something that would help her find the killer. "All right, Mr. Stratton," she said as she reached her car. "But I drive my own car and we split the bill."

"So what else do you want to know?" Cole asked Charlotte as they sat across the table from each other in the restaurant. True to his word, he'd allowed her to grill him over pizza. And grill him she did. He had to give her credit though, she hadn't played coy or tried to be subtle. She was on a fishing expedition for information and made no bones about it. Her questions had been direct and she'd pulled no punches. Neither had he. What he didn't tell her was his own suspicions about who the killer was. In part because for the moment they were just suspicions, and in part because he was praying he was wrong.

"So why give up your career in the navy and come back to New Orleans?"

"Maybe I got tired of risking my neck all the time," he replied.

"All those commendations for bravery in your military record say otherwise. I think you liked all those dangerous commando missions."

He grinned at her perception. "You're right. I did. But most of my assignments were on other continents, which meant a lot of miles between me and my family. I wanted to be closer so I resigned and moved back here."

"By family, you mean your half brothers and sister?" Charlie remarked.

"They're my brothers and sister period. The fact that we have different mothers doesn't make them any less my family."

"You're very protective of them. Why?" she asked.

He took a sip of his beer. "For the same reason you are. We're both the oldest, so we always feel responsible for our younger siblings, and when something goes wrong or happens to them, we blame ourselves for letting them down."

She stiffened and put down her half-eaten slice of pizza. "What makes you think I blame myself for anything?"

"You're not the only one who runs background checks, Detective. After all, I *am* in the security business."

Her expression darkened. "Digging up a few facts and figures about me doesn't mean you know me."

"You're right, I don't know you. But I'd like to."

"This was a mistake," she said and started to rise.

Cole reached over and placed his hand over hers. "The mistake would be to allow good pizza to go to waste." He paused. "Come on, there's got to be something more you want to pry out of me. Please…stay."

Slowly she sat down again. Pulling her hand from beneath his, she picked up her slice of pizza again.

Content to watch her eat, he said nothing and resumed his own meal. Unlike many of the women he knew, Charlotte Le Blanc enjoyed food—which was a refreshing change from watching rail-thin women push salad greens around on a plate and claim they're on a diet. He smiled.

"Something funny?" she asked as she reached for another slice of pizza.

"I was thinking how nice it is to share a meal with a woman who actually eats."

"Don't the women you know eat?"

He laughed. "Now that you mention it, I'm not sure they do."

"Then maybe you need to meet some real women instead of arm trophies. You know, the ones who work for a living instead of marry for it. If you do, you'll find that real women actually eat and breathe and manage to have careers and families."

"So I'm discovering." He picked up another slice of pizza. "So tell me more about Charlotte Le Blanc."

"I thought you had already investigated me."

"I did," he admitted. "But like you said, a few facts and figures don't add up to the whole person. For instance, they don't tell me if you've ever had second thoughts about dropping out of law school."

"If that's your subtle way of asking me if I wish I were a lawyer instead of a cop, the answer is no. I have no regrets. I'm at peace with my decision."

"What about—"

"I thought I was supposed to be the one asking questions," she reminded him.

"Sorry. Ask away."

She wiped her hands with her napkin. "What do you know about the Reverend Homer Lawrence?"

Cole took a swig of beer. "I know that he was Francesca's minister when she was a girl and that for someone who didn't strike me as religious, she saw a lot of him."

"In other words, you couldn't find anything on him either."

"Nope. Just that he left his last church under some kind of cloud, but no one will say why. And I know that I don't trust the man."

"Then that's something we agree on," she said.

Cole sat back in his chair. "So the reverend is on your list of suspects, too."

"A lot of people are on my list of suspects. Including you," she reminded him.

"You know what I think, Detective?"

"No, but I'm sure you're going to tell me."

"I think you would have made a good lawyer, but that you make an even better cop."

"I'm not sure my captain or the police chief would agree with you," she replied. "I still haven't tracked down Francesca Hill's killer."

"But you will."

"You sound sure."

"I am." He leaned forward. "The victims aren't just bodies on a slab to you. They're real people who had families, friends, hopes and dreams, a life cut short. They matter to you and because they matter, you won't stop until you find justice for them."

"I'm no saint, Stratton. The department has a lot of good cops."

"But I suspect that very few of them have your heart and conviction."

"Heart and conviction don't solve cases. Evidence does."

"Then you'll find the evidence," he told her, knowing that she wouldn't stop until she did. The problem was, he couldn't shake the bad feeling he had about where that evidence would lead her.

"You're right, I will," she told him. "And when I have it, I'll have my killer."

"Then I don't have anything to worry about because I didn't kill Francesca."

"You know something, Stratton, I actually believe you." She picked up the glass of tea she'd ordered and drank.

"Thanks."

"Don't thank me too quickly, because I don't have any trouble believing that you're capable of murder. I think you are. I just don't see any woman mattering enough to you for you to resort to that kind of violence."

"I'm not sure if I should thank you or be offended," he told her.

"Neither. It's simply my opinion based on what I've learned about you."

"Speaking of what we've learned about each other, there's something I've been wondering. Which one of your parents was a fan of the Brontë sisters?" When she gave him a skeptical look, he said, "It wasn't that difficult to make the connection, Detective. Your name is Charlotte. Your sister at *Channel 4* is named Anne and your sister who was killed was named Emily. The names of the three Brontë sisters."

"It was my mother. She was an English teacher."

"And the nickname Charlie, where did it come from?" he asked.

"It's what my dad used to call me. I was a bit of a tomboy when I was younger."

He could imagine her as a girl, all long limbs and bravado.

She'd have been the first to take a dare and the last to quit. "I bet you gave the neighborhood boys a run for their money."

She smiled and that simple curving of her lips softened her expression, made her even more lovely. "Let's just say, I was able to hold my own."

And then some, he thought. He studied her face, the delicate features, the too-wide mouth. "I think Charlie suits Detective Le Blanc. But Charlotte suits you."

"I'm perfectly satisfied with Charlie," she assured him and reached for another slice of pizza.

Because as long as she was Charlie, she thought people would see her as a cop and not as a woman. She was wrong. He watched Charlotte bite into the thick crust. When she closed her eyes and savored the tangy tomato, cheese and sausage flavors, Cole's gut tightened. The woman made the simple act of eating pizza a sensual experience, he decided. But then, from the moment he'd first set eyes on her, he'd found the woman enticing on both a physical and emotional level.

Cole reached for his mug of beer and drank deeply, attempting to cool the punch of desire that had hit him. It wasn't working, he admitted. Setting down the mug on the table, he watched Charlotte closely and couldn't help wondering if she made love with the same passion that she did everything else.

As though she sensed him watching her, Charlotte lifted her gaze to his and the sexual tension seemed to explode inside him. Damn, he wanted her. And he intended to have her and for her to have him.

She swallowed and put down the half-eaten slice of pizza. "Something wrong?"

"You've got a little tomato sauce right here," he said and, reaching across the table, he flicked the bit of red sauce from the corner of her mouth with his thumb. Never taking his eyes from hers, he brought it to his mouth.

Her eyes darkened. He heard the slight catch of her breath. And her response did nothing to ease the ache of arousal. Exercising a patience he didn't feel but that he knew was necessary, he sat back in his seat.

"It's getting late. I'd better go," she told him.

"Aren't you going to finish your pizza?"

"I'm not hungry anymore," she said. She pulled a ten from her wallet and put it on the table. "I think that should cover my half."

"It should," he said, even though he intended to leave her money as a tip since he'd already paid for their meal while she had been in the rest room. He stood and came around to her side of the table where she was already on her feet, grabbing her jacket. He helped her into the navy coat. And for several seconds he allowed his hand to rest on her shoulders.

"Thanks," she murmured.

"I'll walk you to your car."

"That's not necessary," she told him.

"I insist," he informed her and rather than argue with her further, he placed a hand at her back and led her from the restaurant. Once they were outdoors, he walked beside her down to the corner where she'd parked her car. He waited for her to unlock her door. "Well, good night," she said, turning to face him.

He leaned in, bringing his body within inches of hers. And slowly, giving her time to protest, he lowered his head. He kissed her. He wanted to swallow her whole. Instead, he forced himself to remain gentle, to allow her to dictate the pace of the kiss. When her lips parted and allowed him entry, he bit back a groan. He wanted her desperately. But she wasn't ready. Not yet. So he would wait until the time was right for both of them. That time wasn't now, he admitted. Lifting his head, he caressed her cheek and whispered, "Good night, Charlotte."

* * *

He watched her drive away from the restaurant. Then he slid behind the wheel of his own car and started the engine. Making sure to keep a proper distance so that she wouldn't spot him, he followed her.

It wasn't the first time he'd followed her to that cramped little cottage on the fringes of the Garden District that she called home. He'd learned a long time ago the importance of proper planning, of knowing your prey, of learning their patterns. And he had learned a great deal about Charlotte Le Blanc.

She had little in the way of a social life because her job consumed her on and off the clock. Outside of her family, her partner and a few friends, she kept to herself. There was no man in her life, which explained why she had no form of birth control in her house. She was neat, but not overly so. She liked both classical music and rock 'n' roll. She wasn't into frills or makeup and didn't waste her pitiful salary on designer clothes. She preferred slacks to dresses—which was a shame since she had great legs. From the dent she'd put into the bag of Tootsie Rolls over the past two days, she had a sweet tooth. Unlike her sister Emily, she wasn't a cook. Her pantry had been practically empty except for cereal, a few cans of soup and a jar of peanut butter. Most of her meals were takeout or leftovers sent by her mother. Breakfast during the week consisted of a bowl of cereal and a cup of coffee. On Sundays, she splurged and picked up fresh doughnuts on her way home after her run.

Charlotte Le Blanc was also a creature of habit. He watched as she pulled her car into the driveway of the corner house and cut the engine. Shutting off his lights, he parked his car beneath the oak on the side street where he had a perfect view of her home. He'd discovered the spot after following her home the first time. He'd needed a vantage point, one

*where he could watch her comings and goings and not worry
about nosey neighbors. Since it didn't connect to any major
streets, there was little traffic. Only two of the houses were
occupied—one with a wheelchair-bound old man and the
other with an aging couple. The rest of the houses sported For
Sale signs, no doubt the owners fleeing to the suburbs to escape the city's high crime rate. The big oak provided lots of
cover and all he'd had to do was use a rock to take out the
overhead light. Pleased with himself, he sat back and watched
Charlotte go through her routine.*

*As usual, she exited the car with a bag that he knew con-
tained case files. She retrieved her mail and then unlocked her
door. The light went on inside the house and he envisioned her
movements. Right now, she would be walking through the living room and dropping her briefcase next to the couch. She
would move on to the kitchen, where she'd go straight to the
pantry and grab a handful of Tootsie Rolls. As she unwrapped
the candy and popped it into her mouth, she would scan her
mail, then place it on the counter to go through later. Now she
would be opening the fridge and reaching for a cola. She
would be popping the top now, he thought, and could see her
putting the can to her lips and drinking deeply.*

*Unable to resist, he eased out of the car. Pulling up the col-
lar of his jacket, he checked the street, saw it was clear and
crossed over to the other side. He went around the side of the
house and looked in the window of the bedroom where he'd
moved the curtain just enough to give him a view of her.*

*He counted down five seconds and right on cue, she en-
tered the bedroom. She turned on the light, kicked off her
shoes and placed the can of cola on the dresser. She removed
her jacket, tossed it across the chair, then she removed her gun
harness and placed it in the drawer of her nightstand. He
smiled as she stretched and her breasts strained against her*

blouse. Oh yes, he thought as she unbuttoned the blouse and then shed her slacks. Her underwear was almost the same color as her skin. But he could just make out the nipples and was surprised by the cleavage. She opted for a bikini brief instead of a thong, much to his disappointment. As she walked back over to the dresser, he could feel himself growing hard.

Patience, he reminded himself. He'd learned the art of patience a long time ago. Waiting would only make it all the more enjoyable when the time came for him to kill her. And he was going to kill her.

When she walked back over to the dresser, his excitement grew, knowing what was to come. She picked up the cola, took another sip and pulled open the center drawer to retrieve the pajamas that she had folded and placed neatly on top. She reached for the pajamas and then she saw it—a black silk stocking. It was his gift to her, a promise of what was to come.

Fifteen

Charlie dropped the pajamas and stared at the black silk stocking. Her stomach pitched. Shock and fear hit her like one-two punches, then she whipped around as her police training kicked in. She ran to the nightstand and grabbed her weapon. Removing it from its harness, she began to check the house. Her heart pounded as she went through the house— the spare bedroom, living room, kitchen, baths. Nothing. Satisfied that the house was empty, she grabbed her coat from the hall closet, slipped it on and then went outside in her bare feet.

She could hear the evening news coming from Mr. Murphy's house two doors down. As always the volume was too loud because the elderly man refused to admit he was hard-of-hearing. But other than that, it was a quiet neighborhood, which had been one of the reasons she'd bought the house. Only two porch lights were burning on the block, everyone else obviously turning in early. Charlie glanced across the street, frowned when she noted that the streetlight on the corner was still out. Using the light from her own porch, she checked the backyard and both sides of the house. Nothing. As she headed back toward the front of her house, she saw the cigarette butt on the grass outside her bedroom window. She shoved a hand in her pocket and was grateful to find a couple of folded tissues. She stooped down and carefully picked up the butt with the tissue. Then she headed back inside.

Once inside she locked the door behind her and went to the kitchen. She dug through the drawers, found a small paper bag and placed the tissue inside. Still holding the bag, she hurried to the bedroom where she set both it and her gun down and grabbed the phone. She started punching in the numbers for the police station, then hit the off button. Still barefoot and wearing her coat, she sank to the bed. If she phoned in the break-in, Vince would have to know and once he found out that the killer had her in his sights, it would be over. He'd tell the captain everything and once the captain knew there was a strong possibility that the Hill murder was connected to her sister's slaying six years ago, he'd pull her off the case.

She couldn't let that happen. Not yet, not when she was getting close. And she was getting close, Charlie told herself. Why else would the killer have left her a warning? Because she knew that he'd left her that black silk stocking for one reason and one reason only—to let her know that he intended to kill her, too.

Reaching over to return the phone to the nightstand, she knocked over one of the photos and sent it tumbling to the carpet. Charlie knelt down and picked up the framed photograph. It was a picture of her and her sisters in costumes on a long-ago Mardi Gras. She had been ten at the time, she recalled, Emily six and Anne four. Sitting back on her heels, she remembered they'd gone as characters from *Peter Pan*. She had been Peter Pan and Anne had been Tinker Bell. Emily was supposed to have gone as Wendy, but when she'd seen the plain costume, she had insisted on going as Cinderella instead.

Even all those years ago, they had carved out their own paths, she thought, noting how their choice of costume reflected their personalities.

Charlie stared at herself in the green costume, the colored tights and pointed shoes. With her hair cut in a pixie, she could almost pass for a boy if it weren't for her mouth and eyelashes. The fake sword in her hand and her defiant stance said she was afraid of nothing. And she hadn't been. She had been the oldest, the protector.

Anne had made a perfect Tinker Bell, she thought as she looked at her baby sister dressed in fairy wings, holding a wand in her hand. With her blond curls and angelic smile, Anne looked like a burst of sunshine, warm and inviting, drawing everyone to her. She still did, Charlie realized proudly.

She stared at Emily. Even at six, her sister had been beautiful. Her brown eyes had been exotic looking in that perfect oval face. Her long blond hair had been swept up atop her head and a tiara woven through the curls. In the blue satin dress and white gloves, she had looked like a real princess. It was no wonder people had stopped them that day to take their picture. Emily had been stunning. And she had known it, Charlie admitted. As much as she'd loved her sister, Emily hadn't been without faults.

Yet, those last six months at college, she could have sworn she'd seen a change in her sister. Emily had seemed less self-centered. Even her switch in majors to premed and her plans to specialize in fertility problems had signaled a shift in her focus from herself to others. So what had happened?

She intended to find out, Charlie told herself as she stood. Because the killer had just made his first mistake, she reasoned as she picked up her gun and the bag with the cigarette butt. He'd warned her that he was going to come after her. And now that she knew, she intended to set a trap for him—and she was going to be the bait.

Hours later Charlie returned to her bedroom. After spending most of the night trying to devise a plan to bring the killer out into the open, she'd come to the conclusion that the only way she could do so was by coming clean with the captain. She placed her gun on the nightstand and kicked off her slippers. She needed the department and its resources if she was going to be able to pull it off, she admitted. And if the department wanted to catch him, they needed her and she intended to use that as leverage with the captain to keep him from pulling her off the case. But before she spoke to the captain, she was going to need to speak with Vince.

First thing in the morning, she promised herself as she crawled into bed. She turned out the light and her head had barely touched the pillow before she was asleep. And as she slept, she dreamed. She dreamed of old-fashioned pizza parlors with red-and-white-checkered tablecloths and candles on the table. She dreamed of a cool March night with a star-filled sky and the scent of night jasmine. She dreamed of a tall dark-haired man with blue eyes and secrets. She dreamed of Cole…

"Charlotte," he whispered her name as he drew her close and covered her mouth with his. Thrusting her fingers through his dark hair, Charlie parted her lips and gave herself to his kiss. His tongue slipped inside to taste her, to tempt her, to drive her wild. And she tasted Cole. He tasted of beer, of the sweetness of the bell pepper and tangy tomato sauce from the pizza. He tasted of desire, of need, of danger. And she wanted him. She wanted him as she had never wanted another.

When Cole broke the kiss, she started to protest. But then his lips were on her again, kissing her jaw, her chin, the sen-

sitive spot behind her ear. He nipped her earlobe with his teeth and she gasped, "Cole."

"Shh." Pushing her hair aside to expose her neck, he kissed her again.

Charlie arched her back, gave him access to her throat. She gripped his shoulders. Her heart raced. Her pulse pounded in her ears while heat pooled in her belly, arrowed downward between her thighs. "Cole," she murmured his name again.

"Tell me what you want, Charlotte."

"You. I want you," she told him.

He lifted her into his arms and carried her to her bed. "You're so beautiful," he told her as he laid her atop the mattress. Slowly, he began to unbutton her blouse. As he did so his fingers brushed her skin and set off new sensations, sharpening her hunger.

Impatient, she reached for him, tearing open his shirt, attacking the button of his jeans. And then he was beside her, his body hot and hard, his blue eyes nearly black with desire. Desire for her.

Charlie sloped his shoulders with her hands, lifted her lips to taste him. All the while he continued to kiss her, to touch her. And when he pressed her back down against the pillow she closed her eyes and gave herself up to the pleasure of him.

Lost in the feel of his mouth and his hands on her skin, it took her a moment to realize that something had changed. The mouth kissing her was no longer tender. The hands touching her no longer gentle. And when she felt something silky slide across her throat, Charlie snapped open her eyes.

His face was in shadow and she could no longer see his eyes. "Cole?"

He laughed and the sound sent a chill through her body. Frantic, she tried to push him away, to buck him off her body, but he was too strong. So she went at his face with her fin-

gers. He slapped her hard, making her head ring for a moment as she fell back onto the bed. And before she could mount another attack on him, she felt the silk tightening around her throat. Gasping for air, she clawed at the stocking, tried to catch her breath. She could feel herself losing consciousness, the world going dark. And then she heard a crash.

Charlie sat up in bed and started to cough. Struggling to breathe, she drew in several breaths. She brought a trembling hand to her throat to see if the stocking was there. It wasn't. A wave of relief rushed through her. She could feel her heart beating at a feverish pace. Her skin felt hot and cold at the same time. As her breathing began to steady, she looked around. It had been a dream. Just a dream, she told herself. There was no man, no black stocking tightening around her throat. She was home. Alone. In her bed.

And that bed was a mess. The sheets had been pulled from the mattress and were a tangle of pale blue fabric at the foot of the bed. The duvet lay on the floor in a heap. The pillows lay beside it. Her alarm clock lay in pieces on the floor next to the photo of her, Emily and Anne. The glass on the frame was cracked.

Leaning over the side of the bed, Charlie picked up the photograph. She stared at the three smiling faces of Emily, Anne and herself all those years ago. Tears welled up inside her. Hugging the picture to her chest, she squeezed her eyes shut for a moment. When she opened them again, she stared over at the dresser and the black silk stocking that had been left for her.

Suddenly last night came rushing back. Shoving aside the tangled sheets, she scrambled from the bed. She placed the photograph back on the nightstand and reminded herself to pick up a new frame. Then she picked up the pieces to her alarm clock, dumped them in the wastebasket and had just picked up her phone to call Vince when her cell phone started to ring. She hurried over to the dresser where she'd left it the night before. Snatching it up, she said, "Le Blanc."

"It's Kossak."

"Hey, I was about to give you a call. I need to talk to you about something. Can you meet me—"

"You need to get down here to the station asap," he told her.

Something in Vince's voice told her something was wrong. "Why? What's wrong?"

"I'll tell you when you get here."

"Tell me now, Kossak."

There was a long pause and Charlie thought he was going to refuse. Instead, he said, "I just got word from the doc. They've got the DNA results back on the Hill case. We've got a match on one of the semen samples."

At last, they'd caught a break, she thought. "Who does it belong to?"

"We don't have a name. But we've got a match to an unknown assailant in the system from another murder case."

Charlie knew what was coming, but still she asked, "Who was the victim?"

"Le Blanc…"

"Tell me."

"Your sister. The semen matched the DNA found at Emily's murder scene six years ago."

During his eight years on the force he had seen the captain angry, Vince thought as he and Charlie stood in the man's office. He'd seen him eat antacid tablets by the handful only a couple of weeks ago. But today was the first time he'd ever seen him chug pink antacid from the bottle like it was a soda.

"What in the hell were you thinking, Le Blanc?" the captain demanded as he paced the length of his office.

"I was thinking that I had a murderer to find, sir."

He whirled around, pinning Charlie with those deep brown eyes. "And you didn't think there was a problem with the fact that the murder you were investigating was connected to your sister's murder?"

"I only thought there might be a connection, Captain," Charlie explained. "I had no way of knowing for sure."

"Don't give me that crap. You had a damn strong suspicion that it was connected."

"It was more of a feeling, sir," Charlie told him.

"Skip the semantics, Le Blanc," the captain told her. "You decided not to tell me because you knew damn well I'd pull you off the case."

"Captain, I'm the one who suggested that Detective Le Blanc not say anything," Vince told him in an attempt to take some of the heat off his partner. "I thought her…feeling about the two murders being connected was off base because of the locations and the differing lifestyles of the victims."

"Then you exercised the same poor judgment that Le Blanc did. I should suspend you both."

Charlie took a step forward. "Detective Kossak is covering for me, sir. The truth is, he wanted me to come forward. I was the one who chose not to."

"That's not true." He looked over at Charlie. Refusing to let her take the fall by herself, he said, "I was aware that there was a good chance the two murders were connected and I didn't say anything either."

"Is that true, Le Blanc?"

She kept her eyes front and center. "No, sir. It's not. Detective Kossak didn't say anything because I asked him not to. If there's anyone at fault here, it's me. I'm the one who deserves the suspension, not him."

"Sir—"

"Quiet, Kossak," the captain told him when he started to protest. He took another swig of the antacid and shuddered. After returning the pink-colored bottle to his desk drawer, Captain Warren sat down. For several moments he said nothing, merely steepled his fingers atop the desk. Finally he looked up at them and asked, "There's no possibility that Doc Williamson is wrong about the DNA?"

"No, sir," Kossak told him.

"Then I have no choice, Le Blanc. You're off the case and on the desk until further notice. Kossak, you need me to assign someone else to work this case with you?"

Before he could answer, Charlie took a step forward, "With all due respect, sir, taking me off of this case would be a mistake. I—"

The captain shot to his feet. "You're damn lucky I'm not suspending you," he fired back. A vein throbbed angrily along his bald head.

"Le Blanc," Vince began.

"Captain, the killer has contacted me."

"What?" Vince said, stunned by the bombshell. "When?"

"He was at my house sometime yesterday," she said, keeping her gaze on the captain. She reached into the pocket of her pin-striped jacket and withdrew an envelope. "He left me this," she said and opened the envelope. A single black silk stocking fell out atop the blotter on the captain's desk.

"When did you find that?" Vince demanded before the captain could react.

"Last night when I got home. I was getting ready for bed and found it in the drawer with my pajamas."

"Dammit, Le Blanc. Are you out of your mind?" Vince

fired at her, furious and worried at the same time. "Why didn't you call it in? Why didn't you call me?"

"Kossak's right. You should have phoned this in last night," the captain told her. "Not only did you put yourself in danger, but he could have still been in the vicinity and we might have been able to catch him."

"He wasn't there, sir. I checked the area. But I did find this," she said and withdrew a bag. Inside it was a cigarette butt. "It was outside my bedroom window. It may not even belong to him, but I think it's worth testing."

"Of all the stupid things…" Vince swore. "Suppose he had been out there waiting for you? He could have grabbed you. Then what would you have done?"

"I'm a cop, Kossak, not some helpless ninny," she said, temper in her voice and her eyes. "I'd have protected myself the way I've been trained to do."

"Put a cork in it. Both of you," the captain ordered. He sat down in his chair again. "Any idea how he got in?"

"There was no sign of forced entry. The doors and windows were locked. But then locks are obviously not a problem for him since he had no trouble getting in and out of the Hill apartment. I don't think there's any point in dusting for prints. He's too smart to have left any."

"We'll send a team out to dust for prints anyway," the captain told her.

"Sir, he obviously knows who I am and that stocking was a message for me," she said.

"Yeah, that he's got you in his crosshairs," Vince told her. But she didn't even look at him, just focused on the captain and the intensity of her expression worried him. He'd seen that look before. "You've got no business on this case."

"It's not your call," she told him and then turned her attention back to the captain. "Sir, this is the first real break we've had on the case. You pull me off now and we may not get another. This guy is smart and he's arrogant. That's why he let me know he intends to kill me. But that was his first mistake. He'll make another—and when he does, we'll be waiting."

"Captain, you can't let her put herself out there as bait," Vince argued.

"He's right, Le Blanc. It's too risky. You're off the case and on a desk for now. I'll assign a police officer to guard your house."

"Then you can have these." She slapped her badge on the desk and after removing her gun from its harness, she placed it beside the badge.

"Don't be stupid, Le Blanc," Kossak told her.

The captain frowned. "Listen to your partner, Le Blanc."

"I became a cop because of this guy and I've spent six years looking for him. If using myself is the only way to draw him out, then I'll do it. I'm not going to be scared off now when I'm so close."

"You do know I could charge you with interfering in a murder investigation," the captain warned her.

"Go ahead and charge me. But I'll make bail and the minute I do, I promise you I'll be right back out there looking for him, daring him to come and get me," she replied. "My sister's a TV reporter. It shouldn't be too difficult to get myself on the news and let him know that I'm going to bring him down. That ego of his won't be able to stand having a woman threaten him. He'll come after me and when he does, I'll be ready."

"Anne would never let you risk your neck that way," Vince argued.

"She'll do it because we both lost a sister when he murdered Emily," she insisted. "I'm going to get him, Captain. I'd rather have my badge and the department backing me up when I do. But if I have to, I'll do it alone."

When it appeared the captain was weighing the decision, Vince said, "Sir, you can't seriously be considering this hare-brained scheme of hers. She'll get herself killed."

"There's a chance she'll do that no matter what I do." The captain sat back in his seat. He rubbed a hand across his bald head and sighed. "I don't like it, Le Blanc. I don't like my people playing these kind of games with a killer. But you're right. None of the other leads have panned out. Even the woman we busted for using the stolen credit cards didn't turn up anything and you still haven't been able to locate Schwitzer."

"And I'm your best shot at finding him," she said.

"Captain—"

He held up his hand. "She stays on the case."

"Thank you, sir."

"Don't thank me yet, Le Blanc. I still need to run this by the chief. And before I do, you better have a damn good plan on how you're going to catch this guy."

She explained her plan. Using herself as bait, she wanted to send a message to the killer, that she intended to bring him down, to challenge his ego by telling him that as smart as he thought he was, she was smarter. She was making it her mission to bring him in and see him locked in a cage like the animal he was. "His ego won't let him stay silent for long. He'll come after me."

And that's what Vince was worried about. That the killer would come after her. He'd been smart enough to get away with it twice now. And as good a cop as Charlie was, she had a personal stake in this one—a personal stake that he feared would get her killed. "What about the FBI, sir? Shouldn't we bring them in?" Vince asked. As difficult as it would be to work with them, it would be added protection for Charlie.

He pursed his lips together. "You've got a point. It might not be a bad idea having them in on this."

"Captain," Charlie said, "you bring them in now and you know they'll take over the case. You remember what happened the last time we brought the feds in on a case like this. Remember the panic that gripped this city when the news got out that we had a serial killer in our midst? We wasted a lot of time chasing down false leads because suddenly every Tom, Dick and Harry who was anywhere near the killings looked suspicious to their neighbors, the people they worked with, even strangers on the street."

"You think not letting the public know they may have a serial killer in their midst won't backfire on the department?" Vince fired back. "What if he kills someone else in the meantime?"

"I'm the one he's after, sir," she argued. "All I'm asking is for you to hold off and give my plan a try. If we go public now and set off another serial-killer panic, he could disappear and no telling how long before he surfaces again."

"I'll talk to the chief. But I'm not making any promises. I may be going along with this plan of yours for now, but I agree with Kossak. I don't like using you as bait."

"I understand, sir," she said.

"All right then, you both have a lot to do. Let's get on it."

"Captain, there's one more thing," Charlie said.

"Yes?"

"Yesterday evening I caught Jason Stratton in Hill's apartment. He said he was looking for a CD he loaned her. But I think he was lying."

The captain frowned. "Should I bother asking what you were doing there in the first place?"

"Just following a hunch, sir. Anyway, whatever he was looking for, he didn't find it. If we're right that Hill was blackmailing the reverend, maybe she had something on Jason Stratton, too. I'd like to put a tail on him."

"All right. But what is it you think you're going to find?" the captain asked.

"I don't know yet. But when I find it, it's going to lead us to the killer."

Sixteen

"Is anything wrong?" Anne asked Vince as she sat across from him in the car.

"No, why?"

"Because you barely said ten words at dinner and you didn't seem to be all that interested in the movie."

"Sorry. I guess I have other things on my mind," he told her.

She'd noticed and it worried her that he had been so distracted all evening. "Want to talk about it?"

"Thanks, but no. It's something I have to work out."

Determined to salvage the evening, she said, "What do you say we go get some coffee and beignets? I bet that'll take your mind off whatever's bothering you."

He glanced over at her. "To tell you the truth, I'd just as soon pass. Would you mind if we just called it a night?"

Anne felt as though she had been kicked. To have Vince slam the brakes on what she had thought was becoming a serious relationship hurt far more than she'd ever dreamed it would. Not that she intended to let him know he'd hurt her. She didn't. If she had nothing else, she did have her pride. "Sure. If that's what you want."

"It's probably better. I'm not exactly good company to-night," he said and turned the car in the direction of her apartment. "Thanks for being such a good sport."

"No problem," she said, feeling another hit to her heart. She stole a glance at him, committed everything about him to memory. The way his dark hair brushed the collar of his shirt. The scar on his chin that he'd told her was the result of being tripped by his older brother and taking a tumble down some stairs. The mouth that had kissed her so hungrily. Realizing that she was torturing herself, she turned away and stared out the window and allowed the radio to fill the silence.

Fifteen minutes later, he pulled the car to a stop in front of her apartment and shut off the engine. "Hang on. Let me get the door for you," he said when she unhooked her seat belt and reached for the door.

"You don't need to get out. I'm fine." Quick as a snap, she was out of the car.

"Anne—"

"See you," she said and slammed the door shut.

"Anne," he called out.

She didn't stop. Holding her head high, she hurried down the walkway to the front door, determined to get inside before the tears burning at the back of her eyes started to fall. She dug in her purse, finally found the blasted key. But in her rush to unlock the door and get inside, she dropped it.

Vince snatched up the key before she could get to it. Inserting it into the lock, he opened the door for her.

"Thanks." Not looking at him, she reached for the key in his outstretched palm, grabbed it and started inside.

"Aren't you even going to tell me good night?"

Anne swallowed hard. Doing her best to school her expression, she turned around to face him. "Good night, Vincent. Thanks for dinner and the movie."

When she started to shut the door on him, he blocked it. "Anne, what's going on here? You act like you can't wait to get away from me."

"I think you're confused, Vincent. You're the one who spent the evening counting the minutes until you could escape. Well, the torture's over. You've put in your time, so you can go to wherever it is you've wanted to be all evening."

He looked at her like she'd lost her mind. Maybe she had, Anne admitted. All she knew was that she felt as if her heart had been stomped on and she felt like an idiot to boot for thinking Vince felt something more for her. But then, she shouldn't be surprised. In the half-dozen times they'd gone out, hadn't she been the one to initiate plans? And hadn't she been the one to kiss him first? She'd even convinced herself that he was being gallant when he hadn't taken things further than a kiss between them when she had all but invited him to do so. God, how humiliating. How could she have been so stupid? Vincent Kossak wasn't interested in her. But being a gentleman and her sister's partner, he probably wanted to let her down gently. Well, dammit, she wasn't a kid and she sure as hell didn't need Vincent Kossak feeling sorry for her.

"I'll admit, I was distracted this evening. But it had nothing to do with you, or me not wanting to be with you."

"It didn't?" she asked skeptically, not wanting to get her hopes up.

"No. There's some stuff going on at work and…well, it's complicated. I should have just canceled tonight instead of making you suffer my company. That was unfair of me and I'm sorry."

He looked at her with genuine regret in his brown eyes and for a moment, she wondered if she'd misread the signs. Maybe she was wrong. Maybe he wasn't giving her the brush-off after all. Hope flickered in her heart. "It's all right."

"No, it's not. But the truth is, Anne, things are a little crazy for me right now. So I'm not going to have much free time—"

Reality came slamming back. "Why don't we stop playing games, Vincent. I like you and I was hoping you'd like me. But obviously, you're not interested," she said and was mortified when she heard her voice crack. Furious with her show of weakness, she hardened her resolve. "So why don't you just say goodbye and skip the lame excuses."

"What in the hell are you talking about?" he demanded.

Her next-door neighbor's porch light came on and Mrs. Guillory stuck her head out the door. "Everything all right, Anne?" she asked, looking from her to Vince.

"Everything's fine, Mrs. Guillory," she said. "I'm sorry if I disturbed you."

"No problem, dear." She eyed Vince again. "I'm right next door if you need me."

"Thank you," she told her. Once the door closed, she turned to Vince. "I don't want to make this any more awkward for either one of us than it already is. So I'm just going to say goodbye."

"The hell you will," he told her and followed her inside. "Anne, I'm not going anywhere until you tell me what's going on."

"Fine," she said and marched into the living room. Turning, she faced him. "What's going on, Vincent Kossak, is that I'm letting you off the hook."

"You're letting me off the hook?"

"That's right," she told him. "You don't have to pretend anymore."

"And just what is it that I'm supposed to be pretending about?"

Anne closed her eyes a moment, steeling herself. She could do this, she told herself. She *would* do this. All she had left was her pride. Her pride would see her through this. "That there's anything going on between us or that there ever will be."

"There isn't something going on between us?"

She glared at him, wondered how he could be so cruel. "We both know that you didn't want to go out with me in the first place and I forced your hand. And now that I've made it pretty clear that I want more than a few kisses from you, you're trying to let me down gently. Well, congratulations. I finally get it. Now, will you please just go?"

"You think I don't want you?"

"I don't think it, Vincent. I know it," she told him. She walked across the room, needing distance from him. Then she turned and faced him. "If you'd wanted me, you never would have walked out of here last night when I made it as plain as the nose on my face that I wanted you to stay."

He came over to her in a flash, shot his arms out on either side of her, caging her between himself and the wall. "Tell me something," he said, his voice dangerously soft, his eyes hot. "Does insanity run in your family? Or is it just you who's crazy?"

"I'm not crazy," she fired back.

He leaned closer until his body was almost touching hers, until she could feel the warmth of his breath on her face. "You must be if you think that I don't want you."

Hope fluttered to life inside her. Her heart beat frantically and when she tried to speak, the words stuck in her throat. Finally, she managed to say, "Vince…"

He crushed her mouth with his. He kissed her long and deep until she wasn't sure where his lips began and hers ended. And when she thought he couldn't possibly shock her more, he caught her hand and pressed it against the front of his slacks. He was hot, hard and definitely aroused. Lifting his head, he asked, "Does that feel like I don't want you?"

"Vince, I—"

He dragged her hand up to his chest, pressed it against his heart. And she felt the rapid *thump, thump, thump* against her fingertips. "Does that feel like the heart of a man who's not interested in you? Of someone who wants to break things off?"

"No," she managed to get out.

"You're damn right it doesn't. I want you, Anne Le Blanc. So much that I can't sleep at night for wanting to make love to you. So much that I can barely go five minutes without thinking about you."

Her heart was so full, Anne felt sure it would burst. She threw her arms around him, kissed him with all the love in her heart. "I'm an idiot," she told him.

"Yes, you are. How could you think for a minute that I didn't want you? Don't you realize how beautiful and special you are?"

"No," she said honestly.

"Well, you are," he told her. He cupped her face in his hands and gently brushed her mouth with his. When he lifted his head, he said, "You're beautiful and special, Anne. And I want you more than I've ever wanted anything or anyone in my life."

"Talk is cheap, Kossak."

He arched his brow. "Is that so?"

She nodded.

"So what do you suggest I do to prove I'm telling the truth?"

She slid her arms up around his neck again. "I suggest you show me."

Charlie watched a repeat of the earlier newscast. For two days now every TV station in the city had been rerunning clips from the press conference called by the chief of police and the captain, giving them an update on the Hill murder investigation. They had been careful that the information released had been truthful. They did have a number of leads in the case, robbery didn't appear to be the motive for the murder even though jewelry and cash had been taken. They also reissued a picture of Schwitzer and a copy of the fuzzy surveillance shot of the man with the dark glasses, saying that both were persons of interest. Then she had capped off the statement by looking directly into the cameras and telling the killer to enjoy his freedom for now because they were going to find him and when they did, she was making it her personal mission to see him locked in a cage like the animal he was.

She had been so sure that his ego would not have allowed him to ignore the challenge from her. But so far, he hadn't contacted her again. And getting the okay to put a tail on Jason Stratton had come too late. The kid had already skipped town. The only good news was that their investigation had church officials looking into the Reverend Lawrence's financial records at the church. Her hunch was that his tenure as a minister was near an end—which, if she was correct and he had been skimming money from the church coffers to pay Francesca, would be a positive thing. And while they hadn't ruled out either the reverend or Jason Stratton as the killer yet, she just didn't see either of them as having the brass to break into her home and leave that stocking. Who did have the temerity to do such a thing was Cole Stratton, she thought. The man certainly didn't let a little thing like her telling him she wasn't interested stop him from calling her and asking her out.

Then again, she wasn't exactly uninterested, she admitted. A fact that she was sure her response to his kiss had told him. The kiss had been a mistake, she told herself. So was this attraction she had for Cole. Getting involved with a murder suspect or even someone connected to an investigation was not only against the department's rules, it was against her own personal ones. Besides, even without the investigation, there was no place in her life for a relationship with anyone, let alone a man like him. She simply couldn't let anyone or anything distract her from her goal—to find the man who killed her sister.

Shaking off thoughts of Cole, Charlie signed onto the department's computer system. She had a lot riding on this, she reminded herself. In addition to her job, which she knew would be on the line if her plan backfired, she also had her promise to Emily. She'd failed her sister once already when she hadn't gone to her that day. She wouldn't fail her again now. She needed the killer to contact her again. But obviously he wasn't going to do so as long as she had a plainclothes officer keeping tabs on her house. She would have to convince the captain to pull the surveillance on her house.

Getting the captain and the chief to buy into her plan in the first place hadn't been easy and she wasn't sure how much longer they would agree to withhold the link between the two killings. But as difficult as it had been selling the plan to the chief and the captain, selling Vince on the idea had been even harder. Her partner had been totally against it and he would, no doubt, be against pulling the officer from surveillance. She would just have to make sure Vince didn't decide to become her shadow instead.

In the meantime, she reminded herself to be grateful that he and Mackenzie were following up on a tip that came in on Schwitzer. It gave her time to press for results on the DNA test on J. P. Stratton and the fetus to see if he was indeed the father of Francesca's baby. If he wasn't, that was another angle she would have to consider.

But thirty minutes later she returned to her desk wishing, not for the first time, that the DNA testing facilities produced results as quickly as the crime labs in the cop shows on TV. Satisfied that she'd at least gotten the lab to refocus on her case, she returned to her desk to do another sweep of the data banks.

Two hours later, she hit pay dirt. Following a hunch, she had gone back to the rap sheet on Schwitzer. He'd done time twice—for insurance fraud three years ago in a country-club prison and six years prior to that he'd served a year in a Florida facility for extortion. It was the Florida conviction that interested her. Several phone calls later, she received the file transfer on the arrest. According to the report, Schwitzer and an underage female had been charged with running a scam whereby they taped the girl having sex with businessmen. In each case, the man had been attending a convention at a beachfront resort when the girl had come on to them and taken them back to her hotel room. Once both parties were undressed, Schwitzer would show up pretending to be the girl's outraged older brother and threatening to press charges for statutory rape because she was underage. Of course, money had made everything go away.

Because the girl was a juvenile, Charlie couldn't get access to her record. But she'd bet her next paycheck that the underage female had been Francesca Hill. Common sense told her that the lessons a sixteen-year-old Mary Frances had learned had been refined and put to use by the grown-up Francesca Hill. She'd had something on the minister, Charlie told herself. While she wouldn't have been able to pull off the underage scam, she would have pulled a scam no less. Whatever it was, she had used it to blackmail the reverend. She was sure of it. And how many others had she been blackmailing? So far, they'd turned up three different bank accounts and all with healthy balances. Who else was she blackmailing? Jason Stratton? she wondered. What had he really been looking for?

Whatever it was, he'd thought it was still in that apartment. Grabbing her jacket, she headed for the Mill House Apartments.

Thirty minutes later, Charlie stood at the door of Francesca Hill's apartment. Try as she might to have another guard placed at the crime scene, the chief had refused, citing the shortage of manpower on the streets. That and the fact that a crime-scene team had already been over the apartment. According to the chief, if evidence had been overlooked, then a closer look needed to be taken at the department. So she had let the subject drop. But there was still something that nagged at her.

She unlocked the door. The place still had the same eerie feeling, she thought as she moved through the apartment. She went from room to room, searching for something she had missed. What was it that Jason had been looking for? she asked herself. But twenty minutes later, she still was at a loss.

She returned to the living room and was about to leave when her eyes went back to the bookcases. Walking over to the wall of black-lacquered shelves, she scanned the titles. She never would have taken Francesca for a reader, Charlie thought as she noted several titles that had graced the best-seller lists, along with some of the classics. Charlie picked up a few, noted the spines hadn't even been broken. Either Francesca Hill had been particularly careful or she hadn't read any of the books.

The woman certainly had eclectic tastes, Charlie thought as she continued to look over the titles. There were several books about sex, pleasure points for the male, and manuals with explicit how-to photos. And sandwiched in between a book about the Kama Sutra and the joys of being a dominatrix was a bible. The moment she saw it, Charlie knew this was what she had been looking for. Francesca Hill hadn't struck her as the type of woman who read many books. And of the books she did read, she doubted that the bible was among them.

Removing it from the shelf, Charlie opened it and began flipping through the pages. She thumbed through Genesis, the Gospels of Paul, John and the two others. Then she found it. Buried between the pages of the Gospel of Luke was a section of the book that appeared to have been removed and glued back. Carefully, she removed the pages and beneath them, she found a hollow section with three discs and two letters.

Pay dirt!

She opened the letters first, skimmed the declaration of love and read the signature. "Jason." So this was what he had been looking for. Quickly skimming the remainder of the letter, she understood why he hadn't wanted his father to see it.

But what interested her more than the love letters were the discs. She took them and popped the first one in the DVD player. Francesca came into view. She was wearing a short plaid skirt, a plain white blouse and Mary Jane shoes. Her hair was pulled atop her head in a ponytail.

"I was a bad girl today," she said into the camera and lowered her gaze.

"Tell me what you did," a man's voice commanded.

"I let a boy touch me."

"Where did he touch you?" the man asked and Charlie thought she recognized the voice.

"Here," Francesca said, touching her breasts. She slid her hands down her body and touched the area between her thighs. "And here."

"Show me, child. Show me how he touched you."

She walked over to the man seated with his back to the

camera and taking his hand, she placed it on her breasts. "Like this," she said.

He squeezed her breasts. Although she couldn't see the man's face, his voice was aroused as he asked, "Is this how he touched you? Through your clothes?"

She nodded. "At first."

"Then what happened?"

"He took off my blouse and I let him touch my flesh," she said.

"Show me how he touched you."

Slowly she stripped off the school blouse and when her breasts were exposed, he filled his hands with them. He squeezed the large milky-white breasts, plucked at the nipples. "What else?"

"He put his mouth on me," she told him.

"Like this?" he asked as he suckled one breast while kneading the other.

"Yes," she whispered. "Then he told me to touch him."

"Show me where you touched him," he commanded.

With her upper body bare, she dropped to her knees and reached for his belt. She freed him and he moaned as she took him into her mouth. Within moments, it was over, his body shook as he climaxed and when he finished, she said, "Are you going to punish me, Reverend?"

"Yes, child. You know I must."

Disgusted, Charlie shut off the machine and removed the disc. She popped in the second and third discs. Both revealed Francesca in sexual encounters—one with a local judge and the other with a man she didn't recognize. She placed all three discs in an evidence bag and exited the apartment. After locking up, she took the elevator down and once she was out on the street, she took out her cell phone.

"Kossak," he answered.

"How quick can you get back to the station?"

"I'm on my way now. Schwitzer had already taken off before we got there. Why? What's up?"

"I think I've found out what Francesca had on the good reverend."

Vince sat in the captain's office with Charlie and Mackenzie. The torrid letters from Jason Stratton made for interesting reading, but murder? He doubted it. Still, he couldn't rule out anything when it came to the lengths people would go in the name of love. What he did think someone might find worth killing for was the discs. He watched with disgust as a man who was entrusted with the spiritual needs of children engaged in what was no doubt a reenactment of his relationship with Francesca as a girl. The other discs showing Francesca engaged in sex with a very married judge and a man he'd recognized as J. P. Stratton's good friend and financial adviser was damning as well.

"The judge certainly looks a lot different without those judicial robes of his," Charlie remarked. "I wonder what the good citizens who elected him on his platform of family values would think of his extracurricular activities."

The captain shut off the machine. "I guess this explains why the Hill woman's bank account was so healthy." He leaned back in his chair. "Do you think there's a chance Stratton knew about the other men?"

"I doubt it," Charlie said. "The man's ego wouldn't have allowed it."

"Le Blanc's right, Captain." Having dealt with the man several times during these past few weeks, Vince was sure that J. P. Stratton would not have taken news of his fiancée's infidelities sitting down.

"These give us enough cause for a warrant," Charlie commented.

"Yes, they do," the captain said. "Go ahead and get the warrants for all three of them and bring them in for questioning."

"And DNA tests," she added.

"All right," he said. "But make sure Kossak goes with you to bring them in. No more going off without backup. Understood?"

"Yes, sir," she said.

The captain picked up the phone. "I'll give the chief a heads-up on what's going down."

After leaving the captain's office, Vince sent Mackenzie to find out who was available in the D.A.'s office so they could work on the warrants. While he and Charlie headed back to their desks, he filled her in on his frustration at not getting Schwitzer.

"Well, at least we caught a break with the discs," she told him.

"Yeah." He paused. "But you shouldn't have gone off alone. We know the guy can get past security at that place. What if he'd been there?"

"He wasn't. And if he had been, I would have handled it. What's up with you, Kossak? I'm your partner, not your little sister. I can take care of myself."

"You're right," he admitted. "It's just that…hell, I don't know. I don't have a good feeling about this one. This is the first time someone's targeted you specifically."

"I know. And I appreciate the concern, but I'm still a cop. You need to remember that and don't go all macho and protective on me."

She was right, he decided. He was acting like a macho ass. When they turned the corner, he saw the cluster of detectives around Le Blanc's desk. And when a few nudges and whispers sent them scattering, Vince saw the reason why. A vase with what had to be two dozen red tulips were sitting on her desk. His first thought was that they were from the killer. But when Charlie marched over to her desk, snatched the card from the arrangement, read it and then crushed it in her fist and tossed it in the trash, he knew that it wasn't. "Problem?" he asked.

"Nothing I can't handle."

But he wasn't so sure. Charlie was pretty closemouthed about her personal life. And while he'd known she'd dated a few guys over the years, he'd never gotten the impression that any of them were serious. Until recently. He hadn't reached the age of thirty-two without being able to recognize sexual chemistry between two people. And there was a boatload of it between his partner and Cole Stratton. The phone ringing at his desk broke into his thoughts. He grabbed it. "Kossak."

"Vincent, it's Anne."

All it took was the sound of her voice and he was like a teenage boy again, suffering with raging hormones and an all-consuming need to see her. "Hi," he finally managed to get out.

"I'm sorry to bother you at work, but your cell went to voice mail. It's about tonight."

Tonight they had planned a quiet dinner at her place. Just the two of them. "Is everything okay?"

"Yes and no. Everything's okay, but I caught an assignment and I'm going to be tied up most of the evening. I'll be lucky to get home before ten. So I'm afraid I'm going to have to cancel dinner."

Disappointed and wanting to see her, he asked, "What about after ten? You have any plans?"

"No," she said and he could hear the smile in her voice. "Did you have something in mind?"

"Yeah. I'll see you at your place at ten." When he hung up the phone and turned around, Charlie was watching him. "That was Anne."

"No kidding," she said dryly. "Sounds like things are getting serious between you two."

"I guess you could say that." The truth was that for the first time since his divorce he could actually imagine himself sharing his life with someone.

"You haven't said anything to her about the DNA match to Emily, have you?"

Vince sobered. Keeping information from her about her sister's killer had made him uncomfortable. It also meant he'd had to walk a fine line. And he thought he'd done a damn good job of keeping his work and his personal lives separate. "You should know me better than that. That information is confidential and part of an ongoing investigation."

She nodded. "You know, she isn't going to be happy with either of us when she finds out."

"Yeah, I know." And he was not looking forward to it.

He fastened the onyx and diamond cuff links in the cuffs of his shirt, then brushed a minuscule speck of lint from the collar of his jacket. After studying his reflection in the mirror, he smiled, satisfied with the result. He had no doubt that the lady he was escorting to the cocktail party that evening would be pleased, too.

Snatching his car keys from the top of the bureau, he was about to leave when his unregistered cell phone rang. The phone had been silent for weeks—ever since the night he'd killed Francesca. Since Francesca had been the only one with the number and he'd gone to great lengths to make sure no one could trace the number to him, the ringing phone now could mean only one of two things. That that bitch Francesca had given the number to someone else and that someone knew about him. Or that Detective Charlotte Le Blanc was even more resourceful than he'd thought. As risky as that would be for him, he hoped it was the latter.

But when he retrieved the phone and saw the caller ID, he was disappointed. "Yes," *he answered and was pleased at how pleasant he sounded.*

"This is Danielle, Francesca's friend," *the woman on the other end of the line said.* "I'm not sure if you remember me."

"Of course I remember you," *he told her.* "I always remember a beautiful woman. What can I do for you, Danielle?"

"Actually I'm the one who can do something for you."

"Is that so?"

"Yes," *she told him but he didn't miss the nerves behind the bravado.*

"As lovely as you are, I don't pay women for sex. I don't have to."

"That's not why I'm calling," *she informed him, the insult hitting her as he hoped it would.* "I'm calling about Francesca and your relationship with her."

"And what relationship would that be?" *he asked.*

"Oh, I think you know," *she told him.* "And seeing as how there's a big fat reward for information about Francesca's murder, I'm thinking the police would be real interested in knowing that you were sleeping with her."

"And what makes you think the police will believe you if I deny it?"

"Because, if you'll recall, Francesca and I were roommates for a while. We were pretty close back then. You know, best friends."

"Francesca didn't have friends. She had people she used," *he reminded her.*

"You're right, she did," *she said, her voice tight.* "So you won't be surprised to hear that she made a little movie starring the two of you."

He clenched his jaw. "You're lying."

"Am I? Then I guess we'll see what the police have to say

when I tell them about the interesting video that I saw on Francesca's digital camera that day when I...borrowed her earrings."

He thought back to a month ago, the new digital camera she'd been so tickled with that had been on her dresser. The bitch. She had taped them, he realized, furious with himself for being so careless. He'd known about the scam she'd been running before her engagement. He'd even known that she had continued to shake down the minister and the others. But he'd gone through that apartment and made sure there were no hidden cameras for her to use against him. "What do you want?"

"I'm not greedy. Not like Francesca was," she said smugly. "All I'm asking is that you match the reward I'm passing on by not going to the police."

"I'm sure the police would be interested in hearing that you tried to extort money from me." He paused, gave her a moment to let his words sink in. "You do know that blackmail is a crime, don't you? That you could go to jail."

"I won't go to jail, not when I tell them what I know," she argued, but she didn't sound quite so confident anymore.

"Are you sure about that? Do you really think the police will just let you walk away when you've withheld evidence in a murder investigation, obstructed justice? Another punishable crime, by the way." He paused. "But I'm not an unreasonable man. If you really do have the disc, I'll give you ten thousand dollars for it."

"Ten thousand! No way, it's worth more than that," she said and lowered her voice and he could hear the background noise of the casino where she was working. "Fifty thousand."

"Twenty and not a dime more."

"All right. All right. I'll take it," she said.

"Shall we meet tonight?"

"No. I'm working until midnight. Bring me the money to-morrow in cash. I'll meet you in the casino's restaurant at noon. We'll do the exchange there."

"Tomorrow at noon it is. And, Danielle?"

"Yes."

"Not a word to anyone."

"No, I won't say anything," she said.

After hanging up the phone, he retrieved the special box from the secret compartment in his desk. Opening it, he removed a pair of black silk stockings. He slipped them in the pocket of his jacket and whistling, he headed out the door.

Seventeen

Charlie poured herself a cup of what passed for coffee in the squad room the next morning. She took a sip and nearly gagged. That jolt of caffeine would certainly wake her up if it didn't kill her first, she thought as she headed for her desk.

"Hey, Le Blanc, what cat drug you in?" Jake Marino called out as she walked by the detective's desk.

"The same one that you tried to pass off as a hair rug yesterday."

"Good one, Le Blanc," someone called out amidst snickers and laughs.

Any other time she would have enjoyed scoring one against the brash Marino, but not today when she was still brooding over yesterday's turn of events. When she reached her desk she sat down, but her thoughts remained on the Hill case. She and Vince had gotten the warrants they'd needed the previous afternoon. For all the good it had done them, she thought, frustrated anew as she recalled trying to round up the three stars of Francesca's sex tapes. Unfortunately, the minister had been out of town, participating in some type of religious retreat in northern Louisiana. The judge had clammed up almost immediately and demanded his lawyer, who, in turn, had given them the name of the hotel in Dallas where the judge had been delivering a speech on the night of Francesca's murder. No fewer than six witnesses had vouched that the judge had been there. While the man may have been guilty of adultery and hypocrisy for preaching family values that he didn't practice, he wasn't a murderer—unless he had discovered a way to be in two places at once.

The moneyman had lawyered up just as quickly as the judge. He'd also given the name of the married socialite he had spent the night with while the lady's husband was away on business. The woman in question had confirmed the tryst, but she had made it clear that if any legal proceedings resulted she would perjure herself before admitting to the affair. She had no intention of risking the loss of her husband and the cushy lifestyle that came with being a rich man's wife. Fortunately for the woman, Charlie doubted it would come to that. Aside from the fact that their alibis checked out, she didn't see the moneyman, the minister or the judge as a killer.

And she had come to that conclusion because of Emily. Not exactly sound detective work, she admitted. But then this case hadn't been just another homicide investigation. It had been personal from the moment she'd seen the black silk stocking. The person who had killed Francesca Hill and her sister had been someone Emily had been involved with romantically. And she knew her sister well enough to know that not one of the three suspects would have peaked her sister's interest. Besides, the man who had left her that black silk stocking would have been too smart to allow himself to be blackmailed by Francesca Hill.

Wondering who that man was, she shifted her gaze to the tulips that had arrived yesterday with an invitation to dinner from Cole. Although she knew she'd done the right thing by ignoring the request, it hadn't stopped her from thinking about him. An image of his face filled her mind. Her pulse quickened as she remembered the pull she'd felt when she'd been near him. Realizing what she was doing, Charlie slammed on the mental brakes. The man was occupying her thoughts far too frequently, she told herself. Determined to get him out of her mind, she took another fortifying sip of her coffee and picked up the phone to retrieve her voice mail. "You have ten messages," the mechanical voice said. "To retrieve your messages, press one."

This is what you get for not rerouting your office calls to the cell phone, Charlie told herself. She punched in the number one on the phone pad and as the messages began to play, she jotted down names and numbers.

"Message ten," the robotic voice announced.

At last, Charlie thought and waited for someone else to tell her they had a lead in the Hill murder case and wanted to collect the reward.

"Detective Le Blanc, are you there?" a familiar female voice asked. "Guess not. This is Danielle Marceau. You came to see me a couple of weeks ago about Francesca's murder. I, um, I have some information that might help. But before I give it to you, I want to talk about the reward."

Charlie gripped the receiver of her phone and listened closely. She thought she could hear a Tina Turner song playing in the background.

"But I'm going to want, you know, immunity for not turning it over sooner," she said anxiously. "Plus the reward. Anyway, give me a call when you get this message," she said and rattled off both her home and cell numbers.

Then the line went dead. Charlie noted the time from the voice mail as twelve forty-five the previous night. After hitting save on the voice mail, she punched in the number Danielle had given her.

She picked up on the fourth ring. "Hello…"

"Danielle, it's Detective Le Blanc—"

"…sorry I missed your call. Leave a number at the beep and I'll get back to you."

At the beep, Charlie hit the off button. When she had a dial tone, she called Danielle's cell phone. "Hi, this is Danielle. Leave a message and I'll get back to you."

"Danielle, it's Detective Le Blanc. I'm returning your call. You can reach me at my office or on my cell." And after she had left both numbers, she redialed Danielle's home number and left the same message.

Charlie didn't leave her desk for the next three hours—not even to go to the bathroom. Every thirty minutes, between calls to the D.A.'s office for the warrants they needed to obtain the bank records of the three suspects, she had tried both Danielle's home and cell numbers, leaving messages each time. She also tried at the casino where Danielle worked, but was told she wasn't scheduled to come in until one o'clock that afternoon. When noon arrived and she still had no word from Danielle, Charlie had a sick feeling that something was wrong.

Picking up the phone, she dialed Vince on his cell. After losing the coin toss last night, she'd been stuck with the leg-work for the warrants while Vince made the three-hour drive to Shreveport, Louisiana, to pick up the Reverend Lawrence.

"Kossak," he answered.

"It's Le Blanc. Any problems picking up the reverend?" she asked.

"Other than a few astonished ministers, no."

"What's your ETA?" she asked.

"We should be back within the hour. Any luck getting the warrants for the bank records?"

"I've got the one for the reverend's personal account. I'm still working on the one for the church," she told him. She went on to explain about the call from Danielle Marceau and her growing concern that something was wrong. "I'm going to take Mackenzie and head over to her apartment. I'll call you from there."

Thirty minutes later, she and Mackenzie arrived at Danielle's apartment building. She pressed the buzzer repeatedly, but received no answer.

"It's possible she's just out, Detective," Mackenzie suggested.

"It's possible." But she didn't think that was the case. When she saw the curtains move in the window of the downstairs apartment where Danielle's neighbor, Mrs. Russell, lived, Charlie said, "I know who can tell us whether she's home or not." Charlie pushed the buzzer with the name R. Russell beside it.

"Yes?"

"Mrs. Russell, it's Detective Le Blanc. My partner and I were here a couple of weeks ago to see Ms. Marceau. I wondered if I could talk to you for a minute."

Mrs. Russell buzzed her and Mackenzie into the building. And once she was satisfied that the baby-faced young man was actually a detective, Mrs. Russell said, "I was debating whether or not I should call you. I'm worried about Danielle. That music has been playing all night, the same records over and over."

It was a tune from the same sound track she'd heard on the phone message left last night, she realized, and her feeling that something was wrong intensified. "Mrs. Russell, have you seen Danielle today?"

"No. I knocked on her door a little while ago to see if she was all right, but she didn't answer. I'm worried she might have slipped in the bathtub and hit her head or something."

"Maybe she went out and forgot to turn off the CD player before she left," Mackenzie offered.

"No, she's home. I saw her come in last night. She had a gentleman friend stop by, but he didn't stay long and he left alone. So Danielle's home."

"Is it possible she left this morning without you seeing her?" Charlie asked.

"Not that one. I was up at six and that girl never stirs before noon. She's up there in the apartment."

And if she was, Charlie had the sick feeling that Danielle was dead. "Mrs. Russell, do you remember what time it was that you saw Danielle come in last night?"

"Let me see," she said and tipped her head to the side. "It was around twelve-thirty. I remember because I had just finished watching a rerun of *Designing Women* on the Lifetime Channel and it's on from midnight to twelve-thirty."

Fifteen minutes later Danielle had placed the call to her. "This gentleman friend of Danielle's, did you get a look at him?"

"I sure did. He was a handsome one, too."

"Can you describe him to me?" Charlie asked. "How old he was? What he looked like?"

"Well, he was young. Very tall, nicely dressed. He had on one of them long coats, but I could see he was wearing a tuxedo underneath," she told her.

"By young do you mean twenty? Thirty?"

She tipped her head. "Older than this young detective, I think. Maybe in his late twenties or early thirties."

"Do you know what color hair he had? What color eyes?"

"It's hard to say. He was wearing one of those dashing hats. You know the kind the detectives in the old movies wear."

A fedora, Charlie realized, which would be ideal if someone was trying to shield their face. "What about his eyes? His features?"

"His eyes were light. Maybe blue or green. I only got a quick look at his face when he passed under the streetlight."

Late twenties to early thirties with blue or green eyes. The description fit both Aaron and Cole Stratton, as well as Marcus Schwitzer. "Mrs. Russell, do you think you would be able to recognize him if you saw him again?"

"Absolutely," she said. "A widow my age living alone doesn't get to see handsome, young men all that often. So when I do see one, I remember him."

"We may need you to come down to the station later," she told her.

"Will I get to ride in a police car?"

"I think that can be arranged," Charlie said.

The woman's eyes twinkled. "Wait till I tell the girls at church." When the door buzzer sounded, she peaked out the window. "It's that nice Detective Kossak," she said and buzzed him inside. She leaned closer and whispered, "If you haven't noticed, he's a good-looking one. Got a nice tush."

Charlie nearly choked at the old woman's comment. And she definitely would have laughed if it were not for the fact that she was fairly sure that the young woman upstairs was dead.

She opened the door to Vince. "Hello, Detective."

He nodded. "Mrs. Russell."

Charlie quickly filled Vince in on the conversation. Then she turned to Mrs. Russell and asked, "Would you happen to have a key to Danielle's apartment?"

"Afraid not, dear. I had one. But Danielle lost hers a few weeks ago and had to use the one she gave me and she never got around to getting another one made."

"No problem," Charlie said and after excusing themselves they went upstairs to Danielle's apartment. Charlie knocked on the door. "Danielle, it's Detective Le Blanc." But the only sound coming from the apartment was the music. She withdrew her weapon. So did Vince and Mackenzie. She nodded to Vince and he kicked the door in.

With weapons drawn, they entered the apartment. But they were too late, Charlie realized. The place had been tossed. Vince hit the off button on the CD player and the sudden silence was disquieting. But even before they went into the bedroom, she knew what they would find. Danielle lying on the bed with her eyes open and staring up at the ceiling, a single black silk stocking lying beside her body. Guilt hit her like a fist. Because she had convinced the captain and the chief to keep quiet about the linked murders, another woman was dead.

"Mackenzie, check the rest of the apartment and make sure you don't touch anything."

Vince turned to her. "You all right?"

She nodded.

"Then I'm going to go call this in."

And while Vince was on the phone with the department, Charlie went back out into the living room. She saw the red light blinking on the answering machine. Donning a pair of gloves, she pressed the button.

"Danielle, it's Ellen," a woman with an accent that was a cross between a Mississippi drawl and a Texas twang said. "Tina, Cissy and I are planning a girls' spa weekend on the Gulf Coast at the end of the month. Do you think you can come? Give me a call and let me know."

The phone beeped and a dial tone sounded, indicating a hang up. The second message began, "Hi, Danielle. This is Sean. We met the other night at the casino. I was calling to see if you're free this Friday for that dinner I promised to buy you for changing my luck at the tables." He left both home and cell numbers.

There were two more calls, both hang ups, one that she knew was hers, Charlie thought. She listened to the rest of the calls on the machine and was disappointed to find that all of them were from her. Picking up the phone, she hit the redial button for the last number that Danielle had called.

After the second ring, a man answered, "Cole Stratton."

After leaving the crime-scene techs to process Danielle Marceau's apartment, he and Charlie returned to the station while Mackenzie arranged to bring Mrs. Russell down to look at mug shots. Vince couldn't help noticing that Charlie had been unusually quiet during the drive back to the station. Even now, standing in the captain's office where they had just related the situation, she had shown no emotion and offered no commentary—both unusual for Charlie.

The captain shook his head. "Tell Doc Williamson we need the body processed asap and we need a DNA comparison yesterday," he commanded. "See if the neighbor can identify anyone and get whatever warrants you need. Where are you with the minister?"

"He's in interrogation. He won't talk until his lawyer gets here," Vince responded.

"Get a DNA sample from him. If he won't give one voluntarily, get a warrant," the captain instructed. "And someone needs to go talk to Cole Stratton, find out what he and the vic talked about last night."

"Sir, I think we should bring him down, along with his brothers, and get DNA samples from them, too," Charlie said. "Mrs. Russell's description of Danielle Marceau's visitor last night could fit any one of them."

"As well as Marcus Schwitzer," Vince reminded her.

"Hell," the captain said. "It probably fits thirty percent of the men in this city."

"I think it's important that we find out where they were last night and get them to submit a sample," she insisted.

"Go ahead then," the captain said. "And find out what the

status is on matching J. P. Stratton's DNA to the Hill woman's dead fetus. If the old man wasn't the father of that baby, we need to find out who was."

"Yes, sir," they each replied in turn.

"I'm going to call the chief and warn him what's coming down. Le Blanc, if the DNA on the Marceau woman is a match, we're going to have to break the story about the murder connection to your sister."

"I understand, sir."

"All right. Get busy," he told them and picked up the phone. "Get the chief on the line for me. It's important."

They exited the captain's office and when she starting walking at a hurried pace toward the squad room, Vince said, "Le Blanc, hang on a second."

She stopped, looked back at him. "You heard the captain. We've got a lot of work to do."

"It can wait five minutes. Come on out to the parking lot, I need to get something from my car," he said for the benefit of anyone who might be listening. Once they were outside, they walked toward his vehicle. It was past three in the afternoon and as was often the case in March the pleasant seventy-degree temperatures at noon were beginning to dip to near sixty. "It's not your fault the Marceau woman is dead. If she'd been straight with us and told us she had something, we could have protected her," he told her. In the three years since they'd been partners, he knew her well enough to realize she was probably blaming herself for not saving the other woman.

"Yes, but I knew she was holding something back when we questioned her. I should have pursued it."

"Come on, Le Blanc, we didn't figure her for the killer and we had real suspects taking up most of our time. In fact, we've got one of them inside waiting right now," he reminded her, referring to Reverend Lawrence.

His words seem to fall on deaf ears. "If only I'd routed my voice mail to my cell phone or even given her the number, I might have been able to save her."

"You also might have gotten yourself killed along with her. Or have you forgotten that little calling card the killer left you?"

She looked at him then out of troubled brown eyes. "I haven't forgotten," she assured him. "I was just so sure I would be the one he would come after."

"He still might," Vince told her. "That's why you need to quit beating yourself up about this and help me find the guy."

"You're right," she said, her voice more determined. "I promised I would find him and make him pay."

He didn't have to ask her who she had promised because he was sure it was her sister Emily.

The back-door entrance to the station opened and Jake Marino stuck his head out and called, "Kossak. Le Blanc. The lawyer for your minister is here."

"We'll be right there," Vince called back. And once the door closed, he asked, "You want to take a go at the reverend?"

"You brought him in. You do it and make sure you nail the bastard."

"I'll do my best."

Once he entered the interrogation room, explained the reason the reverend had been brought in, Vince did his best to nail the man. Not that it had been very difficult, because once the Reverend Lawrence began to talk, not even his lawyer could stop him from spilling his guts.

"You and Detective Le Blanc were right about everything," he sobbed, confessing to being blackmailed by Francesca. "I'd been paying her for months now, taking money from the church's collections so she would keep silent."

"So you admit to stealing $2,500 each week from the Sunday collections to pay Francesca Hill to remain silent about your affair?" Vince asked, wanting the confession on tape to be clear.

"Yes."

"Why that figure, Reverend? Why $2,500?" he asked, curious as to why she demanded that particular amount.

"You don't have to answer that, Reverend," the lawyer who had identified himself as Ducote advised.

"It's all right." The minister lifted his head. His color was off, his eyes bloodshot. The man seemed to have aged ten years since he'd picked him up that morning, Vince thought. "It was some sort of joke to her. She said to think of her as my new church and the money as tithing, ten percent of each week's treasury."

Interesting concept for payback, Vince thought. "Why did you go see Francesca the night she was murdered?"

"To plead with her for mercy. She was marrying one of the wealthiest men in the city. She wasn't going to need the money. I wanted to stop the payments."

"What did she say?"

"She refused," he said, his voice hard. "She said it had nothing to do with whether she needed the money or not and I was to go on paying her until she'd decided I'd done enough penance for my sins."

Talk about Freudian twists, Vince thought. "I guess that made you pretty angry."

"It made me furious," he said. "She had no right to demand that money. It belonged to the church."

"Were you furious enough to want to kill her?"

"Yes, I was—"

"Reverend," his lawyer warned and placed a restraining hand on the minister's arm. "I'd advise you not to say anything more."

"It's all right, Mr. Ducote. The secret is already out. You're right, Detective. I was angry and I did want to hurt her for what she was forcing me to do. But I didn't hurt her. And I certainly didn't kill her. I could never have killed her because to do so would have been a sin against the laws of God."

The hypocritical bastard. "And what about molesting innocent children, Reverend?" Vince asked, his voice softening as his fury built. "Isn't molesting children against God's law, too?"

"Detective, that's enough," Ducote shouted.

Ignoring him, Vince continued, "Because that's when you first started having sex with Francesca, isn't it? When she was just a kid coming to you for guidance?"

"You never saw her as a girl," the reverend spat out, a sudden fire coming into his eyes and demeanor. "Even as a girl she was the devil's disciple, using her beauty and sex to tempt good men."

"And you couldn't resist her, could you?" Vince challenged.

Ducote shot to his feet. "This interview is over, Detective. Either charge my client with a crime or release him."

"Judge me if you will, Detective," the reverend said, his burst of temper replaced by a pious calm. "And as our Lord sayeth, let he who is without sin cast the first stone."

Vince shoved away from the table and banged on the door for the guard to open. He stared over at the creep who had abused the trust of a young Francesca and God knows how many others. "If I were you, Reverend, I'd save the sanctimonious proclamations for prison because that's the only place you're going to be preaching for the next ten years."

The guard opened the door and Vince exited, grateful to put distance between himself and the man. He was in an ugly business, he admitted as he headed to the room with the one-way glass and audio where he knew the captain and Charlie were waiting. But the one thing he found even worse than murder was the abuse of a child. Even if he had to work night and day, call in every favor he had coming to him, he would find a way to make the reverend pay. When he joined the captain and Charlie, he said, "He agreed to give us a DNA sample." He held out the signed release and the captain took it and handed it off to an assistant for processing. "He didn't cop to the murder, but his confession gives us enough to charge him with felony theft and probable cause to get the church to open its records."

The captain looked at Charlie. "The chief is working on a statement for the press. He's going to release the news that the Hill murder and your sister's were committed by the same man and that we suspect he killed the Marceau woman, too."

"I understand, sir," she said. "I appreciate your letting me know. I want to warn my parents and sister."

He nodded. "Now, where are we on the neighbor woman who claims to have seen a man at Marceau's apartment last night?"

"Mackenzie has her looking through mug shots," Vince told him.

"I think we might do better with a lineup," Charlie said.

"You got anyone in particular in mind for this lineup?" Captain Warren asked.

"If we can ever find him, I say Hill's ex-boyfriend, Schwitzer, for starters," she said and repeated the description given by Mrs. Russell. "I also think we should put the four Stratton sons in a lineup."

"Let's get them in here for questioning first," the captain responded. "I'm going to go see what I can do to speed up those warrants."

Once the captain left, Vince said, "Listen, if you want to

go talk to your folks and Anne, I can take Mackenzie and go pick up the Strattons."

"Thanks. But the news will keep a little longer. The Stratton Tower is the closest. Let's go pay Aaron Stratton a visit."

Eighteen

At a few minutes past eight o'clock that evening, Cole answered the door and was delighted to see Charlotte standing on his doorstep. He wasn't nearly as delighted to see her partner standing there with her. "Good evening, Detectives. Would you like to come inside?"

"No, thank you," she said politely. "Mr. Stratton, we'd like to ask you some questions concerning your relationship with Danielle Marceau."

Cole's internal radar that had saved his hide on more than a few SEAL missions went off. "I didn't have any relationship with her," he informed her.

"Are you saying you didn't know her?" Charlotte asked.

"No, I'm saying I didn't have a relationship with her. I met her once, about a month or so ago. Why? What's this about?"

"Ms. Marceau was murdered last night and yours was the last number she called," Charlotte told him.

She kept her eyes trained on him and she was doing a formidable job of showing no emotion. "You think I killed her?" he asked.

"We're investigating her murder," she replied. "We'd like

you to come down to the station with us and answer some questions."

"Do you have a warrant for my arrest?" he asked, angered that she might think him guilty.

"No. But we can get one if necessary," she told him. "Do we need one?"

"No. But I'll drive myself and meet you at the station."

Twenty minutes later, Cole was about to enter the police station when he spied his brother Aaron coming out. "What are you doing here?" he asked, although he suspected he knew already. Charlotte had hauled in all the Stratton men.

"Probably the same thing you are," Aaron told him as he straightened his tie. They stepped to the side and out of the way of the traffic going in and out of the building. "Apparently Francesca's friend Danielle managed to get herself killed and your pretty little Detective Le Blanc thinks one of us Strattons did it."

Cole didn't bite on his brother's dig about Charlotte being his because he'd already begun to think of her that way. "Jason and Phillip are here, too?"

"Just Phillip. Apparently our little brother Jason is nowhere to be found."

That worried him, Cole admitted silently. "What about J.P.?"

Aaron arched his brow. "Don't tell me I finally got through to you and you're actually concerned about Dad."

"You know better than that. You said Charlotte thinks one of the Strattons is a killer. I wondered if that included J.P."

"He called me on my cell and said they questioned him. But I'm guessing they didn't have him come down because they already have his DNA sample. They're supposed to be checking out our alibis for last night. And given the way their captain looks, I sure hope you have a good one, big brother, because they want to pin this one on someone really bad."

He didn't have a particularly good one, Cole admitted. But from his brother's smug expression, Aaron did. "I guess I don't have to ask if you had a good alibi."

Aaron smiled. "I was at the Stratton Arms for a black-tie benefit and was in the company of a luscious blonde until eight o'clock this morning. What about you?"

But before he could answer, Charlotte and her partner, Kossak, walked up to them. "Mr. Stratton, if you'd come inside with us," she began. "We'll try to get this over with as quickly as possible so that you can enjoy what's left of your evening.

Ten minutes later Cole stood in the interrogation room where Charlotte had escorted him. He stared at what he knew was one-way glass. He wondered if she was on the other side. Having her show up on his doorstep to question him as a murder suspect wasn't exactly how he had envisioned their next meeting. But then nothing about his pursuit of a relationship with Charlotte Le Blanc had followed the norm. The woman would drive a saint to sin, but he wanted her. He wasn't sure if that made him a fool or simply a glutton for punishment. Either way, he had no intention of letting her get away. When the door opened, Cole turned around and Charlotte entered. In the harsh lighting of the room, he could see the circles beneath her eyes that he hadn't noticed earlier. The ivory slacks and matching turtleneck she wore seemed to hang on her already lean frame.

"Mr. Stratton, thank you for coming in."

"I didn't think I had an option, Detective."

"All the same, your willingness to cooperate makes things easier for both of us," she said. "Please, have a seat."

Cole took a seat at the table opposite her. "What is it you want to know?"

"Before we get started, I understand you were advised that

you have the right to have legal counsel present during this interrogation and that you waived that right. Is that correct?"

"It is."

"Do you wish to change your mind and request an attorney?"

"Why? Do I need one?" Cole asked.

"I'm afraid I can't advise you on that. I am going to be asking you questions in conjunction with the murder of Danielle Marceau. So if you would like legal representation, it can be arranged."

"That's not necessary," Cole told her.

"Very well. I'm going to be taping this interview. Do you have any objection?"

"None."

Charlotte turned on the recorder. "This is Detective Charlotte Le Blanc with the New Orleans Police Department. I'm interviewing Mr. Cole Stratton, who has waived his right to having counsel present," she stated and reported the date and time of the interview. "Mr. Stratton, would you state your name and the address at which you reside for the record."

"Cole Stratton," he began and gave the street, city and state.

"Mr. Stratton, is it correct that you have been read your rights and advised that you may have legal counsel present, but have chosen voluntarily not to do so?"

"That is correct."

"Would you please tell me the nature of your relationship with Ms. Danielle Marceau?"

Cole sat back in his chair. "I had no relationship with her."

"Did you know her?"

"I met her once. She was introduced to me by my sister, Holly, and I was told she was a close friend of Francesca Hill."

"Then you were acquaintances?"

Cole gave her a tight smile. "Detective, I would hardly call a minute-long introduction at a restaurant an acquaintance."

"So it is your assertion that you didn't know Danielle Marceau?"

"It's not an assertion. It's a fact. Other than a passing introduction to the woman, I know nothing about her."

"Then how do you explain her placing a call from her apartment to your cell phone at twelve-forty last night?"

"Simple. She called me and said she had some information about my brother that could be harmful if it fell into the wrong hands. She suggested we discuss it. I agreed to meet her at the bar in the Royal Sonesta in thirty minutes. But she never showed."

"Did she tell you what this information was?" Charlotte asked.

"No."

"Which one of your brothers did she have this information on?"

"She didn't say," Cole told her, which was true. Danielle had not mentioned Jason by name. She'd merely referred to him as the brother who'd been seeing Francesca behind their father's back. Given Jason's infatuation with Francesca and the fact that he'd been searching her apartment for something, he suspected Jason had done something foolish.

"So let me get this straight. You go to a bar at one o'clock in the morning to meet a woman whom you claim to barely know to discuss evidence that would be damaging to your brother, but you don't ask what that evidence is or which brother she's referring to?"

"I didn't say I didn't ask her, Detective. I did. But she refused to tell me. That's why I agreed to meet her."

She eyed him skeptically. "All right. Where were you between twelve-thirty and two o'clock this morning?"

"Between twelve-thirty and twelve forty-five I was at home. Alone. At twelve forty-five I left my home and walked to the Royal Sonesta where I waited in the bar for Ms. Marceau until one-thirty."

"Why not drive?" she asked.

"It was a nice night and, as you know, the Royal Sonesta isn't far from my home," he explained. "My bartender's name was Wendy. I also spoke with a couple named Ruth and Elliot Portman from Minnesota who were celebrating their anniversary. They were staying in the hotel. Feel free to check with them."

"I intend to," she assured him. "Where did you go when you left the bar?"

"Home, where I arrived around 1:45 a.m. and went to bed."

"Is there anyone who can verify when you left and returned home? Maybe a neighbor, a taxi driver, a pizza deliveryman in the neighborhood?"

"Afraid not."

"All right," Charlotte told him and shut off the recorder. "Would you be willing to give us a sample of your DNA?"

"I'm assuming if I say no, you'll get a warrant."

"That's right."

"Then I'll give you a sample," he replied.

"Someone will be in shortly to get it. Thank you for your time," she said and stood. "Oh, one more thing. You wouldn't happen to know where we could find your brother Jason, would you?"

"No, I don't," Cole told her. He wished he did. "Is he a suspect in Danielle Marceau's murder, too?"

She hesitated a moment. "We need to speak with him. If you should hear from him, I suggest you tell him to contact me."

"I will," Cole told her. She nodded and when she started to leave, he said, "Detective Le Blanc."

She turned back. "Yes?"

"I tried to reach you earlier, but you didn't return my calls."

"If this is about the flowers and the dinner invitation—"

"It's not, but I'm glad to know you received them," he said with a smile. "I was trying to reach you to give you this." He removed a slip of paper from his pocket and handed it to her.

She opened it, read the address. "What's this?"

"I heard you've been looking for Marcus Schwitzer. That's the alias he's using," he told her, referring to the name Mack Sweeney that he'd written on the slip of paper. "You can find him at that address."

She lifted her gaze to his. "How? Why?"

"I put the word out I was looking for him. As to why, I did it because I figured if Schwitzer is the killer, the sooner you lock him up, the sooner you'll remove me from your suspect list and we can move forward in our relationship."

"We don't have a relationship," she informed him.

"But we will," he assured her.

The door opened and in walked a woman wearing gloves and carrying a medical kit. The lab tech looked from him to Charlotte, then said, "I'm here to get a sample of your DNA, Mr. Stratton."

"Thank you for this," Charlotte told him, holding up the slip of paper before turning and walking out the door.

Charlie exited the interrogation room. Leaning against the door, she closed her eyes for a moment. She hadn't expected interrogating Cole Stratton would be so difficult, she admitted. But it had been. She'd seen the disappointment in his eyes when she'd shown up on his doorstep. Then she'd seen that same disappointment shift to anger during the interrogation. She had expected that, had hoped that by bringing him in and treating him as nothing more than a suspect that it would deep-six the growing attraction between them. It hadn't. What was worse was that she knew in her heart that he wasn't a killer. Yet, she had no choice but to treat him as a suspect because it was her job.

"You okay?" Vince asked.

She opened her eyes. "Yes."

"So you buy his story?"

"Yes, I do. He gave me this," she said and handed him the slip of paper with the information on Marcus Schwitzer. "He said Schwitzer is using the alias Mack Sweeney and this is where he's staying."

Vince arched his brow. "I don't suppose he told you where he got this."

"No. But I figure it's worth checking out."

"Why don't I take Mackenzie with me to pick him up and you go talk to your family. The captain says the chief's going to issue a statement in the morning about the murders."

"Thanks," she told him and once Vince was gone, she returned to her desk and placed a call to her parents. When she got the answering machine, she left a message for them to call her on her cell. She left the same message on their cell phone when it went to voice mail. A call to her sister, Anne, had gone to voice mail as well. So much for staying in touch, she thought and left a message for Anne.

Telling her parents and Anne that Emily's killer was connected to her investigation wasn't going to be easy, she realized. She feared the news would drag up the pain and horror they'd all lived through six years ago. She wanted to prepare them for what was to come as best as she could, but it was something she intended to do in person and not by phone.

Charlie considered going home but dismissed the idea. Instead, she remained at her desk and worked while she waited to hear back from her family. For the next hour she hit the data banks, doing another search for other crimes that fit the MO of the three murders. Until now, she had limited that search to the Louisiana and Mississippi area. Now she expanded it to include Florida, Arkansas and Georgia since Schwitzer had operated in those states as well. She came up with two that were possibilities—both in Florida. But until she could speak with the investigating officer, she wouldn't know whether they were related to her cases or not. Since it was half past nine, that conversation wouldn't happen before morning.

She considered calling her parents and Anne again and decided against it. She didn't want to alarm them and be forced to explain everything over the phone. Since nothing would happen before the press conference in the morning, she still had time, she reasoned. She should go home, she told herself. The rest of the department had left hours ago. Even the captain who put in a lot of twelve-hour days had left to have dinner with his wife and kids. She didn't have anyone waiting for her at home. But she knew the real reason she was still there. Once she was alone without work to occupy her thoughts, she would think of Cole.

Not that she had been all that successful keeping him out of her thoughts while she'd been working. She hadn't. Every so often her guard had slipped and he'd snuck into her thoughts again. And each time, she kept seeing his face, his expression when he'd looked at her. The disappointment. The anger. The determination.

Her cell phone rang, breaking into her thoughts. Charlie shook off her dark thoughts and grabbed her phone. "Le Blanc."

"Charlie, it's Anne."

From the grim tone of her sister's voice, Charlie knew at once that something was wrong. "What's wrong?"

"Have you seen the news?"

Charlie frowned. "No, why?"

"Channel 8 just ran a breaking news story, claiming the police are searching for a serial killer who they've linked to three murders—Francesca Hill, Danielle Marceau and Emily."

Oh God, Charlie thought. "Did Mom and Dad see it?"

"Yes," Anne told her.

"Are they okay? Of course they're not okay," Charlie answered her own question. She locked her desk and grabbed her purse. "I'm on my way there now."

"Charlie, is it true?" When she didn't respond, Anne pressed, "Is it true?"

"Yes, it's true," she admitted. "I was going to tell you, to tell Mom and Dad. That's why I left messages for you to call me. I didn't want to do it over the phone. I was going to warn you the chief would be issuing a statement about it in the morning. I never meant for you to find out this way."

"Well, somebody beat your police chief to the punch."

"Listen, I'm on my way now. Annie, I'm sorry. Tell Mom and Dad I'm sorry y'all had to find out this way."

Ending the call, Charlie raced from the building to her car. She stuck the emergency siren on the roof of the car and tore out of the parking lot. In record time, she was turning onto her parents' street. Her stomach clenched when she saw the news trucks parked out front. She pulled to a stop in front of the house and slammed on the brakes. She ran toward the house and spying her, the reporters converged on her with microphones in hand, cameras rolling.

"Detective Le Blanc, is it true that you've linked the killer of Francesca Hill to your sister's murder six years ago?"

"No comment," Charlie said and pushed her way up the walkway.

"Do we have a serial killer on our hands?" another reporter asked.

"Detective Le Blanc, do you have any suspects?"

"This is private property and you're all trespassing," she told them.

"Come on, Detective, you have to give us something. Is the story true?"

Charlie whirled around, stared at the platinum blonde with the hard mouth sticking a microphone in her face. "I don't have to give you anything. And neither does my family. They've been through enough."

"The public has a right to know if they're in any danger," the woman insisted.

"Right now the only person in danger is you. Because if you don't get off my parents' property and get that microphone out of my face, I'm going to make you eat it."

And without waiting for a reply, Charlie ran to the front door. Anne opened it and she hurried inside. Slamming the door behind her, she turned the lock.

"Charlie, are you out of your mind?" Anne asked her. "Every station in the city is going to run that sound bite and accuse you of threatening bodily harm to the press."

"Let them," Charlie told her. "Where're Mom and Dad?"

"Upstairs. Dad gave Mom a sedative and I fixed him a tall scotch. The story caught them off guard. Seeing Emily's picture on the TV screen was tough. But I think they're all right. How are you?"

"Angry," she said and headed upstairs to her parents' bedroom. She tapped on the door.

"Come in," her dad called out.

Her mother was lying on the bed, a compress on her head. Her father sat in a chair beside her, holding her hand. The tall scotch Anne had fixed him remained untouched. She entered the room that looked nearly the same now as it did when she'd been a child. The old-fashioned bedspread stamped with cabbage roses, the matching drapes. The cedar chest at the foot of the bed that she, Emily and Anne had pretended was a treasure chest filled with pirates' gold and jewels. She recalled sneaking into her parents' bed on Saturday mornings to snuggle and make plans for the day. Guilt enveloped her like a cloud as she thought of all they had lost. She walked over to them, knelt beside her mother's bed. "I'm so sorry," she told them both because she didn't know what else to say. "I was going to tell you. That's why I left messages for you to call me. I'm so sorry," she said again.

"You have nothing to be sorry about. We took in a movie and had a late dinner," her father explained as her mother pushed the compress away and sat up.

"Your father's right, honey. You have nothing to be sorry about. We're the ones who didn't turn our cell phones back on when we left the theater. It's not your fault you couldn't reach us. None of this is your fault."

But it was her fault. It was her fault for not telling them sooner. It was her fault for not going to Emily's that day when she had called and said she needed her help. And it was her fault for not being there when Danielle Marceau had called her.

As though reading her thoughts, her mother said, "Quit blaming yourself for something that you had no control of, Charlotte. Your father and I will be fine. It's you we're worried about."

The phone rang. "Don't answer that," she said. "It's probably reporters." When the doorbell sounded, she stood. "I'll get rid of the reporters outside. Do you want me to stay here tonight?"

"No, honey," her mother said. "You look tired. Why don't you go home and rest. And we'll talk tomorrow."

She hugged them both, then left the room. Once she was on the other side of the door, she leaned against it and shut her eyes, bracing herself for what she would have to face.

Then she headed downstairs. The first thing she did was to check to see if the reporters remained out front. Most had cleared out, but she noted a suspicious-looking van and two cars parked across the street a few doors down. Using her cell phone, Charlie called the station and requested a cruiser to check out suspicious characters in the neighborhood. Then she went in search of Anne.

Charlie found her in the kitchen, seated at the blond-and-white wooden block table, cradling a mug in her hands. When Anne looked up and saw her, she asked, "Mom and Dad okay?"

"They seem to be. I'm sorry, Annie."

Anne pushed out one of the matching chairs with her foot. "Have a seat."

Charlie sat down. "I should have told you sooner. I'm sorry. It must have been awful for you and them to have all that stuff about Emily's murder dredged up again."

"No harder than it's been for you I imagine. As a matter of fact, I'd say it was a lot worse for you because you've been the one dealing with the murder investigation, all the while knowing that the man you're looking for is the one who killed Emily."

She shrugged. "It comes with the job. I just wish I'd had the chance to prepare you," she said. "What I can't figure out is how the press found out. No one outside of the police department even knew there was a connection. I didn't tell a soul and I know Vince didn't say anything."

"If that's your subtle way of asking if the leak came from me via pillow talk with Vince, the answer's no. He and I have a rule not to talk shop with one another."

"Sounds like a smart rule."

"It seems to be working," Anne said, a satisfied smile on her face.

For the first time in her life, Charlie envied her younger sister that happiness, that sense of sharing. It made her think of Cole, made her wonder if she might find that same contentment with him.

"As far as the source, I can tell you it came from within the police department."

"But who?" Charlie asked, surprised.

"Word is that you've got a new tech working in the lab who's seeing a reporter at Channel 8. Apparently, he wanted to impress his girlfriend about how in the loop he is."

"You never cease to amaze me, Anne. How do you find out this stuff?"

"I have my vays," she said in a mock-Russian accent. She got up and went to the stove and refilled her mug and poured another one, which she plopped down in front of Charlie. "Drink up."

Charlie sniffed. *Hot chocolate.*

Hot chocolate parties had been a mainstay of the Le Blanc girls' childhood. From the time that they had been old enough to discover the girlie world of Barbie dolls, the three of them had held hot-chocolate parties. All through the winter months and right up until they pulled out their white shoes for Easter, they had indulged in the rituals and dreamed about the lives they would lead one day. It had been ages and ages since she had had hot chocolate. Not since the winter before Emily had been killed.

"Thinking of Emily?" Anne asked.

She looked up from the cup in which she'd been staring. "I was remembering the three of us having hot-chocolate parties at this table. We had so many dreams, so many hopes for the future," Charlie said. "I miss her."

"So do I," Anne told her. "But the person I miss most of all is you."

"Me? What are you talking about? I'm still here."

"No, you're not, not the person you were. When Emily died it was like a part of you died with her." She leaned forward, elbows on the table. "What happened to the Charlie who loved life and hot-chocolate parties? What happened to the Charlie who laughed and knew how to have fun? What happened to the Charlie who had so many dreams and hopes for the future?"

"She found out that life isn't a fairy tale, that the world is filled with evil people and that dreams can be snatched away in an instant."

"Whose dreams are we talking about, Charlie? Yours? Or Emily's?"

Charlie stiffened. "I'm not going to sit through another one of your analysis sessions of me," Charlie said and started to rise.

Anne caught her by the wrist. "When are you going to stop running away?"

"I'm not running."

"Aren't you? You've been running ever since Emily died. It's as though you believe that since Emily didn't get to live out her dreams, then you don't deserve to live yours either. That you don't deserve to be happy."

"You don't know what you're talking about. That's not true."

"No? Then why did you drop out of law school and become a cop? Why do you bury yourself in work day and night instead of having a normal life? Why do you push away everyone who tries to get close to you?"

"I don't."

"Yes, you do. I've watched you do it for years. With me, with Mom and Dad, with your friends. With every man who shows any interest in you," Anne told her, her expression filled with sadness. "Why can't you accept the fact that Emily's death wasn't your fault?"

"Because it was my fault," Charlie cried out. "If I'd gone over to her apartment that day when she called me, she might still be here. I knew she was upset, that something was wrong. But I still didn't go. I was angry with her for expecting me to drop everything and rush over. All I cared about was acing that exam when I should have been taking care of my sister. It's because I was selfish that Emily's dead."

"For God's sake, Charlie. You were her sister, not her bodyguard."

"I'm the oldest," Charlie insisted. "It was my job to look out for her."

"No, it wasn't."

"How would you know?" Charlie snarled. "You've always been the baby. No one has ever depended on you. You've never had to worry about looking out for a younger sister. You've never had to make sure that she got home all right, that she didn't get hurt or get into trouble at school."

"You're right. Maybe I don't understand all those things because I am the youngest. But the fact is, Emily wasn't your responsibility. And Mom and Dad were wrong to lay all that on you and make you believe that she was." Anne got up, came over to her side of the table and put a comforting arm around her. "You've got to listen to me. Emily's death wasn't your fault."

"But I feel like it was," she tried to explain.

"Then your feelings are wrong. It's time to stop punishing yourself and move on with your life. If you won't do it for you, then do it for me and Mom and Dad and the people who love you. Don't keep pushing everyone away."

For a long time she didn't say anything. Neither did Anne, who returned to her seat while they finished their chocolate in silence. Was Anne right? Had she been pushing everyone away? Shutting herself off from the people she loved most because she felt she didn't deserve to have a life, didn't deserve to be loved? Finally, Charlie said, "Thank you."

"For what? The kick in the butt?"

"That, too," Charlie said. "But mostly for making me see that by being so hard on myself, I've made things hard on you and everyone else."

"Anytime. And the next time you need a swift kick in the pants, just holler."

"I will," Charlie told her. Feeling as though a weight had been lifted, her heart felt lighter, too. For a second, she considered telling Anne about the stocking left in her home, then dismissed the idea. Her sister had enough to deal with. "So you and Vince, huh?"

Anne's lips curved in a secretive smile. Her eyes brightened. "Yep."

"Just how serious are you two?"

"Oh, I'd say about as serious as it can get. I'm going to marry him and have a half-dozen little Kossaks with his dark eyes and my blond hair."

Charlie nearly choked. "You're engaged? When did that happen?"

"It hasn't. At least he hasn't asked me yet. But he's going to," she said confidently.

And Charlie believed her. "I'm happy for you, Annie. For both of you."

"Thanks," she said. "So what about you? I thought I picked up on something between you and Cole Stratton."

"It's complicated. Putting him and half his family on my list of murder suspects doesn't exactly lend itself to romance."

"Do you think he's the killer?" Anne asked.

"No." Because she didn't. She never had.

"Then tell him that and see where it goes."

"I can't do that. I shouldn't even be having these feelings

for him, not while I'm investigating a case that involves him and his family. It's against every rule in the book and my own personal rule about mixing business with pleasure."

"Some rules are worth breaking," Anne told her. "I'm sure there's probably some unwritten rule somewhere that becoming involved with my sister's partner is wrong. Suppose I hadn't taken a chance? Look what Vince and I would have missed."

She shook her head. "I couldn't take that kind of risk. It could cost me my job."

"Some things and some people are worth the risk," Anne told her.

It was insane, Charlie told herself. She'd had a growing suspicion that the killer could be Aaron Stratton. The man was intelligent and certainly would know his way around security systems. He was a narcissist. He was arrogant and there was something about him that left her cold. What kind of relationship could she and Cole possibly have if his brother had killed her sister?

"How would you feel if you never saw Cole Stratton again?"

Charlie's heart sank. "Empty."

"Then why don't you go tell him that?"

Nineteen

Cole slammed his fists into the punching bag over and over again until, finally, he couldn't hit it anymore. Breathing hard and sweating profusely, he collapsed against the bag, holding on to it with his gloved fists. When he was able to get his breath again, he stepped back. He snatched up a towel from the workout bench in the gym he'd set up in the family home. After wiping the perspiration from this face, he draped the towel around his neck.

Despite his efforts to reach Jason, his brother hadn't answered his cell phone. And according to Phillip, he didn't know where his twin had gone—only that some of his clothes were missing. Resigning himself to the fact that there was little else he could do before morning, he had hit the gym to work off some of his frustrations. And while he was worried about Jason, he knew him well enough to know the kid wasn't capable of murder. Whatever it was though, it had him running scared. But at the moment, his greatest source of frustration was Charlotte Le Blanc.

When she'd walked out of that interrogation room this evening, he'd told himself to forget her. But she hadn't been gone five minutes before he admitted that he wasn't going to forget her or give up on them. He had never been a quitter. What he would do, he decided, was give Charlotte space, some time to deal with the demons. Then he would go after her as he had gone after everything else in his life that mattered.

She mattered to him. More than his business, more than besting J.P.

Unlacing his gloves, he pulled them off with his teeth and set them aside. Picking up the remote to the wide-screen TV mounted on the wall, he turned it on and flipped through to the cable channel running a repeat of the late-night news. The *Channel 4 News* logo came onto the screen and after announcing that this was a repeat of the ten o'clock news broadcast, Bill Capo's friendly face came into view.

"This is Bill Capo filling in for Karen Swensen who is off tonight. At the top of tonight's news is a frightening twist in the unsolved murder of Francesca Hill, the fiancée of multi-millionaire Realtor and hotelier J. P. Stratton, who was found robbed and murdered in her apartment three weeks ago."

Cole grabbed a bottle of water from the minifridge. Straddling the workbench, he turned up the volume and watched the report.

"Earlier this evening an unnamed source reported that DNA evidence found at the murder scene of Francesca Hill also matched DNA found at last night's murder of Danielle Marceau, an acquaintance of Ms. Hill."

Cole twisted off the top to the water bottle and drank deeply, quenching his thirst as his body cooled down while pictures of both Francesca Hill and Danielle Marceau came onto the screen.

Continuing his report, Capo said, "The DNA found at both murder scenes has also been linked to a third murder that occurred in Baton Rouge, Louisiana, six years ago when the body of nineteen-year-old college student Emily Le Blanc was found in her apartment." A picture of a pretty blonde with Charlotte's smile came onto the screen. "Emily Le Blanc was the sister of New Orleans homicide detective Charlotte Le Blanc and our own investigative reporter Anne Le Blanc. When contacted at her parents' home this evening, Detective Le Blanc refused to comment."

The TV screen flashed to a news clip of Charlotte arriving at her parents' home and being hounded by reporters before hurrying inside. Cole hit the remote and turned off the TV. "Jesus!" He couldn't imagine what Charlotte was going through, to see her sister's face splashed on the news, to have the details of the crime recounted.

He needed to get to her. No point in calling, he reasoned. With the press hounding her, she'd avoid the phone. Hurrying from the gym, he raced to his bedroom, threw on some jeans and started toward the den to get his car keys, when the doorbell sounded. He snatched the keys from the table and ignoring Goliath's meows, he ran to the front door, determined to get rid of whoever it was.

He pulled open the door and there she was. "Charlotte."

She was already at the bottom of the stairs and turned at the sound of his voice. "I didn't think you were home," she said.

She looked exhausted, her brown eyes tormented. She had on the same ivory turtleneck and pants she'd worn earlier. Despite the chill in the air, she wore no jacket.

Her gaze dropped to the keys in his hand. "I'm sorry. It looks like I caught you on your way out. I'll go."

"Charlotte, wait," he said. "I was on my way to find you."

"You were?"

"Yes. I just saw the news reports."

She remained at the bottom of the stairs and although he wanted to reach for her, Cole forced himself to wait, to let her make the decision. She'd come this far. He needed to let her choose for herself.

"I wasn't sure you would even want to speak to me after this evening."

"You were doing your job. I may not always like it, but I understand it," he told her. "I just wish you had a little more faith in me to understand. I want you to trust me."

"Everything is such a mess. All I know is that I didn't want to go home and Anne said some stuff that kind of made sense, but was confusing, too," she rambled. "Then I wasn't sure what to do or where to go and the next thing I knew I was here. I'm not even sure why I came here. I'm not even sure where I belong anymore."

"I'm glad you came. Because you belong here…with me."

She came to him then and Cole wrapped her in his arms. After shutting the door, he took her into the den. The March nights were still cool enough to chill the air so he lit a fire in the fireplace. And while the flames licked at the logs, they spread out on the rug in front of the hearth and he held her in his arms and let her talk. She told him about finding her sister's body all those years ago. She told him of the guilt that tormented her still. She told him of her fear that the killer might get away again because of her mistakes.

For a moment Cole had the feeling she wanted to say something more. But she didn't. So he kissed her forehead. "Did you eat today?"

"Yes. I had a burger and fries…or maybe that was yesterday. I can't remember. All the days seem to have blurred together."

"Why don't I fix us something. I do wonderful things with eggs," he boasted.

"I don't want eggs."

His repertoire of meals was limited. But he offered, "What about a cheese sandwich? Frozen pizza?"

She crawled up to her knees, pressed a kiss to his lips. When she lifted her head, she said, "It's not food I'm hungry for."

Cole felt his body go hot and hard in an instant. There was no mistaking the look in her eyes. "You've had an emotional day and you're vulnerable right now. I don't want you to do anything that you'll regret in the morning."

She pushed him down onto his back and straddled him. "The only thing I'll regret in the morning is if you and I don't make love tonight." Then she pulled off her turtleneck and tossed it aside.

His mouth went dry at the sight of her. Milk-white breasts spilled from the cups of a piece of ivory lace. Her torso was smooth and long, her waist narrow. When she reached for his sweatshirt, he caught her hands. "Make sure this is what you want," he told her. "Because there'll be no going back."

"I want you," she told him.

"Then you'll have me. And I'll have you."

She stripped off his sweatshirt, unfastened his jeans. And as her fingers skimmed his stomach, he groaned. He reached for the clip on her bra, released it and filled his hands with her breasts. Then he took her nipples, one at a time, into his mouth.

"Cole," she cried out and he flipped her onto her back. Taking his time, he kissed and tasted his way down her rib cage. He stripped off her slacks, and using his mouth, he continued his journey down her belly, along her hips, to the edge of her panties, inside her thighs. He rid her of the wisp of silk and spread her legs.

He tasted her. She arched her hips, groaned at the touch of his tongue. She curled her fingers into his hair as he continued to feed on her. She was wild and wanton, everything he'd known she would be. When the first spasm hit, she cried out and he held her hips, waited for the tremors to settle. Then he took her up again.

She clawed at him. "Now, Cole. I want you now."

"Not yet." He refused to rush this, refused to let her rush them. He wanted her. All of her. And not just for tonight. He took her up again and again, found pleasure in giving her pleasure. And when he could wait no longer, he entered her in one long thrust and the groan he heard was his own.

Determined to go slowly and extend their pleasure, he slid in and out of her, nearly withdrawing each time only to thrust deeply into her again and again. And finally when he could hold back no longer, he thrust into her a final time and together they shattered like the falling embers from the logs.

Later, after he'd fed her, he carried her upstairs to his bed and they made love again. And while she slept in his arms, he thought he finally understood why his mother had tried so desperately to hold on to love. Because he would move heaven and earth to hold on to it now.

Charlotte awakened slowly. As she stretched, memories of the previous night came flooding back. She felt a flush come to her cheeks as she remembered all that she and Cole had done. Smiling, she reached for him.

But she found the bed empty. Opening her eyes, she glanced around the room. Then she saw the bud vase with three pink tulips on the nightstand. An envelope with Charlotte written across the front was propped in front of it. Sitting up, Charlie pulled the sheet up to cover her breasts and reached for the envelope. She removed the single buff-colored paper and the key with it. His script was strong, bold, sure.

Charlotte—Something important has come up that can't wait. Coffee and croissants are in the kitchen. Eat! Take the key. This is your home now and so am I. See you tonight. Love, Cole

Charlie stared at the key a moment, then closed her fingers around it. She waited for the guilt to come flooding back, for that voice in her heart that told her she didn't deserve to be happy. A flicker of guilt tugged at her. Closing her eyes, she thought of her sister Emily, of the life she had never gotten a chance to live.

I'm sorry, Emily. I'm sorry I let you down, that you never got to do all the things you wanted to do. That you never got to live the life you planned. But I can't give those things back to you. What I can do is find your killer. I'm close, Em, I'm close to finding him. And once I do, I want you to forgive me and let me get on with my life. Because I'm still here, Em. I want a life with Cole. I want to believe in dreams again. I want to believe in love again. I want to live.

And as she headed for the bathroom, she told herself she would have all those things because she wanted to live life again and the person she wanted to live that life with was Cole. But the first step to having that life was finding Emily's killer.

Charlie stared through the one-way mirror into the interview room and waited for Vince to take a stab at getting a confession from Marcus Schwitzer. Beneath the blond highlights, glib manner and designer shirt, the guy was slime. His rap sheet proved that. He'd done time for blackmail and fraud and he should have done time for pimping Francesca. The man was a user. He'd used Francesca and God knows how many other girls. He had also been in the Baton Rouge area around the time of Emily's death. As Vince entered the room, she turned on the audio.

"More questions?" Schwitzer asked with a sneer as Vince sat down. "I must be real important for you guys to keep wanting to talk to me."

"Just need to clarify a few things," Vince told him.

"My attorney here yet?"

"No. But if you'd rather wait for him, we can," Vince told him and started to rise. "I'll just have the guard take you back to your cell until he gets here."

"No," Schwitzer said. "What do you want to know?"

Vince eased back down in his seat and flipped open his file. "According to your statement, you said that you knew about Francesca Hill's blackmail scheme. Did she tell you she was blackmailing someone?"

"She didn't have to. I saw the way she was living all high and mighty."

"She was engaged to a very rich man," Vince pointed out.

"She was living the good life before she even met him."

"How do you know that?"

"Because her friend at the casino told me. She said Francesca wasn't in town no time before she was wearing expensive clothes, buying herself a car, and she didn't even have a job yet. Doesn't take a genius to figure she was running a scam."

"Maybe she came into some money," Vince offered.

"From who? That holy-roller mother of hers? The woman didn't have a pot to piss in and the old man took off when she was just a kid. She was running a scam."

"She was about to marry one of the wealthiest men in the city. If she was running a scam as you say, she wouldn't have had to much longer."

He sat forward, his expression cocky. "You didn't know Francesca. The woman got off on the power. She could have married the richest man in the world and that wouldn't have stopped her from bleeding some poor slob dry. She wasn't giving that up for nobody."

"And you wanted a piece of the action."

"I deserved a piece of the action," he corrected. "I'm the

one who taught the bitch how to run a scam in the first place. She owed me."

"But Francesca didn't agree with you, did she? Like you said, she was into power. Must have made her feel real powerful telling you to get lost. She wasn't the least bit grateful when she should have been, was she?"

"Damn straight," he said. "She owed me."

"And you weren't going to leave town without getting your share, were you? That's why you went to her apartment that night, isn't it? What happened? Did she laugh in your face? Is that when you grabbed her by the throat?"

As Vince spoke, Charlie noted the way Schwitzer wrapped his hands around the soda can in a death grip. Was he imagining it was Francesca's throat? Had he used those hands to pull the black silk stocking tight, then tighter until she could no longer breathe? Had he done the same to Danielle Marceau? To Emily?

"I wanted to strangle the bitch all right and maybe I would have, but somebody beat me to it. She was already dead when I got there. So I took her money and credit cards and some jewelry and split. But if you think you're going to pin her murder on me, you can forget it. I didn't kill her."

"You mentioned her friend at the casino. I suppose you're talking about Danielle." When he nodded, Vince asked, "How well did you know her?"

He shrugged. "She and I had a few laughs, nothing special."

"When was the last time you saw her?" Vince asked him.

"I don't know, maybe about a month ago. Why?"

"Because she's dead," Vince informed him. "She was murdered two days ago."

"Well, there's no way you're pinning that on me. I was at that casino in Mississippi where you found me."

"Can anybody verify that?"

"Damn right. Two nights ago, I was at a craps table. I had

a run and was there from seven at night until seven the next morning. Just ask the croupier."

"I will," Vince told him. "In the meantime, if you're willing to give us a DNA sample, we can rule you out on these murder charges."

"If I do, you'll cut me a deal on those other charges…you know, taking the money and jewelry and selling the credit cards?"

"That's not up to me. It'll be up to the D.A."

"Then I'll wait for my attorney."

"Suit yourself," Vince said and exited the room. When he joined Charlie, he said, "I think that's all we're going to get out of him until his lawyer gets here."

"I think we should put him in a lineup and see if Danielle's neighbor, Mrs. Russell, can ID him. I think we should put Aaron Stratton in that lineup, too."

"If we demand Aaron Stratton be put in a lineup, we need to have his brothers, too." When she started to object, he said, "You're the one who said the profile could fit any one of them."

"You're right," she admitted. "But I'd like to be the one to tell Cole."

"It'll be better if you let me handle it."

Once again, she knew her partner was right. "Okay."

"I'll go talk to the captain about the lineup. Why don't you give Mrs. Russell a call and see if she'd like to take another ride in a police car."

"Take your time, Mrs. Russell," Charlie told the woman as she stood with her, Vince and Schwitzer's attorney to view the lineup that consisted of Cole, Schwitzer, Phillip and Aaron Stratton and a police officer. The only one missing was Jason Stratton, who was MIA. According to Vince, the Stratton men had complied with the request to participate in the lineup. It was their father, J. P. Stratton, who had been outraged by the request. No doubt both the chief and the captain would get the same earful Vince had about their incompetence in the running of the murder investigation. But it wasn't J. P. Stratton who'd concerned her. What concerned her was the fact that she hadn't spoken to Cole.

"You're sure they can't see me?" she asked.

"I'm sure. This is one-way glass. We can see them but they can't see us. Just look closely and tell us if you see the man you saw at Danielle's apartment the night she was killed."

She adjusted her glasses on her nose and stared for a long time. "It could be number two," she said.

"Number two, step forward," Vince said.

Marcus Schwitzer stepped forward and Mrs. Russell looked at him hard. "Could he take off the glasses? The man I saw wasn't wearing glasses."

"Number two, remove your glasses."

Schwitzer took off the glasses and stared at the mirror, his expression defiant, a smirk curling his lips.

"Could you have him turn around so I can have a look at his tush?"

Vince coughed and Charlie bit back a smile. But he schooled his expression quickly and said, "Number two, turn around."

Schwitzer complied. Charlie looked at the older woman. "Mrs. Russell?"

She shook her head. "His tush is too flat."

"Are you sure, Mrs. Russell?" Charlie asked her.

"You heard her," Schwitzer's attorney said. "It's not him."

Disappointment settled over her like a heavy fog and Charlie realized she'd been hoping that Mrs. Russell would identify Schwitzer as the man she'd seen that night. If she had and the DNA matched, she'd have Emily's killer. She didn't want it to be Cole's brother. He was close to his siblings and protective of them, feelings she understood. For Cole's sake, she hadn't wanted it to be his brother.

"Could you have number four step forward so I can get a closer look at him?" Mrs. Russell asked.

"Number two, you can step back. Number four, step forward," Vince said.

Aaron Stratton looked like a fair-haired prince, Charlie thought. He was handsome and the resemblance between him and Cole was evident. He was smart and personable, the type of man a girl would want to bring home to her mother. But something about the man rubbed her wrong.

"That's him," she said.

"Mrs. Russell, are you sure?" Charlie asked.

"Yes."

"I need you to be sure, Mrs. Russell," Charlie told her. She looked at Vince. "Have him turn around."

"Number four, turn around," Vince said.

Aaron Stratton turned around.

"That's him. A nice tight tush. He wasn't wearing that overcoat when he left, so I got a good look at it."

"That's all," Vince said and pulled the curtain closed. He turned back to Mrs. Russell. "We'll need you to give us a statement."

"You heard the lady," Schwitzer's attorney told them. "Now we need to discuss setting bail for my client."

"Your client isn't going anywhere," Charlie told the lawyer. She hadn't believed it possible, but Schwitzer had managed to come up with an ambulance-chasing attorney who was every bit as sleazy as his client. "We're still waiting on the results of the DNA test and we have him on theft charges and credit card fraud."

"About those charges—"

"Save it for the D.A.," Vince told him and he opened the door for her and Mrs. Russell to exit.

Once they had Mrs. Russell's statement and had advised the captain of the outcome of the lineup, he sat at his desk and shook his head. "Aaron Stratton, a killer. It just doesn't make any sense."

"Most murders don't," Charlie pointed out.

"But where's the motive?"

"I don't know. Usually it's sex, money or power," she said.

"And the man's got all three." He let out a breath, looked up at her and Vince. "You think the old woman's ID will hold up?"

"If it was anybody but a Stratton, I'd say yes," Vince replied. "But with the Strattons involved, it could be tough. They'll bring a team of attorneys in here who'll point out that the woman is in her seventies, she wears glasses, it was late at night."

"She said she was sure," Charlie reasoned.

"Before we charge him with anything, see if they've got the DNA test results yet," he told her. "They promised we'd have them back today."

"Yes, sir."

"Kossak, go have another chat with Aaron Stratton. Tell him about the old woman's ID and see what he has to say for himself."

Aaron Stratton had little to say, Charlie noted as she watched Vince finish up the interview. If anything, he seemed to find the entire situation amusing. Just as he had apparently found the DNA test amusing. Either the man was as innocent as the angels in heaven or he was one cool customer.

"Thank you, Mr. Stratton. I'll have the officer escort you out," Vince said as he closed his file folder, turned off the recorder and headed for the door.

"Detective?"

Vince paused with his hand at the doorknob. "Yes?"

"Any results yet on the DNA tests?"

"I'm heading to the lab now to find out," he told him.

"I'd be very interested in knowing the outcome when you get them. So would my father. We'd both appreciate it if you'd let us know what they reveal."

"I'll try to work it into my schedule," Vince replied, not bothering to hide his annoyance with the man.

"Maybe you can have Detective Le Blanc call me when you get the results."

Vince didn't bother to answer him, simply walked out of the room. "The smug bastard," Vince snarled when he joined her.

"Don't let him get to you," Charlie told him, although she certainly would have loved to wipe that smirk off his face herself. "He was just trying to get a rise out of me because he knew I was watching."

"I'd still like to knock a few of those expensive caps off his teeth."

"So would I," she told him. "Let's see if the lab can help us bury the jerk."

"You're telling me none of them were a match?" Vince said as he and Charlie met with Dr. Williamson the next day to obtain the DNA test results. She'd confirmed that J. P. Stratton was indeed the father of Francesca's baby, but that neither he nor the others tested were a match to the killer's DNA.

"I said none of them were a match to DNA found in the three victims," Dr. Williamson told him. "But I can tell you that your killer is related to J. P. Stratton. The evidence points to a male relative. Possibly a father, a brother or another son."

"J. P. Stratton is an only child and his parents are dead,"

Vince said. "That leaves his other son, Jason. He's the only one we didn't test."

"Dr. Williamson, are you sure? There's no mistake?" Charlie asked.

"DNA doesn't lie, Detective. None of those men we tested is your killer."

"Thanks, Doc," Vince told her and guided Charlie from the lab. "I was hoping we could nail Schwitzer or if not him then that jerk Aaron Stratton."

"So was I," Charlie said.

"Unless J.P. has another son no one knows about, it has to be Jason. But I gotta tell you, Le Blanc, I just don't see it. The kid might have a giant-size chip on his shoulder, but I'd never have pegged him with the brass to kill anyone, let alone three women. Hell, he would have only been seventeen when he killed Emily." He shook his head. "It just doesn't make any sense."

Charlie stopped midstride. "Kossak, there's got to be another explanation. Do you think that it's possible J.P. has another son no one knows about?"

She was grasping at straws, Vince realized. She didn't want to believe Jason Stratton was a murderer and he understood why. Because if she did accept it, that meant that Cole's youngest brother was responsible for her sister's murder and the murders of two other women. "Do you really think a man with his ego wouldn't want to let everyone know just how virile he is? The man already had five kids with four wives and was expecting another. Even if he hadn't married the woman, he'd have made sure the world knew he had another son—if for no other reason than to brag."

"I suppose you're right. But for the life of me, I just can't see Emily with Jason." She looked up at him. "Emily liked older guys. She barely looked at guys her own age, let alone one who was two years younger."

"Maybe she didn't know he was younger. Women aren't the only ones who lie about their age, Le Blanc. In my younger days I tacked on extra years when I wanted to score with an older woman."

"Do yourself a favor, don't tell my sister that story," she advised him.

"The point I was making is that it's possible. I'll see about getting a warrant to search his house and see if we can get a sample of his DNA from something. In the meantime, we're going to have to put out an APB on Jason Stratton and have him picked up for suspicion of murder."

"I know," she said and Vince knew she wasn't happy about it. "I'll tell Schwitzer's attorney that his client is off the hook on the murder charges, but I'm going to see if we can hold him on the theft and credit card fraud."

"I'll contact the Strattons," he told her.

"But I—"

"It's better if I do it," he told her. "Le Blanc, you heard the man at that press conference yesterday. He's out for blood. He's already demanding an investigation over us withholding the link to Emily's murder. When he finds out we don't have anything, he really is going to try to get your badge. Probably mine and the captain's, too. But the one he really wants is yours."

"But we do have something," she said. "We know that his son Jason is a killer."

Twenty

For the second time in as many days, Cole found himself at the police station in the same room with J.P., three of his siblings and Sylvia Stratton. And for the second time that day, he had been told that Charlotte wasn't available. He looked over at the captain and Vince Kossak and decided he wouldn't want to find himself in a poker game with either man.

"We have the results back from the DNA tests," Captain Warren informed them. "The tests were negative. None of your DNA matched that found in the three victims."

"Of course they didn't match. You could have saved us all time and the department the expense if you'd listened to me in the first place," J.P. gloated. "You've already got your killer. Schwitzer's the one responsible."

"Schwitzer's DNA didn't match either," the captain informed him.

Some of J.P.'s bravado dimmed. "Then I suggest you get your people out on the street to look for Francesca's killer. You might have had him by now if you hadn't wasted precious time harassing me and my family."

"I said there wasn't a match to any of your DNA," Captain

Warren told him. "But there was a match to your family line, Mr. Stratton. I won't give you all the technical terms but the bottom line is the killer is a male related to you. Since none of your sons here were a match, we're going to pursue your son Jason. We were unable to retrieve any DNA at his home and, as you know, we've been unable to locate him."

"Captain, you're sure there's no mistake?" Cole asked.

"Of course there's been a mistake," J.P. said. "Besides the fact that the boy doesn't have the balls to kill a bug, let alone three women, he wouldn't dare cross me. He knew Francesca belonged to me. It's obvious that the people in your lab are just as incompetent as your detectives."

"There's no mistake, Mr. Stratton. The tests were run twice," Kossak advised him. "DNA doesn't lie. The person who killed your fiancée and the other two women is a male related to you. Since you have no brothers and your father is dead, that leaves your sons. The three here weren't a match, that only leaves Jason."

"But where's the motive?" Aaron asked.

Cole saw the captain give a nod to Kossak, who said, "Your brother was infatuated with Ms. Hill, Mr. Stratton. He wrote her some love letters. We think she may have threatened to turn them over to your father."

"I want to see those letters," J.P. demanded.

"I'm afraid that isn't possible. They're evidence in a murder investigation," the captain said.

Sylvia Stratton gasped. She clutched J.P.'s arm. He shook her off. "You're either crazy or you're lying. Jason would no more know what to do with a woman like Francesca than Holly would know how to read a financial report."

Holly looked as though she'd been struck and Cole wanted desperately to plant his fist in J.P.'s face. But to do so would only make things worse for his sister. He placed an arm around her shoulders. "You don't need to be here for this. Why don't you wait outside?"

"I want to stay." She tipped up her chin. "Go on, Detective. Explain to my father how his beloved fiancée obviously encouraged his son's feelings for her."

Cole gave his sister marks. She didn't even flinch when J.P. turned on her and said, "You should take a lesson from your mother. Look pretty and keep your mouth shut because every time you open it you prove just how stupid you are."

"The only one showing any stupidity here is you," Cole told him.

J.P. looked as if he was ready to explode. Sylvia touched his arm again. "I'm sure there's some mistake, J.P. Jason adores you. He'd never betray you."

"Save it. I'm finished with the little prick, his brother and you," J.P. said and walked out of the office.

"J.P., wait," Sylvia cried out, racing after him.

The undercurrents in the room reverberated in the wake of J.P.'s exit. "We'll give you and your family some privacy," the captain told them. "But if you know where your brother Jason is, I suggest you have him turn himself in."

Once the captain and Detective Kossak left the room, Cole walked over to Phillip and placed a hand on his shoulder. "You don't need J.P. or his money," he told him. "You've got a place at CS Securities and I'll help you with anything you need."

"I know," Phillip said. "But it's not me I'm worried about. It's Jason. It's true he had a thing for Francesca and wrote her a couple of dumb letters. And he was really nervous when she threatened to show them to Dad. But he didn't kill her. And there's no way he killed those other women."

"I know that. But the only way we're going to be able to prove it is to find him." He looked into his brother's eyes. "You're sure you don't have any idea where he is?"

Phillip shook his head. "I've checked all of his usual spots and he's not answering his cell phone."

Because he wasn't using his cell phone, Cole thought silently. He'd already hooked into the phone systems searching for activity that would lead him to his brother. But wherever Jason was, he wasn't using his cell phone or his credit cards.

The door opened and Sylvia said, "Aaron, your father needs you."

"I better go see what he wants and try to get him to settle down," Aaron told him. "I'm with you on this, Cole. I can't see Jason as a murderer. If there's anything I can do to help, let me know."

"I will. Thanks."

"Is there anything we can do?" Holly asked him once Aaron had left with Sylvia.

"Just let me know if you hear from Jason, or if you think of any other place he might have gone."

"We will," Holly replied. "Come on, Phillip, I'll give you a ride home."

Alone, Cole stood for several minutes, considering where to look for Jason next, when he heard a tap at the door. When he turned around, she was there. Charlotte. And his chest tightened at the sight of her. The dark circles were gone and there was color in her cheeks that hadn't been there yesterday. Her eyes had lost that haunted look, but she looked troubled. "I've been looking for you," he told her.

"I know. But all things considered, the captain thought I should keep some distance." She shut the door but held herself back. "I'm sorry, Cole. About Jason. I know how close you are to him. I wanted to be wrong."

Cole went to her, held her close. "None of this is your fault and no matter what happens, you're not going to lose me. I meant what I said the other night. We belong to each other now. There's no going back—for either of us." He eased her from him so that he could see her eyes. "Agreed?"

"Agreed."

And because he needed to, he kissed her. It wasn't a passionate kiss, not like the ones they'd shared that night when they'd made love. This kiss was gentle and short, just enough to tell her that he loved her and to sustain him for what lay ahead. When he lifted his head, he said, "I need to find Jason before the police do. Wherever he is, he's scared. Having the police arrest him will only make things worse." He paused. "I know my brother. He didn't kill your sister or the others. I think in your heart you know it, too."

"But the DNA—"

"The DNA is wrong. I don't know how, but something's not right. And once I find Jason, I'll prove it."

"Cole—"

A tap sounded at the door and Charlie looked over at Mackenzie. "Excuse me, Detective. But this just came for you," he said and held out a manila envelope to her. "The front desk said one of those messenger services dropped it off and said it was to be given to you right away."

"Thanks, Mackenzie," she said and took the envelope from him. She looked at her name, which had been printed in big black letters across the front with the address of the police station.

"Aren't you going to open it?" Cole asked.

Turning it over, she used her thumbnail to tear the sealed flap. She looked inside. It was another envelope, this one smaller in size but with a slight bulge to it. She pulled it out and written across the front in the same print was EMILY. Charlie sucked in a breath.

"What is it?" Cole asked.

Turning the envelope over, she pulled open the flap and inside was a single black silk stocking.

"Mom, are you sure you and Dad don't want to get out of
town for a few days until things die down?" Charlie asked as
she sat in the kitchen with her parents and Anne. With the APB
out on Jason, it was only a matter of time before every TV
station in New Orleans would be frequently splashing photos
of Jason, Emily and the other two victims on-screen. And if
they were able to link the two cases in Florida to him, the
media frenzy would be even worse. Already the chief was
talking to the FBI. She hated the thought of her parents going
through the details of the murder again.

"Your father and I will be okay. It's you we're worried
about. This hasn't been easy for you either."

"I'm all right."

"I don't know how you can be when you're still blaming
yourself for Emily's death," her mother told her.

Charlie didn't know what to say. It was something they had
never discussed, not even at the time of Emily's murder. She
looked over at Anne and from her guilty expression she knew
her sister had told them about their conversation.

"Somebody had to tell them," Anne said in her own defense.

"And we're glad she did," her mother told her. "Honey,
don't you think your father and I know it's the reason you quit
law school and joined the police force? We just didn't realize
that you were still blaming yourself because we never did.
What happened to Emily was tragic, horrible, but it wasn't
your fault."

Charlie swallowed hard as emotions welled inside her.
"I'm the oldest. I was supposed to look out for her."

"You were her sister. You were supposed to love her and
be a friend to her, and you were. But Emily was never your

responsibility." Her father reached across the table, placed his hands atop hers. "I'm so sorry if we made you feel that she was."

"We're both sorry," her mother said. "And as much as we will always miss Emily, we're just grateful that we have you two girls. We love you."

Charlie hugged her mother and then her father. "I love you, too."

She touched Charlie's cheek. "I almost feel sorry for that young man's mother. To know your son is capable of such a thing," she said, referring to Jason Stratton.

"One thing's for sure, all of his father's money isn't going to be able to buy him out of this. I know we're supposed to be forgiving, but I hope they toss him in prison and throw away the key," her father said.

"He's obviously an unhappy and twisted young man," her mother said.

Unhappy and confused? Yes, Charlie thought. But twisted and a murderer? She didn't think so. True, Cole's certainty of his brother's innocence had impacted her. But her own instincts had told her the same thing. While she didn't know who had sent her that stocking, she didn't think it was Jason. The gesture was a sign of arrogance, the need to show her how clever he was. Jason hadn't struck her as someone confident enough to risk being caught by doing something so bold. If she'd had to choose any of the Stratton men as a killer, it would have been Aaron. But how could the DNA be wrong?

"Sick or not, he's going to pay for what he did to our daughter and to those other women," her father said.

"We still don't know for sure it's him," she told them. "I mean, we still have to test his DNA."

"But you said the DNA proved it was him," her mother said.

"No, I said the DNA proved that it was a male related to

J. P. Stratton and that since his other sons had been eliminated, they think it's Jason Stratton," Charlie explained.

"You sound like you have doubts," her father remarked.

"To be honest, I do. I know it sounds crazy and that DNA doesn't lie, but I just don't think he's the murderer," she admitted.

"All this DNA stuff is so confusing," her mother remarked and fidgeted with the napkin under her glass of tea. "Even when Emily was taking those courses and tried explaining it to me, it never made any sense."

"I didn't know Emily took any courses about DNA," Charlie said.

"Actually, it was one of those premed classes. She said she needed to know everything there was to know about fertility if she was going to specialize in obstetrics and there was a section in the class on DNA," she explained. "As smart as she was, Emily didn't spend a lot of time studying. I guess because it always came so easily to her. But for this class, she was very serious, very conscientious."

"Do you know why?" Charlie asked.

"Well, I'd like to think it was because she was getting serious about school and her future, but the truth is I think it had something to do with that girl she was friends with in one of her classes. The poor thing had been raped. Apparently she identified the man responsible, but he got off because the DNA didn't match. Emily was very upset about it. She said the young woman withdrew from school and forfeited her scholarship because of it."

Charlie had a vague recollection of her sister mentioning the incident. She'd made some remark about hoping Charlie would be a better attorney than the ADA who had refused to prosecute her friend's case and had allowed a man to get away with rape. At the time Charlie had been so involved in her own studies, she hadn't given it much thought and had forgotten about it.

"Anyway, I remember Emily was all excited about this one class she was taking where they were studying DNA. She became almost obsessed with the subject. That last time she was home, she spent half of her time at the library or on the computer and writing stuff in her notebook."

Alarm bells went off in Charlie's head. "Mom, do you remember the name of Emily's friend? The one who was raped?"

"Let me see," she said, her brow creasing. "It was Lisa something…a name that began with a W I think."

"Walters? Weldon? Wright?" Charlie asked, tossing out last names that began with the letter W. "Williams? Whitney? We—"

"Whitman. It was Lisa Whitman."

Her sister had always kept a diary, but they hadn't been able to find one in the apartment after her murder. But she did remember packing up Emily's notebooks along with some of her books. "Mom, do you still have Emily's stuff from school? Her notebooks and things that I packed from her apartment?"

"Yes. It's in the closet of her room with all the other boxes of mementos that she kept through the years. We never…" Her mother's voice grew husky with emotion. "We never could bring ourselves to get rid of any of her things."

"Would you mind if I went through them? I'd like to see if I can find that notebook. It might help me find her killer."

"You do whatever you need to do," her mother told her.

"Thanks," she said and after hugging both her parents, she raced upstairs.

Entering her sister's room after all these years was strange, Charlie admitted. Nothing had changed. The room looked exactly as it had when Emily had left for college. The brushes, lipsticks and perfume bottles were still on the vanity as though waiting for her to return any minute to fluff and pretty her-

self. Snapshots of Emily with her friends goofing around
were still tacked on the bulletin board. Even the pink unicorn
that she'd gotten when she was six rested atop her bed.

She missed her sister, Charlie admitted. As she looked
around the room the happy memories came flooding back and,
for the first time in a long time, she could think of Emily without regret and guilt. And just as it so often happened to her at
a crime scene, she could almost sense Emily's presence. It was
as though she'd been waiting for her to come, waiting for her
to find the key to set her sister's spirit free and on its way.

"Need some help?"

At the sound of Anne's voice, Charlie shook off her
thoughts of the past. "Sure."

Together they went to work. "Exactly what is it we're looking for?" Anne asked, then sneezed as she handed her another
dusty box from the shelf of Emily's closet.

"A box with notebooks, cards, letters and some books,"
Charlie said as she pulled the fifth box down.

Seated on the floor, she ripped off the sealing tape and began
digging through the boxes. Anne did the same. Thirty minutes
into it, they were surrounded by stacks of notebooks and papers.

"Good Lord! She saved her workbooks from grade school,"
Anne exclaimed.

"I can beat that. Here's a stack of Valentines that, judging
by the crayon-printed signatures, must be from first or second grade," Charlie commiserated.

"I never realized what a pack rat our sister was."

"She always did like commemorating every event. Especially once she started dating," Charlie said.

"True. And Emily certainly had her share of admirers. Remember how she insisted on pressing her corsages in that
scrapbook?"

"Let's not forget the pictures of her with her dates, the name of the song they danced to and a copy of the menu from whatever restaurant they ate in before the dance," Charlie recalled.

Anne laughed. "She really did know how to have fun, didn't she?"

"Yes, she did."

"I miss her," Anne said.

"Me, too."

"I guess I always thought of Em as being so into herself. I was surprised to hear Mom say how upset she was about what happened to her friend."

"Maybe we didn't give her enough credit," Charlie admitted. She opened the next box and spied the calendar with old movie scenes that she had taken from Emily's apartment and packed away with her things. "I think this is the box," Charlie told Anne.

She began taking out all the things she had hurriedly stuffed inside the carton all those years ago. She pulled out various cards, a grocery list, a note to call for a dental appointment. Then she saw the spiral notebooks. There were four in all. She went through the first one. It contained poems, a short story, a guest list for a party titled Spring Break. The second one contained notes for a psychology class. It was in the third one that she found what she was looking for.

"Did you find it?" Anne asked when she saw Charlie sit back and begin going slowly through the pages.

"I think so." She flipped through page after page of notes in Emily's flowery script. There were facts and figures about fertility problems facing today's women that hadn't faced their ancestors. A list of drugs and procedures to aid couples trying to conceive was listed. Another section dealt with the increase in multiple births as a result of fertility drugs and in vitro procedures. She flipped through more pages, skimmed notes about twins, triplets and multiple births. DNA was listed and underlined. Dozens and dozens of pages followed, too much for her to read right now. "This must have been the notebook Mom was talking about," Charlie said and put it aside.

"What are you looking for?"

"I'm not sure. But I'll know it when I see it." Charlie glanced at her watch. "I need to go. Can you help me put this stuff away?"

After leaving Charlotte and the police station, Cole suggested Phillip and Holly meet him at home for dinner. He had seen that the encounter with the police and J.P. had disturbed them. He'd also hoped that maybe he could get Phillip to tell him where Jason had gone. He knew his younger brother well enough to know when he was keeping secrets. He also knew that if Jason would turn to anyone, it would be his twin. He already knew that Jason had left the state. What he didn't know was where he had gone. And it was just a matter of time before the police picked Jason up.

Shifting the bag containing the three barbecue dinners, Cole fished out his house keys. While it hadn't taken much coaxing to get his siblings to stay and join him for dinner, he hadn't wanted to chase them off because of his poor cooking skills. With luck, they would stuff themselves with the barbecue ribs and maybe, just maybe, he could get Phillip to open up.

Inserting the key into the lock, he opened the door and went inside. Goliath came trotting down the hall, meowing that he wanted to go out. "Not tonight, pal," he said and after deactivating the alarm, he started for the kitchen. And as he moved, he could hear Holly and Phillip arguing. Evidently, they hadn't heard him return, Cole realized.

"You need to tell Cole," Holly insisted.

"I can't. I promised I wouldn't tell anyone," Phillip responded.

Cole placed the bag with their dinner on the kitchen table and headed for his home office where the argument was in progress.

"You heard what Cole said. The police think he killed Francesca and those other women. The only way he can prove he didn't is if he turns himself in. After he takes the DNA test, then he'll be in the clear."

"Jason said not to trust Cole, that he heard Dad and Aaron talking and they said he's sleeping with that lady detective."

"Well, that's good then," Holly pointed out. "He can get her to help Jason."

"You heard what Dad said. The cops are trying to pin Francesca's murder on one of us because they're too dumb to find the real killer. They resent us because we're rich and they don't have anything. That's why those two detectives keep coming around, asking us all kinds of questions and treating us like we're the criminals," Phillip told her. "If I tell Cole where Jason is, he'll make him come back. You know he will. And then Jason will have to go to jail."

"Cole won't let that happen," Holly argued.

He'd heard enough, Cole decided as he stepped through the doorway. "Holly's right," he told them as both Holly and Phillip swung their gazes toward him. "I'm not going to let anyone lock Jason in a jail cell for something he didn't do. But the only way I can stop that from happening is if I find him first and have him come in on his own."

"We didn't hear you come in," Phillip said.

"Obviously. Did Jason contact you on the Internet?" he asked Phillip. When he didn't answer, Cole said, "You know how good I am on the computer. I'll be able to trace the connection back to where he is. But I'd rather have you tell me and save me the trouble and the time."

"I promised him I wouldn't tell anyone," Phillip said.

"I'm not anyone. I'm his brother and right now he's in a lot of trouble. I want to help him, but I can't do that unless I know where he is." When Phillip remained silent, he said, "I need you to trust me, Phillip. It's going to be a lot worse if the police find him first and believe me, they're going to find him."

Phillip stared at him and the gray eyes behind the round frames were tormented. "I gave him my word."

"And I would never ask you to break it if I didn't believe it was necessary."

"He's in Chicago."

"Chicago?" Holly repeated. "What's he doing there?"

Cole held up his hand to silence his sister. "Where in Chicago?"

"I don't know. I swear it. He contacted me from one of those Internet cafés. He doesn't want to use his credit cards. He wanted me to send him some money."

"Where are you supposed to send it?" Cole asked.

"To a Western Union office. Here's the address and the in-structions," he said, withdrawing a slip of paper from his pocket. "Once I've sent the money, I'm supposed to go to a bulletin board on this Web site called trainlovers.com and post a message that says the New Orleans Special is on time."

Cole took the slip of paper, read it and committed it to memory. "I want you to wire the money to him like he asked, then post the message. I'll take care of the rest."

"What are you going to do?" Phillip asked.

"I'm going to Chicago to convince Jason to come back and turn himself in."

Twenty-One

After spending most of the previous evening poring over Emily's notes, Charlie yawned as she watched the exits on the interstate leading to the Louisiana State University campus in Baton Rouge. A search of the databases had revealed no charge of rape being filed by Lisa Whitman. Since she had been unable to find any listing for a Lisa Whitman in the Baton Rouge area, she'd decided to try her luck at the university.

She still wasn't sure what all of Emily's research notes meant or how Lisa Whitman's rape and her sister's murder were connected. She only knew that somehow they were. It was why she'd called both the captain and Vince that morning and told them she would be out on personal business. She'd felt guilty about lying to them. But she'd told herself it was a white lie, one that was necessary because if either her captain or her partner knew she was following a lead on the murderer, they would have thrown up roadblocks. She didn't want any more roadblocks.

Her cell phone rang and Charlie retrieved it from her bag. "Le Blanc."

"It's Cole."

"Good morning," she said.

"How did things go with your folks last night?" he asked.

"Good. Better than I expected. What about you?" she asked, knowing he had planned to have Phillip and Holly join him for dinner.

"Better than I expected," he repeated back to her. "Listen, I just wanted to let you know I had to go out of town. I should be back within twenty-four hours."

"I don't suppose you're going to tell me where you're going."

"It's better if you don't know," he told her. "But I'll call you when I get back."

"Okay."

"Charlotte?"

"Yes?" she replied.

"Be careful."

"I will," she promised and after she ended the call, she took the exit to Louisiana State University in Baton Rouge. Fifteen minutes later, Charlie pulled into the parking lot. She locked her vehicle and headed for the administrative offices where she'd made arrangements to speak with Mrs. Shaw, whom she had been referred to when she'd called earlier and asked for information on a former student.

"Can I help you?" the woman at the reception desk asked her.

"Yes. I'm Detective Charlotte Le Blanc with the New Orleans Police Department. I believe Mrs. Shaw is expecting me."

"Yes, Detective, you can go right in."

"Thank you," Charlie said and entered the office.

"Good morning, Detective. I'm Myra Shaw," the woman behind the desk said as she rose to greet her. "Please have a seat."

As Charlie sat down, she studied the other woman. She was of average height, with toffee-colored hair cut in a neat bob, dark eyes and a friendly smile. Charlie pegged her to be somewhere in her late fifties. "Thank you for agreeing to see me."

"You made it sound so urgent. You said it had something to do with your sister's murder six years ago. That was such a tragedy. You have my sympathies."

"Thank you," Charlie responded.

"Now, how is it that I can help you?"

"I was hoping you could give me some information about a former student at the university. Her name is Lisa Whitman."

"Lisa Whitman. Lisa Whitman. That name's familiar."

"She was a student at the university around the time my sister was here."

"Let me see what I have in the system." Mrs. Shaw tapped away at the computer keyboard. After a few moments, she said, "Here she is—Lisa Whitman. She had an academic scholarship but left after her freshman year."

"Do you have an address for her?" Charlie asked.

"We don't usually give out that kind of information…"

"It's really important that I speak with her, Ms. Shaw. I can get a warrant, but it would waste precious time that I don't have."

"Can you tell me why you want to speak with her?" she asked.

"Because I think she might be able to help me find out who murdered my sister and two other women in New Orleans."

"But I thought…the news reports said they had a suspect, Jason Stratton, the son of that hotel tycoon in New Orleans."

"I think they're wrong. But the only way I can prove it and save an innocent young man from going to jail is by talking to Lisa Whitman."

She hesitated a moment, then returned her gaze to the computer screen. "I have an address for her parents' home in Atlanta." She jotted the information down on a slip of paper and handed it to her. "The address is over six years old. So I'm not sure if it's any good."

"Thank you, Ms. Shaw," Charlie said as she took the sheet of paper from the other woman and stood. "You've been a great help."

"I hope you catch the man you're looking for, Detective."

"I intend to, Ms. Shaw," Charlie said as shook the other woman's hand.

Unfortunately, locating Lisa Whitman had taken the better part of the day. After leaving Baton Rouge, she'd returned to New Orleans and taken the first plane out to Atlanta. The address for Ellen and John Whitman was no longer good. They had moved two years earlier to the suburbs. Once she had located them, Mrs. Whitman had advised her that Lisa was now married and had a small child and she'd been reluctant to give Charlie the information. Finally, after speaking with her daughter by phone, Mrs. Whitman had relented and given Charlie the address.

Lisa Whitman Fenmore lived in a yellow house with white shutters, a picket fence, a small garden of roses and lilies and a yapping ball of white fur named Missy that was dancing around the woman's feet when she opened the door. The woman was a pretty, blue-eyed blonde who appeared to still be carrying a few extra pounds, no doubt courtesy of the toddler perched on her hip. "Lisa Fenmore?"

"That's right. You must be Emily's sister. I can see the resemblance. But she never mentioned that you were a police detective."

"That's because I wasn't back then," Charlie explained. "Thank you for agreeing to see me."

"My mother said you wanted to talk to me about Emily's murder. She was a good friend to me at a time when I needed a friend. How can I help you?"

"By telling me what happened to you six and a half years ago."

A cloud came over the other woman's eyes. "That's something that I've tried very hard to forget, Detective Le Blanc. It was a dark time for me, one I've put in the past. I have a wonderful husband now and a beautiful son. I don't want that ugliness to touch us in any way."

"I understand and I hate to ask you to relive it. But I think what happened to you might be connected to my sister's murder. But to prove that, I need details that only you can give me." When Lisa remained silent, she said, "You said my sister was a good friend to you when you needed one. Don't you at least owe her that much?"

"All right," she said and released a sigh. "But let's go in the backyard so Jack can play while we talk."

The backyard was as pretty as the front. It was small, but the grass was green, the trees provided some shade, more lilies and pink azaleas added color. A children's playset constructed of sturdy plastic in bright yellow, red and blue provided a slide and swing. A sandbox with pails, shovels and trucks completed what was Jack's play area. The moment his mother put him down, the little boy ran on wobbly legs toward the sandbox with Missy chasing after him.

Lisa offered her a seat at the white wrought-iron table on the patio area and then asked, "What is it you want to know?"

"I need you to tell me what happened to you."

"Where do you want me to start?" she asked.

"From the beginning."

"I went with my roommate to the Capitol for a political debate. I'd turned eighteen the year before and was going to be voting in my first election that fall. So I wanted to look at the candidates and the issues," she said. "The place was packed, standing room only. The debate was exciting and I felt so grown up and sophisticated. There was this gorgeous man standing near me who had been exchanging looks with me all evening. When the debate ended, the question-and-answer session was running long and I had to go to the bathroom. He apparently had the same idea because when I came out of the ladies' room, he was coming out of the men's room. We laughed about it and he introduced himself to me. His name was Aaron Stratton."

Charlie went still.

"I see you know the name," Lisa remarked.

"Yes."

"Jack, don't chase Missy," she called to her son. "Why don't you go build Mommy a sand castle." And once the toddler went back to the sandbox, she continued. "He told me he was a law school student at Tulane University in New Orleans and that he had driven up for the debate. Of course I knew who his family was. I'd seen pictures of his father and his family in the society pages of the newspaper. I couldn't believe this rich, sophisticated and gorgeous man was interested in me."

"What happened?"

"My roommate found me. She said she was going with some kids from her political-science class for burgers and to talk about the debate. But it was late and I had an exam in the morning and didn't want to go."

"So Aaron Stratton offered to take you home," Charlie said.

She nodded. "Normally I would never have gotten in a car or gone anywhere with someone I'd just met, but he was so charming and his family was so well known, I thought it would be okay. Besides, I liked him and wanted to see him again." She stared over at her son, shoveling sand into a bright green pail. "I was so naive. I agreed. I thought I was so lucky to be sitting next to him in that fancy red Porsche."

"He made an excuse to come inside, didn't he?"

She nodded. "A couple of blocks from my place, the engine warning light came on, telling him not to drive the car.

Once we got to my apartment, he popped the hood and fooled around under it. Then he shut it and I could see by his face that it wasn't good. When I asked him what was wrong, he said it looked like the transmission fluid was leaking and that he would need to call a tow truck."

"You offered to let him use your phone," Charlie surmised.

She gave her a wry smile. "I did, but he said no. He had a cell phone, you see. He placed a call to a towing service. Or at least that's who he said he called. And when he hung up, he said they would be about thirty minutes. He said he would wait outside, but asked if I minded if he washed his hands because they were covered in grease. Of course, I said yes."

"What happened?"

"Once he'd washed up, it seemed stupid to make him wait outside. So I told him he could wait inside and then I offered him something to drink. Since he was driving he said he'd stick to cola. So I poured us each a glass and brought them into the living room. Only, when I handed him his, the glass slipped and he spilled cola all over the front of his shirt. Naturally, I ran to the kitchen for some towels so he could clean himself up. I could see the shirt was expensive and didn't want him to ruin it. He kept apologizing for being clumsy and I thought it was sort of cute for such a sophisticated man to be embarrassed. I insisted on getting him another glass of cola. And while I was gone, he put something in my drink.

"The last thing I remember was sitting across the couch from him drinking a glass of cola. When I woke up the next morning, I was in my bed naked and there was blood on my sheets and bruises on my body. I freaked out and my roommate came running in. When she saw me, she took me to the hospital. From the vaginal tearing and bruising, they determined I'd been raped."

"I'm so sorry, Lisa."

Tears filled her eyes. "I was a virgin. I had planned to save myself for marriage and instead—"

Charlie touched her arm. "It wasn't your fault. Men like him prey on innocent women."

"That's what the rape counselor said, too," she said with a sniff.

"What happened when you went to the police?"

"They took my statement and questioned him. He admitted that he had met me at the debate and had given me a lift home. He even admitted to having some car trouble and coming inside to wash his hands. But he said he left right after that because he was worried about his car breaking down on the drive back to New Orleans."

"And the tow truck?"

"He said he never called one and there was no record of any call on his cell phone."

"So it came down to your word against his," Charlie pointed out. "Why didn't the D.A.'s office file charges?"

"Because Aaron volunteered to provide a DNA sample, hardly the actions of a man guilty of rape was what the police officer told me."

"And the sample didn't match," Charlie added.

Lisa nodded. "The police thought I was lying, that I'd had sex with someone else and afterward I was afraid. They thought I'd made up the charge against him because of his family's money. I guess his father pulled some political strings, because they never even arrested him."

Despite the strides that had been made to clean up the political corruption and the good-old-boy network in the state, Charlie knew that the changes were slow in coming. After her encounters with J. P. Stratton, she didn't doubt for a second that he had used his influence to help his son—

which explained why there was no record of the charges in the system.

"Anyway, the D.A. said I had no case and refused to take it to trial. But it was him. I swear to you on my son's head, it was Aaron Stratton who raped me."

"I believe you," she told her. And she did.

"Emily did, too. She was my biology lab partner and when I didn't show up for class for a week and wouldn't take any calls, she came to see me. I told her I was dropping out of school and going home. She tried to convince me not to quit. She knew it meant giving up my scholarship and plans to teach. She said she'd help me, that she'd find a way to prove he was guilty. But all I wanted to do was leave and forget everything that had happened. Not long after I went home, my dad requested a transfer and we moved to Georgia to be near my aunt and cousins."

"Did Emily say how she was going to prove he was guilty?"

"No. I just didn't want to discuss it. She called me twice after I moved. She wanted to talk about it, but I told her I couldn't. She said that she wasn't giving up, that she had a plan and when she proved that Aaron Stratton had raped me, she wasn't going to take no for an answer and that I'd have to get my butt back in school."

"And that was the last time you heard from her?" Charlie asked.

She nodded. "I guess it must have been about a year later that I heard she'd been killed. Do you think Aaron Stratton had something to do with her murder?"

"I think it's possible. I'm just not sure how to prove it. Do you have any idea what this plan of Emily's was?"

"No. All she said was that she'd come across something in one of her premed classes that might explain everything. But she didn't say what it was." She looked in the direction of her son. "Jack, don't eat the sand!" She shook her head. "Sorry about that. He's almost two and at this age he thinks everything goes in his mouth."

"I know this was difficult for you, Lisa. Thank you for talking to me."

"I wish I could have been more help."

"You were a big help," she told her and stood. "Take care of your son, I can see myself out."

"Detective Le Blanc?"

Charlie turned, looked at the other woman.

"Aaron Stratton is an evil man. I hope you find a way to nail him."

"I will, Lisa. I will," Charlie said. She'd do it for Lisa, for Francesca and Danielle, and most of all, she'd do it for Emily.

Cole sat inside the café directly across from the Western Union office where Phillip had wired the money to Jason. He'd chosen a table by a window so he could see when Jason arrived.

"What'll you have?" the waitress asked.

"A cup of coffee and a slice of apple pie," he told her.

"Coming right up."

Once the woman was gone, he turned his attention back to the street. From what Phillip had told him, Jason had spent the first night hiding out in the park and then hopped a train to Chicago. Since he'd used most of his cash and was afraid to use his credit cards, he'd called his twin for help.

The kid must be terrified, Cole thought. He wasn't surprised that Jason hadn't gone to J.P. or even Sylvia. But he couldn't help wishing that Jason had trusted him enough to come to him. Keeping his eyes peeled in the direction from the train station, Cole watched several people walk past, huddled in jackets because of the late snowfall and overcast skies. Twice he thought he saw Jason, only to be disappointed when they came closer.

"Here you go," the waitress said and served him both his coffee and pie. She slapped a bill on the table facedown. "Just let me know when you're ready."

"Thanks," Cole said and went back to monitoring the foot traffic across the street. After ordering another refill, he was beginning to think that Jason had found out he was there and was going to be a no-show. Then he saw a young man wearing a beige jacket, khakis and sunglasses. He'd dyed his hair a dark brown, but it was his brother Jason. Once he entered the Western Union office, Cole fished out several bills and dropped them on the table, then went outside to wait for his brother.

Jason was still stuffing the cash in his wallet when he exited the building and started down the street. When he reached the corner, Cole stepped into his path. "Excuse me," Jason began without looking up and started to move around him.

"Jason."

Jason started. "Phillip told you," he accused. "I should never have trusted him."

"He told me because he knows you're in trouble and that I want to help you."

"I don't need your kind of help. Now get out of my way," Jason said and started to move past him.

Cole caught him by the arm. "What do you mean, you don't need my kind of help?"

"I know you lied to me about you and Francesca. You were the one with her that night. It was you in the other room."

Still holding his brother by the arm, Cole muscled him to the side of the building out of the wind and out of the pedestrian traffic. "I never lied to you. I was never involved with Francesca," he told him.

"Quit lying," he said and tried to break free of his grasp. "Aaron saw the videotape of the two of you."

"What videotape?"

"The one with the two of you in bed. You were having an affair with her. And she taped it just like she did with those other men."

"You're wrong," he told him. "If I were having an affair with her, where's the tape? Why didn't they find it when they found the others and the letters from you?"

"Maybe you had that lady detective you're sleeping with destroy it and rig the DNA tests so that they'd pin Francesca's murder on me instead of you."

His brother's accusation stunned him. And he knew who was responsible for it and why. "Jason, I want you to listen to me. I was not having an affair with Francesca. If Aaron told you he saw a tape of the two of us, he's lying. There was no tape. There was no affair."

"Why should I believe you?"

"Because I've never lied to you. I'm not lying to you now."

Cole could see his brother waver. "But Aaron was trying to help me. He's the one who told me they were looking for me and that I should leave town. Why would he lie to me about you and Francesca?"

"That's a question I intend to ask him." He'd ask Aaron that, and a great deal more. "But the first thing we need to do is get you back to New Orleans. Once you give them a DNA sample and they rule you out, you'll be in the clear."

"Phillip said Dad thinks I'm guilty. And when he reads those letters I wrote to Francesca, he'll hate me. You know how powerful he is, all the friends he has. He'll make sure they put me in jail."

"J.P.'s not the only one with friends," he assured his younger brother. "Come on. If we hurry, we might be able to get an afternoon flight home."

"Cole, if there was no tape of you with Francesca, why would Aaron say there was one and that he'd seen it?"

"I don't know." But he had a sick feeling that he knew why.

Seated on the airplane traveling from Atlanta to New Orleans, Charlie pulled out her sister Emily's notebook. Once again, she went through it page by page, trying to make sense of the notes. There was lots of stuff on fertility, more about multiple births and how they were more common now due to the fertility drugs many couples turned to in order to conceive a child. She reread Emily's notes about twins.

Identical twins—formed when one fertilized egg splits in two. Identical DNA.

Fraternal twins are the result of two separate eggs being fertilized by two different sperm. Separate placenta. Do not look alike. Can be male and female or male and male or female and female. DNA differs.

Jason and Phillip were fraternal twins. But how did this relate to Aaron? she wondered. She continued to go through the notes, study the drawings of what were obviously representative of eggs. She flipped through the pages, skimming other entries, and stopped once again on a single page with the word *CHIMERA* that was followed by a question mark.

A creature from Greek mythology made up of three distinct body parts. The head of a lion for the front, the body of a goat for the middle and the tail of a snake for the end.

Suddenly something clicked. Charlie flipped back to the page about multiple births as the result of fertility treatments and reread her sister's notes.

The increased use of fertility treatments and drugs has resulted in a greater number of multiple births. Most of these are not identical twins because one fertilized egg is not splitting. Rather, it is the result of multiple eggs fertilized by different sperm that result in fraternal twins. In many cases one of the fraternal twins die in embryo and is absorbed into the surviving egg. How does this affect DNA? Is it possible to have multiple DNA in one person?

Was it possible that Aaron Stratton had started out in vitro as one of a set of fraternal twins? Twins ran in the Stratton family. If he had been a twin at conception and Emily's theory was right, he would have absorbed his fraternal twin's DNA when it died in embryo. If that was true, then maybe it would make it possible for him to leave one DNA from a semen sample but have an entirely different one from a buccal swab. Or was that wishful thinking? Checking her watch, Charlie waited impatiently for the plane to reach New Orleans so that she could follow up on her theory.

And as she waited, she went back over the details of the case. If Emily had set out to prove Aaron guilty of rape, maybe she had stumbled on a way to expose him. And if he had found out, would he have killed her sister to silence her?

Yes. He would have. There was something about him, something that had rubbed her wrong from the start. Beneath all the charm and good looks there was a cunningness, a coldness about him that she had found repulsive.

The minute her flight landed, Charlie was off the plane and

dialing her cell phone. "Come on, come on, it's not closing time yet. Answer the phone."

"Lab."

"This is Detective Le Blanc. Is Dr. Williamson in?"

"She's at the scene of a hit-and-run, Detective. You might try her on her cell."

"Thanks, I'll do that." Charlie ended the call and called the doctor's cell phone.

"Dr. Williamson," she answered on the fourth ring.

"Doctor, it's Charlotte Le Blanc. I need to ask you some questions about DNA."

"All right. I should be finished up here in about thirty minutes. I'll meet you back at the station," she said.

"Dr. Williamson, I can't wait that long. It's important."

"Hang on a second then," she said and Charlie could hear the people in the background, the street noise, the bystanders no doubt gaping at the tragedy. "Go ahead and bag him while I take this call," she said. "Okay, what do you want to know?"

"You said that DNA doesn't lie. But what happens when there are fraternal twins involved?"

"I assume this has something to do with your sister's murder and our testing of the Stratton men."

"Yes, it does."

"Well, fraternal twins are formed by two separate eggs that are fertilized by two separate sperm. The DNA is different."

"Have you ever heard of something called a chimera?" Charlie asked.

"It's a fire-breathing monster in Greek mythology that's made up of three different creatures. A lion's head, goat's middle and serpent's tail," she said. "But I'm assuming it's not the creature in mythology you're asking about but rather the medical term."

"Then you've heard of it?"

"Yes. It's usually used to refer to an individual, organ or organism consisting of more than one genetic compound. For instance, if someone were to have an organ transplant, that organ would have DNA different from the recipient."

"What about when there isn't a transplant?" Charlie asked as she exited the airport and headed for the parking garage to get her car. "I found some research notes that my sister made about fraternal twins and how when one of the twins dies embryo, the surviving twin absorbs it."

"We refer to it as Mother Nature messing up. The second twin is never formed and it's absorbed by the other egg. I read about a case where a rape suspect had two different DNA—his own and that of the twin whose egg had been absorbed before birth."

"Then it is possible for a person to have one DNA for, say, his hair and another for semen?"

"Yes, it's possible. And not as uncommon as you might think because of fertility drugs and treatments. Of course, there's not much documentation, because the second egg usually dies early in the pregnancy and the mother never knows about it."

"Is there any way to tell if someone is one of these chimera?" Charlie asked.

"In the case I mentioned, supposedly the rapist was exposed when they discovered Blaschko's lines. Those are V-shaped lines on the back and it's what can identify a person who is a chimera."

"So if we were to examine the back of a suspect and saw these lines, then that would mean he's a chimera? That he has two DNA?" Charlie asked for clarification as she reached her car and unlocked it.

"Yes. But the lines are only visible under ultraviolet light or sometimes if the lighting is right, a camera flash might have the same effect."

Charlie went still behind the wheel of her car. Suddenly she had a flashback to Emily's apartment, to the camera with the big flash that was on the counter. There had been no film in it, so she'd packed it along with the strange-looking lamp with the rest of her sister's things. She'd even wondered at the time why her sister had picked such a plain lamp.

"Detective, are you still there?"

"Yes. I'm here. Thank you. You've been a big help. It all makes sense now."

After she ended the call, Charlie started the engine and joined the line of traffic exiting the airport. As she drove, she considered all that she had learned and tried to put the pieces of the puzzle together. If Emily had tried to expose Aaron and he'd found out, he would have killed her.

But why kill Francesca and Danielle?

Money? Francesca marrying his father and having a child would mean one more slice in the Stratton money pie. But that didn't explain Danielle's murder. She would have posed no threat to him in that regard. Unless the information she'd had incriminated Aaron Stratton. It made sense.

What if Francesca had one of those tapes of Aaron Stratton? How would a man like him react to her threatening to exercise power over him?

He would kill her, Charlie concluded. There had to be another tape. That's why Danielle's apartment had been trashed. He was looking for the tape. Aaron was his father's golden boy. With Cole already out of the picture and now Jason accused of murder and Phillip disowned, the only person Aaron would have to contend with was Holly. And according to Holly, Aaron was the administrator of her trust if something happened to her father.

Oh my God. That had to be it, Charlie thought. Because of Mother Nature's screw up, Aaron Stratton had a virtual license to kill without any fear of being caught. Given all that had happened with the case already, she doubted that the captain or the D.A.'s office would agree to bring Aaron in again to test the theory. The entire case had been a political nightmare thanks to J. P. Stratton, and she and the entire department were skating on thin ice because of it. Even if she could convince the captain to go along with her plan, if for any reason she was wrong again, it wouldn't be just her job lost. It would be the captain's and Vince's jobs, too.

What she needed was hard evidence. She needed to find the video that Francesca had made with Aaron Stratton. Since they hadn't found anything at Danielle's, it meant the video had to be hidden somewhere in Francesca's apartment. Pulling her car onto the Interstate 10 on-ramp, Charlie headed back to the scene of the crime, back to Francesca's apartment.

Twenty-Two

During the entire flight home, Cole had tried to think of another explanation for Aaron's actions, but he hadn't been able to come up with one. Finally he'd accepted that Aaron was somehow involved in the murder. He'd known when they'd been kids that Aaron had resented him and he'd tried to understand. He was J.P.'s firstborn and J.P. had still been married to his mother when Aaron had been born. Even after J.P. had married Aaron's mother, Aaron had still been unable to accept him as a brother. During those rare times when Cole had visited, the anger had remained. It just had been more subtle. But then he'd left for the navy and when he'd returned because of Holly, Aaron had changed. For the first time, he'd felt like they were real brothers. But if he was honest, he had never trusted him. Apparently, his instincts had been right. What he couldn't figure out was how Aaron had managed to ace the DNA tests. DNA didn't lie. Yet, if Aaron was guilty as he suspected, then the DNA had lied. He just had to figure out how. But first, he had to clear Jason.

Cole walked into the police station with Jason at his side and approached the front desk. "Sergeant, I'm Cole Stratton. I'd like to see Detective Le Blanc."

"She's not here," the sergeant said and it was obvious from the way he was eyeing Jason that he knew who he was. "She took a few days' personal time."

He hadn't known that. But then he hadn't spoken to Charlotte since very early this morning. He hadn't gone into the details of what he was doing but now he thought perhaps he should have. "What about Detective Kossak?"

"Vince is here. I don't know where, but he's here in the building. I'll see if I can find him for you." After making a call, he said, "He's sending someone up here to bring you back. You'll both need to sign the visitors' log."

Cole signed the book. So did Jason and they clipped on their visitor badges just as Officer Mackenzie came up. "Mr. Stratton, if you'll follow me."

As they started back through the station, Jason said, "Maybe we should wait and come back tomorrow when Detective Le Blanc is here."

Cole could see his brother was not only tired from the strain of the past few days and the trip back to New Orleans, but he was also scared. What he didn't want to tell Jason was there was little chance that he'd be able to walk out of the station now. His brother's picture had been splashed across every TV screen in the metropolitan area as well as in the newspapers. "It'll be better to go ahead and get this over with. Try to relax, buddy. Everything's going to be all right."

More than an hour later after Jason had surrendered to Detective Vince Kossak, Cole had Jason arraigned, bail was set and Jason was released into his custody. The worst of it was over. All they needed to do now was wait for the DNA test results. "How long before you get the results?" Cole asked Dr. Williamson, who had taken the sample.

"I've put a rush on it. It could be as early as tomorrow, but it could be as long as a week. Everyone wants DNA testing these days," she said.

"Thanks, Doc," Kossak told her. "Looks like we're going to have to arrange another dinner for you at Commander's."

"I want one from you *and* one from Le Blanc. She's the reason I got back here so late."

"You've seen Charlotte?" Cole asked.

"No. She called me. As is usually the case, she had some questions that needed answering asap," she replied.

"Patience is not one of Charlie's virtues," Kossak said dryly.

"I thought she was on personal leave," Cole said. When Kossak didn't reply, he pressed, "Is there something I should know?"

"She gave the captain some song and dance about needing personal time, but Anne said she's hot on some theory. My guess is it's connected to her sister's murder," he said. "I tried calling her, but she's got the phone going to voice mail. Anne hasn't heard from her either."

"Doc, what kind of questions did she ask you?" Kossak asked. When she hesitated a moment, Kossak said, "It's okay to talk in front of him."

"She was interested in some research notes that belonged to her sister about a phenomenon known as the chimera. It's sort of a screwup by Mother Nature where fraternal twins are conceived but one of the eggs doesn't form completely and it's absorbed by the surviving twin. The result is one person with two different DNA."

Suddenly everything fell into place. Cole whipped out his cell phone, tried Charlotte's number. Her voice mail came on. So he tried her home phone and got the answering machine. "Damn." He looked up at the doctor. "Kossak, any idea where she might be?"

"She's not at Anne's place or her parents," he said. "She's been wound pretty tight lately."

"Here's my cell number," he said and jotted the number on a slip of paper. "If you hear from her, call me. Let's go, Jason."

"Where are we going?"

"To Aaron's."

For the most part, they made the drive in silence. He suspected Jason knew his thoughts were elsewhere. When he was a block from Aaron's house, his cell phone rang. Cole snatched it up, hoping it was Charlotte. "Charlotte?"

"No, Mr. Stratton. It's Harry at the Mill House Apartments."

"Hi, Harry. Listen, this isn't a good time," he began.

"You said you wanted me to let you know if your brother showed up here. Well, he's here now."

He started to tell the man he was mistaken, that Jason was seated next to him. Then he asked, "Which one of my brothers, Harry?"

"Mr. Aaron," he said. "He said your father wanted him to check Ms. Hill's apartment to see about having it redone so they could release it."

"Thanks, Harry."

"Mr. Stratton, he's not the only one here. So is that lady detective."

He stood in the shadows and watched her. Hidden by the massive ficus tree in the corner of the dining room, she hadn't seen him when he'd arrived and found her searching the apartment. He'd known it was only a matter of time before she figured everything out. She was like a dog with a bone— just like her sister. She simply wouldn't let go. That was why he'd known that sooner or later she would find the video for him. So he had waited. And while he waited, he anticipated the power and pleasure of witnessing Cole's anguish when he found her dead.

But first, he needed her to find the disc. Kneeling on the floor of the living room, she opened the CDs one by one, checked to make sure the disc inside matched the case, no doubt. He'd already done that and come up empty.

She sat back on her heels and ran her hands through her hair. When she suddenly went still and turned to look in his direction, he pressed his body against the wall, slowed his breathing and waited. For a moment, he thought she'd seen him and that he would have to kill her before she found the disc, but then she turned away. Relaxing again, he continued to watch her.

For several seconds she just glanced around the room. Then her eyes went to the bookshelves again. He'd known she had found the other discs and Jason's letters in the bible. It had been a clever hiding place, he admitted. He'd thought so himself when he'd first discovered it the night he'd killed Francesca. That's why he had left them for the police to find.

And just as he had known she would, Detective Charlotte Le Blanc had found them and all hell had broken loose. He smiled to himself, pleased that she had helped his plan along so wonderfully. Thanks to her, the minister, the judge and his brother Jason had all come under suspicion. It hadn't been hard to convince that twerp Jason not to trust Cole or the cops and to run. Like putty in his hands. They all were—even Cole. Just as he'd known he would, Cole had run off to find Jason. Which only served to prove that his big brother wasn't nearly as smart as his father and everyone else thought he was. He had always been the smarter one and now he had proven it.

By the time Cole found Jason and they discovered that his DNA didn't match, the damage would have already been done. Both Jason and Phillip were out of the picture now, and Holly...Holly was never any threat. And the best part of all was watching Cole running to the rescue and failing, not only the twins and Holly, but his lover, too.

He couldn't wait to see Cole broken, left with nothing but his arrogance and guilt. And what would make it all the more enjoyable was knowing that he had been the one to engineer the mighty Cole Stratton's fall. God, how he hated him, had hated him for as long as he could remember. He wanted to destroy him, erase all trace of him. He didn't want him to exist. And while using his brothers and sister to hurt Cole had proved satisfying, killing the woman Cole loved would be the ultimate revenge.

But first, he needed her to find him the damn disc.

Growing impatient, he continued to watch her, standing in front of the bookshelves, staring at the titles. Slowly she went from shelf to shelf, considering each title. She skipped over Francesca's sex manuals, the bestsellers that he knew she'd bought but never read, the volumes of Shakespeare, poetry and books by the Brontë sisters. She reached for East of Eden *by Steinbeck and began flipping through the pages of the book. He'd already checked the books and found nothing. He wanted to shake her, tell her she was wasting time, that the disc wasn't there. But he knew if he showed himself too soon, it would be over. And he needed her to find the disc first— before he killed her.*

Taking the book, she sat down on the couch and began running her fingers around the binding. She retrieved her purse from the coffee table and took out a metal nail file. Using it, she worked at the edge of the binding. Then she set down the file and eased the leather cover apart…and pulled out the disc.

Aaron's heart surged with triumph. She'd found it—just as he'd known she would. She studied the small square and then apparently realized it was the cartridge for the digital camera. He watched her walk over to the table and retrieve the digital camera. She inserted the cartridge and flipped the switch and watched the video of him and Francesca.

Francesca lay on the bed wearing only a black thong and black silk stockings. He could feel himself growing excited as he watched her watch them. He stepped out from his hiding place. "Tell me, Detective. Do you think I'm photogenic?"

Charlie whipped around at the sound of Aaron's voice and saw him step out of the shadows. He came toward her. She reached for her gun and started to aim it when she saw the gun in his hand already pointed at her.

"I wouldn't try it. Not unless you want me to shoot you now. And I'd hate to do that when I have such a fun time planned for the two of us."

Her stomach pitched at his words. She stared at the gun he had pointed at her, debating what to do. At this range, even if he was a bad shot, she doubted that he'd miss her. And while she might get off a shot, so would he. In those brief seconds, her future flashed before her eyes. Her parents burying a second daughter, a life that she had begun to hope she could share with Cole gone.

"I mean it, Detective. Put down the gun—now. Or I will shoot you."

"All right," she said and put down the gun.

"Good girl. Now slide it over here."

She did as he instructed.

"Now I want you to remove the cartridge from the camera and put it on the table."

Once again, she followed his instructions. And as she removed the cartridge and placed it on the table, she glanced around the room, searching for something to use as a weapon, searching for some way to distract him.

Keeping the gun on her, he came forward, picked up the disc and slipped it into the pocket of his jacket. He smiled at her then, an evil, cold smile that sent chills down her spine.

"Would you believe I didn't even realize that bitch Francesca made this? But Danielle was kind enough to tip me off. Too bad I wasn't able to find out where she hid it before I killed her. But then, I knew I could count on you to find it for me."

"Forgive me if I don't say you're welcome," she tossed back.

He laughed. "I must say, I hadn't thought to check the binding. That was very clever of you. But I'm curious as to how you knew to look there."

"Because of the story. *East of Eden* is the retelling of Cain and Abel. Two generations of brothers—Charles and Adam and Caleb and Aron—the manipulative and evil brother so jealous of his good and honorable brother that he tries to destroy him. Anyone who bothered to look close enough could see how jealous you are of Cole and that you want to destroy him."

"Interesting analogy. And you're correct, of course," he admitted. "I do want to destroy him and I intend to. But not because I'm jealous. It's because I loathe him. I have from the first time I set eyes on him as a child. It was because of him that my mother and I had to suffer all those years of shame, of coming in second, of having people treat us like trash because my father was still married to Cole's mother, Margaret. It didn't matter to my father that people talked about my mother, called her a home wrecker and worse. It didn't matter to him that I was the one who was born a bastard and had to wait years to legally claim the name that should have been mine from the start. All that mattered to him was his precious son Cole. He wouldn't leave that bitch Margaret because he didn't want to give up Cole. So we had to wait all those years until Margaret finally had the good sense to slit her wrists before he would marry my mother and acknowledge me as his son."

Charlie stared at Aaron, realized how twisted by hate he was.

"But even after he married my mother and declared me his son, Cole ruined everything. My father never made any secret that it was Cole he cared about the most. Even though Cole hated him, to my father Cole always came first. Everything was about Cole and I was the afterthought. But I found a way to get even. I made sure he got blamed for things I did, and of course, he would never rat me out. He was too good to do that. I was his little brother and he loved me."

"And you hated him even more because he did, didn't you? Because he was everything you wanted to be but never could be," she said, angered on Cole's behalf.

"Careful, Detective," he said, his expression hardening and his grip on the gun tightening. "I'm not ready to kill you yet, but I will."

"You'll never get away with this," she told him. "I know about the chimera, the double DNA."

He arched his brow as though surprised. "I hadn't realized you'd figured it out. A remarkable little gift, don't you think? I can do anything I want and the DNA never traces back to me."

"How long have you known?" she asked him.

"Since I was in high school. I raped a little tease who'd been asking for it for weeks. The bitch and her parents filed charges. Of course, the DNA swab didn't match the semen sample and I was home free. And since I was a juvenile and J. P. Stratton's son, I had no problem having the record expunged."

He was proud of it, Charlie realized, and she knew then just how truly sick he was. "My sister figured it out, too. Didn't she? That's why you killed her."

"Yes. Emily was too smart for her own good, just like you. I hadn't realized she'd been friends with Lisa. I also hadn't known she'd been researching DNA and was trying to find a way to pin the rape on me."

"And she found a way, didn't she," Charlie said, wishing she had realized long ago just how smart and caring Emily was.

"She would have. It was a foolish mistake on my part underestimating her. When she spilled wine on me in her apartment that night and tricked me into taking my shirt so she could rinse it, I had no idea she was setting me up. Even when I saw the lamp, I didn't realize what it was at first or what she was up to. Of course, she saw the V-shaped lines on my back and she pretended not to know what they were or what they meant. But I could see that she did. Since I couldn't have her blabbing my little secret and screwing up my future, I had to kill her. And now I'm going to kill you."

"You won't get away with it. I'm not the only one who knows," she bluffed. "I've told my partner and Cole. They're probably looking for you right now."

He smiled. "Nice try, Detective. But I know for a fact that Cole's in Chicago looking for Jason and that your partner is at the station. You see, I called there looking for you and they patched me through to him."

Charlie's heart pounded and she scanned the area, seeking a means of escape.

"Come, come now, Detective. It won't be that unpleasant. We'll have a little fun first and you can see for yourself that I truly am the better man."

"You don't even come close to measuring up to Cole," she fired at him. "He's a man and you're nothing but a petulant boy."

He slapped her and Charlie's head rang. She could taste her own blood. But she refused to back down. She had no intention of going down without a fight.

He pulled a pair of black silk stockings from his pocket. "Put these on," he ordered and tossed them at her.

Charlie let them fall at her feet. "Go to hell."

The car had barely stopped when Cole jumped out and hit the pavement running. Ignoring Harry's shout, he raced inside the building. The elevator showed it was on the third floor. Unwilling to wait, he ran to the stairwell.

"Cole," Jason called after him.

"Stay here and wait for Kossak and the police." Then he took the stairs two at a time. When he reached the fifth floor, he took care opening the door. If Aaron had Charlotte, he didn't want to risk him hurting her because he heard someone coming. Charlotte was smart, he told himself as he moved silently down the hall. She would stop him or stall him until help arrived. At least that's what he'd been telling himself the entire drive over. He couldn't lose her—not now when he'd just found her.

He reached the door, turned the handle. It was locked. Pressing his ear to the door, he could hear Aaron's voice say, "Pick them up."

"I told you, go to hell."

He heard a blow struck and fury raged in his heart. Brother or not, he would kill Aaron for hurting her. But first he needed to make sure Charlotte was out of range. Glancing at the window at the end of the hall, he recalled the fire escape that led to the picture window in the living room.

Moving quickly, he went out onto the fire escape, maneuvered himself so that he was outside the window of the living room. The drapes had been drawn, but there was a slight gap between them that allowed him to see inside. Aaron's back was to him, but he had a gun aimed at Charlotte. She stood so that she was facing in his direction. Her mouth was bloody. A bruise was already forming on her cheek. But her amber eyes were defiant, her stance strong as she faced down Aaron.

He tried the window, found it locked. Fishing out his pocketknife, he prayed he'd have time to work open the latch. Charlotte must have sensed him because she stole a glance in his direction. Her eyes met his. He pressed his finger to his lips and went back to work on the latch.

Aaron grabbed her by the hair, yanked her to him and took her mouth in a brutalizing kiss. When he released her, she spat in his face. This time when he lifted his hand to strike her, Cole couldn't wait. Shielding his face with his arm and jacket, he kicked in the window. Glass flew everywhere. Cole felt shards of glass nick his hands as he pulled on the drapes, sent them tumbling down as he lunged at Aaron's back.

They went down. He and Aaron were closely matched in size and skill. But he was better, Cole knew. When Aaron struggled to get up and tried to kick him, Cole grabbed his leg, pulled him down onto the floor again. As he did so, Aaron reached for the gun. Cole kicked it away. It slid across the floor and it landed at Charlotte's feet.

"Get off of him."

Cole looked over at Charlotte. She had the gun aimed at Aaron. Aaron rolled off of him, came to his knees and started to rise. "Go ahead, Detective. Shoot me," Aaron dared. "Shoot me and avenge Emily's death. That's what you want, isn't it?"

"Shut up," she all but growled. "Cole, get away from him."

He could see from the anger in her eyes that she had been pushed to the breaking point. "Charlotte, don't do it. He's not worth it."

"He murdered my sister," she said, never taking her eyes from Aaron.

"Then let the courts deal with him. Let them sentence him to prison," Cole reasoned, not wanting her to do something she would regret.

Aaron laughed. "Do you really think I'll serve time? We both know that the name J. P. Stratton means something in this town. I'll walk away from this one just like I always do."

"You deserve to die," she told him.

"Maybe I do. But I won't. We both know that. And there's not a thing you can do about it."

"Oh yes there is," Charlotte told him and aimed the gun.

"Charlotte, don't!" Cole shouted. "Can't you see that's what he wants? You're not a cold-blooded killer. Don't let him bring you down with him."

She was torn. He could see the torment in her eyes, the tense way she held her body. "He murdered my sister."

"And I had a wonderful time doing it," Aaron taunted.

"You bastard," she said and continued to hold the gun with both hands.

"I want a future with you, Charlotte. Don't let Aaron steal that from us."

She looked over at him and slowly began to lower the gun. And before he could stop him, Aaron lunged at her. Then he heard the blast as she pulled the trigger.

Cole watched his brother fall to the floor. The look of surprise on his face said everything. "Why, Aaron? Why?" Cole asked him.

"Because I hate you. I always have. I always will."

Charlie stood in the cemetery with her parents and Anne. Once her mother had finishing arranging the roses on Emily's grave, she walked back over to her husband. Together they stood, her father with his arm around his wife, and the two of them looked at peace. "Charlotte, we'll see you back at the house?" her mother asked.

"Yes. I'll be along in a few minutes."

"Bring that young man of yours with you," her father said. "I think it's time he and I had a talk."

"I'll see what I can do," she said.

Anne touched her arm. "Do you want Vince and I to wait for you?"

"No, I'm all right. I just want a few minutes first."

"Okay. But don't be long," Anne said and with Vince at her side, she watched her sister walk away.

Once she was alone, she knelt beside Emily's headstone. "I found him, Em. Just like I promised. They've got him in prison and I don't think they'll ever let him out." She swallowed. "I'm so sorry, Emily. I'm so sorry I wasn't there when you needed me. And I'm even sorrier that I never told you how much I loved you, how beautiful and smart I always thought you were, how proud I was of you."

Tears slid down her cheeks as she thought of the past, of the happy times, the fights, the love. "I miss you, Em. And I'll never forget you. But I've met someone, someone really special. I think you'd approve of him. And I want a future with him," she told her sister. "All these years I've felt that I didn't deserve to have a future, that I didn't deserve to be happy, because you didn't have a future and it was my fault for not being there to protect you."

She wiped her cheeks. "But I was wrong, wasn't I, Em? I realize now that you never blamed me and that I need to have that happy life for both of us. And I will, Em. I promise you I will."

Charlie placed the yellow rose across her sister's grave and stood. And as she turned she saw him. Cole was waiting for her by the street. She stared at him, felt her heart quicken because she knew he was her future. So she ran to him, ran toward her future, and Cole met her halfway. He caught her in his arms, kissed her and said, "I love you."

"And I love you," she told him.

And as Cole took her hand in his and they started to walk away, Charlie stopped and looked back at Emily's grave. For a moment, she thought she saw her sister standing there, waving at her and smiling.

"Everything all right?"

She smiled at her sister, then turned back to Cole. "Everything is wonderful."

NEW YORK TIMES BESTSELLING AUTHOR

STELLA CAMERON

Emma Lachance is taken by surprise when she runs into her old friend and high school crush Finn Duhon on a construction site in Pointe Judah, Louisiana. But the last thing she expects to find is the corpse of her friend, a local journalist whose relentlessly scathing articles have enraged every lawmaker and opportunist in town, including the mayor—Emma's husband.

When more bodies are found, Emma and Finn wonder if the link is an eclectic support group for women in which all the murder victims were members. But in their search for the truth, Emma may become the next body of evidence....

Body of Evidence

"Cameron returns to the wonderfully atmospheric Louisiana setting of *French Quarter*...for her latest sexy-gritty, compellingly readable tale of romantic suspense."
—*Booklist* on *Kiss Them Goodbye*

Available the first week of March 2006, wherever paperbacks are sold!

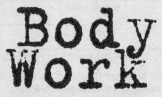

If you enjoyed what you just read,
then we've got an offer you can't resist!

Take 2 bestselling novels FREE!
Plus get a FREE surprise gift!

Clip this page and mail it to MIRA®

IN U.S.A.
3010 Walden Ave.
P.O. Box 1867
Buffalo, N.Y. 14240-1867

IN CANADA
P.O. Box 609
Fort Erie, Ontario
L2A 5X3

YES! Please send me 2 free MIRA® novels and my free surprise gift. After receiving them, if I don't wish to receive anymore, I can return the shipping statement marked cancel. If I don't cancel, I will receive 4 brand-new novels every month, before they're available in stores! In the U.S.A., bill me at the bargain price of $4.99 plus 25¢ shipping and handling per book and applicable sales tax, if any*. In Canada, bill me at the bargain price of $5.49 plus 25¢ shipping and handling per book and applicable taxes**. That's the complete price and a savings of over 20% off the cover prices—what a great deal! I understand that accepting the 2 free books and gift places me under no obligation ever to buy any books. I can always return a shipment and cancel at any time. Even if I never buy another The Best of the Best™ book, the 2 free books and gift are mine to keep forever.

185 MDN DZ7J
385 MDN DZ7K

Name	(PLEASE PRINT)	
Address	Apt.#	
City	State/Prov.	Zip/Postal Code

*Not valid to current The Best of the Best™, Mira®,
suspense and romance subscribers.*

Want to try two free books from another series?
Call 1-800-873-8635 or visit www.morefreebooks.com.

* Terms and prices subject to change without notice. Sales tax applicable in N.Y.
** Canadian residents will be charged applicable provincial taxes and GST.
All orders subject to approval. Offer limited to one per household.
® and ™are registered trademarks owned and used by the trademark owner and or its licensee.

BOB04R   ©2004 Harlequin Enterprises Limited

METSY HINGLE

32096 DEADLINE   ___ $6.50 U.S. ___ $7.99 CAN.

(limited quantities available)

TOTAL AMOUNT	$ _____
POSTAGE & HANDLING	$ _____
($1.00 FOR 1 BOOK, 50¢ for each additional)	
APPLICABLE TAXES*	$ _____
TOTAL PAYABLE	$ _____

(check or money order—please do not send cash)

To order, complete this form and send it, along with a check or money order for the total above, payable to MIRA Books, to: **In the U.S.:** 3010 Walden Avenue, P.O. Box 9077, Buffalo, NY 14269-9077; **In Canada:** P.O. Box 636, Fort Erie, Ontario, L2A 5X3.

Name: _____
Address: _____ City: _____
State/Prov.: _____ Zip/Postal Code: _____
Account Number (if applicable): _____

075 CSAS

*New York residents remit applicable sales taxes.
*Canadian residents remit applicable GST and provincial taxes.

MIRA®

www.MIRABooks.com   MMH0306BL